THE IRISH GOODBYE

THE IRISH GOODBYE

A Novel

AMY EWING

alcove
press

This is a work of fiction. All of the names, characters, organizations, places, and events portrayed in this novel are either products of the author's imagination or are used fictitiously. Any resemblance to real or actual events, locales, or persons, living or dead, is entirely coincidental.

Published in the United States by Alcove Press, an imprint of The Quick Brown Fox & Company LLC.

Alcove Press and its logo are trademarks of The Quick Brown Fox & Company LLC.

Library of Congress Catalog-in-Publication data available upon request.

ISBN (paperback): 978-1-63910-781-0
ISBN (ebook): 978-1-63910-782-7

Cover design by Ana Hard

Printed in the United States.

www.alcovepress.com

Alcove Press
34 West 27th St., 10th Floor
New York, NY 10001

First Edition: June 2024

10 9 8 7 6 5 4 3 2 1

For Ali
Who believed in this story from the very beginning.

1

"Ladies and gentlemen, welcome to Dublin. The local time is 8:45 AM. Please remain seated until the captain has turned off the 'Fasten Seat Belt' sign."

Cordelia rubbed her eyes, bleary from a sleepless flight, and peered through the small oval window as the plane crawled its way toward the gate. The sky overhead was covered in thin gray clouds, wispy enough to give hope that they may break at any moment and let in the cheerful rays of the June sun. But for now the weather was as muted and shifting as her feelings.

She'd been jittery with excitement when she boarded the plane at JFK but now that she'd landed in Ireland, her stomach was tying itself in knots. Was this a mistake? Leaving her home, her friends, everything she knew in New York and crossing an ocean to spend the summer on a tiny island in the middle of nowhere? It had seemed like such a perfect opportunity when she'd made the decision all those weeks ago.

"You need a break," her best friend Liz had declared one afternoon as Cordelia sat on her couch going through some photos she'd taken in the West Village that day.

"I'm fine," Cordelia had insisted, despite every photo on her reel being all wrong, as if she'd forgotten the basics—the rule of three, negative space, everything that made a photograph interesting.

"Cord, if your frown gets any deeper it's going to become permanent. You should go to an island somewhere," Liz had said. "Get away from New York for a while. Live on a beach. Sip fruity cocktails. When was the last time you had any real fun? Or did anything that wasn't photography-related?"

That wasn't fair, Cordelia thought. Liz knew better than anyone how hard these past two years had been for her.

She used to be so confident in herself—Cordelia James, street photographer. Star of her graduating class at the School of Visual Arts. Mentored by the great Philip Watson. She'd spent days on end walking the streets of New York with her camera, waiting for the right moment to capture and share on her popular Instagram feed. And with that popularity came financial success: She'd had a show in a gallery in Chelsea, where her work had been purchased by rich housewives desperate for something "cool and edgy" to hang on their walls. And she'd gotten a deal for a coffee table book: *New York Minute*, it was called. It did okay. But the publisher never asked for a second one.

And then Cordelia's father died. Her biggest champion and her fiercest advocate. He'd inspired her love of art, lifted up her dream of being a professional photographer, and never insisted she get a "real job" like her mother always harped on about. His death was brutally sudden. One day he was texting her about getting tickets to the latest Broadway revival and the next he was just . . .

gone. A brain aneurysm right in the middle of his Intro to Shakespeare class.

For months, Cordelia could barely stand to pick up a camera. By the time she finally surfaced from the ocean of grief and began crawling back toward normal, Philip had moved to Chicago, the gallery had moved on to other up-and-comers, and her Instagram following had dwindled. Worst of all, her camera had felt like a stranger. She'd look into her lens but she couldn't *see.*

She'd lost her patience. Street photography was all about patience. That and good humor. Cordelia had been seriously lacking in both for a while. She felt like a wet rag wrung dry too many times, damp and crumpled and pathetic.

So she'd taken Liz's advice and started looking into vacation spots. But all the places in Bermuda or the Bahamas were massively expensive. She had some savings and a modest inheritance from her father, but she didn't feel like blowing it all on one extravagant summer vacation.

Then a listing had caught her eye. *Cozy cottage nestled in the heart of Ireland's picturesque Inishmore,* the ad had read. A quick Google search told her that was the largest of the three Aran Islands off Ireland's western coast. *Rent free and small stipend if willing to do some menial housework and look after elderly neighbor. Must stay from 1 June–31 August.*

Cordelia had jumped to book it.

As the plane came to a jolting stop, Cordelia's mind began to spin fantasies of learning life lessons she never would have if she'd stayed in New York. This "elderly neighbor" appeared in her mind as a wizened sage taking Cord under her wing, encouraging her the way her father used to, the way her mother never seemed to be able to do. Spending her days roaming the green hills of Ireland with her camera (she'd never been to Ireland before, but wasn't everything green there?), reconnecting with herself as an artist, taking stunning shots of craggy vistas that would have the photography world melting at her feet. And in the evenings, she'd sit by a fireplace with the old woman and soak up quaint Irish words of wisdom. She'd come back changed. Happier and more at peace with the world.

This is going to be great, she told herself as she unfastened her seat belt.

She reached under the seat in front of her for her striped canvas tote bag that contained the two most precious things in her possession. The first was her phone, the lifeline to her friends and family. She turned it off airplane mode and waited for her international plan to connect so she could text Liz and her brother.

The second was her Fujifilm X100V. It was small, perfect for street photography and well-suited to travel. But more importantly, it was the last gift her father had given her, one month before he died.

"Have you ever thought about maybe, like, taking a break from photography altogether?" her brother Toby had asked hesitantly when she told him about the trip.

As if that were possible. Going without her camera would be like leaving her leg behind—it was a part of her. Besides, Ireland was going to rejuvenate her love for her craft.

The thought put a spring in Cordelia's step as she made her way to the baggage claim. Her phone finally pinged.

HELLO HAVE YOU LANDED YET???

She grinned at Liz's enthusiastic greeting.

Just got off the plane. Getting my bag now.

Ten bucks says it's raining, Liz wrote back.

Cordelia laughed. Liz had insisted it would be raining the whole time she was there. Even though she was the one who'd come up with the idea for Cordelia to take a vacation, Liz couldn't fully hide her disappointment that Cordelia would be missing their summer trips to Jones Beach, tanning in Central Park (as if Cordelia was capable of getting a tan), outdoor concerts at SummerStage, and watching the sunset from her rooftop. In turn, Cordelia had reminded Liz of all the crap parts about being in the city for the summer—the oppressive humidity, the smell of rotting garbage, the unexpected drips from air conditioners.

Nope, she wrote back with a winky face. *But it's cloudy.*

While she waited for her suitcase, Cordelia messaged Toby to let him know she'd landed, then reviewed her travel itinerary. Getting to the Aran Islands wasn't easy; she had to take a taxi to Dublin, then a train all the way across the country to Galway, and then a bus to Rossaveel, where she would catch the ferry to Inishmore.

It was a lot to do in one day and now that she was off the plane, the jitters were coming back. Not because of the trip ahead—she had plenty of time to catch the train. Cordelia liked to be fastidiously early, another trait she'd inherited from her father. No, these were nerves of hope and possibility, of the certainty that this summer, things were going to change.

By the time she arrived at Heuston Station, Cordelia's stomach was growling. She paid the cabbie and thanked him, then bought a sandwich and a coffee from a vendor and had just enough time to scarf it all down before they were calling her train for boarding. Once her bag was stowed, she settled in to watch the Irish countryside roll past.

It looked exactly like someone would imagine it if they were told to picture the Irish countryside: lush green pastures and small winding roads, tiny houses and gray-bellied clouds dotting the sky. Sheep everywhere. The weather couldn't make up its mind; the sun and clouds played tug-of-war so that sometimes the world was muted in dull greens and browns only to suddenly grow jewel-bright, the grass shining in brilliant patches of emerald, the trees limned in gold.

Cordelia instinctively took her camera out of its sling. She'd gotten the image of her father's thumbprint laminated and pressed as a sticker on the spot where her own thumb rested when she held the camera up to her face. She touched it now and sighed.

A moment later her phone pinged with a picture from Toby, and she smiled at the faces of her niece and nephew. Perfect timing.

Miles with his glasses and mini afro puffing out around his face, Grace with her long delicate features, her hair braided into pigtails. Cordelia wondered how long those would last—Grace was leaving childhood behind and fast approaching the dreaded tweens.

Grace and Miles say we miss you, Aunt Cordie!

Tell them they have to stop growing over the summer, she texted back. *Grace looks so big!*

Tell me about it, Toby wrote. *Nikki says hi.*

He sent another picture, this one of him and his wife, a beautiful Black woman with box braids hanging loose around her face, her smile bright but her eyes faintly exasperated. Toby had insisted on communicating with lots of pictures, as if three months in Ireland were a decade on another planet, but now Cordelia was grateful for it.

Three months in a new country. Cordelia couldn't believe she was actually doing this.

There'd been a photograph on the job listing of Alison Murphy, a pretty woman who looked to be about Cordelia's age—late twenties—with thick auburn hair, freckles, and a large toothy smile. *I run the Tigh na Mara Bed and Breakfast in Kilronan,* Alison had written after Cordelia had asked for more details. *The summer months there are busy so I won't be able to make it home much. I need someone to stay in the cottage in case my gran needs anything—she's nearing eighty and I don't like the thought of her alone with no one nearby. She gets her mail delivered at the cottage so if you could take it up to the house that'd be grand. I mostly wanted someone to keep the cottage clean and help out Gran while I'm living at the B&B. Her name is Róisín.*

Róisín was pronounced Ro-sheen, apparently—Cordelia had had to look that one up.

The job sounded pretty straightforward, though. And in her down time she could clamber around the island with her camera. Her work generally centered around people and city life, but shaking things up wouldn't hurt. Maybe she would discover an unknown penchant for landscape photography.

The bus ride was less pleasant than the train, with lots of lurching and sharp turns. They drove through simple Irish suburbs, on roads that seemed too narrow to hold such a large vehicle.

The clouds had officially won the tug-of-war by the time she reached the ferry; she boarded the boat alongside a tall man with jet-black hair and blue eyes, talking in a low, irritated voice on his phone. Cordelia caught the words "I said I'd do it, Da, isn't that enough?" before he walked up to the next level. Her heart pinched—what she wouldn't give to have an argument with her father again or hear his voice over the phone. She found a seat and stared out across the rolling waves, slate-gray and gloomy blue.

The ferry ride was an hour and Cordelia got herself another coffee from the little café on board. The jet lag was setting in, her eyelids drooping, her brain turning to mush. She hoped she wouldn't be expected to do anything grandma *or* cleaning related today. A light rain began to fall, leaving a pretty pattern across the waves, but by the time the ferry had pulled into the dock at Kilronan Harbor, it had faded to a gentle mist.

Cordelia's heart kicked up a notch as she got her bag and waited in line to disembark. Alison had said she would pick her up, and as she walked down the gangplank, Cordelia saw the same black-haired man descending from the upper deck, still on his phone.

She stepped down onto the concrete pier and headed toward the lot full of cars. Kilronan was the largest town on the island, but that wasn't saying much. There were several brightly painted houses surrounding the harbor, squares of yellow and pink. She saw a big stone building with large white letters declaring it the Aran Sweater Market.

The harbor was as picturesque as she'd hoped it would be—and bustling with people. *See, Liz?* Cordelia thought smugly. This was perfect. Two old women were chatting outside the market while a small brown dog sniffed at the entranceway. A young man was leaning against the pink house smoking a cigarette.

Her fingertips tingling with excitement, she reached into her bag to take her camera out. This was the moment. Her photography was about to change, she could feel it.

As she was lifting the strap to secure the camera around her neck, she stepped six inches to her left to get the exact right framing of the two market women. But she was so excited by the prospect of the photograph that she didn't look where she was going, and she collided with the person behind her. She watched in horror, like an out-of-body experience, as her camera jolted out of her hands and clattered onto the concrete, rolling once, twice, and then coming to a stop, face down on the cement.

"Watch it," the black-haired man muttered as he pushed past, barely even glancing at her, his stupid phone glued to his ear.

For a second Cordelia was too stunned to speak. She found her breath and shouted, "Hey!" but he was already gone, vanished into the crowds now streaming from the ferry. Cordelia dove to protect her most precious possession from the feet of a hundred tourists, cradling it gently like a baby bird.

She turned it over. Her heart stuttered, and the world shrank in her vision, pinpricks of light making her dizzy.

The lens was cracked.

She brought it to her eye, not caring what she was pointing it at, desperate to know it was okay. But no matter how she adjusted the aperture, the camera wouldn't focus. Everything was blurry, formless.

Her camera was ruined.

2

Niall O'Connor did *not* want to fucking be here.

He was already in a black mood when some dumb tourist stepped right in front of him in the middle of the bloody walkway to take a picture of the stupid sweater market—an American, probably, they were always stopping in inconvenient places to take the most inane pictures. Her elbow jammed into his ribs and he muttered a terse, "Watch it," and kept talking to Colin.

"Yeah, I'm just off the ferry, mate," he said to his best friend. "Where are you?"

In response he heard a car horn honk and saw Colin waving at him with that big dopey grin of his. Niall sighed. At least Colin would be here for the summer as well. Niall didn't think he would have been able to handle this forced homecoming otherwise. He was already missing Dublin, and his favorite pub, and the crowded streets, and the walk down Grafton Street in the mornings to—

His thoughts glanced off the memory like a stone skipping over smooth water, skittering away toward safer shores.

He should have stopped taking that walk a month ago, but apparently he was a closeted masochist. What a fun personality trait to discover at the ripe old age of thirty-one. After weeks of Niall ignoring phone calls and sleeping during the day and watching far too much reality television while eating far too much takeaway, Colin had stepped in and staged an intervention. What was the word he'd used to describe Niall's behavior? Self-indulgent? Toxic? Insane?

You're off your fucking head is what he'd said. Out of his mind, more like it. But how else was he supposed to react? Niall had lost everything—his plans, his dreams, his future, the love of his life—all in one fell swoop. He'd been crushed and then trampled and then sliced into bits like chum. He was surprised no one had thrown him overboard on the ferry to feed the gulls.

He passed Alison Murphy on his way to Colin's car. She was peering into the crowds, looking for someone.

"How's it going, Alison?" he said.

Her eyes went wide before she quickly smoothed out her expression. "Hiya, Niall," she said.

His stomach twisted—she knew. They all knew, everyone on this godforsaken island knew his whole story by now. *Thanks, Da*, he thought bitterly. Though maybe it was better he wouldn't have to sort out a way to tell people. That would have been torture. He could just imagine it.

Hey Niall, how's that fancy pub in Dublin coming along?

Oh well, you'd have to ask my former business partner and my cheating ex-fiancée. They're having a go of it together now, cut me out completely. Lost my whole investment and life savings to boot. They'd been carrying on behind my back for months, apparently. Anyway, cheers, thanks for asking!

"Picking up a new lodger?" he asked before she could make some trite comment about *hanging in there* or *keeping his chin up*.

"Got someone taking the cottage for the summer," she said.

"The whole summer?" Niall asked.

Alison nodded.

Who in the world would want to stay on Inishmore for the entire summer? They'd go bored out of their mind. If Niall could have gone anywhere else, he would have. But his father needed help with the pub—or at least, that's what his mother had said. Niall didn't really think his father wanted him home at all, and if he did, it was only so he could rub Niall's nose in his failures. *Too big for his boots* was one of Owen O'Connor's favorite sayings when it came to talking about his son. As if wanting to start a gastropub with elevated Irish fare was somehow the equivalent of opening a Michelin starred restaurant.

But his mother was far craftier, and she'd done the one thing that could make coming home with his tail between his legs palatable—she'd hired his best friend to be the musical entertainment at O'Connor's for the summer. The pub had been in the family for generations and while good beer and a hearty meal were its blood, music was its beating heart. And Colin was exactly the sort of happy-go-lucky, see-where-the-wind-takes-him kind of guy to accept her offer instead of making a go of touring the cities.

"I need someone to keep an eye on Gran," Alison explained. "Since I'll be busy at the Tigh na Mara."

Jesus. Niall didn't envy that poor sod, whoever they were. He loved Róisín dearly but Alison's grandmother was a prickly old codger who didn't take shite from anybody. He couldn't imagine who would be willing to spend a whole summer looking after her. Alison must have sugarcoated the deal quite a bit. Or flat out lied. He bet she hadn't told Róisín a damned thing about it—Róisín would be furious thinking of Alison hiring someone to watch her like a nanny.

The thought almost made Niall smile. He'd have to stop by Róisín's house later and see what she thought of the arrangement. He bet she'd have a few choice opinions to share.

He had only taken another handful of steps before he was engulfed in one of Colin Doyle's famous bear hugs. Colin was a lean, lanky guy but he did everything with so much enthusiasm it could feel like he was twice his actual size. Niall felt himself relax for the first time in far too long. For weeks there'd been an iron spring in his chest winding tighter and tighter, keeping him from breaking into pieces.

"Good to see you," he said gruffly.

Colin released him and patted his shoulder. "You look shite. Come on, let's get you home and unpacked." He glanced at the duffel bag hanging over Niall's shoulder. "Is that all you brought?"

Niall shrugged. The truth was, it was all he had taken from his and Deirdre's place five weeks ago after walking in on her and Patrick fucking on the pristine floor of the newly renovated kitchen in what was supposed to be his dream pub. He'd gone straight back to their place, thrown whatever was closest into a bag, and left. He'd stayed at a hotel for the first week, then a mate who was out of town generously offered to let Niall stay at his flat. But that arrangement had ended, and the thought of finding a new place to live, alone, with no prospects, was agony. Dublin itself seemed to have turned against him—the city he once loved was now haunted by Deirdre at every turn. He'd moved to Dublin as soon as he possibly could, the moment he turned eighteen and left school. It was his chosen home, his sanctuary, a place where he could be himself and live his dreams. He'd worked in more kitchens than he could count, learning as much as he could, saving and scraping by while secretly hoarding the hope that one day, he might run his own place, make his own menu.

All those years of hard work were meant to finally be coming to fruition. Until the day he caught Deirdre going at it with Patrick.

His throat closed up at the memory, the iron spring tightening another inch. Colin didn't press the issue, instead gesturing to Niall's mother's old green Volkswagen, which Colin had borrowed to pick Niall up.

"God, this car makes me feel like I'm twelve again," Niall groaned, tossing his bag in the back seat. The Volkswagen still smelled like oiled leather and peppermint. Niall had a sudden image of himself as a boy, his mother laughing and passing one of her hard candies to him as they drove home on Sundays after church.

"Just like old times, isn't it?" Colin said cheerfully, hopping in the driver's seat. "When was the last time we lived together in the same city?"

"Please don't call Kilronan a city," Niall said as Colin put the car into gear.

"Are you going to be such a delightful ray of sunshine all summer?"

"Yes." Niall folded his arms across his chest and glared out the window.

"Grand," Colin muttered, and they left the crowded harbor behind and drove up into the hills of Inishmore. The car puttered along Cottage Road, low stone walls breaking up the rich green landscape. There were tourists with cameras hanging around their necks, peering around in the rain—Niall was reminded of the woman on the docks. The locals were hurrying about their business or stopping along the roadside to chat with one another.

"Alison Murphy said someone's rented the cottage for the whole summer," Niall noted absently. "To watch Róisín."

"Ha! Well good luck to 'em," Colin said. "I bet it's one of those hippie Aussies. Alison probably wants someone close by in case Róisín falls off her cart."

"Is she still doing pony and trap tours?"

"Do you think there's a man, woman, or sea creature on this island who could stop her?"

Niall's lips twitched. Róisín Callahan was a lover of all fairy stories—mermaids and banshees and púcas. He remembered how she would scare the shit out of the children during Pátrún—Niall's father would tell her every year not to bring up the Dullahan, and every year she'd tell the tale of the headless rider on a black horse whose coming would mean death if he stopped in a village.

All these years later, Róisín was still doing as she pleased. Nothing ever changed on this island.

They drove past the cheery yellow farmhouse where Niall had spent his youth, and sure enough, his mother was standing in the open doorway waving to them as they passed.

"I told her we'd stop by once you'd settled in," Colin said, returning the wave. "Your da's at the pub with Pocket."

Niall appreciated the heads up. He wasn't ready to face his father quite yet. Though he couldn't wait to see the family dog. The last time he'd visited was two Christmases ago.

"How's the house?" he asked.

"It's not bad, actually. Old Fagan kept it pretty tight. It's not the Ritz but it'll do fine. You'll like the kitchen," Colin added. "Lots of counter space."

He winked and Niall's mouth twitched again. He did love a well-fashioned kitchen.

"Bless me, was that a *smile*? And honest to goodness Niall O'Connor smile? Didn't think I'd be seeing one of those for a month at least."

"Har har. You're a regular comedian, Colin. Maybe you should change professions."

"Think your da would let me do a standup night at the pub?"

Colin let out a bellowing laugh and even Niall gave a small chuckle, imagining Owen O'Connor's face at the mention of standup comedy and his precious pub in the same sentence.

The house they'd rented had once belonged to an old friend of Colin's father, but he had moved to Doolin to be closer to his daughter and her children. It was tucked in between his parents' house to the south and Róisín's home high up on the hill to the north. The house was sturdy and white, two stories with a red door and slate roof. It had been years since Niall and Colin had roomed together—back when Colin was studying music at Trinity and Niall was working in a pub called the Crooked Antler. Eventually they'd gotten their own flats. Colin was often traveling to whatever city would pay him to play at their pubs and then Niall had moved in with Deirdre. It felt a bit like old times to be living with his best friend again, though the house promised to be more comfortable than the tiny flat they'd once rented in Ranelagh. Colin parked the car and Niall grabbed his bag from the back.

"Home sweet home," Colin said, opening the door with a flourish. It was simply but neatly furnished—a large main room, a narrow hall that led back to the kitchen, and a set of stairs going up to the second floor.

"I took the best room," Colin joked. When Niall got upstairs he realized both bedrooms were identical, square with two windows each and brass beds. He dropped his bag on the bed and opened the narrow, creaking wardrobe door. Inside smelled like mothballs, and the memory of Deirdre came unexpectedly, like a punch to the gut, surprising him with its ferocity. The one time in their three-year relationship that he'd brought her home from Dublin to the island to visit, she'd gone to hang up her clothes in his old room at his parents' place and wrinkled her nose.

"Does your mam own stock in mothballs?" she'd quipped. "I'm going to smell like my gran this whole trip!"

Niall's jaw clenched, the spring tightening again as he slammed the wardrobe door shut. He left his bag unpacked on his bed and wandered down to the kitchen. The appliances were old but well maintained. There was more counter space than he'd expected, despite Colin's description. A small island with a teak top sat in the center of the room, a couple of high stools on one side, copper pots and pans hanging from a rack above it. A block of knives was next to the gas stove—Niall took one out and examined it. It needed sharpening.

"Unpacked already?" Colin asked, standing in the doorway.

Niall shook his head. "I'll do it later. Probably should wash everything anyway." Somehow Deirdre's scent still lingered, like she was perched on his shoulder or hidden in his pocket, following him wherever he went. He scraped his hand over his two-day-old stubble. Even here, even as far away from Dublin as he could get without leaving the bloody country, he could still smell the faint trace of her jasmine perfume.

"We should go see my mam," he said, though he was already tired at the thought of going anywhere, doing anything, seeing anyone.

Colin walked over and clapped a hand on his shoulder. "Before we go," he said, "you're taking a shower. You look a mess, Nie. You don't want your mam to see you like this."

Once he'd showered and shaved and borrowed a shirt from Colin, Niall drove them to the old farmhouse down the road.

They could've walked over, but the rain had picked up again.

"I hope Fiona's making a roast," Colin said, rubbing his hands together. "I'm starved."

"It's Sunday," Niall reminded him. "She always makes a roast on Sundays."

Colin grinned. "I know. Why d'you think I made friends with you in primary school? Your sparkling personality?"

Niall punched him on the shoulder.

His mother hurried out the front door as he parked, waving eagerly, and Niall's heart softened. Fiona O'Connor had big blue eyes, like her son, but wild brown curls that were always escaping whatever band or scarf or hairband she tried to tame them with. She wore a flowered apron over her gray slacks and a red Aran jumper.

"Gorgeous day, isn't it," she said with a grin as Niall got out of the car. She threw her arms around him. "My sweet boy."

"Hi, Mam." He breathed in the scent of soda bread and rosemary. "What's cooking?"

"Well, the bread's in the oven and I'm working on the roast for dinner. But there's a bit of lamb stew if you're feeling peckish. The kettle's on and I've got some jam and scones if you like." She glanced up at the sky. "Róisín said she'd stop by with carrots and a cabbage or two, but I hope she doesn't, not in this weather." She smiled at Colin as he came to give her a hug. "Colin Doyle, you look peaky. I'll set up a bowl of stew for you."

"That'd be grand, Fiona," Colin said, throwing Niall a wink.

As soon as he stepped into the house, Niall was hit with a thousand memories—the upright piano where his mother would play in the mornings, the sheet music open to some hymn or other. Niall could still see the small lines on the doorway where Fiona had marked his height by age. A newspaper sat folded on an armchair by the window, reminding Niall of the Saturdays when he would beg his father to put it down and kick the football around with him in the yard.

But the smells—the smells were this house's true treasure. Stewed meat and baking bread and fresh herbs, roast potatoes and garlic and the faint sweet scent of tea, all mingling together and calling to mind so many dinners at the simple dining room table. Watching his father season a whole chicken. Learning how to cut onions the proper way. Laughing as he punched an enormous mound of bread dough, a fine dust of flour clinging to his hair.

Niall swallowed hard. This kitchen was where he had first begun experimenting with his own recipes—his father never would have allowed him to try new things in the sacred hallow that was the family pub's kitchen. Fiona had been his first guinea pig when trying out a newly invented recipe after researching ingredients and dishes from all over the world, like making colcannon with wilted kale and Mexican crema or glazing a good fillet of Irish salmon with gochujang sauce to give it a kick. Once they'd left the island to live in Dublin, Colin had filled the guinea pig role.

And then came Deirdre. She had been the one to breathe real life into his dream. His own gastropub, a place in Dublin where he could serve his unique recipes. Peeking out from beneath his father's oppressive shadow of what an Irish pub *should* be like.

She'd believed in him so hard that he'd finally believed in himself. And right when he was on the cusp of actually having it, she'd punctured that dream with a massive needle, leaking all the color and joy out of his life. She and Patrick had strong-armed him out of his own damn restaurant—not that he would have wanted to work there with the two of them. But it was *his* menu they were going to be serving. He was meant to be preparing for the soft open right now, not back on fucking Inishmore pouring pints for imbecilic tourists. It had been a month since he'd cooked anything. He lived on takeaway and sadness now.

But as he sat down at the table and his mother pushed a bowl of stew and a slice of fresh bread in front of him, Niall realized he was famished. The lamb was tender, the gravy rich and well-seasoned, the carrots holding the perfect amount of firmness. He shoveled the food into his mouth like a dying man with his last meal; his mother's voice washed over him as she chatted about what Cian Byrne was doing now that he had taken over the Seaview restaurant and how Aoife O'Shea had been since her husband died last fall. And then suddenly, Niall's spoon clattered into the bowl and he dropped his head in his hands and began to cry.

His stomach was full for the first time in ages and his chest loosened as the iron spring unwound a fraction. He felt his mother's arms wrap around him, her murmured shhhs in his ear, and he didn't even care that Colin was here to see this. He felt drained, broken.

"There you go now," his mother murmured, rubbing his back. "Let it out. There's a good lad. Let it all out. You're home now. It's going to be all right. You'll see."

Niall wished he could believe her. But from where he was sitting, it didn't feel like anything would be all right. Something inside him had been shattered and he didn't see how he would ever be able to put the pieces back together again.

3

Cordelia was in a state of complete and utter shock.

She barely heard Alison talking to her as they drove up into the hills. It had taken all of her willpower to introduce herself in a somewhat normal manner at the dock. Now she felt her lungs compress, squeezing themselves up into her throat and choking her. Her camera was broken, and she was miles away from any store that could possibly repair it.

"Are you all right?"

Cordelia started and realized the car had stopped. They were sitting in front of the tiniest cottage she'd ever seen, gray stone with a thatched roof, rain pattering down the windshield and blurring her vision.

"I'm sorry," she said thickly.

Alison's cheerful face creased with worry. "Don't be sorry," she said. "You've had a long day. Is it . . . are you tired from the travel?"

Cordelia held up her camera. "It's broken," she said and her voice cracked. "Some jerk coming off the ferry bumped into me and I dropped it and now . . ." She swallowed hard. "My dad gave me this camera before he died."

And that did it—something broke in her chest, the long trip, the exhaustion, the distance from home, the loss of her most precious possession, all of it came crashing down on her. She sobbed into her hands and Alison sat beside her quietly, patting her shoulder. At last, Cordelia took a deep shuddering breath.

"I'm really sorry," she said with a hiccup. She wiped her nose on the back of her sleeve. "This isn't how I wanted to meet you."

"Don't you apologize. That's an awful thing to happen after such a long day." Alison's eyes were full of pity. "We could all use a good cry from time to time, and this seems like a fair reason for one. But as my gran always says, the sun shines brightest after a storm. Let's get you inside. A hot shower is what you'll be needing. I'll make some tea and we'll sort out what to do about your camera." She gave her a small smile. "We aren't completely cut off from the outside world, y'know."

"Thank you," Cordelia said with a sniff. "Sorry, was I meant to meet your grandma now or . . ."

"Oh no, it's fine," Alison said quickly. She glanced up the hill where a large stone house loomed, bleak against the clouds. "There's no rush."

She grabbed Cordelia's bag from the trunk and they hurried inside the cottage, shaking the rain from their coats and hanging them on pegs by the door.

The inside was as tiny as it had seemed in the pictures online—the front of the cottage was a living and dining area squished together, a faded blue sofa against one wall and a lamp with a butterfly print shade sitting on top of a stack of old books. There was a chipped wooden table with three chairs and a braided rug on the floor. White eyelet lace curtains hung in the windows, and there was a small fireplace with an armchair beside it. Alison showed Cordelia to her bedroom, then went to make tea. A window over the bed looked out onto a back garden and up to a green field surrounded by low rock walls.

She could practically hear her father's voice in her ear. "It's like you've stepped into *The Secret Garden*, Cordie. Now don't you cry over spilled milk—get up, get out there, and enjoy the day." But she couldn't enjoy the day. How could she enjoy anything now? Who was she without a camera?

She took out her phone and texted Liz what happened. She wasn't ready to tell Toby yet—she didn't know what would be worse, him acting like this was some kind of sign or him saying something trite like *You keep Dad in your heart, not in a camera.*

Before she could put her phone away, it pinged. She checked the screen and her stomach dropped. She'd completely forgotten to text her mother.

Toby says you got there ok.

Oof. That was some quality Louise James shade right there.

Sorry Mom, it's been crazy, Cordelia wrote back. She sighed and added, *How's Gary? How's the vacation?*

She didn't really care how her mother's boyfriend was, but Toby was constantly insisting she be nice. She was trying. Not always succeeding, but trying.

Ever since Louise had started dating Gary six months ago, she'd become some kind of zealot about romance. She was constantly nagging Cordelia about her lack of a love life. As if the only possible way to be happy was to be paired up with someone.

And okay, maybe Cordelia had assumed that Dad had been the love of Mom's life, and when you found the love of your life you didn't just get over it and start dating an ex-marine you met on an "older singles" website.

Oh it's wonderful! her mother wrote back and then sent a picture of the two of them on a boat. They were spending a week at Gary's house in the Florida Keys. Her mother had a faint sunburn on the bridge of her nose and wore a big floppy hat. Gary was wearing a Hawaiian shirt and Ray-Bans, his arm thrown casually around her mother's shoulders.

You guys look great! Cordelia wrote back, adding the exclamation point as an afterthought. *So there, Toby,* she thought to herself. *I can be nice.*

Her mother sent back a red heart emoji and a cat with a kissing face and a rainbow. Cordelia rolled her eyes—Gary had been teaching her about emojis and now she couldn't have a text conversation without them. Nikki thought it was cute. Toby thought it was funny. Cordelia thought it was weird.

The bathroom was en suite, and Cordelia stripped off her travel-worn clothes, turned on the water, and stepped gratefully into the low porcelain tub wedged between the narrow walls. If she were in New York, she'd take her camera to Leslie Greer over on 58th Street, to the shop where she got all her equipment. If anyone could fix it, Leslie could.

The initial shock was beginning to wear off beneath the soothing rush of hot water—of course it could be fixed. It was just a lens, plus the focus was off. Surely Leslie could handle that. Cordelia could get it sorted out when she got back to the city.

The problem was, that was months away. Cordelia had made an agreement with Alison—she couldn't break it and run home because of a cracked lens. But there was no way she could spend three months without a camera. Photography was a secondary system of veins and capillaries running straight to her heart. A week without a camera was doable, maybe. But not an entire summer.

She sighed. She *really* didn't want to spend the money, especially since she was already dipping into some of the inheritance her father had left her to come on this trip in the first place. But it looked like she was going to have to.

She turned off the tap and wrapped herself in a towel, wiping the steam from the mirror over the sink and staring at her reflection. There were deep shadows under her eyes and her hair hung in a rope over her shoulder. The scattering of freckles across her left cheek seemed stark against her pale skin. Her Andromeda, her father used to call it, because they were patterned in a shape similar to the constellation, curving under her left eye and leaving a trail to her jawline with a little sprinkling upward across her cheek.

She took a calming breath. It was time to make a slightly better impression on her new landlord. As she changed into a pair of sweatpants and an oversized tee, the smell of frying bacon filled the room and Cordelia's stomach roared. She followed her nose to the kitchen.

It was as snug as the rest of the house, with a window that had the same view as her bedroom, a tiny sink and stove, a humming little fridge, and mint green cabinets lining the walls, the paint peeling in some places.

"Bad news wants food," Alison said, pointing at the bacon sizzling in a pan on the stove. "That's another of my gran's sayings."

"I'm excited to meet her," Cordelia said politely.

Alison chuckled. "I'll warn you right now, she's a character. Don't be put off if she's a bit . . . strange at first."

"Oh," Cordelia said. "Okay."

An electric kettle was heating up on the countertop beside the bacon and Alison had cracked some eggs into a large clear bowl and was whisking them enthusiastically.

"Did the shower help? You look like you've got some color back."

"It did," Cordelia said. "Thank you so much, I'm sorry about all that. I—"

Alison waved the whisk at her. "No need for sorrys, like I said. I lost my da and my mam when I was just a little girl. I still have a good cry about them sometimes. I understand completely."

Cordelia was surprised that Alison was being so open with her, but it turned at once to gratitude. Here was a kindred spirit—another child in the horrible Dead Parent Club. "You didn't have to do this," she said, gesturing to the stove.

"It's no trouble. I stocked the fridge well enough for a day, but there's a shop in town you'll want to visit tomorrow. There's bikes you can use, they're in the shed up at the house. How does an omelet sound? I'm only proficient in breakfast food, I'm afraid—that's all I make at the Tigh na Mara."

Cordelia felt so many things at once—starving and sad and overwhelmed and exhausted. So she just nodded. There was a tiny table with two stools in the corner, and she sank into one. The kettle began to steam and Alison switched it off, putting another pan on the stove for the omelet, sliding some mushrooms on to cook, and pouring them each a generous cup of tea. The scent of black tea filled the room and mixed pleasantly with the mushrooms and bacon.

The whole story poured out of Cordelia then, why she had been eager to come to the island for the whole summer in the first place, the frustration she'd been feeling in New York, the sense of being stuck after her father's death, of being a failure.

"Right," Alison said when she'd finished. "Okay. I was wondering why a New Yorker would be agreeing to my offer. It sounds to me like you need a break. And this is as good a place to take one as any."

She added the mushrooms and some goat cheese to the eggs, then folded the omelet in half. She slid it onto a plate, sprinkled it with chives, and slapped two pieces of bacon next to it.

"Eat," she said. "You'll feel better. Now let's see what we can do about this camera."

"There's a woman I know back in the city who can fix it," Cordelia said. "But I think I'd rather buy a new one while I'm here."

Alison took out her phone as Cordelia picked up her fork. She took one bite and groaned, losing herself in the delicious flavors. She'd eaten half the omelet before Alison had finished typing *camera shops* into her search bar.

"We can order things from the shops in Doolin to be sent here. It might take a few days. What sort of camera is it?"

"A Fujifilm X100V," Cordelia said through a mouthful of bacon.

Alison did a search for the camera and blanched when she saw the price. "That's some piece of equipment you brought," she said.

Cordelia was feeling the wholesome effects of home cooking on an empty stomach along with the cheer of friendly company and she finally managed a smile.

"Good cameras are pricey," she said. "Even when they're small."

Alison frowned. "It looks like you'll need to order it from Dublin. That'll take about a week, at least."

A week? Cordelia's full stomach lurched. But hadn't she just been thinking she could go a week without a camera? It might turn out to be a good thing. Plus she could rub it in Toby's face.

Her phone buzzed and Cordelia looked down to see that Liz had responded in classic Liz style.

OH MY FUCKING GOD CORD WHAT THE FUCK WHO WAS THIS ASSHOLE WHO BUMPED INTO YOU I WILL COME FOR HIM AND HAUNT HIM TO THE ENDS OF THE EARTH OH BABES I AM SO SORRY. And then almost as an afterthought she added, *Are you ok???*

I'm okay, Cordelia wrote back. *Over the initial shock. Alison is helping me order a new camera from Dublin. I'll take Dad's to Leslie when I get back.*

OH YAY! Liz was a big fan of all caps. *Omg so proud of you, handling this like a champ. How's the cottage? How's the grandma? Is it raining yet?*

Cordelia chuckled. "It's my best friend," she explained to Alison. "She thinks I'm crazy to come here. She's sure it will rain the whole summer."

Alison grinned and gestured to the window, where the rain was now lashing against the panes. "She's not fully wrong. Though there will be sunny days too, don't you worry." She took out a thick folder and laid it on the table. "This has all the information about the island, the things to do, sightseeing, all that. The Wi-Fi password and such is in here too. And there's a map of the town and the key to the cottage. Like I said over email, if you don't mind keeping the cottage tidy and bringing the mail up to Róisín. She gets some deliveries too, fertilizer and animal feed, you can leave that in the shed. And just, you know, knock on the door once or twice a day to let her know you're there."

"I don't need to, like, take her for walks or anything?"

Alison laughed. "You could try," she said.

Cordelia opened her mouth to speak but instead gave an enormous yawn.

"You need rest," Alison said. "It's been a long day. But if you'd like, tomorrow I can take you to dinner at O'Connor's. It's the place where all the locals go. It's in walking distance and it's always good craic."

"Sorry, did you say *crack*?" Cordelia yelped, wondering if she'd stumbled on some kind of *Breaking Bad* situation.

"Craic means fun," Alison explained, smiling.

"Oh. That sounds perfect, then," Cordelia said, returning the smile.

"I wrote down the name of the shop in Dublin. Have that camera shipped to the B&B, that way it'll come straight to me."

After Alison left, Cordelia grabbed another slice of bacon and refilled her tea before crawling into bed and FaceTiming Liz.

She picked up on the second ring.

"Oh, Cord," Liz said. "Are you sure you're okay?"

Liz had light brown skin and sleek mahogany hair, shaved on one side and cut at an extreme angle down to her chin. She wore her signature bright red lipstick and her nose ring glinted in the muted colored lamps in her apartment. Seeing her face had Cordelia's heart pinching all over again.

"I wasn't, but I'm better now." Cordelia sighed. "Not the best moment to be blowing over a grand on new equipment, but I can't be here without a camera, Liz."

"I know, babes," Liz said sympathetically. "Ugh. What a shit way to start your summer. Have you at least met any hot Irish guys yet?"

Cordelia narrowed her eyes. "I'm sorry, I didn't realize I had called Louise James's number."

"Okay, okay, I deserved that. How's the place? It's raining, isn't it?"

"It *is* raining and the place is really cute." She switched her camera view so Liz could see the bedroom, then switched it back.

"Oh my god, Cord. It's like you're living in Snow White's cottage or something."

"I know."

"Oh shit." Liz frowned. "I gotta run, I'm meeting Meena for lunch. Get some sleep. You'll feel much better tomorrow, I bet."

"Yeah," Cordelia said. "Maybe. Give Meena my love."

Liz hesitated, as if Cordelia didn't always send her love to Liz's girlfriend. But before she could wonder too much about it, Liz smiled brightly. "Will do," she said. "Love you."

"Love you too."

She hung up and stared out the window at the darkening gloom. One phone call with Liz and she was already homesick. She finished her tea while she placed her order for the new camera, sending it to the Tigh na Mara B&B as Alison had instructed.

It was only seven o'clock, but Cordelia didn't care. She placed her broken camera on the nightstand and touched her father's thumbprint. "Love you, Dad," she murmured. Then she slid under the covers and played an old *Forensic Files* episode on her phone. But within five minutes, she'd fallen into a deep, dreamless sleep.

She awoke early the next morning with a jolt.

Sunlight streamed in through the window. For one disorienting second, she forgot where she was. Her camera sat on the nightstand staring at her through its broken lens, and Cordelia's heart sank to settle somewhere around her knees.

Get up, get out there, and enjoy the day. Nothing a brisk walk couldn't fix, that was Christopher James's motto. She checked her phone—she had a couple of new texts and pictures from Toby: Grace all dressed up and going off to gymnastics camp and Miles holding up a tooth he'd lost. And from her mother, a link to an article titled "Five Top Tips to Find Romance on Vacation." Cordelia didn't feel like responding to that.

She showered and dressed, then checked the fridge and cupboards to see what food she had. Her spirits were lifting a little—she opened the kitchen window and was pleased to feel a warm breeze on her face. The scent of thyme and basil wafted in from the herb garden behind the house. The sun was bright in a pale blue sky, not a cloud in sight. She snapped a picture and sent it off to Liz, then pored over the information Alison had left for her.

There were boat schedules for travel to the other two islands, Inishmaan and Inisheer, along with things to do like cycling and visiting monuments, cliffs, and beaches. She studied the map of the town of Kilronan and was pleased to find it pretty straightforward—Alison had marked where the cottage was, and it seemed like she was living off the one main road that led down to the central thrust of the town. She saw the pub, O'Connor's, clearly marked.

Cordelia decided to pop down to the market, then see if she could finally meet this Róisín. She could feel the missing weight of her camera as she hiked her bag over her shoulder. She touched her dad's thumbprint one last time before heading out.

As she walked down the main road, her phone pinged with a text from Alison.

How are you feeling today?

Much better thanks, Cordelia replied. *Heading to the market then I'll bring the mail up to the house.*

Great, cheers. Meet at the pub at six tonight? Sorry if it's on the early side—I have to be up to get breakfast ready for the guests.

An early dinner sounded perfect.

See you then! Cordelia wrote back.

The market had a striped awning and baskets of produce outside. Cordelia grabbed some essentials, and by the time she returned to the cottage, the jet lag fog was setting in again. The only mail was a copy of *The Irish Times* addressed to Róisín Callahan. Cordelia walked up the dirt path to the big stone house—it was like a much larger version of the cottage, with a wreath of daisies hanging on the heavy wooden door.

She knocked but got no reply. A low bench was placed to the side of the door. Cordelia sat on it for a bit, wondering if maybe Róisín would return home, but after a while she gave up and wedged the paper under the doormat, heading back to the cottage to nap before dinner.

O'Connor's was full but not crowded when she arrived that evening at five minutes to six. There were Guinness posters and soccer jerseys on the walls and a long sleek bar with a dozen gleaming metal taps. Mirrors hung behind neat rows of liquor bottles, and antique lights glowed overhead. There was a smattering of tables, about half of them occupied, along with a sofa and a couple of armchairs crowded around a dormant fireplace. In one corner, there was a small, elevated platform that served as a stage—a lanky man with thick brown hair was playing guitar and singing a cover of "Trouble" by Ray LaMontagne. He was talented, his voice rich and clear. She hovered in the doorway, looking for Alison. When she didn't see her, she decided to grab a seat at the bar.

An old man with a bulbous nose and red cheeks two seats away tipped his cap to her. Cordelia gave one of her long-practiced New York half-smiles, the kind that said, "I acknowledge your existence but don't talk to me."

It didn't work.

"And what might your name be, missy?" he asked.

"Leave the girl alone, Darragh," a rough voice said. "Can I get you something to drink or d'you want to look at the menu?"

Cordelia turned, thinking she'd take the largest glass of wine they had to offer, and instead found herself staring straight into a pair of aquamarine eyes beneath a thick mess of black hair.

"You!" she cried. "You fucking *asshole*!"

4

Niall wasn't quite sure what to say to that.

"Sorry, do I know you?" he asked, as Darragh chuckled and a few other regulars turned to watch the action.

"You broke my camera!" the woman shouted. Half the bar was looking now. Niall was mortified but still confused as to why this stranger seemed to hate him so much.

"I don't know what you're talking about," he said.

"Yesterday, getting off the ferry." She was so mad he could practically see steam shooting from her ears, her cheeks puffing out in a way that was more comical than intimidating. "You bumped into me and made me drop my camera and it *broke*."

She said this with the ferocity of a victim of some truly great crime, like armed robbery or running over a beloved cat. But he remembered her now.

"I believe it was *you* who bumped into me," he snapped.

"I definitely did not."

She definitely *did*, but Niall didn't want her causing more of a scene. Sure, maybe he'd been walking too fast but it wasn't his job to pay attention to every tourist coming off the ferry. "Look, I'm sorry, it was an accident, okay?"

The woman glared. "Do you have any idea . . . *any* idea—"

"Hey, it's just a camera right?" Niall forced a chuckle. He wanted this drama over so the regulars would stop staring. They'd stared at him enough already since he'd started work this afternoon. Seamus Donovan in particular had been making all manner of snide remarks. "How about I replace it for you? What was it, a hundred euro or something?"

Not that he had much cash to speak of, but Colin might lend him the money.

"It cost one thousand four hundred dollars," she spat at him. "But that isn't the point."

"One thousand—Jesus Christ!" Niall exclaimed. "What are you tossing something that expensive around for?"

"I wasn't tossing it around," the woman hissed. "You were barging down the docks like a bull in freaking Pamplona."

The door opened and Niall saw Alison Murphy step in. "Oh, thank god," he muttered, eager to get away from this angry American. "Need a table, Alison?" he called, but to his dismay, she hurried over and took the seat beside the girl.

"Sorry I'm late—" she said, then stopped when she saw the expression on the woman's face. Niall didn't blame her. She could probably melt metal with those eyes. "What's going on?"

"This"—she hooked a thumb violently in his direction—"is the asshole who broke my camera."

Darragh and a few others snorted into their beers.

"Now look," Niall said, leaning forward. "That's the second time you've called me an asshole and there won't be a third! I said I was sorry about the camera."

"No, you didn't," she snarled. "You said the word sorry. That doesn't count as an apology."

"Well, I *am* sorry, all right? But could you please . . . keep your voice down? First drink's on the house."

"Do you like wine?" Alison asked, inserting herself in to smooth things over. "They've got a good cabernet here."

The woman sniffed. "Yeah. Fine."

"Niall, this is Cordelia James. She's the one I told you is staying at the cottage for the summer. Cordelia, this is Niall O'Connor."

Cordelia blinked. "As in *O'Connor's* O'Connor?"

Niall spread his hands out wide, his teeth gritted into a bad imitation of a smile. "The one and only. I'll get that wine." Then he hurried down to the opposite end of the bar before Cordelia could insult him again.

Colin finished his set and joined him.

"Sweet mother of Mary, what did you do to make that American so upset?"

"We bumped into each other coming off the ferry and she dropped her camera and it broke. It was pricey, apparently. And my apology was shite, so I've been told." Niall couldn't believe someone would spend so much on a camera when an iPhone would work just as well.

Colin whistled. "You better give her free drinks all night."

"That's the plan."

"She's easy on the eyes, though, isn't she," Colin said, casting an appreciative glance in the direction of the two women.

"You think everyone is easy on the eyes," Niall said. He meant that literally—Colin was bi, and though he'd never had a serious relationship, he'd certainly slept his way through half the population of Dublin, both male and female.

"Don't be such a prude, Niall. You've had your heart torn out, yes, but you're not dead. At some point, you're going to have to get back on that horse."

"When I do, it won't be with an American who called me an arsehole twice in the span of ten seconds," Niall snapped.

"Okay, okay, fair enough. Why's she talking with Alison?"

"She's the one who's taken the cottage."

"Oh grand!" Colin said brightly, then adjusted his expression when he saw Niall's face. "Right, not grand."

"Let's hope she finds another place to have dinner after tonight," Niall said. "Darragh and the others were already giving me those looks and innuendos, and Seamus was being an outright tool. Look at poor Niall, can't keep a woman. Poor Niall, couldn't get his pub started. Poor Niall, can't keep his fucking father's customers happy. I don't need more fuel added to that fire."

"Poor Niall needs to get laid, I think." Colin raised an eyebrow at the look on Niall's face. "What? That'd shut Seamus up right quick."

"Niall!" His father's voice came bellowing from the kitchen.

Niall clenched his jaw and inhaled sharply through his nose. "Be right there," he called, taking the two wineglasses over to Alison and the angry American. He slammed them down harder than he should have and some wine slipped over the top of one. "Sorry," he muttered, avoiding eye contact. "Be back in a few to take your order."

"Take your time!" Alison called after him. He could feel Cordelia's glare like a dagger between his shoulder blades as he stalked off to the kitchen.

His father was ladling seafood chowder from a huge pot on the stove into two glazed crock bowls. "Get these to table twelve," he said brusquely. "And what was the temperature on that steak for table five? You've got to write this stuff down, Niall. Where's your head at?"

Back in Dublin, where I should be opening my own pub and marrying Deirdre, Niall thought acidly. But he just grabbed the soup bowls and muttered, "Sorry, Da." When it came to his father, Niall had long ago learned it was easier to give in than to fight. Owen always won anyway.

He left the kitchen and saw Alison and Cordelia deep in conversation over their wine. Cordelia's eyes flitted to him briefly—she *was* pretty, he supposed, in an American sort of way. Big hazel eyes, honey-blonde hair, creamy skin that flushed pink at her cheekbones. But he knew all about her kind of tourist from working at various pubs in Dublin. Americans were self-entitled and demanding and loud, and this one seemed worse than any other he'd ever met. He gave her a glare worthy of the one she'd given him and went to deliver the soup to the waiting table.

"His fiancée cheated on him with his business partner?" Cordelia said, probably a little too loudly. She couldn't help herself—it was such wild gossip, like something out of a movie.

Alison gave a solemn nod and took a sip of wine. "Such a dreadful thing. He left the island when he was eighteen and never looked back. His father's a bit hard on him, always has been. It was the talk of Kilronan when news came that he was opening his own place in Dublin. But then a month ago, it all fell to pieces. So he's come home for the summer."

"That's so sad," Cordelia said. Niall came bursting through the kitchen doors with two bowls of soup and she shot him what she hoped was a more sympathetic look. He glared at her. "Jeez, is he always such a jerk?"

Alison chuckled. "He's always had a giant chip on his shoulder, if that's what you mean. We were friends all the way up through secondary school—not many year-rounders on the island and even fewer kids. Colin, he's over there with his guitar—oi, Colin!" She waved the musician over. "The three of us grew up together. When we got older and Niall started working in the pub, the tourist girls would be falling all over themselves blushing and laughing and batting their eyelashes. He's a fine thing."

"Talking about me again, are you?" Colin said, coming up and throwing his arm around Alison's shoulders as she introduced them.

"Cordelia is a photographer," Alison said. "From New York."

"New York! That's grand. I'd love to go to New York one day. Been my dream to play at one o' those cool little venues they've got."

The wine was making Cordelia more relaxed, and she felt friendlier now that the specter of Niall had been removed. "There's one I love on Bleecker Street called the Bitter End," she said.

"Do they have seisiúns there?" Colin asked with a wink.

"Uh, sessions of what?" Cordelia said.

"A seisiún is like when a whole bunch of musicians show up at a pub and play traditional Irish music," Alison explained.

"How cool," Cordelia said. "I don't know. But it's New York, so I'm sure they have them somewhere."

"We're having a seisiún here next week," Colin said. "You should come. Alison will be here. Róisín too. Have you met Róisín yet?"

Colin was a whirl of energy, and Cordelia found she couldn't stop smiling—his cheerful mood was infectious.

"Um, no," she said. "I dropped her mail off today but when I knocked, nobody was home."

Colin whistled. "You're in for a right treat. Róisín's a legend. Get her to take you out in her cart. She'll tell you everything you need to know about this island. And Inishmaan. And Inisheer. And the púca. And the banshees. And—"

"Hey!" Niall called from the end of the bar, tapping on his watch.

"Right, right," Colin said. "Sorry, I'm up again. We'll see you next week for the seisiún, eh, Cordelia? Fergus is bringing his bodhran. It'll be good craic."

"Oh, I . . ." Cordelia glanced at Niall. His face looked carved out of stone, his eyes like chips of ice when they met hers.

"Ah, don't worry about him, he's all bark and no bite," Colin said. "He's going through an *adjustment period*, shall we say."

"I told her," Alison said. Cordelia felt a twinge of embarrassment, but Colin just shrugged.

"I told him everyone would know," he said. "Can't keep a secret on Inishmore." He clapped Cordelia on the shoulder. "Anyway, I'll expect to see you. A week from Friday. Seven PM sharp." He wagged a finger at Alison. "Make sure she doesn't chicken out."

"Go on, you," Alison said, kissing him on the cheek. Colin winked and then jogged off between the tables.

"What can I get for you?" Cordelia jumped as Niall appeared behind them.

"I'll have the burger, thanks," Alison said.

Niall nodded. "And you?"

He'd thrown a dishrag over his shoulder, his blue eyes catching the light. They were startling, Cordelia thought, and in such contrast to his jet-black hair. There was a shadow of stubble across his angular jaw, which had a permanently clenched look. She wondered if that was a residual effect from the horrible end to his recent relationship or just how his face was. She guessed she could see why the tourist girls had fallen over themselves to flirt with him. But Cordelia could never imagine being attracted to someone who was that broody—someone who could be so unapologetic after destroying something so precious.

"I'll have the mussels, please," she said politely.

Then she picked up her wine and turned away from him to watch Colin play beneath the softly glowing lights.

5

Niall was wiping down the tables and putting up the chairs when his father came out of the kitchen with two bowls of chowder.

"Sit," he directed his son. Niall stopped wiping and sat down. His father set the bowls on the table and went to pour them two pints of lager. "Eat," he said, taking the empty seat beside Niall.

I'm not a fecking dog, Niall thought. But he ate the chowder anyway—he was too tired to fight. It wanted salt and some fresh herbs, but Niall wasn't about to say that. He took a long drink of his beer and waited for his father to speak his piece and be done with it. He wanted to be back at the house with Colin and Pocket. After weeks of lying about, his first day back working had left him knackered.

Owen took his time, eating the chowder in slow spoonfuls, then sipping his beer thoughtfully. Finally, Niall couldn't stand the silence any longer.

"Christ, Da, spit it out already."

Owen raised one bushy black eyebrow. "Beg your pardon?"

"I know you've got something to say so just say it. Otherwise, I'm going home."

"All right then," Owen said, sitting back and folding his arms across his chest. "I told you that girl was trouble."

"Here we go," Niall muttered, leaning forward and putting his head in his hands.

"I told you she was no good. City girl with all her big ideas, filling your head with notions that made you look down upon your family."

"She didn't make me look down upon you," Niall said through gritted teeth. "The pub was *my* idea. It was my dream. Deirdre made me feel like I could actually achieve it."

Owen snorted. "Well, she certainly achieved something, didn't she."

"What is the point of this conversation?" Niall demanded. "To make me feel more shite than I already do?"

"Alls I'm saying is, when you get too big for your britches—"

"Christ almighty, Da, wanting to do something different than you isn't too big for my goddamn britches! And I don't care if you didn't like Deirdre because I loved her. I *loved* her, okay? I was meant to marry her and we were meant to be happy together. And it's gone now, y'see? It's all fucking gone. So the last thing I need is you sitting me down to have some talk about how right you were and how wrong I was. I *know* I was wrong, Da. I know it every day. I know it in my bones. But living in Kilronan and running this pub is your dream, not mine."

Owen slammed his hand down on the table. "There you go again, with all your talk of dreams," he snapped. "D'you think my father cared a whit what my dreams were? D'you think I could have fed you and your mother on dreams? No. Good plain work is all you need in life. You'll find someone here, start a family of your own, then you'll see."

"No, I won't!" Niall cried, springing to his feet. "I won't see. I won't find someone here and I'm not starting a bloody family. I don't want to be here at all and I'm off as soon as the season's over. When are you going to get it through that thick skull of yours that *I'm not you*?"

"Don't you be taking that tone with me, boyo," Owen said, standing as well. He was as tall as Niall but with more girth, and he leveled his son with a dark look. "I know you're not me, that's plain as day. And your mother seems to think that bringing you home will sort everything out. But we know, son—we know you were living in some mate's flat in God knows what seedy corner of Dublin. We know you haven't got any money left."

Niall blinked. He thought he'd managed to keep that a secret from his parents. *Colin*, he thought in a flash.

He felt himself deflate. He was too tired for this fight. He was too damn tired of everything. "You're right, Da," he said. "I'm broke. I'm a loser. I've got no money, no prospects, no home, no relationship. I'm nothing."

This sudden about-face seemed to take his father off guard. "Well now, I didn't mean—"

"Yes, you did," Niall said, throwing the rag down on the table. "I'm going home. Close up yourself."

He grabbed his jacket and strode out the door.

Pocket was waiting for him outside. The border collie cocked her head to one side and trotted over to nuzzle his leg. He patted her head.

"Does Colin know you snuck out?" he asked as they began the walk back up to the house. Niall took out the torch he kept in his jacket—the roads were very dark at night. Pocket padded along beside him and Niall found his thoughts drifting back to the days of his childhood, when his father had seemed like such a hero, a big burly man, the king of Kilronan. When had it all changed?

Probably when Niall had started thinking for himself. And learning to cook his own sort of food. Dublin coddle, or corned beef, or champ with bacon were far too boring for him. It wasn't that he didn't love a good stew—he just thought there could be other things on a menu at a pub. But it was like even the thought of trying something different was the equivalent of slapping his father in the face.

Well, you don't have to worry about that anymore, Da, Niall thought bitterly as the lights of the house appeared in the distance. Deirdre had sapped the life right out of his dream. He would gladly serve whatever O'Connor's had to offer, get through this summer, and get as far away from Inishmore as he possibly could. His father should be happy—Niall had lost all desire to create new recipes. He'd lost the desire to cook ever again.

Cordelia awoke on her third day on Inishmore, got dressed, and went up to the house, wondering if she could finally meet the mysterious Róisín—but when she knocked, there was still no answer. She thought she saw a flash of movement inside, so she waited on the bench again but Róisín never appeared.

Alison texted Cordelia and asked if she could pull up some of the weeds in the cottage's front garden, so Cordelia headed back down the road.

It was chilly and windy outside. A quick assessment told Cordelia that she had no idea which were the flowers and which were the weeds. After perusing the living room, she found a book that listed various species of Irish wildflowers. By lunchtime she'd named honeysuckle, oxeye daisies, harebells, common milkwort, and cross-leaved heath and had pulled up quite a few of the weeds that sprouted up among them.

A truck stopped by to deliver a big bag of fertilizer for Róisín. Cordelia hoisted it up on her shoulder and stumbled back to the house on the hill. Alison had said to leave it in the shed, which Cordelia found off to one side, its red paint chipping, its wooden doors unlocked. Inside there was a wheelbarrow, various gardening tools, some buckets, a rubber hose, and two bicycles, one with a basket between the handlebars, a plastic flower stuck to its front.

She dumped the fertilizer in the wheelbarrow, then went to explore the other side of the house, wondering if maybe Róisín was in the backyard. She found a paddock for horses and a breathtaking view of the ocean. The paddock was empty.

Cordelia went back to the shed and decided to take the bike with the basket on it into town to grab some lunch. She texted Alison that she had delivered the fertilizer but had seen no sign of Róisín.

Was there a horse in the paddock? Alison replied.

No, Cordelia wrote back.

She's off giving a tour then. Thx for bringing up the fertilizer!

When Cordelia stopped by the cottage to grab her bag, she emerged and was surprised to find a border collie sitting on the dirt path, looking at her with shockingly intelligent eyes.

"Hello," she said, glancing around. "Who do you belong to?"

The dog padded forward and sniffed her pockets, then her bag. When she discovered that Cordelia had no treats hidden on her person, she nudged at her right hand for a pet. Cordelia laughed.

"Are you hungry?" she asked, scratching behind the dog's ear. "Hold on."

She went back inside to retrieve some of the leftover bacon Alison had made and found the dog sniffing around her bike.

"Here you go," she said, holding it out. The dog came forward and the bacon vanished in an instant. She cocked her head, one ear flopping, then looked in the direction of the road.

"Is that where your home is?" Cordelia asked. "Okay, let's go."

She climbed onto the bike seat and began to pedal. The dog trotted happily along beside her and Cordelia soon realized that this creature was a bit of a celebrity.

"All right, Pocket!" a man in a truck called as he passed.

A woman walking along with an umbrella said, "Made a new friend, have you, Pocket?"

"So your name is Pocket, huh?" Cordelia said.

When they passed the large yellow farmhouse, Cordelia saw a woman with wild brown curls taking laundry down off a line. It was such a perfect picture, stockings dancing in the whipping wind, the pale sunshine color of the farmhouse behind. Cordelia's fingers ached for her camera. The woman dropped the sheet she was holding and put her hands on hips.

"Pocket!" she shouted, and the dog perked up as the woman came hurrying over.

"I'm sorry, she wasn't bothering you, was she?" the woman asked. "Come here, you scoundrel. You're meant to be up at Róisín's place."

"I think she was," Cordelia said. "I'm Cordelia, I'm renting the cottage from Alison for the summer."

"Oh, the American girl!" the woman said.

"That's me." Cordelia grimaced. "News really travels fast."

The woman chuckled. "Not much else to do in a small place like this except talk. I'm Fiona." They shook hands over the stone wall that lined the property. "So you're staying the whole summer, eh? I hope you don't get bored. I know you young folks like to party and such."

"I'm not really a partyer," Cordelia said.

"Well, that's good. Have you met Róisín yet?"

"No," Cordelia said, puzzled. "She doesn't ever seem to be home."

Fiona laughed. "She's always got something or other going on. Does a lot of cart rides for the tourists. Where are you off to then?"

"I thought I'd go down to the harbor for lunch."

"If it's food you're after you should go to O'Connor's. All the locals love it."

Cordelia smiled. "I know, Alison took me there last night."

"And how did you find it?" Fiona was giving her a stern look that made Cordelia certain there was only one appropriate answer.

"It was wonderful," she said. *Angry, jerk-face, camera-breaking bartenders aside*, she added mentally.

Fiona pushed her wild curls out of her face where the wind caught them. "Now listen, it can get awful lonely up at that cottage all by yourself. Why don't you come over for Sunday dinner? Alison and Róisín always come for my roast. Give you a break from the whistling wind and the sound o' rain."

Cordelia was delighted by the offer. Alison would be there and she could finally meet Róisín, if she still hadn't by then. Sunday was five days away—it would be nice to have something to look forward to.

"I'd love that," she said. "Thank you."

Fiona clapped her hands together. "Grand! Dinner's at six thirty. Róisín can take you down in the cart, I imagine. Or the walk is easy enough as long as the weather holds." She turned to the dog. "Now come on, Pocket, I've got to be getting these clothes off the line before the rain comes."

"Is it going to rain?" Cordelia asked, looking up. The sky was cloudy but not particularly threatening.

Fiona patted her thigh. "Got two screws in this knee," she said. "It always aches before the rain."

Cordelia wished she'd brought her rain jacket. She said goodbye to Fiona and Pocket and carried on down to the center of town.

She didn't know any other restaurant besides O'Connor's and, jerk-face bartenders notwithstanding, it really was a nice place. And the mussels had been fantastic.

So she gathered her courage and pushed her way through the doors, instinctively glancing at the bar for any sign of black hair or blue eyes. But there was only a cheerful middle-aged woman with curly red hair pouring some drinks for a couple of tourists. Cordelia exhaled with relief and took a seat at a free table.

The bar had great lighting. *If I had my camera*, she thought with a grumble, *I could be taking pictures right now. I wonder where those tourists are from. Maybe they'd let me shoot them. Give a fresh start to my Instagram.*

She hadn't posted anything or even looked at her feed in a month. A detox, she'd told Liz, but the truth was she was too scared. She was tired of the negative comments, tired of feeling like she'd lost her spark. But now she'd give anything to feel the gentle weight of her camera slung across her chest.

She ordered a beet salad from the woman, who introduced herself as Shauna and definitely knew who Cordelia was already. Cordelia took out her true crime book and sipped a club soda while she waited for her food, losing herself in the Keddie Cabin murders. Liz had tried to insist that she bring some light beach reads, but to Cordelia true crime *was* a beach read.

A group of young American men came in and sat at the bar. Cordelia cringed—they were loud and obnoxious, ordering whiskey shots and high-fiving. It was people like them that gave American tourists a bad name.

The door opened again, letting in a gust of chilly air, and Cordelia froze when she saw the tall, lean form of Niall O'Connor striding into the room.

Shit, she thought as he caught sight of her. Niall's cold blue eyes widened a fraction, then Shauna appeared at the table with Cordelia's food.

"Here's your salad, dearie," she said. "Oh, Niall!" she called. "This here is Cordelia from New York. She's staying up—"

"I know," Niall said as he strode past them, behind the bar, and through the swinging kitchen doors.

"Don't mind him," Shauna said. "He's going through a bit of a rough patch."

"It's fine," Cordelia said primly because she did not care one bit if Niall freaking O'Connor was nice to her or not. She picked at her salad, and when she looked back at the bar, Niall was pouring more shots for the loud Americans and glaring at the whiskey bottle like it had personally offended him. How could someone radiate so much fury and not spontaneously combust? Cordelia could feel the tension rolling off him all the way across the room.

She was halfway through her meal when her phone began to ring with a call from her mother. Usually when her mom called, Cordelia was overcome with a sinking dread, but today she rushed to answer. The homesickness was really starting to get to her, and she found herself eager to hear her mother's voice.

"Hello? Cordie? Hello?"

"Hi, Mom!" Cordelia said with an enthusiasm that probably surprised them both. "How's it going? What time is it there?"

"I don't know, it's seven or something, we got up early to catch the sunrise on Gary's friend's boat. Gary! Say hi!"

"Wait, Mom—"

Cordelia wanted her mother, not Gary, and she gritted her teeth as a deep male voice said, "Hi, Cordelia," on the other end.

"Hi, Gary."

"How's the island?"

"Oh, it's great. You know. Quiet. Rainy."

Gary chuckled. "I told Louise—I said I hope she brings some rain boots! Or what do they call them there? Wellingtons, right?"

"Yup, that's right, Gary." Why had her mother called her at all if she was just going to pass the phone off to her boyfriend?

"Can I talk to Mom real quick?" she asked.

"Oh sure, sure, hold on. Louise!"

The next minute her mother's voice came through. "Hi, darling. You did bring rain boots, right?"

"Yes, Mother, I brought rain boots." She did know how to read weather reports and pack appropriately.

"So," Louise said. "What's it like over there? Have you met any men?"

Ohmyfuckinggod. "Yeah, Mom, I went to Inishmore's weekly speed-dating session last night," Cordelia joked. She didn't want to fight. But why couldn't her mother simply respect her wishes and stop freaking asking about guys?

"Really?" Louise sounded painfully excited.

"No, not really. Jesus, Mom, there aren't that many people here. They don't do speed dating."

"Now see, this is what I was worried about," Louise said. "Mary Ellen was telling me, if you'd gone to London, or maybe even Paris, there would be so many more suitable people your age to make friends with."

"Suitable people? This isn't a Regency romance novel. I'm not here to snag myself a man from a reputable family."

"Well, there's always the apps," her mother continued. "Mary Ellen's daughter met her fiancé on an app called Summr of Luv. But that's Summer without an E, so when you look it up don't use the E! You girls today are so lucky, there's so many ways to meet someone. And you know, Cordie, you *are* going to be thirty next year."

"Yes, Mom," Cordelia said through gritted teeth. "I am aware."

"Are you done?" Niall appeared at her elbow, his expression as grim as ever.

"Sorry?" Cordelia said as her mother cried, "Who's that, he sounds handsome!"

"Hold on a second, Mom," Cordelia hissed. She covered her phone with one hand and said, "I'm sorry, what?"

Niall jerked his chin at her plate. "Are you done with the salad?"

"Oh. Yes." She wasn't, actually, but she didn't want him coming back to the table. What had happened to Shauna? Niall swooped the plate away and strode off to the kitchen. *Even his back looks angry*, Cordelia thought, her eyes tracing the hard set of his shoulders as she put the phone up to her ear.

"Before you say anything else, Mom, that was the bartender," she warned. "I'm out having lunch."

"He still sounded handsome. And what's wrong with dating a bartender? At least he's got a job. That Sam, he was always mooching off of you."

"Yeah, there were a lot of problems with Sam," Cordelia said with a sigh.

She hadn't dated anyone since her dad died, and the two boyfriends before that had been . . . less than great. Sam, the unemployed former hedge fund manager, had refused to acknowledge they were actually, you know, in a relationship. Which, she supposed, was better than Luke, the boyfriend before, who had constantly leaned on her for emotional support while never making time to listen to her own worries, or come to her shows, or even take more than a brief glance at her photos. All he wanted was to bitch about his office job and force her to sit through boring indie movies.

"I'm only saying," Louise said, "a whole summer away from home . . . something good has to come out of that, right?"

Cordelia's nostrils flared. "Mom, finding a man does not equal *something good*. I can find something good all on my own. I'm not here to catch myself an Irish husband."

"I only mean you've been so sad since your father died . . . I think you'd feel a bit better if you had someone special in your life."

"That's how *you* deal with things, Mom," Cordelia snapped. "Not me." She heard her mother's sharp intake of breath and said, "Look, I gotta go, I'll talk to you later."

She hung up before her mother could say anything else.

By the time she left, it had started to rain.

6

When Sunday finally rolled around, Cordelia was extremely grateful for Fiona's offer of dinner.

She had been on Inishmore only one week and the homesickness was killing her. It might have been easier to bear if she had a camera, but her new one had been delayed in shipping. She hadn't gone back to O'Connor's since that lunch, and though she hadn't planned on actually going to the seisiún Colin had invited her to this coming Friday, now she was desperate for it. She needed a night out. Hell, she needed human interaction. The mysterious Róisín was still never home, or if she was, she never answered the door when Cordelia knocked. It was getting hard not to take it personally.

She was beginning to wonder if Róisín actually existed.

And then there was the rain. Inishmore had more kinds of rain than it knew what to do with: hard lashing rain and soft misting rain and big fat drops of rain that slipped down the neck of her jacket if her hood blew off in the wind. It rained during the day and it rained at night. And in the brief moments it wasn't raining, the air was so heavy with dew that it felt like it was raining then too.

Every time she'd make a plan to explore the island, whether it was the Seal Colony or just Kilronan Harbor, the rain got in the way. She was trying to stick to her father's mantra of *Get up, get out there, and enjoy the day*, but it was hard to do when the day kept pouring buckets of water on her plans. She'd taken the bike out on the one slightly less rainy day to see some of the island, and it really was lovely: rolling hills and slick black rock and shaggy ponies and sheep. But just as she'd been about to take some photos on her phone, the rain had turned into a blinding sheet and driven her back to the cottage, soaked and shivering, cursing Ireland and wishing she was on a beach with a cocktail like Liz had suggested.

Toby kept sending a stream of photos, which Cordelia clung to, grateful for the reminders of the people she loved back in New York. But they also made her more homesick.

She was FaceTiming with Liz now as she got ready for dinner, trying on outfits with her phone propped up on the lamp next to her broken camera. She'd emailed Leslie, who had assured her she could fix it no problem once she was back.

The summer was stretching out in front of her like the sea. A rain-soaked, depressing, endless sea.

"You need to get a hobby," Liz said as Cordelia held up a silky pink blouse. She shook her head and Cordelia tossed the blouse aside.

"There aren't any hobbies here," Cordelia said. "Except maybe fishing."

"Learn to fish!"

"That's boring."

"Cord, you can literally sit in the same spot for five hours when you're waiting for the right picture."

"That's different."

"How is that different?"

"It just is." She ducked into her closet and returned with a knee-length shirtdress, white with thin blue stripes.

"Yes!" Liz exclaimed. "Do you have a wide belt? And boots. That would be perfect."

"You don't think it's too New York?" Cordelia asked, slipping her sweatshirt off over her head.

"Uh, I don't know if you remember this, but you're *from* New York. Do you think this woman is going to expect you to come in waders and a wool sweater?"

"I don't want to be too city-mouse," Cordelia said, buttoning up the dress. But when she'd added the belt, she had to admit she looked cute.

"Yes, girl!" Liz crowed. "Minimal makeup, gloss on your lips, and leave your hair down. You're the perfect blend of casual and class."

"I love when your interior design skills can apply to people," Cordelia said wryly.

"That reminds me!" Liz clapped her hands. "I was talking to my boss the other day and she said they were looking for a new photog to do some promotional work. Can I give her your info? I'll tell her you're out of the country till September, of course."

"Oh," Cordelia said, her stomach lurching. "Um. Yeah."

Liz pursed her red-painted lips. "I know it's not really what you want to do, babes," she said. "But it's work, right?"

Cordelia swallowed. "Right. No, of course. That's amazing, Liz. Really. Thank you."

Liz smiled. "Okay, before I go, I need details on the guy situation. Like how many age-appropriate hotties might there be living on Inishmore? Or cute tourist guys. I'm not picky."

"Liz . . ."

"I'm not pulling a Louise on you, I swear," Liz said. "I don't care if you get married and have babies or whatever. But Cord, you're young, you're hot, you're in a foreign country for the summer—you must let me live vicariously through you while you fuck a bunch of Irish island boys. Please please please." She made big eyes at the camera and batted her lashes.

Cordelia laughed. "You want to vicariously have sex with men?"

"Ew, no, not the men part. Just the sex part. Vacation sex, Cordie! The best kind there is."

"I think you're confusing Inishmore with Cancún," Cordelia said. "Besides, I'm here to look after an old lady, not hit up the clubs. There aren't any clubs anyway."

"I don't think Róisín is real," Liz declared. "I bet she's some old ghost that haunts the cliffs and only the locals can see her. But seriously, Cord. Don't keep those walls you've built up so high. Be open to the possibility of some adult fun times. Maybe you'll meet Cillian Murphy 2.0."

"For a lesbian, you have a very bizarre obsession with Cillian Murphy."

Liz shrugged. "He's so femme."

Cordelia saw the time and her heart jumped. "I have to go."

"Let me guess—you're going to be only five minutes early instead of ten?"

"Ha ha. Bye, Liz," Cordelia said, hanging up her phone. She put on a little eye makeup and mascara, a dab of gloss on her lips, and flipped her hair over her shoulder.

"Liz, you're a genius," she muttered. Then she threw the nice bottle of wine she'd bought yesterday into her bag and headed out the door. Her father always said you should bring something when you get invited to someone's house.

The rain that had been pattering against the windows all day had miraculously subsided, so she didn't need to put the hood of her raincoat up. The air held a faint chill, but it was kind of refreshing. The sky was deepening to twilight colors as she walked, the lights of the houses in the distance shining like patches of gold over the verdant fields. The scent of grass and ocean brine filled her nose.

When she came upon the yellow farmhouse, it was so picturesque that her breath caught. Lights shone through white-curtained windows and a curl of smoke rose up from the chimney, mixing deliciously with the grassy sea scent. The faint strains of a guitar could be heard, and then the cheerful bark of Pocket. Cordelia smiled. Home for her had always been the brownstone in Carroll Gardens and then her apartment in Morningside Heights. This was the home of some ancient fantasy world.

Her dad had dreamed of moving to the country when he retired, buying a house upstate by a river with lots of land. He would have loved it here. Cordelia's throat tightened and she blinked the tears back quickly. No need to arrive on Fiona's doorstep crying.

She walked down through a break in the stone wall and across the grass to the front door. She could hear voices within as she raised her hand and rang the doorbell.

Niall could not. Fucking. Believe it.

He'd come to Inishmore to get away from Deirdre and Patrick, and now their faces were staring up at him in his mother's kitchen.

"I'm so sorry," Fiona was saying. "We thought you'd seen it already."

"No," Niall said, gripping the copy of *The Irish Times* so hard it shook. There was a big splashy article about the opening of Dublin's newest gastropub—the Fallen Star. The name *he* had chosen, inspired by one of his favorite Neil Gaiman books. Deirdre and Patrick smiling at the camera, Patrick's arm around her in the place where Niall's had always been. Glowing reviews about the food—*his* food, the menu *he* had created.

His head spun. He couldn't read it. He could barely look at it. He threw the paper down onto the kitchen table and turned away.

"Oh, Niall," his mother said, putting a hand on his shoulder. He shrugged it off.

"It's fine."

"No, it's not," she said emphatically. "It is *not* fine. If I could, I'd go right up to that—that—*floozie* and I'd give her a piece of my—"

"Don't, Mam," he said. The iron spring was winding up into his throat now, tightening around his esophagus. How long could he go on like this? When would the pain stop?

The doorbell rang.

"Fiona!" his father called from the living room where he and Colin were sitting while Colin picked out a tune on his guitar. "That'll be Alison and Róisín!"

Niall rolled his eyes. Like his father was incapable of walking five steps to the door.

"Coming!" his mother said, but Niall put a hand on her arm.

"I'll get it." He stormed out of the kitchen and down the hall to the front door. Thank god Róisín was here—she would keep everyone entertained and distracted and no one would ask him how he was doing. Maybe no one else had seen the papers yet.

Fat chance, he thought bleakly.

He opened the door, expecting Róisín's pointed, discerning face and instead was completely thrown by the sight of the last person he would've possibly imagined.

"What are you doing here?" he asked Cordelia, who was staring up at him in equal shock.

"What are *you* doing here?" she retorted.

"This is my parents' house," Niall hissed.

Cordelia's hand flew to her mouth. "Oh my god," she said. "You're Fiona's son?"

"Mam!" Niall shouted back toward the kitchen as Colin scampered over to see what was happening, Pocket at his heels.

"Cordelia!" he cried. "Didn't know you were coming."

"Um, Fiona invited me." Cordelia glanced behind her like she was considering making a run for it. Niall wished she would. Tonight was already miserable enough; he didn't particularly care to spend it in the company of the woman who'd called him an asshole twice in one sitting. Pocket trotted up and shoved her little black nose into Cordelia's hand. Cordelia smiled and scratched her behind the ears.

"Hello again," she said.

Traitor, Niall thought at his dog as Colin said, "I see you've already met Inishmore's most famous celebrity."

"Yeah, she showed up at the cottage a few days ago."

Colin laughed. "She does that sometimes. Likes to make herself acquainted with everyone. Doesn't she, Niall?"

He elbowed Niall in the stomach and Niall forced his mouth into a rough approximation of a smile.

"Who's this?" his father said, finally getting his arse up off the couch.

"Is that Cordelia?" Fiona said, hurrying in from the kitchen. "Well, bless me, what are you all doing standing around with the door open and leaving the poor girl out in the cold? Come in, child."

She pushed the gathered men out of the way and shepherded Cordelia inside, Pocket bringing up the rear.

"Let me take your coat," she said, helping Cordelia out of her rain jacket.

Colin gave a whistle. "Cordelia, don't you look marvelous."

She was wearing a knee-length dress, like a men's shirt but belted, with high brown boots. Who did she think was attending this dinner? The bloody king?

"Thanks," Cordelia said, blushing and looking around at everyone else wearing normal Sunday clothes, his mother in slacks, himself in just a T-shirt and maroon hoodie. "Sorry, maybe I overdressed, I didn't know—"

"Not at all!" Fiona said. "I love your dress. Is it from New York?"

"Yeah," she said and her blush deepened so that it actually spread down her neck and across the deep V of skin exposed beneath her collarbone. Niall hadn't known people were capable of blushing that hard.

"Owen O'Connor," Niall's father said, pushing himself forward and holding out his hand. Niall groaned inwardly—Owen had that stupid da thing about handshakes.

Cordelia gripped his father's hand, looked him right in the eyes, and said, "Cordelia James. Pleased to meet you."

Owen's face brightened. "Now, there's a proper handshake," he said, pumping her hand up and down twice before releasing it.

"My dad taught me," she said, almost shyly. "He said you can tell a lot about a person by their handshake."

"Smart man he is, then," Owen said.

Cordelia bit her lip and reached into her bag. "I brought wine."

"Aren't you lovely," Fiona said, taking the bottle. "Isn't she lovely, Niall?"

Niall did not want to be dragged into this conversation. "I'll open it," he said, grabbing the bottle and striding off down the hall, Pocket at his heels.

"Now where's all this attitude coming from?" Fiona asked, entering the kitchen as Niall removed the foil from the bottle.

"That's the woman from the pub," he hissed. "The one I told you about."

Her eyes widened in surprise. "The one whose camera you broke?"

"Shhh, keep your voice down."

Fiona closed the kitchen door. "I'm sorry, Niall," she said. "I didn't know."

"How many other Americans d'you think are staying up at Róisín's cottage?"

His mother crossed her arms over her chest. "Now don't you be taking that tone with me. I know you're in a right state, but it may come as a surprise to you that other people are living their lives and have their own cares and worries and can't be bothered to remember every little thing you say or every pub customer you get in a tiff with."

Niall felt himself immediately cowed. "You're right," he said. "Sorry, Mam."

She handed him the wine opener. "She seems like a lovely girl," Fiona said, looking at the label on the bottle. "Oooh, and she brought us an excellent wine. How could I leave her all alone up at that cottage on a Sunday? No, that's no way to spend the evening. You be nice to her now, d'you hear?"

Niall sighed and kept his eyes averted from the paper on the table. “Yes, Mam. I’ll be on my best behavior. Promise.”

She patted his cheek. “That’s my boy.” The doorbell rang again. “Oh lord, that’ll be Róisín. Better open a second bottle while you’re here. Pocket, come.”

She loaded up a tray with glasses and headed back to the front room, Pocket padding at her heels.

7

Róisín Callahan turned out to be real after all.

Cordelia had just gotten herself settled in a chair by the piano when a tiny woman with a puff of white curls burst through the door without waiting for anyone to answer it. Alison followed behind her looking harried.

"Owen O'Connor, you dumb bastard," Róisín said, stomping into the living room. "How many times have I told you to pave that driveway?"

"It's *gravel*, Róisín, for god's sake," Owen said. Cordelia was quite startled by this entrance and for a second she wondered if a fight was going to break out. But then the two of them embraced, Niall's father towering over the tiny woman, both chuckling like this was how they always greeted each other.

"Let me take your coat," Owen said.

"That'd be grand. Alison, darling, go fetch me a whiskey."

Cordelia was having a hard time reconciling this firecracker of a woman with the friendly old grandma she'd pictured in her head. Róisín wore a plaid shirt under a pair of overalls, heavy brown boots, and a no-nonsense expression. Cordelia felt even more overdressed than she had before.

"We've got wine, Róisín." Fiona appeared with a tray of glasses, Niall behind her, an open bottle in each hand.

Oh thank god, Cordelia thought, and gratefully accepted a glass from Fiona.

"So." Róisín snatched her own glass and stomped over to peer into Cordelia's face. She was so small she barely had to bend to be even with Cordelia sitting. "You're the American who keeps banging on my door."

"Oh, I—" Cordelia wasn't sure what to say to that. She looked to Alison for help.

"She's renting the cottage for the summer, Gran," Alison said, exasperated.

"Is she paying you to spy on me?" Róisín snapped at Cordelia.

"Sorry?" Cordelia said, bemused.

"All I get from her is *You can't live up there by yourself, Gran* and *What if you fell?* and *You can't drive with that eyesight.* As if I need a car! Who needs a car when they have Brigid?"

"Who?"

"My horse! Christ on a bike, I thought Americans were meant to be smart."

Colin snorted into his wine.

"I'm a New Yorker," Cordelia said tartly, feeling a little irritated that she was being chastised for things she couldn't possibly know.

"Is that supposed to mean something to me?"

"No, I—I'm not a spy, I'm here to help!" Cordelia said. Wasn't she? She didn't feel like she was helping anyone, though. She didn't feel like she was doing anything useful at all.

"Niall, what did you tell Gran?" Alison demanded.

"Nothing," Niall said. "Well, nothing Róisín hadn't already guessed. Just that you'd brought someone to the cottage to keep an eye on her."

"Like I needed him to tell me," Róisín said. She turned on Cordelia. "I don't need anybody's help, you hear me? I don't need anybody coming around *my* house and prying into *my* business."

Róisín was poking a finger in Cordelia's face and she felt her last nerve snap. She was tired, and overdressed, and jerk-face Niall was smirking, and she could hear the goddamn rain starting up again outside.

"You know what?" she snapped. "You're right. I am a spy. Alison asked me to come all the way from New York to spy on your very fascinating and interesting life, which I assume it must be since you are *never* home, and guess what, it turns out I suck at spying, so if you could just answer your fucking door from time to time that would make things a lot easier for me, okay?"

There was a split second of startled silence in which her words hung in the air—then Cordelia began to feel the mortification wash over her. What had she just said? Alison was going to send her packing for sure.

But suddenly, Róisín threw her head back and cackled.

"Oh, I like this one," she said to Alison. "Go fetch me a whiskey, girl," she said to Cordelia, who stood almost on instinct until Alison said, "Gran, there's a glass of wine in your hand."

Róisín looked at it, surprised. "Ah, so there is." She took a long drink, draining half the glass. "This is damn fine wine, Fiona. Damn fine."

"Cordelia brought it," Fiona said.

"Who the feck is Cordelia?"

Cordelia gave a little wave as Colin said, "The American, Róisín."

Róisín raised an eyebrow. "She's got cheek *and* she knows wine. Colin, you should marry this girl. Or are you still a pouf?"

"Half pouf," Colin corrected her. "But I'll take the instruction under advisement." He grinned and gave Cordelia a nod as if to say *well done*. But Cordelia's head was still spinning. She'd shouted at this tiny old woman and everyone seemed . . . totally cool with it.

"Did you bring Brigid this evening?" Owen asked. "Niall can put her up in the back field."

"Course I didn't," Róisín grumbled. "Alison picked me up in the damn car." She pointed another finger at Cordelia. "You aren't going to be harping on at me about cars, are you, girl?"

Alison barely repressed a sigh.

Cordelia frowned. "I'm a New Yorker," she said again.

"Is that your fecking answer to everything? Fiona, is that her fecking answer to everything?"

"Róisín, why don't you help me in the kitchen," Fiona said, giving her husband a significant look.

Owen got the hint. "Come, Róisín." As they passed by Niall, Róisín stopped and reached up to pat his cheek.

"It's good that you're home, boyo," she said tenderly. "I saw the papers this morning. That fecking trollop."

Some strong emotion spasmed across Niall's face, and for a moment Cordelia saw bleak pain in his eyes. Then it was gone and they were hard as gemstones again.

Once the trio had gone into the kitchen, Alison collapsed on the couch and Niall poured her a drink.

"Cheers," she said, taking the wine. "I love her," she added to Cordelia. "I love her more than anyone else in the world. But she's a lot."

"She's like a tornado," Cordelia observed. "Or . . . a Tasmanian devil."

Colin and Alison had a good laugh at that.

"I'm glad she likes you," Alison said.

"Are you sure about that?" Cordelia asked doubtfully.

"Oh yes," Alison said. "You spoke her language. No beatin' around the bush. She won't be hiding from you anymore, I promise."

Now that she'd met Róisín, Cordelia wasn't sure if she wanted this ornery old woman to stop hiding from her.

"So," Colin said. Niall had taken a seat on the far side of the room, as far as he could be from Cordelia, thank god. "How's your first week on the island been?"

"Oh, um . . ." Cordelia searched for the right words, then gave up and told the truth. "Kind of awful. Sorry. I don't mean to be rude. But I'm homesick, and it's raining all the time."

Colin was laughing again. "No, that sounds about right for Inishmore. Tourists usually come for the day, or only stay a night or two."

"Have you been to Dún Aonghasa?" Niall asked in what Cordelia felt was an unnecessarily demanding tone. "Or the Seal Colony? Or taken the ferry to Inisheer?"

"Um, no," Cordelia stammered. "I mean . . . it's been raining. Like, every day."

"Welcome to Ireland," Niall said coldly. "Did you think it would be all beaches and sunshine?"

"Jesus, Niall," Alison said. "Give the girl a break."

"I'm just saying. She hasn't even done any of the bland tourist stuff. What's she complaining for?"

"I wasn't complaining," Cordelia said.

"Sounded like complaining to me," Niall replied with an infuriating shrug.

"Never thought I'd live to see Niall O'Connor defending Inishmore," Colin said, shaking his head. He turned to Cordelia. "You'll get used to the rain. And you should go check out Dún Aonghasa—or Dún Aengus, as you tourists call it." He winked at her. "The views are incredible."

"Everyone goes to Dún Aengus," Alison said. "But I prefer Dún Dúchathair. You can even walk there from the cottage, though a bike is faster."

"What's a dún?" Cordelia asked, feeling stupid and looking anywhere but at Niall.

"It means castle or fort," Alison explained. "Dún Dúchathair means the Black Fort."

"Okay. Well, maybe I'll go tomorrow then." She jutted out her chin and added, "Things will be better once my new camera comes. It's been hard losing the one I brought with me."

Her eyes flitted to Niall, who suddenly seemed very interested in his wineglass. Well, good. She hoped he still felt bad about the whole situation.

"Yes, when should it arrive?" Alison asked. "I'll keep an eye out."

"Thursday."

Alison nodded. "Niall, did you know Cordelia is a professional photographer?"

"Grand," Niall muttered.

She knew Alison was only trying to be nice, but her words left Cordelia feeling empty and insecure.

"I'm not," Cordelia said. It was her turn to stare into her wine. "Not really. Not anymore."

There was a heavy pause, and Cordelia wished she hadn't spoken at all. What did it matter anyway? Let them believe what they would. Let them think she had some amazing life in the city and not the truth of her sad days in her apartment alone, missing her father and doubting herself, living on ramen and true crime shows.

When she lifted her gaze again, Niall was looking at her with an expression she couldn't decipher. Judging her, no doubt. She turned away.

"Cordelia, I was thinking—when that new camera comes, maybe you'd consider photographing Pátrún," Colin said. "I'm sure the town can pay you for your trouble."

"Yes, that's a great idea!" Alison exclaimed. "You know how Cian Byrne is always saying they need more publicity. He'd blow his load if he could have a famous New York City photographer taking shots this year."

"Thanks for the image, Al," Colin said, shuddering.

"What's Pátrún?" Cordelia asked.

"It's a three-day festival at the end of June," Alison explained. "To celebrate St. Enda, the patron saint of Inishmore."

"There's music and boat races and tug-of-war and sandcastle competitions and dancing and such," Colin added. "And food. O'Connor's is always at its best at Pátrún, right, Niall?"

Niall shrugged and took a drink. "Da will serve whatever he wants," he said quietly. "As usual."

"He certainly will with that attitude."

"What d'you want from me, Colin?" Niall snapped, standing. "Just get off my back for one fucking second, would ya."

He drained his glass and stormed out of the living room. Cordelia heard a door slam.

Colin sighed. "You saw the paper?" he said to Alison, who nodded.

"What paper?" Cordelia asked, but then Fiona and Róisín emerged from the kitchen.

"Right, you all better get seated, it's time to eat," Fiona said. "Owen's bringing the roast. Where's Niall?"

"Just stepped out for some air," Colin lied smoothly.

Cordelia stood. "Fiona, could I use your bathroom?"

"Course, dear. It's down the hall to the left." She pointed and Cordelia scurried out of the living room.

The hallway was dim and quiet. She could hear Owen rattling around in the kitchen. Cordelia pressed her forehead against the wall and squeezed her eyes closed. She wished she were back in New York, snuggled on Liz's couch while they watched some cheesy romantic comedy and gorged themselves on Jiffy Pop. She wanted city streets and sunshine. She wanted to wear a tank top and sit outside at Oxomoco with Toby and Nikki and stuff her face with guacamole.

It wasn't that these people weren't friendly—well, Colin and Alison and Fiona were. But Cordelia felt like a weird extra appendage, flapping about uselessly, unsure of what she was even doing here. She'd yelled at an old lady. She'd made an enemy out of a man she barely knew.

Get up, get out there, and enjoy the day!

She wrapped her arms around her ribs in an attempt to keep herself together. *I'm trying, Dad.* With a heavy sigh, she unstuck her forehead from the wallpaper.

That's when she noticed the framed photographs hanging on the wall. There was one of Fiona and Owen on their wedding day, with eighties hair, Fiona wearing a dress with big puffy sleeves, Owen sporting a mustache. The next few photos documented the early days of their marriage. Then Cordelia recognized Niall; first as a boy with chubby cheeks and black curls standing in front of a church and then as a teen, in some kind of sleek canoe, rowing along with two other young men. The last one was of him laughing happily with his arm around his mother at a party—white lights were twinkling in the trees overhead and they were both dressed in nice clothes, champagne flutes in hand. The change in Niall was startling; it was like looking at a completely different person. When he smiled, a dimple popped in his left cheek. His eyes glowed. With his jaw not clenched so tight, there was something alluring in the lines of his face.

"She should have taken that down."

Cordelia whirled around. Niall stood in the bathroom doorway, silhouetted against the bright light. He strode forward and snatched the frame off the wall.

"It was from my engagement party," he said, not looking at her, his voice strained. The line of his jaw stood out with tension. His breath hitched.

It hit Cordelia then that this was a man in deep pain. That his story wasn't fodder for gossip, but real, and awful, and something he was living with every day. She suddenly felt ashamed. Here she was, snipping and picking fights, still blaming him for the camera even though it was fixable. It wasn't Niall's fault she had chosen to come to this island.

"I'm sorry," she said, the words tumbling out before she could think too hard about them. "I—I shouldn't have yelled at you like that before. And called you an asshole. I didn't . . . know. Your situation, I mean."

"So if you'd known my fiancée was a lying cheat you would have been nicer to me?" Niall said acidly. "Grand. I'll make sure to spill my heart out in the future to ensure the kindness of strangers."

"That's not what I—" Cordelia threw her hands in the air. "You know what, forget it." She didn't know why she was even trying. If he was so determined to be a prickly, defensive jerk, there wasn't much she could do about it except stay the hell away from him.

Niall sighed. "Fuck, no, I'm sorry. I got some . . . bad news before you came tonight." He looked at the photograph and his mouth quirked. "I wasn't always such an angry asshole. I used to be quite pleasant, you know."

Cordelia didn't know what came over her, but something about the way he was looking at that picture, the utter desolation in his eyes, like he didn't recognize that version of himself either . . . it tweaked her heart and she found herself blurting out, "I could take another one, you know. Picture, I mean. Of you and your mom. To replace this one. If you wanted."

Niall blinked at her.

"I *am* a photographer," she kept going. "A professional one. Well, street photographer, but it's really all about people. Or sometimes not, I guess, but . . . candids. That's what I do. Candid photos. I could take a few if you wanted. When I get my new camera."

Niall frowned and opened his mouth.

"Or not," Cordelia said quickly. "Never mind."

"No, that . . . that'd be sound," Niall said. "I'm sure she'd love that."

Cordelia didn't miss that he said *she* and not *we*. She felt foolish and wished she'd never made the offer in the first place.

"Okay. Great. Well, I've got to pee!" She pushed past him, ran into the bathroom, and slammed the door behind her.

Niall stared at the closed door for a second.

Then he looked down at the picture again. He was mortified that she'd seen it, but now that she was gone, he was crumpling beneath the weight of the memories it brought. How happy he'd been. How certain his future had seemed. He gripped the frame, his knuckles white, and strode over to the sideboard where his mother kept the doilies and good linens, shoving the picture inside a drawer, then slamming it shut.

His father was carving the roast and his mother was pouring more wine as he entered the dining room. There were only two seats open, next to each other.

Perfect, he thought grimly. He didn't know what to make of Cordelia's offer, or why he'd accepted it, and he was wishing now that he hadn't. The last thing he wanted was this woman poking around in his private life, making him feel like even more of a failure. Miss New York City Photographer. He bet her schedule was full of parties and bottomless brunches and glamorous events.

But then he remembered how she'd stared at her glass and insisted she wasn't a photographer anymore. The fragility in her expression, like an eggshell about to crack. He hadn't thought her capable of vulnerability—weren't all Americans annoyingly confident?

"I like that American," Róisín declared as Niall sat down. "Cordelia!" she called as Cordelia came hurrying back from the bathroom. Her cheeks were flushed again, her eyes bright, and for a second Niall wondered if she'd been crying. Christ, he hadn't made her cry, had he?

She stumbled for a fraction of a second when she saw where she'd been seated, then walked in an exaggeratedly calm manner to slide into the chair next to him. She smelled like bergamot and something faintly piney. It was unexpected—he'd pegged her for a high-end, flowery perfume kind of gal.

"Now see here, Cordelia," Róisín said, grabbing the bowl of boiled potatoes and scooping a large helping onto her plate. "Alison's been telling me you've seen hardly any of this island or done anything to write home about—that's going to change. Starting tomorrow."

Colin was grinning as he helped himself to the Yorkshire pudding. Cordelia's lips had formed a small O as if she wanted to say something but couldn't decide what. Niall's father passed her a plate of pot roast.

"O—okay," Cordelia stammered.

"There's no use arguing with her," Alison said. "Right, Gran?"

Róisín patted Alison's knee. "No use at all, my darling. I always get my way. So you come on up to the house tomorrow and we'll get started."

"Uh, started on what?"

"I wouldn't ask if I were you," Colin said in a mock whisper, handing her the platter of sautéed mushrooms. Once his plate was full, Niall ignored the chatter and dug in. His thoughts drifted back to the newspaper in the kitchen, then skittered to the image of Deirdre on top of Patrick on the floor of the pub. He squeezed his eyes shut and when he opened them, Colin was watching him, worried.

"Your parents must be very proud of you, Cordelia," Owen said, leaning back in his chair. "Making a go of this photography thing."

Cordelia choked on a mouthful of potato and then cleared her throat. "Yeah."

"And that makes you money, does it?"

"Owen," Fiona said.

"What? I'm just asking a question."

"How did you get into photography?" Alison interjected.

Cordelia fiddled with her napkin. "Um, I was always into arty things. I used to drive my mom crazy, drawing on my sneakers with magic marker and getting glitter glue all over the couch. Then my dad brought home this old Polaroid camera and I fell in love. Took pictures of everything. And it kind of grew from there. I got accepted to SVA—that's the School of Visual Arts in New York. Then I got mentored by this really famous street photographer and things just took off."

"I'm surprised you're able to make a living," Owen said. "Seems awfully risky to go to school for that sort of thing."

Cordelia gave a little half smile. "You sound like my mom. She wasn't a fan."

"It worked out wonderfully I would say," Fiona said. "Look at you now. Traveling the world."

Two pink spots appeared on Cordelia's cheeks. "Yeah," she said, but her mouth turned down.

"Took a lot of hard work, I'll wager," Owen said. "And determination. And making the *right choices.*"

Niall felt his blood begin to boil. As if losing the Fallen Star had been a choice. As if Deirdre leaving him had been Niall's *choice.* Fiona was shooting daggers at her husband, but he didn't seem to notice.

"It definitely took hard work," Cordelia said, taking a cautious sip of wine.

Owen drained his own glass and pointed a thick finger at his son. "Now, Niall here—"

Colin groaned and Róisín said, "For fuck's sake, Owen, give the boy a break."

"What? He seemed to think he could just swan into Dublin and start up his own pub like that." He snapped his fingers.

Niall was clenching his jaw so tight he thought his teeth would crack. Images flashed across his eyes. Crafting the menu, bringing out dishes for Deirdre and Patrick to try. Noticing they were sitting close, but it was a booth, and they were friends after all. Deirdre giggling and licking the melted butter from her fingers, declaring Niall's lobster risotto the best she'd ever tasted. Had they already been sleeping together, even then? He tried to remember how to breathe.

"He did not," Fiona said. "He worked hard, Owen, and you know it."

"Could you all stop talking about me as if I'm not here?" Niall muttered.

"I bet Cordelia's father instilled a strong work ethic in her along with that handshake," Owen said jovially. "Didn't he, Cordelia? He must be a great man with a good head on his shoulders."

Cordelia put her napkin on her plate. "My father's dead," she said tersely. "And I don't think my work ethic was what mattered to him. Just that I loved him and he loved me. He gave me the courage to follow my dreams, and he supported me unconditionally. So I think that whatever Niall has or hasn't achieved, it shouldn't be a measure of how much love he deserves. And you're lucky you still get to have dinner with him. I'd give anything to have one more dinner with my father. Excuse me."

She took her empty plate and fled to the kitchen. Niall was stunned. It was such an effortless and subtle way to eviscerate his father's argument. He felt a twist of guilt—that she'd been willing to share something that caused her pain, in defense of Niall. And he'd been acting a right prick to her ever since they met.

"Now you've gone and put your big fecking foot in it, haven't you," Róisín said.

"I didn't know," Owen said, blinking.

"Well, you weren't stopping to think either," Fiona said. "Just plowed ahead like you always do."

Niall couldn't sit there anymore. He got up and took his own plate to the kitchen. Cordelia was standing at the sink, gripping the counter with both hands.

"Hey," he said. He gestured back to the dining room. "Sorry about my da."

"It's fine," she said but her voice cracked. "Is he always like that?"

"Like what? A complete and utter arsehole?"

Her lips twitched. "Always that hard on you."

"Oh." Niall shrugged. "Yeah."

Silence hung between them. Niall shifted from foot to foot. The kitchen was spacious, but right now it felt far too small. Cordelia seemed to think so too. She moved away from him, over to the table. She picked up the little ceramic salt and pepper shakers his mother kept, shaped like ducklings.

Niall wanted to tell her thank you. That no one had ever stood up for him like that—not even Deirdre. Not even his mam. That he hadn't known she was in pain. That he hadn't thought anyone else's pain very important besides his own recently. But the words wouldn't come.

"I'm sorry about your da," he said instead. "When did he die?"

"Two years ago." She must have seen the surprise on his face because her expression soured. "You probably think I should be over it, huh? So does my mom. So does my brother. Join the club."

"No, that's not what—" Niall stopped himself. "I didn't know, is all."

"Why would you?" She rubbed her thumb over the salt duckling. "I hope I didn't make things weird out there, with your family."

"Nah, we've been making things weird just fine on our own for years."

Her mouth twitched again. Niall suddenly wished he could find the right words to make her smile. To ease some of the sadness from those big hazel eyes. He felt like he'd been tramping around the entire evening like an angry ram, lashing out at anyone close by. He *was* capable of being nice. Even if he was out of practice completely.

"I really am sorry," he said softly. And he meant it—he was sorry for breaking her camera, and sorry for his crap apology, and sorry for all the digs he'd made at her earlier. It wasn't her fault that Deirdre left him. It wasn't her fault that his life had fallen apart.

He was surprised when she put the shakers down and glared at him.

"I don't need your pity," she snapped. Her eyes landed on the paper open to the article and the picture of Deirdre and Patrick. His heart somersaulted, the iron spring snapping around his lungs. As she picked it up, Niall wanted to throw himself between Cordelia and his shame. But it was too late.

"Oh," she said. "Bad news. The papers. The trollop. I get it now." She held it up as if he needed to see it to confirm. "This is, um, her?"

"Yeah," Niall said coldly. Deirdre's face stared at him, filling the room, mocking him. He marched over and snatched the paper from her hands, tossing it in the dustbin. "And I don't need your pity either."

He heard her sharp intake of breath and cursed himself, staring into the bin. What the fuck was he doing?

He turned around in time to see a curtain of blonde hair disappearing out the kitchen door.

8

Since dinner had come to an abrupt and early end, Alison offered to drop Cordelia off at the cottage.

She went straight to her room and called Liz.

"Hey, girl! How'd it—oh my god, Cordie, what happened?"

Cordelia sank onto her bed. Her hands shook as she reached for her broken camera, holding it against her stomach, her thumb pressed to her father's print.

"I'm so . . . so . . . homesick," she sobbed. "I'm lonely and it rains all the time and I have no camera and I made a total fool of myself at dinner and . . . I miss you, Liz, I miss everyone, it wasn't supposed to feel like this, I'm trying to do what Dad would want, I'm trying to enjoy the day, but I . . . I can't . . ."

And then she dissolved into tears. When she was finally able to take a few deep breaths, she wiped her eyes and mumbled, "Sorry."

"Cord. Don't apologize. It's only natural that you'd be homesick. Remember when we were reading about culture shock?"

Cordelia nodded.

"This'll pass," Liz said gently.

"Will it?" she said. "It doesn't feel that way."

Liz chewed on her lower lip for a second. "Can I say something you might not love to hear?"

Cordelia sighed. "Sure."

"You're holding on so tight. I want you to know . . . it's okay. It's okay to let go a little bit. Of your dad, of your work, of all the things you think define you."

"What if I forget him?" Cordelia whispered.

"That will never happen."

"What if I never sell a photograph again? What if I can't be a photographer anymore?"

"Also never going to happen. Selling your photos isn't what makes you a photographer, babes. That's as much a part of you as your love of packaged ramen or your weird obsession with murder shows."

Cordelia let out a shaky laugh and stared down at the camera. This trip was meant to push her forward in life, but nothing seemed to be going the way she'd planned. When she looked up, Liz had a guilty expression on her face.

"What?" Cordelia asked warily. "Is there another thing you need to tell me that I won't like?"

Liz half smiled. "No. I'm feeling bad. I shouldn't have—I'm really sorry if I was pushing you with the whole vicarious sex thing. There's no pressure for you to do anything there you don't want to do. I didn't mean to stick my nose in."

Cordelia gave a watery chuckle. "I don't think we need to worry about me having sex." She gestured to her face—puffy, red-rimmed eyes and blotchy cheeks.

"You're beautiful," Liz said. "Inside and out. Crying or not."

"Thanks, but that's not even what I mean."

"What *do* you mean?"

Cordelia fiddled with her belt buckle. "I'm too scared to feel those feelings. Like I've sealed myself up in wax and even one small crack will make me crumble."

"Oh, Cordie, no. You're still hurting, that's all. Don't push yourself. But don't cut yourself off from everything either. It doesn't have to be all or nothing. Baby steps. Taking the space and time to be you. Isn't that what this trip was supposed to be about?"

Cordelia sniffed. "Yeah. I mean, I guess. Who even knows anymore."

"What happened at dinner?" Liz asked.

"Ugh." Cordelia adjusted herself on the bed. "It turns out Niall the breaker of cameras is Fiona's son."

"No!"

Cordelia relayed all that had happened.

"Wow," Liz said when she was finished. "What a night. Mystery Grandma sounds amazing, though."

"She's going to take me to a castle tomorrow," Cordelia said. "With this horse and cart she uses for tours. I guess she's done hiding from me."

"That's so great! I think you'll feel better. You need another badass bitch in your life since I'm not there. And at least you know people now—Alison and Colin sound really nice. And maybe Niall isn't as terrible as we first imagined. You don't have to be so alone there."

Cordelia's chest pinched and she gave a small nod. "Maybe you're right."

"I'm always right."

Cordelia laughed and rubbed her eyes. "I should get some sleep. Love you."

"Love you too. Let me know how it goes tomorrow."

"I will."

She ended the call and the tears welled up again. But as she lay back on her pillow and let them trickle down into her hair, her thoughts turned to that photograph on the wall, the one of Niall smiling so happily, looking like a different person. And she saw now why it had tugged at her so strongly—because that was her, too.

She had her own before and after, just like he did. Her smile hadn't been the same since her father died.

It was strange to think they might have something in common.

Niall walked home with Colin in silence.

He felt Colin's glances but ignored them until they were across the threshold, Pocket sniffing around at the baseboards as Colin propped his guitar up in the corner.

"What?" he said finally. "Spit it out, Coll."

"You okay, mate?" Colin said. It was direct and bleak, not his usual lighthearted inquiry.

"No," he said. "I'm not." He rubbed his hand across his forehead. "I'll try, okay? I'll try not to be such an utter prick all the time."

"I bet the pub fails," Colin said thoughtfully. "They can't do it without you. Not that menu. Not that spot. It was your baby, Nie. It was—"

"I know what it was," Niall snapped. Then he sighed. "It was seeing them together. And his fucking arm around her . . ."

He tried to swallow back the bile that rose at the thought of them living the life that was meant to be his. He stroked the top of Pocket's head and looked anywhere but at Colin.

"Cordelia set your da straight, though, didn't she," Colin said.

That brought an unexpected chuckle out of him. "She did."

"Never seen him so quiet as he was after dinner."

"No." He scratched his ear. "I was a prick to her all night too."

"Yup."

"Didn't know that about her da."

"Neither did I. Alison did, apparently."

Niall looked up. "Did she? Well, I guess that makes sense." Alison's parents had died in a car accident when she was six. "She saw the picture of me. From the engagement party."

Colin cocked his head. "Sorry?"

"Cordelia." Why did her name feel so strange on his tongue? "She was looking at all the family photos and Mam still had that fucking picture of us from the engagement party hanging up on the wall."

"Oh," Colin said, his face creasing.

"I didn't even recognize myself. It was like looking at a total stranger."

"You're not a different person, Niall. You're hurting, is all."

"Yeah. Sure." Niall felt suddenly, overwhelmingly tired. "I'm off to bed. Come, Pocket."

"See ya," Colin said. Niall climbed the stairs to his room, stripped down to his boxers, and got under the covers. Pocket curled into his side and he waited for Deirdre's face to blossom in the dark.

But he found his thoughts wandering to what Cordelia had said, and he turned her words around and pointed them at himself—his father still had a son, yes, but Niall still had a da. His family dinners weren't missing a member forever like hers. His father hadn't always been such a wanker. There was a time when Niall had idolized him.

I'd give anything to have one more dinner with my father.

Maybe, Niall thought as he drifted off to sleep, even though his life was shit, even though he'd lost everything he cared about . . . maybe he did have one or two things to be grateful for.

Cordelia was awakened the next morning by a furious pounding on the front door.

She sat up, startled. The crying jag with Liz had helped, she realized. She felt better. Lighter. Like maybe some part of her had let go a bit.

The pounding came again and Cordelia got out of bed and threw on her robe. There was something different about the light in her room, and it took her a moment to place it—*the sun was out.* She skipped to the door and flung it open to find Róisín standing on the doorstep, wearing a gardener's hat and a thermal under her overalls.

"Still in your nightclothes?" Róisín cried. "Jesus, girlie, you'll miss the best part of the day."

"What . . . part is that?" Cordelia blinked around, her eyes so unused to sunshine.

"All of it!" Róisín stomped past her into the house, leaving a bemused Cordelia to trail in her wake. Róisín whirled around the kitchen, opening drawers and rifling through the fridge. When she saw Cordelia in the doorway she said, "Well, don't stand there staring, go put some clothes on. I'll make us a coffee and eggs." She picked up a spatula and waved it. "Off you go."

Cordelia stumbled back to her room and tied her hair up in a loose bun. She rinsed herself off in the shower, then put on a pair of shorts—it might be tempting fate but she didn't care. Her legs wanted fresh air and sun. She threw on a white tee and her favorite rust-colored cardigan with big brass buttons and deep pockets on the front. Slipping her feet into her rain boots, she walked back to the kitchen, where Róisín had made coffee and was scrambling eggs.

"Do you live on cheese and chocolate?" Róisín said. "Christ, child, there's hardly a scrap of real food in this house."

"I don't cook," Cordelia said.

Róisín shook her head and muttered something that sounded like "Fecking Americans."

Cordelia poured herself some coffee and took a seat at the table.

"Quite a dinner last night, wasn't it," Róisín said. "And I'm not talking about the food."

Cordelia froze with the milk jug in her hands.

"Mm," she said noncommittally.

Róisín smirked. "We don't need to go having a deep discussion so early in the morning," she said. "But I'm glad of what you said to Owen. That man's been far too hard on Niall for far too long. No wonder the lad ran off to Dublin first chance he got. You know about what all happened with him I suppose?"

"Alison told me," Cordelia said.

"Good. If she hadn't, someone else would, and lord knows the way folks on this island love to exaggerate. Niall's a good man, and there's many in Kilronan would do well to remember that." Her face crinkled, her eyes going sad. "I'm sorry to hear about your da, though." Cordelia looked down and finished adding milk to her coffee. Róisín busied herself around the stove, then turned back to place a plate of eggs in front of Cordelia. "Eat," she said. She sat down beside her. "So. You're a photographer."

Cordelia swallowed a mouthful of food. "Yeah, but I don't have a camera at the moment."

"But you're an artist."

She shrugged. "I guess."

"Christ on crutches, girlie, why are you acting like this is some shameful thing you've got to be hiding from everyone? Are you an artist or aren't you?"

Cordelia bristled. "Yes," she said firmly. "I am."

Róisín slapped the spatula against the table. "That's more like it. I've got a job for you and then we'll hook Brigid up to the cart and head to Dún Aengus. It's a tourist trap to be sure, but a rite o' passage. It's going to be a fine day for it too. I called Fiona earlier and she said her knee's feeling grand. The sun'll hold. Go on, eat up!"

The light in the kitchen was growing brighter. Cordelia ate quickly, wanting to be outside. She was glad to be off the subject of Niall—her ribs had gone oddly soft when Róisín brought him up.

After breakfast they walked to the house. Róisín kept up an endless stream of chatter, sometimes talking to Cordelia but sometimes talking to the grass, or a passing butterfly, or cursing one of the locals.

"Cian Byrne has taken over the Seaview, and you just know he's going to ruin all its sparkle. Not that it has a patch on O'Connor's. Oh, get off with ya, damn bee, there's pollinating to do in the garden back down the cottage." She swatted at a bee floating past.

Cordelia found she couldn't stop smiling. The sky was a brilliant blue, the air fragrant and sweet. The sun was so warm she wanted to reach up and hug it, or roll around in the grass like a dog. They reached the house and Róisín stomped around toward the back. The sun glinted off the ocean, Brigid was grazing in the paddock with the shed to one side, and it was such a perfect moment—the composition, the colors, the light slicing across the field. The whole scene was calling out to be remembered.

Cordelia reached into her pocket and pulled out her phone. She snapped a few quick photos, then the breeze caught the scent of lavender and she hurried to catch Róisín.

There was a marvelous garden in the back, part vegetable, part wildflower, part herb. Róisín plucked a strawberry off a low plant bursting with red fruit and pointed at a bush with small yellow flowers.

"St. John's wort," she said, popping the strawberry in her mouth. "Used to treat depression and anxiety. Niall could do with some of that, couldn't he, poor lad." Without waiting for Cordelia to respond, she walked up to another plant with larger yellow blossoms. "Evening primrose. Good for treating symptoms that come along with your monthlies. Not that I've got any need for that now." She cackled. "But some of the girls still come asking for it. It can treat acne too. Those purple flowers there, that's echinacea. Good to take when you've got a cold."

"It's a lovely garden," Cordelia said, wondering what the point of all this was.

"I know that! I didn't bring you here for compliments."

"What did you—"

But Róisín had disappeared through the back door to the house, returning with a sketchpad and a charcoal pencil.

"I haven't got any paints yet," she said. "But I've asked Alison to order some." She thrust the pad and pencil into Cordelia's hand.

"Um . . ." Cordelia stared down at them. "What exactly do you want me to do?"

"You're an artist, aren't you? Draw!" She waved her hand in the direction of the plants she'd named. "I'm making a book, you see," she said proudly. "For meself and others who want to know about herbal remedies. But I can't draw for shite."

Cordelia opened her mouth to say she really wasn't that kind of artist. But then Toby's words came back to her, from before she flew to Ireland, when he was trying to convince her to leave her camera behind.

You used to make those cool charcoal sketches and do watercolors and stuff.

She did used to do that. She used to try all sorts of mediums.

"Well," Róisín said, hands on her hips. "What are you waiting for?"

"Do you have a stool?" Cordelia asked.

Róisín grinned. "In the shed. I'll fetch it."

And so Cordelia spent her morning sitting on a three-legged stool, a horse grazing nearby, the warm June sun shining down on her back, a sketchpad in her hands for the first time since college. Her first attempt at the St. John's wort wasn't very good, but the second was better. The third was perfect. Róisín puttered around her garden, sometimes talking to Cordelia, sometimes talking to the plants, sometimes talking to Brigid. The horse was a shaggy brown mare with a blaze like a sunburst and wise old eyes that seemed to understand every word the old woman uttered. Cordelia took off her cardigan and started on the echinacea.

By the time she got to the lavender, the sun was high overhead. Róisín made them tea and ham sandwiches, and they ate in her roomy kitchen with flowered wallpaper and a woodburning stove. She talked to Cordelia about the history of the island—the small settlements called clachans that had contained anywhere from two to fifteen houses and given the early settlers a sense of security during hard times.

"These islands were built by families sticking together," Róisín said. "The bonds of those of us that live here year round are strong and old and deep. Some say it makes us stubborn. I don't know about that."

She then launched into tales of the sea, the danger of the surrounding waters, and the hardiness of those who fished them.

"My own husband died out on the Atlantic," she said. "Storm came and swept his boat away. Never found him or his crew."

"I'm so sorry," Cordelia said.

"It was many years ago." Róisín took a sip of tea. "But it's kind of you to say."

She told Cordelia about currachs, the traditional boats that were once the only way to get from the islands to the mainland.

"First they used cowhide on the currachs," she said. "Then it was calico. Then canvas."

Her description jogged something in Cordelia's memory.

"I saw a picture of those!" she exclaimed. "On the wall in Fiona's house. They look like canoes, right?"

"They do indeed. Niall used to race in the summers—that's what they're mainly used for now. Though some still fish with 'em. You'll get to see the races during Pátrún. Niall was a great rower back in the day. Strong arms. Broad chest." She winked. "He's a fine thing, isn't he?"

Cordelia flushed. "Oh, um . . ."

Róisín laughed and put her teacup down. "I'm just teasing you, girl. He's all doom and gloom now. I wouldn't imagine any young girl, much less one so lovely as yourself, would go near him with a ten-foot pole."

"He seems to have a pretty good reason for the gloom, though," Cordelia pointed out.

"Yes," Róisín said sadly. "That he does."

After lunch, Róisín showed her how to hook Brigid to the cart. Cordelia climbed up to sit beside her in the driver's seat and with a crack of the reins, they were off. The cart rumbled and bumped along the roads, and Róisín pointed out this house and that, telling Cordelia about who lived there, and who their grandparents were, and bits of small gossip. They passed the ruins of an old church and a beach where a few daring swimmers were kicking around in the surf. Everyone seemed to know Róisín and by extension Cordelia.

"Fine day, innit, Róisín?" a man called from the doorway of his house.

"Grand, Brogan," she called back.

"Hello, American girl," he said. Cordelia smiled and waved.

They were turning a bend in the road when a teenage boy ran out right in front of them chasing a soccer ball.

"You fecking eejit!" Róisín cried. "Watch where you're going, Rory, or I'll tell your mam you've been messing about with the Sullivan girl."

"Sorry, Róisín!" the boy said, scampering away to safety.

Cordelia had quite forgotten where they were going by the time they reached a road packed with other carts, all headed in the same direction.

"Too nice a day," Róisín grumbled. "The tourists coming out of the woodwork like termites. I know this island needs tourism but I wish they wouldn't clog up the roads. All right, Darragh!"

The man with the bulbous nose from O'Connor's was driving a cart in the opposite direction, a family in the back chatting away in German.

"American girl!" Darragh cried, waving at Cordelia. "Good t'see you again."

"Hi," Cordelia said. It was weird that everyone knew her, but it was also kind of nice. A little less lonely, maybe. There was a cluster of whitewashed buildings with thatched roofs huddled around a cobblestone square, selling various trinkets and hats and scarves made of Aran wool.

"There's the entrance," Róisín said, pointing. A wide path wound its way over a vast expanse of grass dotted with gray stones, leading up to where a larger, higher stone wall spread out across a cliff. The ocean sparkled in the distance.

Cordelia hopped off the cart. "Are you coming too?" she asked. Róisín chuckled.

"Not on these old stumps, lass."

Cordelia joined the throng of people making their way along the path.

The wind picked up as she walked, whipping her hair about her face. The air was turning colder and goose bumps spread across her bare thighs. She climbed through a break in the larger wall and stepped out into a wide semicircle of ancient stone. The grass receded into smooth slabs near the edge of the cliff. The view was spectacular—waves crashed against the high cliff walls, the water a shocking turquoise at their base then dulling into slate gray as it spread out toward the horizon. Every now and then a wave would smash into rock and send up a violent spray.

She tried to take it all in but there were so many people peering over the cliffs and taking pictures and talking loudly. Cordelia headed back, and by the time she reached the cluster of shops, dark clouds were creeping across the sky, the air turning chilly and damp.

"It's good you came back so soon—I don't like the look of those clouds," Róisín said, snapping the reins. When they reached the house, Cordelia helped Róisín untack Brigid then walked down to the cottage. As soon as she stepped inside, it began to rain.

"Perfect timing," she said with a smile. She headed to the kitchen, humming to herself as she boiled water for pasta and heated up the sauce in a small pot. She poured herself a glass of wine while the pasta cooked, and when the meal was ready, she sat at the table in the front room with her book as the rain pattered against the windows.

Suddenly, she remembered the pictures she'd taken earlier. She grabbed her phone and opened her photos. Her breath caught and she put her fork down. Róisín's house with Brigid framed by the blue sky and green grass . . . she felt like she could step inside it and relive the day all over again.

She sent it off, first to Liz then to Toby. And then, after a moment's consideration followed by a heavy sigh, she brought up her mom's thread and added the picture there. They hadn't spoken since the fight at lunch.

Great day on the island, she wrote.

She put her phone down and gazed out the window, the rain obscuring the fields outside, the world blurring to muted grays and greens. It didn't bother her so much, not after the day she'd had. It was sort of beautiful even. She picked up her wine and opened her book, a deep contentment washing over her.

It took her a moment to place the feeling.

It felt like home.

9

Niall wasn't sure what was going on.

Ever since that Sunday dinner, his father hadn't mentioned Deirdre, or the Fallen Star, or the everlasting shame Niall had brought down upon his family.

He'd barely spoken to Niall at all. Working at the pub had become much easier now that Niall wasn't being snapped at or reprimanded all the time. Though he did wish his father would say more than just *Hello* or *Get this curry out to table three.* Cordelia's words had clearly struck a nerve.

"He's doing some hard thinking, is all," his mother had said when Niall brought it up. "About damned time too, if you ask me." Then she'd patted his cheek. "You want feeding. Let me set you up with a bowl o' stew."

He hadn't spoken to Cordelia since that night, though he had seen her driving past the pub in the cart with Róisín. And one time he saw her at the shop but he was ashamed to admit he'd hidden in the frozen food section. He didn't want to invite another awkward situation where he'd end up feeling a right eejit.

With the pressure from his father off and the routine of work settling in, Niall found that the spring in his chest was unwinding, no longer necessary to keep him together. He was remembering how much he actually *liked* working in a pub. He liked the constant flow of conversation, the eager questions from the tourists and the tall tales from the locals, the laughter that came from people enjoying a good drink and a hot meal. The regulars had long gotten over the scandal of his return, and the article in the paper was old news now too. With no more gossip to be had, they joked with him more often, and engaged him in conversation when they came in for a pint or a bowl of potato leek soup.

When he was home, Niall found himself wandering into the kitchen more and more. He didn't make anything. Sometimes he poked around the fridge and judged Colin's grocery choices. Or he'd make sure the knives were sharp and the stove clean. Or he'd peruse the spice rack, which was shockingly bare.

That Friday was the seisiún and Niall got to work early for his dinner shift. It was sure to be a busy night; the pub was already filling up with both islanders and tourists. His mam was there at the table reserved for her.

"Hiya," he said, bending down to kiss her cheek. The sky was growing dark, the rain a steady patter outside. It was cold enough that his father had started a fire in the fireplace, and it crackled merrily, each opening of the door bringing a blast of chilly wet air. "Sauvignon blanc?" he asked.

"That'd be lovely. Oi, Aoife!" she called as Aoife O'Shea, who owned the shop, entered, waving her over to say hi. Niall left to get her wine but first poked his head into the kitchen.

"All right, Da?" he said. His father was sniffing a bunch of wilted parsley.

"Parsley's gone bad," Owen said, tossing it in the bin in disgust.

"Just use some carrot greens," Niall suggested.

"Really?" Owen looked up and their eyes met. Niall shrugged. "That or celery leaves. Either would make a fair substitute."

"Huh." Owen looked away. "All right. I'll try that. Cheers."

"Yup." Niall left quickly before the moment was ruined.

He took a few orders from the bar, then went to pour his mother's wine.

"It's bucketing down out there," Colin said, coming up to get himself a water. The rain was beginning to lash against the windows. "Did you see Cordelia made it?"

Niall slopped some of the wine onto the bar and hurried to wipe it up. There were three figures at his mother's table, all peeling off their raincoats and hanging them on the backs of their chairs. Róisín was in her usual plaid shirt and dungarees but Cordelia was wearing an Aran jumper, soft white in a honeycomb stitch—it looked like one Róisín had made. It was a little too big for her, falling to the middle of her thighs, and she wore it over soft gray leggings, her damp hair sticking to her neck in places. She was laughing with Alison as she pushed the sleeves up to her elbows and sat beside his mother.

He finished pouring the wine and turned to see Colin watching him.

"What?" he said.

"Nothing," Colin said. He took a sip of water, eyeing Niall over the glass. "Maybe you'll want to be a bit kinder to her this time. She got your da off your back."

"If you're going to stay behind the bar, then take some orders and pour some pints," Niall said. "Otherwise get your arse on that stage."

Colin grinned. "It's a fine arse, though, isn't it," he said and he swung his hips in an exaggerated manner as he walked back to tune his guitar. Niall chuckled and went to take the wine to his mother.

He passed a table with two young female tourists, a blonde and a brunette looking at something on one of their phones. "Be right with you," he said.

The brunette eyed him up and down. "Take your time," she called, then whispered something to her friend and they both giggled.

Americans, Niall thought and rolled his eyes.

"Here you are then, Mam," he said, placing the wine in front of her. "Hiya, Alison. Róisín." He cleared his throat. "Cordelia."

But Cordelia didn't seem interested in glaring at him today. "Hi," she said with an exuberant smile.

"Can we have some cabernet please, Niall?" Alison asked.

"And a whiskey," Róisín added. "Neat." She was smiling too.

"Right," Niall said, looking around at the happy faces. "You all celebrating something or what?"

Cordelia reached down into her bag. "My new camera came," she said excitedly.

"She took some pictures of me and Brigid this morning," Róisín said. "Show him, girlie. She's got an eye, this one. Going to be the next—what was his name again?"

Cordelia laughed. "Henri Cartier-Bresson. And no, probably not, but it's easy to take good photos when I've got a good subject."

"Go on," Róisín said, but she looked pleased.

Cordelia held the camera out to Niall. "Don't break this one," she said. He started, about to argue, when he realized she was teasing him.

Oh. Well. That made for a nice change. He gave her a half smile and took the camera with exaggerated care.

"Just press that button there," she said. "To see the other ones."

But Niall was looking down at one of the most expressive and moving photographs he'd ever seen. It was black and white. Brigid was nuzzling her nose against Róisín's face, Róisín's hand curving about her long neck. There was such raw intimacy—it was framed in a way to give a hint of the thick impending clouds in the top right-hand corner.

"Jesus," Niall said.

"It's grand, isn't it?" Alison said. "She said she'd take a few of me and Gran. I'd like to hang one in the cottage."

Niall couldn't stop staring at the picture. It was like Cordelia had seen into Róisín's soul and brought it forth, capturing her very essence. Without thinking he said, "She offered to take some of me and mam as well."

"She didn't," Fiona said, sitting up and pressing her hand to her chest. "Oh, Cordelia. That would be lovely."

Cordelia's eyes widened.

"But maybe you're busy," Niall said quickly.

"No, no, it's fine," she said. Then she smiled at Fiona. "I'd love to. After a week of drawing plants, I'm itching to get back to photography." She looked down, her smile softening, like the sentence had a deeper meaning than Niall could guess.

"I'll get that wine for you," he said, handing her back the camera. Their fingers brushed together and Niall felt a jolt like static zipping across his skin. He put his hands in his pockets and headed back to the bar.

He didn't have much of a chance to talk to anyone as he hurried around taking orders, delivering food, and pouring drinks. Once he thought he caught Cordelia looking at him, but she turned away so fast he couldn't be sure.

Why does it matter? he thought to himself. Who cared if she looked at him? He decided he was glad she wasn't glaring at him anymore, that was all. The brunette American, on the other hand, kept glancing over with hungry eyes.

He brought a second round of drinks to his mother's table, catching a whiff of Cordelia's bergamot-and-pine scent as he leaned over to take her empty wineglass. Fiona ordered some food for the table as Colin crouched down by Alison and Cordelia, chatting away. Niall tapped his watch.

"Right, let's get this started," Colin said, standing.

Cordelia slipped her camera strap over her head. "Is it okay if I take some pictures?" she asked.

"That'd be grand!" Colin exclaimed. "Shoot from the left, that's my good side." He winked and Cordelia rolled her eyes, grinning. Colin jumped up onto the stage and Niall settled in behind the bar to watch.

"Welcome, friends from near and far," he said into the microphone and the crowd hushed. "Thanks for coming out on this fine Irish evening." Rain slapped against the windows and there was a smattering of laughter. "I'm Colin Doyle, Inishmore's grandest and sexiest musician."

There were some cheers and Darragh shouted, "Boyo, I've known you since you were a wee lad who didn't know which hand to piss with. Get on with it!"

"Thanks for that reminder, Darragh," Colin said dryly. "Next pint's on me."

He slipped his guitar strap over his head and took his seat next to Fergus and his bodhran. Fergus perched the drum on his knee, beater at the ready. There was a woman Niall didn't know playing the flute and old Cormac Kelly with his fiddle. Eoghan Sullivan had brought his melodeon, an Irish button accordion, and Saoirse Ryan had her mandolin.

Colin nodded at Fergus, who started up a beat on the bodhran. They began with "The Wind That Shakes the Barley," and as the music filled the room, Niall saw Cordelia slip from her chair and crouch by the door. She brought her camera to her eye and Niall wondered if she thought this seisiún some kind of quaint, silly tradition or if she found the music at all appealing. He hoped Colin would play "Out on the Ocean" at some point. That was one of Niall's favorites.

It had been a while since he'd been to a seisiún. It'd been a while since he'd done anything fun at all, to be honest. The music flowed and rippled and lightened the room, keeping at bay the gloominess from outside.

Darragh signaled for his next pint and then a few orders had to be taken and some food run out to the tables. When Niall looked again, Cordelia was in a different spot, in the far corner of the room, taking a photo of the bar. He hoped she wouldn't take his picture—he should have asked her not to. Niall didn't much like seeing himself in pictures anymore.

When the musicians had finished "A Fig for a Kiss," Colin signaled it was time for a quick break. Niall poured them all drinks, on the house, of course.

"So," said Cormac, taking a sip of his Guinness. "Looks like you've settled in nicely."

"Mm," Niall said.

"Will we be seeing you in the currach races over Pátrún?"

"Oh, I—"

"Of course, Cormac, you daft prick," Colin said, throwing his arm around Niall's shoulders. "We'll be on a team as usual. Inishmore's Finest Rowers."

Cormac laughed. "Colin Doyle, I could beat you in a currach race with one arm tied behind me back."

"All right, you two," Niall said, shrugging Colin off and handing him a pint of Galway Bay. He poured one for himself—this was a night of good craic, after all. Colin and Cormac clinked glasses as Alison and Cordelia approached the bar.

"Another glass of cabernet?" Niall asked them.

"Yes, please," Cordelia said.

"No, thanks," Alison said. "I've got to be getting Róisín home." They looked over to where Róisín was dozing at the table, her chin drooping to her chest, her hand clenched around an empty tumbler. "Could one of you make sure Cordelia gets to the cottage okay?"

"Course!" Colin said.

Cordelia beamed. Her cheeks were pink and her eyes bright—she was quite pretty, Niall had to admit. Colin had been right about that. Her camera still hung from her neck and she pushed the sleeves of her sweater up where they kept slipping down.

"Thanks. You guys are amazing!" she gushed to Colin and Cormac.

"Excuse me!" The brunette was waving her hand to catch Niall's attention.

"Looks like somebody's got himself an admirer," Cormac said.

Niall shrugged and motioned for Shauna to take the table. "No use in playing around when you're not interested in the game."

"If I had your looks, boy," Cormac said, "I'd be playing in every game there was to be had."

"Yeah, yeah," Niall said, waving him off, embarrassed. He watched with relief as the American girls paid their tab and left, then took a long drink of his beer.

"We'd best be getting back on," Colin said. The two of them grabbed their drinks and headed back to the stage.

"Is it okay if I sit here?" Cordelia asked, gesturing to the open barstool.

"If you like," Niall said.

She hopped up and started looking through the pictures she'd taken.

"Anything good?" Niall asked, pouring her wine.

"Mm," she said, distracted. She frowned in concentration and a little crease appeared between her eyebrows.

"You didn't catch any of me, did you?" he asked.

"No. Why?" She looked up. "Did you want me to? I figured you'd rather not—you seem like the type who hates having his photo taken."

"Do I now," he said, surprised to feel a smile on his face and hear a note of teasing in his voice.

She grinned. "I have a sixth sense about these things. When you're a street photographer, you learn to pick up on people's vibes."

"I have vibes, do I?"

"Oh yeah. You've got major fuck-off vibes." Her expression froze but Niall laughed and took another drink.

"That does sound like me. Nowadays at least." He realized he was veering into dangerous territory—Deirdre territory—and quickly changed course. "What about you? I thought all New Yorkers were meant to give fuck-off vibes as well."

"For sure," she said. "I give even better fuck-off vibes than you, if you can believe it."

"I cannot," Niall said. "I don't think there's ever been a grumpier bastard than me, thank you very much. I am the King of Fuck-Off Vibes. Don't come for my crown."

"You've never seen me on the D train during rush hour," Cordelia said, gesturing to herself with a flourish. "Let me tell you, fuck-off vibes *abound*."

Niall laughed again and Cordelia giggled. Then she tilted her head thoughtfully.

"It's a shame," she said.

"What?"

"You'd make a good subject. The contrast between your hair and eyes. The dimple in your left cheek." Her eyes flew wide and her face turned bright red, the blush creeping down her neck. "Oh my god. Wow. What a creeper. Sorry. I just . . . it's hard to turn it off sometimes. Being a photographer. Looking at things like . . ." She waved a hand at him, then hid her face in her wineglass.

"Are you saying I should take up modeling then?" Niall asked. He struck a vogue pose and Cordelia nearly spat out her drink.

"I wouldn't quit your day job just yet," she said.

"Ouch."

"Oh please. I saw those girls eye-fucking you over there. Were they American? They looked American. I feel like I'm developing a spidey-sense for my own people now. We can be such cringey tourists, right?"

"You're not all bad," he said. "You've seemed to fit right in. How did you manage to charm Róisín so quickly?"

"I'm drawing her medicinal plants as illustrations for this book she's writing."

"Ah," Niall said, nodding. "She's using you for free labor."

"It's fine with me. I like listening to her talk. She has this crazy stream of consciousness thing going. Sometimes she talks more to a horsefly than she does to me. But I don't mind. She's so unapologetically herself."

"That she is," Niall said. "No one more so."

Cordelia fiddled with the stem of her glass. "I used to think I was like that."

The sentence hung in the air, but Niall didn't know if she really wanted to talk about personal things and if she did, if she'd want to talk to *him* about them. But before he could say anything, she continued.

"It's been nice to draw again. I think I needed a break. From photography. I needed to remember there are lots of ways to be creative. I needed to remind myself that I'm not just one thing." She looked at him, half shy, half teasing. "I suppose I should be thanking you. If you hadn't broken my camera, I might not have gotten the space I needed away from my work." She fingered the strap around her neck. "It might even be better. Using a new one. One that wasn't his."

"His?" Niall asked.

"My dad's," she said. "He gave me the one that broke a month before he died."

Niall's heart plummeted and his face blanched. "I broke your *da's* camera? God, Cordelia, I'm so—"

She held up a hand. "It's fixable. I'm taking it to my local shop when I get back. And I think we've said enough sorrys, haven't we?" She tapped on the camera with her fingernail. "You were right," she admitted. "I did step in your way. I'm always adjusting myself to put things in the right frame. It drives Liz crazy. My best friend," she explained but Niall was still stuck on the part where he'd broken her dead father's camera. "We'll go out for drinks or have coffee in Central Park and I'm always tilting my head or scooching to the left so that her face is in perfect composition with the background. Like, even just a moment ago, I moved a little so that the greenish brown light from those bottles fills the negative space and the line of the mirror frames you on the right-hand side." She shrugged. "Can't help myself, I guess."

"Can I—pay for the repair or . . ." His voice trailed off.

"No, it's okay. Really," she said when she saw his doubtful look. "I mean, if it couldn't be fixed that would be another story."

"If it couldn't be fixed, I'd jump off the cliffs of Dún Aengus," Niall said.

"Róisín took me there!" Cordelia exclaimed. "It was nice. Really crowded, though. What was the one Alison had mentioned?"

Niall felt his face snap shut. "Dún Dúchathair," he said tightly. The memories that came with those ruins weren't ones he wanted to recall now, not on this night, when he was finally having fun.

Cordelia seemed to sense his shift in mood. She picked up her camera and busied herself in the photos. Then the music started up again.

"Niall!" Shauna called from the other end of the bar, gesturing for him to help her with the customers.

"Right, I'd better get back to it," he said.

"Okay," she replied.

As he walked away, Niall felt as if the floor was shifting beneath his feet, each step uncertain where it might land.

10

That Sunday during dinner, Niall's father finally started speaking to him again.

It was just the four of them this week—Alison had called and said she and Cordelia were having dinner at Róisín's.

"I've been thinking," Owen said, cutting into his chicken while Pocket sat patiently by his chair, waiting for scraps. He paused for so long Colin and Niall exchanged a glance.

"About?" Niall asked.

"Pátrún," Owen said. Fiona seemed very interested in her champ all of a sudden, pushing the mashed potatoes around on her plate. Niall's eyes narrowed.

"What about Pátrún?" he asked.

"Well, we've been thinking—" Owen glanced at Fiona and her nostrils flared. "*I've* been thinking," he corrected himself. "That maybe . . . in addition to our usual fare . . . we could serve up something special for the occasion. Something, you know . . ."

He gestured with one hand and Pocket followed the movement with laser-like focus.

"Something . . . ?" Niall prodded, unsure exactly what was going on here.

"One of your *fusion* things. Dishes. Whatever." Owen said the word fusion like it was a curse. Fiona looked pleased. Niall was stunned.

"Oh," he said after a moment. "Sure. That'd be grand."

"Right. Well." Now that the big talk was over, Owen was eager to get back to his food. "There you go, you wee beggar," he said to Pocket, holding out a piece of chicken. She devoured it in half a second and turned to Niall expectantly. "But you'll run the recipe by me first," Owen said.

"Course," Niall said. "No problem."

Colin raised an eyebrow and Niall shrugged. He was as surprised as anyone.

He should thank Cordelia. Whenever he saw her again.

Niall woke up the next morning and, for the first time in months, he felt like cooking.

"Got any plans this evening?" he asked Colin as he poured himself a cup of coffee. Both of them were off that day and Colin was sitting at the island picking out a new song while Pocket eyed his bacon.

"I was thinking of hitting up the Seaview. Check out what Cian's done to the place. Maybe find a cute tourist to charm." He waggled his eyebrows.

Niall sat down on one of the high stools. Pocket rested her head against his knee and he stroked her ears thoughtfully, sipping his coffee.

"What's that mile-long stare about?" Colin said.

"I was just thinking . . ." Niall began.

Colin waited. "For fuck's sake, Niall, the suspense is killing me."

Niall scratched behind his ear. "I thought I might cook dinner."

Colin put his guitar pick down on the table. "Plans canceled. Count me in. Christ, man, I've been wondering when you'd start making good use of this kitchen. Should we call Alison and invite her? Cordelia too?"

He should say yes. It would give him an opportunity to let her know how much her words had helped mend things a bit with his father. But the thought of asking her to come to his house had his stomach squirming.

"No," Niall said. "I don't want to make a big thing. Maybe next time, though."

"All right, suit yourself. Whatcha making?"

"I'm not sure yet," Niall said slowly. "Thought I'd go down the market and see what's fresh."

Pocket followed Niall as he walked to the market and then left to do her own thing. She was always keeping track of the animal life on the island, checking in on sheep and cow and horse alike—as well as popping by the houses for pets and treats. Niall took his time, letting the menu slowly come together as he perused the fresh vegetables, sniffed bunches of herbs, and examined the butcher's stock. As he walked back to the house with a full tote bag slung over his shoulder, the cloud cover broke and the sun shone down on the road, dew drops on the grass glittering like crystals.

Maybe, Niall thought to himself, coming home for the summer hadn't been such a terrible thing after all.

Cordelia returned from a long bike ride, exhausted.

The sun had decided to make an appearance and she hadn't wanted to miss out on the opportunity. She was getting better at biking too—today she'd finally made it to the Seal Colony. Róisín had been hired by a group of Australian tourists for two days of sightseeing and Cordelia felt ready to do some exploring on her own.

The seals had been marvelous subjects, sleek bodies lounging on the rocks, plump tummies facing the sun. Their eyes had a startling amount of depth, like wise old souls who knew the untold secrets of the sea. It really did feel like she was getting a fresh start with this new camera. She parked the bike in the shed and walked back to the cottage, perusing some of the pictures she'd taken as she went. She knew she should start posting on her Instagram account, but she didn't know if she was ready yet. She was rediscovering the simple love of photography again. She didn't want to ruin it.

Just then her phone began to ring.

"Hey, Toby. Shouldn't you be in school?" she teased. Toby taught English at a public school in Brooklyn.

"Last day was this past Thursday," Toby said. "I'm officially on summer break. How's it going over there, little sis?"

"Oh, grand," Cordelia said in a poor imitation of an Irish accent. Toby laughed. "I just got back from this amazing place called the Seal Colony. It was—"

"Full of seals?"

"Ha ha. I was going to say incredibly cool but yes, it was also full of seals. How are things with you? How're Nikki and the kids?"

"We're going away next weekend. I booked an Airbnb in the Berkshires. With a pool. The kids can't wait."

Cordelia laughed. "I bet. That sounds great."

"Mom and Gary are coming too."

"Oh."

Silence hung between them.

"Look, Cordie, I know you don't like Gary but—"

"Gary's fine," Cordelia snapped. "Who said I didn't like Gary? I never said that."

"No, but your dislike is literally pouring out of the phone and slapping me in the face from an ocean away."

Cordelia pursed her lips. "What's your point, Toby?"

"My point is, it's hurting Mom's feelings."

"I highly doubt that," Cordelia said. "When does she have time to have her feelings hurt? Aren't they always going off on some adventure together?"

After Key West, they'd spent a week at Gary's son's villa in Tuscany. Apparently the son was a winemaker, married an Italian, divorced her, but kept the villa. Her mother had sent photos, Louise in white linen with a glass of rosé in hand, Gary giving a thumbs up from the middle of a crystal blue swimming pool, his nose white with sunscreen. And, of course, the photos had come with a new dating app suggestion. This one was Irish-specific, called Mo Rogha. Cordelia had deleted the text immediately.

"That's not the point," Toby said. "Why are you holding that against her? Is Mom not allowed to have fun anymore?"

"Of course she is," Cordelia said, but something about his words made her stomach pinch.

"Yeah, I definitely don't believe you. Mom is happy, Cord. Isn't that what you're trying to do over there? Find happiness, especially after Dad?"

"Yeah, but I'm not using a man to find it," Cordelia snapped.

"Okay, first of all, Mom isn't *using* Gary. She actually likes him. Secondly, what's wrong with finding a new purpose with a relationship? Just because it's been decades since you've been in one—"

"Oh, very funny, Toby."

"Well? Your last boyfriend was who, Sam? That was almost three years ago."

"So you're pulling a Mom on me now? Want me to settle down and pop out some kids like you did?"

"Jesus, Cordelia, stop being so goddamn defensive. That's not what I'm saying."

"What *are* you saying?"

"I'm saying can't you stop looking at everything through your own narrow lens and see things from her side? Just because you're unhappy doesn't mean Mom should be too. And just because she's found happiness in a way that you don't like doesn't mean it's not valid."

"I AM HAPPY!" Cordelia shouted into the phone. "Look, I'll . . . reach out to Mom this week, okay? I'll ask about Gary. Maybe we can all FaceTime when you're on vacation."

"Sure," Toby said. "That would be great."

But he didn't sound like he really thought that. Since when was Toby on Team Gary? Cordelia hated feeling like the odd man out in her family. She wondered if Toby weren't already married, if her mother would be pushing dating apps on him too. She doubted it. Another thing Toby just didn't understand.

"I have to go," Cordelia said, even though she didn't. "Give my love to Nikki and the kids."

"Yeah, sure," Toby said. "Bye."

They hung up and Cordelia walked into the cottage and slammed the door. Her stomach was beginning to rumble. She headed to the kitchen and stared into the fridge. Eggs, milk, cheese. She'd run out of pasta. There was a can of tomato soup in the cupboard. She had one slice of bread left.

You could go out to eat, a small voice whispered. *O'Connor's has good food.*

It did, she had to admit. Better than any other restaurant she'd tried. Colin might be there—she could show him some of the photos she'd taken from the seisiún.

Is it really Colin you're hoping to see?

Yes, she thought firmly even as a pair of startling blue eyes flashed across her mind. It had been nice to finally put the whole camera incident with Niall behind her. And sure, he wasn't glowering so much anymore, which softened his features. And yeah, it turned out he kind of had a sense of humor. But the guy was recovering from possibly the worst breakup in the history of ever. Even if Cordelia *was* thinking about dating—which she wasn't—she for sure would not choose a broken-hearted dude with daddy issues.

She was still staring into the empty fridge and wondering if she should just have chocolate for dinner when there was a scratching at the door. It couldn't be Róisín. Róisín never knocked—she burst into the cottage as she pleased, without warning.

Cordelia closed the fridge and went to open the door.

"Oh," she said. "Hello."

Pocket was smiling up at her, tongue lolling out.

"What are you doing here?" Cordelia said. "I don't have any food, sadly." Pocket gave a little huff, turning her head to the road, then looking back at Cordelia. She butted her head against Cordelia's knee.

"Okay, hold on, let me get my shoes. I'll walk you home."

Cordelia slipped into her boots, threw on her raincoat, then grabbed her camera and sling out of habit. The rain wasn't bad, only a light mist, and Pocket wove around Cordelia's legs, herding her to the side of the road whenever a car or horse-drawn cart passed. Cordelia assumed they were going to Fiona's house, but Pocket shepherded her off down the long driveway to the white house.

Niall and Colin's house. Her knees locked and she stopped walking.

Well. She was just dropping off the dog. She didn't need to be such a coward about it. Maybe he wasn't even home. He was probably working.

But there were lights on in the front room.

Who cares if he's home or not? They'd had a perfectly pleasant conversation the other night at the session. She didn't need to be tiptoeing around him or walking on eggshells. He was her neighbor, for god's sake.

Pocket circled around and nudged the back of her calf, pushing her forward.

"Grow up, Cordelia," she muttered to herself.

She stomped to the red front door, took a deep breath, and knocked.

11

The door flew open and Niall stood staring down at her with a look of complete surprise.

His hair was disheveled and he wore a red-and-white striped apron over a blue button-down with the sleeves rolled up to his elbows, a bottle of olive oil in one hand.

"Oh. Hello," he said, his eyes going wide. They were clear blue today, like a summer sky.

Stop staring at his damn eyes, Cord.

"Hi," she said, shifting from one foot to the other. "Pocket was at my house and I thought I'd . . ." She gestured feebly.

"Ah. Trying to sneak in a pre-dinner snack, were you?" Niall said to the dog, who came up and licked his free hand.

Cordelia chuckled. "It was a futile attempt, I'm afraid. I've got, like, zero food in the fridge. I was planning on chocolate for dinner."

"What's this about no food?" Colin came bounding up to the door. "Cordelia! Aren't you a sight for sore eyes. Come in! Niall's cooking. Fecking finally, if you ask me. There's plenty. I think he got enough fillet steak to feed all of Kilronan."

"I did not," Niall said. "I bought what looked good."

"Yeah, a whole cow, it seems." Colin smiled at her and brushed his brown hair out of his eyes. "Come on then. You can't be eating chocolate for dinner. Can she be eating chocolate for dinner, Niall?"

"Please come in or I'll never hear the end of it," Niall muttered to her. "No, she can't be eating chocolate for dinner, Colin, will you get off my fecking back now? Here, make yourself useful and take this to the kitchen with the dog."

"Come, Pocket," Colin said, grabbing the olive oil from Niall's hand and heading down the hall.

"You can leave your boots here," Niall said pointing to the neat row of shoes lined up by the door. "I'll take your coat."

His fingers brushed the bare skin at the nape of her neck as he helped her out of her jacket and goose bumps blossomed across her shoulders.

"Thanks," she said. "You really didn't have to invite me, you know."

"Nah, Colin's right. I bought far too much food." He hung up her coat and turned. "Are those . . . avocados on your socks?"

"Oh." Cordelia flushed. "Yeah. Liz got them for me."

The socks were purple with happy dancing avocados on them, some with pits in their bellies and some without. Cordelia felt a little embarrassed. But then Niall smiled so wide his dimple popped.

"Cute," he said.

For some reason, that word in his brogue made her toes curl.

They entered the kitchen and Cordelia gasped. Every inch of counter space was covered in green. There were herbs of every variety, a neat line of asparagus on a cutting board, and scallions sitting in a colander. A huge strip of steak was laid out on brown paper next to the stove.

"See what I mean?" Colin said. He was filling a glass with ice. "Gin and tonic? That's what we're having, but I can make you something else if you'd like."

"No, that's perfect," Cordelia said. "Wow." She glanced at the countertops again, feeling dazed. "This is—"

"Far too much food?" Colin said, pouring a healthy amount of gin into the glass and filling the rest with tonic.

"Oi," Niall said, raising a knife so that it glinted in the overhead lights. "Don't be slagging me. The chef is armed, remember."

"Can I help with anything?" Cordelia asked.

"Do you know how to cook?" Niall said brightly.

"Um . . . no," she admitted. "Róisín thinks I live on cheese and chocolate."

Colin laughed, squeezing some lime into her drink and pushing it into her hand.

"Sit with me," he said, hopping onto a stool and patting the one beside him. "See, now what I like to do when Niall cooks is, I pretend I'm a judge on one o' them cooking shows like *MasterChef*."

"Oh god, *please* do not do that again," Niall said as he rinsed the scallions and put them aside. Then he grabbed the salt and pepper and started to season the meat.

"Seasoning is key," Colin said gravely, putting on a studio announcer voice. "But let's see if Niall O'Connor can get the temperature right. A fillet steak is a tricky thing."

"No, it's not," Niall said, exasperated.

Cordelia giggled. She took a sip of her drink—it was tart and fresh and the bubbles filled her nose.

"What's this?" she asked, picking up a bunch of what looked like long thin blades of grass.

"That'd be tarragon," Niall said. "For the chimichurri."

"Chimi-who?"

"Oh, lord," Colin said. "Now you're going to get him started and he'll never fecking stop."

"She should know what it is she'll be eating," Niall said. "Now, a classic chimichurri is like a green sauce to put on meat or fish. Usually only has parsley, coriander, and oregano, but I like to add as many herbs as I can."

He stood at the island across from them, peeling a large shallot and dicing it, then smashing a clove of garlic flat with the side of his knife and mincing it. It was fascinating to watch—Cordelia sipped her drink and wondered how he didn't cut his fingers off. Niall's movements were fluid as he switched out tarragon for parsley, then coriander, and on and on. The scent of mint and basil filled the air. Niall put the chopped herbs, shallot, and garlic in a bowl, doused it all with olive oil, added some red wine vinegar and chili flakes, and wiped his hands on his apron.

"That's one thing done," he said.

Colin pointed to the camera she'd placed on the island. "Show us the photos you took at the seisiún. I want to see how devilishly handsome I look."

She gladly obliged, but her eyes kept drifting to Niall. The process of cooking had always seemed dull and arduous to Cordelia. But Niall made it look fun. Like an adventure. Or creating a piece of art.

He sliced the meat into several pieces, then set a large pan on the stove. Cordelia hadn't realized how long she'd been staring at him until he glanced up and caught her. His eyes glinted merrily, a lock of raven hair falling over his forehead. He pushed it back with his wrist and said, "Have I got something on my face?"

"No," she said, flushing. "Watching you cook, it's like . . . like a dance."

Colin let out a guffaw but Niall seemed oddly touched.

"I'm a bit out o' practice," he admitted. "It's been a while since I . . . danced."

"You can't tell," Cordelia said.

"I want this one," Colin said, thrusting the camera toward her and pointing to a photo of himself sharing a laugh with Fergus the drummer.

"I'll email it to you," she promised, taking the camera back. She lifted it to her eye to gaze at the kitchen through the lens, the darkening night outside the window a perfect contrast to the warm light inside. She found herself focusing on Niall, who was now leaning over some potatoes and carefully slicing into them.

"Sorry," she said, when he looked at her again. "No photos. I remember."

"Oh, go on then," he said. "I don't mind. Oi, Colin, make yourself useful and play us some tunes."

"Right on it, brother," he said and disappeared, his footsteps going up the stairs. Cordelia lifted the camera again and the shutter clicked as she took a few shots in quick succession.

"Do I still make a good subject?" Niall asked.

Cordelia blushed so hard her ears turned red. "I was shooting the potatoes," she said primly.

Niall laughed. She'd never imagined such a relaxed sound could come from his throat. He was the complete opposite of the man she'd bumped into on the docks. She got up off her stool and walked over to see what exactly he was doing.

"These are called hasselback potatoes," he explained. "They were first created in a Swedish tavern and they'll look gorgeous once they're done. I'm making small slices crosswise, like little incisions, very very thin. Only cutting about two-thirds through so that the potato stays together. See?"

Cordelia nodded. She snapped a few pictures as he sliced—his hands were large and strong, his forearms surprisingly muscular. Well, maybe not surprisingly—she hadn't ever really thought about his forearms one way or another before. But now, standing so close to him, she was deeply aware of the broad set of his shoulders, the curve of his biceps beneath the button-down, the black hairs exposed where the undone buttons gave a peek of his chest before the apron covered it.

She stepped back to get a full shot of him leaning over the countertop and then, feeling a bit awkward, she took a picture of Pocket sniffing around by the sink.

"So what made you get into cooking?" she asked.

"My da," he replied, placing the finished potato on a baking sheet and taking a sip of his drink before starting on the next one. "If you can believe it. Visiting him in the kitchen at O'Connor's and watching him run the show. Learning how to properly season things and the right way to use a knife. He taught me everything I know about cooking. But after a while I wanted to try making something myself. Got ideas about how certain flavors might mix together, or how different spices would suit different proteins. Not all of them worked. Mam was a good sport about it. So was Colin—we lived together in Dublin when he was going to university."

"Where did you go to school?" she asked.

"I didn't," Niall said. "No money to speak of and no inclination really. I worked. Probably worked in half the pubs in Dublin.

First collecting glasses, then as a bartender, then I got a job in the kitchens and worked my way up until I was running one myself. But it was someone else's kitchen and I was serving someone else's menu, always making the same thing—lamb stew, fish and chips, colcannon—"

"Sorry, what?"

"It's like mashed potatoes with herbs and cream and cabbage," he said. "Anyways, then I met, um, Deirdre."

Silence fell, and for a moment Niall focused very hard on the potatoes. Cordelia searched around for another subject. She hadn't meant to make him uncomfortable. But she'd never known Niall's ex's name. It was weird hearing it—like it made her real, somehow, instead of a picture in the paper and a figure from a gossip story.

"You don't . . . have to talk about . . ." she stammered.

"No, it's all right. Can't go avoiding her forever." Niall picked up the final potato and began to slice. "It was Deirdre who encouraged me to start my own place. It was a dream I'd always had but never thought I could actually realize. She said we'd go in on it together, that I had the skills, the talent, and the discipline, and she had the connections. I'd saved up quite a bit of money at that point and she had—well, her family's rich, so money wasn't ever a problem on her side. We found a business partner through her dad. Thought he was the perfect fit."

His mouth twisted and his eyes darkened. Cordelia felt a flash of anger toward this woman she'd never met. She didn't just break his heart—she built up his dream and then broke that too.

"I meant to thank you," Niall said softly.

She blinked. "For what?"

"For all that you said to my da. He's gone quiet, which is unusual for him, but not unwelcome. It's been a bit of a relief actually. And he's letting me cook something for Pátrún. Never thought I'd live to see the day me da actually asked me to cook something. So. Thanks for that."

"Oh," Cordelia said, her throat swelling up. "I . . ."

The kitchen suddenly felt very warm and Niall seemed very close. Cordelia jumped when something touched her leg, but it was only Pocket.

"Sometimes I don't think before I speak," she said, turning to get her drink, needing an excuse to look away from those aquamarine eyes.

"It serves you well."

"Ha," she said, remembering her fight with Toby. "Not always. I can really put my foot in my mouth."

She turned to see Niall looking at her curiously, but before he could ask, there was a knock on the door.

"Bloody hell, what is this, visiting day?" he said as Colin called, "I'll get it!"

They heard footsteps running down the stairs, then voices coming up from the living room. Cordelia turned to see Alison enter the kitchen, a bottle of red wine in one hand and a chocolate cake in the other.

"Colin said you were cooking!" she exclaimed, coming over to kiss Niall's cheek. "God, doesn't this look grand. I brought wine and dessert. Colin, fix me up a G&T, would ya? Cordie, don't you look lovely."

Did she? She hadn't really thought about what she was wearing. She hadn't intended to be anywhere but home alone for dinner. Alison wrapped her up in a warm hug, Colin started to play a Sam Cooke tune on his guitar, and Niall popped the potatoes in the oven. As she and Alison danced while Colin sang "Another Saturday Night," Cordelia couldn't believe how much had changed in such a short amount of time.

And she couldn't imagine any place else she'd rather be.

Niall was feeling quite light-headed.

And it wasn't just Colin's heavy hand in making a drink.

He hadn't wanted anyone here for his first foray back into the kitchen, but now he was grateful that Pocket had wandered over to the cottage, and that Colin had called Alison. What had he been so afraid of? It was steak and potatoes, for Christ's sake. He'd forgotten the pure joy of cooking, not only the mixing of flavors, and the scent of herbs, and the sizzle of meat, but the joy at having friends around to share it with. There was music, laughter, silly chatter about nonsense—Niall wasn't taking everything so goddamned seriously for once.

He was glad he'd told some of his story to Cordelia. It had been like drawing poison from a wound. The memories didn't quite have the sting they used to.

She did look lovely, as Alison had noted, in her soft gray top with a scooped neckline. And those socks. Niall didn't know why, but every time he looked at them he chuckled. They were utterly ridiculous. And utterly adorable.

His brain screeched to a halt as he thought the word, then veered away toward safe waters. *Meat. Cook the meat. Asparagus. Is the griddle hot enough? Don't burn the potatoes.*

"Can I help with anything?" Cordelia asked, skidding to his side, flushed from all the dancing. "Anything not cooking related?"

"D'you mind setting the table?" he said. The heat of her body was radiating against his left arm. She'd put her hair up in a messy bun, but a few strands stuck to her jaw. His eyes snagged on the pale gold freckles scattered in a unique pattern across her left cheek.

"Why, I'd love to," she said in a very bad Irish accent.

He laughed. "Doing impressions now, are we?"

She grinned and her freckles danced with the movement. Colin was leading Alison in a rendition of "Chain of Fools." Niall bent down to take the potatoes out of the oven.

"Whoa!" Cordelia said, coming over with her hands full of cutlery. "Those look so cool!"

The skin had crisped up nicely and the potatoes looked like little fans. Niall sprinkled them with rosemary and salt, then set them aside.

"Now to cook the steak," he said. He placed two strips side by side in the pan and watched the concern in Cordelia's eyes when she heard them sizzle.

"Are they burning?" she said.

"Never," Niall said. "You need the pan to be hot to get a nice sear on the outside and keep the steak pink on the inside." He shot her a wary look. "You're not one of those Americans who eats their steak so well done it's basically rubber, are you?"

Cordelia shook her head so hard her bun flopped about. "Medium rare. Always."

"That's what I like to hear," Niall said. "Weren't you going to set the table?"

"I wanna see you flip them," she said. Her eyes were bright, her expression openly eager in a way that made Niall's chest go strangely soft.

"It's not that exciting, I promise you."

"I still want to see."

He smiled. "Okay." They needed to cook for a few minutes first, and he thought about telling her she had time to do both, but he found he liked having her there.

Just then, Alison's phone rang.

"Hello?" she said, breathless. "Hiya . . . What? . . . Aw shite. No, it's fine, I'll go . . . All right. Yup, cheers, bye."

"Everything okay?" Colin asked.

"We've got a big party coming this week with lots of dietary restrictions and the order just arrived and it's fucked. Not the right things at all. I'll have to go to Galway tomorrow and get supplies meself." She turned to Cordelia. "I'm so sorry, I can't take you to Dún Dúchathair like we'd planned."

"That's all right," Cordelia said. "I've got a map, I can go by myself."

"I can take you if you like," Niall said.

Christ, what did he say that for? Colin's eyebrows were raised so high they were disappearing into his hair. Niall stared intensely at the steak in the pan, trying to come up with some way to take it back without being rude.

"That would be great," Cordelia said after a pause. "Thanks."

He couldn't tell if she was just being polite, so he ducked his head and said, "Cool." He threw a quick, desperate glance at Colin, and his best friend started up an old Everly Brothers song. The energy in the room seemed to relax again. What had he been thinking? It sounded like he was asking her on a date, which he definitely was not—he wasn't dating. He was heartbroken and sad and *not* dating.

He didn't feel heartbroken though. Not at this moment anyway.

The steaks were going to overcook, he realized with a start.

"Are you ready to watch me flip 'em?" Niall asked, chancing a look at her.

Cordelia's cheeks were faintly pink, her eyes brimming with excitement. She had a small button nose that twitched when she smiled, like a rabbit. She clapped her hands and nodded. Niall took the tongs and, with exaggerated movements, turned the steaks.

"I told you it's not that impressive," he said.

She shrugged. "It is to me."

Their eyes met. Niall was about to say he hadn't meant to push himself in on her plans, and if she wanted to go to the fort alone that was fine. But then Colin called out, "Oi, don't forget I like mine medium!"

"You'll have medium rare, you bugger, or none at all," Niall said. He turned back in time to see Cordelia fleeing the kitchen with the cutlery. Alison grabbed some plates and went to help her. Colin stopped playing and came over to where Niall stood at the stove.

"Dún Dúchathair, huh?" he said.

"Mm."

"With Cordelia."

"Mm."

Why was his face so hot? It didn't mean anything. And his issue with the Black Fort was stupid, really. It was past time he went back there.

He could feel Colin's eyes on him.

"What?" Niall said at last.

Colin shrugged. "Sounds grand." He strummed the guitar and walked out of the kitchen to join the women, but he picked up the Everly Brothers song again as he left. "When will I be loved . . ."

12

Cordelia was meant to be brushing down Brigid, but she kept stopping every few minutes to tuck the curry comb under her arm and take out her phone.

She'd already written and deleted several texts to Niall.

Hey, you really don't have to come today if you don't want to.

Didn't mean to put you on the spot last night, you still up for the fort?

Should be fun today amirite lol.

What even was that last one? She never used "lol." She was not a lol person. She was a hahaha or laughing emoji person.

"Christ, girl, is there a ball you're attending later?" Róisín cried. "You can't brush Brigid properly if you're staring at that infernal contraption every two minutes."

"Sorry," Cordelia said. She was being stupid. It wasn't like this was a date or anything. Niall was a friend now. She'd exchanged numbers with both him and Colin. Niall had said they could head out around two since he had to be at work at the pub at six.

She slipped the curry comb back into her hand and started brushing Brigid's neck in the circular motions Róisín had shown her. But her mind kept wandering. Niall had been relaxed and laughing last night, looking more like the person in the old photograph with his mom than the clench-jawed, irritable guy she'd bumped into on the pier.

And his eyes. They were nothing short of mesmerizing. There seemed to be endless shades to them, reflecting his mood. There was that startling blue that flashed like sapphires when he'd talked about his ex and then brightened to aquamarine when he thanked her for what she'd said to his father. They were intensely cerulean when he was cooking and a gentle azure when he teased her about photographing him. She had taken a couple of pictures of his face, leaning over the potatoes in utter concentration. She hadn't looked at them yet, though.

"Right, that's it." Róisín threw down the bunch of carrots she'd pulled up from the garden and stormed over to Cordelia. "At this rate, I may as well teach Brigid to brush herself. What has gotten into you, child? Has the púca come and taken your shape in the night?"

Cordelia gave her a wry look—the púca was a mischief-making shapeshifter of Irish legend that Róisín had told her about. Every rural county had one. The bench beside Róisín's front door was for the púca, Cordelia had been informed. A good púca always sits on the right, apparently, but the bad ones like the left. The way Róisín told it, she and Inishmore's púca were old friends.

"No," Cordelia said. "But if I *was* the púca, I wouldn't tell you, would I?"

Róisín chuckled. "I've taught you well." She peered up into Cordelia's eyes. "Ah, you're no púca, you're too mopey. What's on your mind? Spit it out now."

"I'm going to the Black Fort with Niall this afternoon," Cordelia said in a rush. "I was meant to go with Alison but she's gone in to Galway so Niall said he'd take me and I said yes."

Róisín stared at her for a long moment. "And?"

Cordelia shrugged and went back to brushing. "I don't know." She tried to come up with something to say that wasn't *He laughs now* or *I think his eyes are kind of beautiful and it makes me nervous.* "He's a little intimidating."

Róisín let out a loud belly laugh. "Miss New York City intimidated by Niall bloody O'Connor? I never. Come on, girl, let's get Brigid hooked up then."

"Hooked up?"

"I'll take you both to Dún Dúchathair in the trap," Róisín said.

"We aren't meant to go until two."

"What, you think Niall's got some more pressing business to attend to today than spending time with a lovely girl at a bleak and wondrous ruin? No, he'll be sitting at home staring at his phone, same as you. Young people these days and their phones." She clucked her tongue and headed over to the shed to get Brigid's tack. "You stay right there, ya damn carrots, I'll be back for you in a wee minute!" She saw Cordelia still hovering by the horse. "What are you waiting for? I didn't show you how to tack up Brigid just to do it all meself."

And so ten minutes later, Cordelia found herself bouncing in the cart beside Róisín as they rode up to the white house. Róisín, without bothering to get down, shouted, "Oi! Niall O'Connor! We've come to fetch you to Dún Dúchathair, now get your lazy arse out here so we can make it before those clouds turn to rain."

Cordelia heard footsteps inside and then the door was thrown open. Niall stood there, bemused, with Colin right behind him, grinning.

"All right, Róisín," he called.

"Morning, Colin. Fine day for a trip to the Black Fort, is it not?"

"It's a grand morning," Colin said, glancing up at the grayish cloud cover overhead. Niall was hurriedly pulling on a white cable knit sweater—as he lifted it over his head, his T-shirt rode up to expose a line of skin above the waist of his jeans. Cordelia blushed so hard her eyes stung and she looked down, fiddling with her camera. What was wrong with her? It wasn't like she'd never seen a man's stomach before. She hated how easily she blushed. Liz told her it was charming, but Cordelia found it mortifying.

"We were set to meet at two, Róisín," Niall said, grabbing his jacket.

"She told me as much. But no need to put off to the afternoon what can be done in the morning."

"Let me guess," Niall said to Cordelia. "She gave you no choice."

"None whatsoever," Cordelia replied.

He smiled and Cordelia felt an odd jerky sensation, a tightening in her shoulders combined with a looseness in her chest. Niall went to climb into the back of the cart and Róisín said, "Get your bike, you daft bastard. I'm only driving you there, not back. Got things to do."

Niall shook his head, then went to get his bike from under a tarp on the side of the house. He lifted it into the back of the cart alongside Cordelia's then climbed up.

"All right, I'm in. Enough of your harping. Let's get a move on."

"Is that any way to talk to your elders?" Róisín said as she cracked the reins and Brigid made a slow circle back to Cottage Road.

"Eh, you're not *that* old."

Róisín cackled. "Damn right, boyo."

Cordelia was glad that Niall seemed totally chill about this. She'd been worried he might turn back into the dour man she'd first met. Brigid clopped through the center of Kilronan and Róisín greeted everyone with her customary blunt manner, sometimes speaking in English, sometimes in Irish. They passed the Aran Sweater Market and started down a road that skirted the harbor, seaweed gathering in great slimy bunches around the jagged stony shore. The ocean was a melancholy blue today, and on the far side of the harbor Cordelia could see clusters of houses, white and mauve and pale yellow; behind them rose the gentle hills of Inishmore, green grass divided up by endless stone walls.

They reached a fork in the road and began to climb up into the hills. Sheep watched them with impassive eyes. The stone walls weren't like the ones surrounding Cordelia's cottage—those were thin smooth stones laid flat, one on top of the other. These ones had enormous craggy rocks at their base with smaller stones piled on top haphazardly so that some were standing on end while others were tilted at angles. It made the tops of the walls as uneven and rolling as the hills surrounding them.

Cordelia was struck by the raw beauty of it all. More than once she raised her camera to take photos—she wasn't much of a landscape photographer, but she *was* a tourist who wanted to remember this ride. She was trying to remind herself that sometimes photographs could be for fun. They didn't all have to be perfect.

But she was keenly aware of Niall in the cart behind her. A few times the nape of her neck prickled and she thought maybe he was looking at her.

Who cares if he's looking at you or not? You're just friends. Friends look at friends all the time.

"I heard your da's letting you put something on the menu for Pátrún," Róisín said.

"And how would you be knowing that?" Niall asked.

"The púca told me," Róisín said, winking at Cordelia. "All right, no, it was Fiona. So." She turned to fix him with a stern look. "What are you makin' then? And will you be needing any taste testers, because I'm happy to offer my services."

Niall laughed and Cordelia peeked over her shoulder. He had one knee up on the bench, his forearm resting on it, and he bounced with the roll of the cart's wheels, his black hair tousled by the wind. The road stretched out behind him, a thin black line among grass that was lushly green even in the drab light. His eyes looked navy today.

She couldn't help herself—she lifted her camera and took a picture. He shot her a wry grin and she captured that too before lowering the camera and returning the smile.

"Force of habit," she said.

"Enough pictures, I mean to talk about food," Róisín said.

"I haven't sorted that out yet," Niall replied.

"Well, you'd better get on it. You know your father will be expecting nothing less than absolute perfection. But not too fancy. Nothing that'll scare the pants off the likes o' Darragh O'Grady. But it must be good enough to impress the tourists."

"Oh, is that all?"

"No. Most important, you must be making something *I* like."

"You like everything I cook."

Róisín waved her hand. "I didn't much care for whatever that was you did with colcannon."

Niall rolled his eyes. "That's because you have a bizarre resentment against kale."

"Why's it got to be so chewy?" Róisín demanded. "And it tastes like grass. No thank you. It's fine for Brigid, not for people."

"I like kale," Cordelia volunteered.

"See?" Niall said.

"She's American. Besides, have you seen her kitchen? Cheese and chocolate, this one lives on. I think I saw one lonely egg in a carton. No meat. No potatoes. I'd give her some of me carrots but she wouldn't know what to do with them."

"Hey," Cordelia said. "I have apples."

"Oh, she's got apples. You hear that, Niall?"

"I heard it."

"What's an apple going to do for you? Can't make a dinner out o' apples and chocolate."

Cordelia made a silent vow never to tell Róisín about her obsession with fifty-cent ramen packets. The road climbed higher and she could smell the salty tang of the ocean and hear the crashing of waves in the distance. The clouds were growing heavier, pressing down toward the earth like thick curls of smoke.

They rolled to a stop in front of a faded wooden sign written in Irish. Niall hopped down and took the bikes out of the back. Cordelia had almost forgotten that Róisín wasn't coming to the fort with them and that soon it would be her and Niall alone together.

She climbed from the cart on trembling legs and reminded herself that this was no different than hanging out with Alison or Colin. She worried at her hair, then at her camera strap, and then fiddled with the buttons on her jacket until she realized she was doing everything she could not to look at Niall, and that didn't really go along with her whole *I'm not nervous* mantra.

When she turned back, Róisín was watching her carefully.

"All right, lass," she said. "I'll see you at the house." Then she clucked her tongue and Brigid trotted forward. Cordelia's heart leaped to her throat and fluttered there like a moth. Niall stood with a bike on either side of him, looking almost as apprehensive as she felt. He was probably realizing they were going to be alone together too. Maybe he was regretting this. Maybe she should clarify that he didn't need to feel awkward because *she* certainly didn't feel awkward, not in the slight—

"Er, shall we?" Niall asked.

"Yeah. Um, let's go," she said.

He leaned the bikes up against the street sign.

"We can leave them here," he said. "We won't be needing them to get to the fort. Couldn't ride 'em there if we tried."

"Okay."

Niall jerked his head toward the sound of the water. "This way, then."

She followed him off the road and onto a plain of thick grass, her rain boots squelching in the mud. For a moment, neither of them spoke.

"That's so great that—" Cordelia began as Niall said, "So Róisín's been—"

"Sorry, what?" they both asked in unison.

"You first," Cordelia said, smiling shyly.

He grinned back at her. "Róisín's been telling you all her stories, has she?"

"Yes. I like them a lot. She's a wonderful storyteller."

"She is that. Which is your favorite so far?"

"I like the púca. Because it doesn't feel like a story. It feels like she's telling me about an old friend."

Niall laughed. "It does, doesn't it? Sometimes I wonder if he's real. Who knows, right? She used to scare the shite out of all us kids with her stories, but I loved them. Even the ones that gave me nightmares."

"She certainly loves *you*," Cordelia observed. "Like you were her own grandson."

Niall's cheeks turned pink. "Yeah, she does. I love her too. My da's parents died before I was born and my mam's live in Cork. She was like my gran growing up." He sighed. "I know it hurts her, that I haven't come back as much. Especially not since . . . well." He rubbed the back of his neck. "I got so busy with other things. Other people. You know."

Embarrassment tugged at his features, and the last thing Cordelia wanted was to bring up painful memories.

"I liked the one about the children of Lir too," she said. "Those poor kids getting turned into swans."

"That one's a bit dark."

"I like dark stories. My dad used to read us Greek myths at bedtime. And I read a lot of true crime. Doesn't get much darker than that."

They reached a low stone wall and Niall stepped over it. Cordelia followed him and saw a vast expanse of flat black stones stretching out toward the horizon, like huge paving stones some mythical giant had placed among the tufts of grass. They walked slower now that the landscape had changed. The slabs were deceptively high so that Cordelia found herself stepping up to cross one and landing on the wet grass for a few paces before stepping up to cross another one.

"What was he like?" Niall asked.

"Who?"

"Your da. Sorry, you don't have to talk about him if you don't want to. Just seemed like the two of you were quite close."

"We were." She found she didn't mind that he'd asked. Another stone wall traversed their path and they climbed over it to another plain of black rock and wild grass. "He was creative, like me. He wanted to be an actor. Loved Shakespeare. He taught English lit at New York University, but he would always be auditioning for local productions in Westchester or whatever. I remember when I was maybe ten he got cast as Prospero in the Yonkers community theater's production of *The Tempest.* I think that was the proudest moment of his life—even more than when my brother and I were born. He named us after Shakespearean characters."

"Did he? I only know, like, *Romeo and Juliet* and *Hamlet.*"

"Yeah, I'm named after the youngest daughter in *King Lear*—the favorite child, as I would always remind my brother Toby. He's named after Sir Toby Belch from *Twelfth Night.*"

"That's cool," Niall said.

"What about you?"

"Ah, Niall is a family name. My da's grandfather was a Niall and his grandfather before him. Nothing special."

"Do you have any siblings?" Cordelia asked.

Niall shook his head. "My parents wanted more but . . . well, me mam had lots of miscarriages. Wasn't in the cards for them."

Cordelia paused. "That must have been so hard for her. For both of them."

"Yeah, she keeps her chin up, but I know she wishes she had a whole brood. My da too. Probably wishes he had a son who was just like him. Never wanting to leave Inishmore, never wanting anything more than to carry on running O'Connor's."

"He's asked you to cook for Pátrún," Cordelia pointed out, stepping off a stone slab and landing in a deep puddle of mud. "Oof." She tried to pull her leg out but the mud sucked at her boots. "Oh no, I'm stuck."

"Here, give me your hand," Niall said. A shiver ran through her as she placed her hand in his—his palm was rough and warm, his grip firm. As he pulled her out of the muck, she stumbled into his chest. Their faces were so close and her breath caught, transfixed by his aquamarine gaze. She could feel hard muscle beneath his wool sweater and her heart thumped unevenly.

"Thanks," she said, breathless. Niall released her and she quickly tried to put some space between them. She searched for the thread of the conversation. "What are you thinking of making? Or do you really not know?"

"I really don't know," he said, grimacing. "Róisín was right. It's got to strike the perfect balance."

"If it's anything like last night's dinner, you'll be fine."

His face brightened and his eyes shone. She made the mistake of looking directly into them and nearly lost her footing again.

"You liked the meal, then?" he asked.

"Liked it? I had a wet dream about those potatoes. Oh god. Sorry. That was inappropriate." Her skin prickled as blood rushed to her cheeks, but Niall threw his head back and laughed.

"I think that's the best review I've ever received," he said. They reached another stone wall, this one the highest yet. Niall easily clambered over it and offered his hand again. Cordelia took it eagerly—she needed the help, she told herself. It was nothing to do with the way his fingers curved around her palm. Nothing at all to do with the feel of his skin against hers.

The wind was picking up and she landed with another wobbly thud.

They'd reached the edge of a vast cliff. The stones had sunk deep into the grass and the shoreline of Inishmore stretched out before her, jutting cliffs in both directions. She felt like she was standing on a puzzle piece waiting to be fitted snugly into a larger picture. The ocean was as smoky as the sky, vast and gray and churning, but at the base of the cliffs the water shone aquamarine, like the eyes of the man standing beside her.

Off to her right rose the ruins of Dún Dúchathair, crumbling walls of black stone. The ones at the back of the fort were larger and higher than others, and at the very front there were a series of half circles, the shapes of long forgotten rooms.

Cordelia had the sensation of stepping into the past, like if she listened close enough she could hear the ancient whispers of this place and learn the secrets it still held. Standing amid the ruins of a fortress built during the Iron Age, Cordelia felt like she'd reached the edge of the world.

And, unlike on Dún Aengus, here they were completely and utterly alone.

13

"D'you like it?" Niall asked.

He didn't know why he was nervous. He'd been nervous all damn day in fact. He was glad when Róisín showed up early with the trap—he'd spent the morning pacing around the house, checking his phone, and declaring he was going to cancel. He was driving Colin bonkers.

He'd been pretty sure Cordelia regretted letting him shove his way into her plans, though the conversation wasn't as awkward as he thought it would be. They'd never spent any time alone together, but the more they chatted, the more it felt like hanging out with any other friend. *See, Colin?* he thought. *We're friends, is all. I can still make friends.* He tried very hard not to think about the way his stomach had flipped when he held her hand, so small and soft. Or the feel of her palm on his chest when she'd stumbled into him.

Why did it matter if she loved this spot as much as he did? It didn't. It wasn't *his* spot, after all. It belonged to Inishmore. But it held so many memories for him.

It took Cordelia a moment to answer.

"Oh yes," she said at last, her voice hushed like she was in church. "I like it very much. I love it, actually." Niall felt a tug of pride. She glanced at the ruins and then said, "Can I touch them?"

"Course. We aren't in a museum," he teased. They walked among the black walls and Cordelia let her palm run over the stones.

"It's so *old*," she murmured. "It has this presence like . . . I don't know. Can you feel it? Am I crazy?"

"No," he said. "I feel it too. I love it here. Used to play in this fort when I was a kid. Pretend I was Aragorn, son of Arathorn, off to vanquish Sauron and all that."

Cordelia giggled. "Wait, I'm sorry, are you a nerd?"

"What? No," Niall said defensively.

"You said the word vanquish. You said Aragorn, son of Arathorn. Oh my god, Niall, I did not have you pegged for a fantasy nerd!"

"Lots of people like those books," he protested. She was beaming at him.

"This is amazing," she said. "I'm not making fun, I swear. I just never would have guessed."

Niall shoved his hands in his pockets and gazed out at the water. "Being up here by myself, I felt I could be anyone or anywhere. I could be in King Arthur's court or Middle Earth. When you grow up in such a small place, everybody knowing everybody, everyone in each other's business . . . it was my own little escape, I s'pose. To feel part of something bigger. To imagine I could go on a grand adventure."

Cordelia's smile faded and her expression turned thoughtful. "I love that," she said. "Growing up in New York, you're always part of something bigger. But it can feel like you might get swept away by it. Or left behind." She closed her eyes and inhaled deeply. "I wish I'd had a place like this to come to. It's healing."

She opened her eyes. They were more green than brown today, he noticed.

"I was going to propose to Deirdre here."

Shit. Why had he said that? Why had he brought fucking Deirdre into this moment? Cordelia's eyebrows rose up her forehead.

"Oh." She looked around awkwardly, then started tracing a pattern of lichen on the stones. "That must have been some proposal. Very romantic, I imagine."

"It wasn't," he said quickly. "Because I didn't. She didn't like it here."

"She didn't *like* it?" Cordelia yelped. "But it's so . . ." She struggled for the right word. "Timeless."

"It's also cold and windy," Niall said. He remembered that day vividly. It was the first (and last) time he'd ever brought Deirdre home to Inishmore, and he did it so that he could propose to her here on this very cliff. He remembered the ring burning a hole in his pocket, remembered eagerly waiting for Deirdre to be struck by the untamed beauty of the cliffs so he could drop to one knee and surprise her. "I thought she'd love it like I do. But she just complained on end that her hair was getting wet and her legs were killing her from the walk, and it looked like Dún Aengus only colder anyway."

"What?" Cordelia cried. "It's nothing like Dún Aengus."

He nodded. "I know. But that's what she said. So I didn't even try." His throat constricted at the memory, the disappointment that had washed over him, the brave face he'd had to put on so she wouldn't suspect anything. "I waited until we got back to Dublin and proposed in some posh restaurant she'd been wanting to go to."

Cordelia's lips pulled together in a frown and her nostrils flared. She looked like she was trying very hard not to start shouting. It made Niall's chest ache in a tender sort of way.

"Guess it didn't matter in the end, did it," he said. The waves were smashing against the steep faces of rock, sending up huge sprays and churning bright blue in the coves. He loved that no matter how cloudy or rainy, the cliffs always had swirls of turquoise at their base.

"I didn't want to come back home, you know," he said quietly. "Me mam said Da needed help with the pub, but I'm pretty sure she was only worried about me, staying at a friend's flat with no place of my own. I'm glad I came, though. I needed to get away. From Dublin, from all the streets and parks and pubs that reminded me of her. Everything there seemed to be stamped with Deirdre. Every alley haunted me with her face, every strain of music reminded me of her. Even places we'd never been to, it would be like, oh I could imagine takin' her there. Sorry," he said, flushing. "You don't need to hear about this."

"No, it's okay. I was kind of feeling the same way." Cordelia moved to sit on an outcrop of stone. "In New York, everything reminded me of my father. I felt so stuck. I would walk the streets of the city, sometimes for an entire day, trying to find a place where I wouldn't be reminded of him." She cocked her head. "But now I wonder if I should have been doing the opposite. Searching out the places he used to love, the spots in the city where he would linger the most in my mind. Maybe I can do that when I go back. I think I've been so afraid to let go of him, but also afraid to really face that he's gone. Being here, it's like I have the space to process it all. He can be distant and close at the same time. There's no pain in the memories." She patted the rock. "He would have loved this spot, I'm sure of it. Very evocative. Very Shakespearean."

"It is that," Niall said. He sat beside her and for a while they listened to the waves and watched the clouds swirl across the sky. Niall felt as if the world had shrunk to this one cliff and they were the only two people left on it. He shot Cordelia a surreptitious glance to see if he could read her face and wondered how he had ever thought her merely pretty. Her hair was like honey flowing over her shoulders, her high cheekbones tinged with the palest pink, her full lips pressed together in a line. Her eyes were ever so slightly narrowed and she was turning her head a fraction of an inch one way. She shifted her weight infinitesimally to the left, then lifted her camera to her eye.

"I thought you were going to do that," Niall said. "Saw you shifting about."

Cordelia blinked then smiled. "You remember that?"

"Yeah." Niall looked away, embarrassed. It was a fascinating way of looking at the world. Of course he'd remembered it.

"I still need to take those pictures of you and your mom," Cordelia said.

"You do," Niall agreed, latching onto a safer topic. "And what about your mam?"

"What about her?"

"Haven't heard you talk about her much."

"Oh." Cordelia stood up and stretched. "I don't know. We're . . . going through a rough patch."

Niall stood too. "How so?"

They started to wander along the edge of the cliff, away from the ruins.

"Well," Cordelia said. "She has a boyfriend now."

And without needing any further push, Cordelia launched into a tale of a man called Gary whose only flaw as far as Niall could tell was that he was dating Cordelia's mother and was not Cordelia's father.

"Toby says I'm being difficult. He said I should be happy for her," she finished in a huff. "And I *am*!"

Niall laughed. "Sorry, but when you say it like that, I'm thinking maybe you're not, actually."

Cordelia huffed again. The huffing was almost as adorable as the avocado socks.

Not adorable, he told himself. He needed to banish that word from his vocabulary.

"She's the one who's being difficult," Cordelia insisted. "Ever since she started dating Gary, she's been pushing me about getting a boyfriend, throwing dating apps in my face and acting like that will solve all my problems." Cordelia kicked at a tuft of grass.

"Did it work?" Niall asked, his stomach lurching. "I've never used a dating app before."

Cordelia blushed so hard even her forehead turned red.

"No," she said, not looking at him. "It did not. Hence the pushiness. Do you know what she sent me the other day?" She took out her phone and held the screen up to him. It was an article titled "Ten Ways to Find a Man and Keep Him."

"Wow," Niall said.

"Exactly." Cordelia's mouth turned down at the corners and her brows knit together in another expression of comical fury.

"Toby says I'm not *living my life*." She used air quotes. "He thinks I'm hurting Mom's feelings by not being one hundred percent on Team Gary. That just because I haven't been happy doesn't mean Mom has to be miserable too. I mean, yeah, it's been like three years since my last relationship, but relationships aren't essential to happiness. I can be perfectly happy without one."

"And are you?" Niall asked. "Happy?"

Cordelia opened her mouth and then closed it. "No," she admitted. She stopped walking and stared out over the ocean. "But it's not because of my lack of a boyfriend. God, the two boyfriends I had before Dad died were . . ." She shuddered. "No thanks. I'd rather be single."

Niall felt his jaw clench, wondering who these men were and how they could have treated someone like Cordelia so terribly.

"That bad, eh?"

"Liz says I don't have the best taste in men."

"I'm delighted to hear it. I thought I was the only one who had terrible taste."

"But you and Deirdre were going to get married," Cordelia said.

It was very strange to hear Cordelia say Deirdre's name.

"Yes, but you know, that was before she shagged my business partner and stole my pub out from under me. So. I think I have you beat in the crap relationship department."

She shot him a full smile, the freckles on her left cheek dancing. Niall wanted to reach out and touch one of them with the tip of his finger. He wanted to cup his hand around her neck and let her hair spill across his knuckles, to see if it was as soft as it looked. Cordelia turned away, flustered, and raised her camera to her eye. Niall put his hands back into his pockets.

"Go on then," he said. "I know you prefer takin' pictures with people in 'em. You can use me if you like—since I make a good subject and all."

She laughed. "I should never have told you that," she said, shaking her head. "Okay, go stand over there." She pointed and Niall willingly scampered over the rocks. "Now walk around," she called. "And talk to me. And don't think about the camera."

"Easy for you to say," Niall called back. "You're not the one in front of it." He bent down and picked up a small round pebble, then chucked it off the cliff. "You know, Colin and I used to come up here and see who could throw stones the farthest."

"Was Colin pretending to be Frodo?" Cordelia asked.

He snorted. "I never should have told *you* that."

She tapped her temple. "It's in the vault now."

He laughed and she raised the camera again. He tried to ignore it—he wanted to be a good sport. And okay, maybe it was nice knowing that she was looking at him, piecing him into the minor adjustments she made as she crouched or turned or stepped to one side. The clouds roiled overhead and thin drops of rain began to spit down on them. Cordelia pulled up the hood of her raincoat.

"D'you want to go back?" Niall asked.

"What for?" she said. "It's just a bit of rain." She took one more picture, then tucked her camera away inside her jacket.

A swooping sensation looped around his ribs. He rubbed his chest and remembered the iron spring that used to live there, winding tighter and tighter until he could hardly breathe. When had it disappeared? He couldn't quite recall.

But as he climbed over the rocks, bantering with Cordelia and tossing stones out into the ocean, he found he wasn't missing it one bit. He kept himself together now.

Healing, Cordelia had called this place.

Well, he thought as he watched her pick up a stone and throw it out into the sea, *maybe she was onto something there*.

Niall noticed Cordelia coming into O'Connor's more and more over the following week.

"Cordelia seems to have finally acknowledged O'Connor's is the best pub on the island," Colin said one night. She was hunched over her book, but glanced up, her fork suspended over a plate of spaghetti and clams.

"Yep," Niall said, wiping down pint glasses with a clean rag.

"She's looking at us now."

"Stop staring at her," Niall said, elbowing him.

"She's not looking at me, that's for sure," Colin said. "Howya, Cordelia! Whatcha reading?"

She held up her book. Colin squinted at the title.

"*The Lazarus Files*," he read. "What's that about?"

"It's fascinating, it's about this cold case from the eighties—a woman was murdered in her own home and it took them thirty years to solve it. Turns out it was her husband's ex-girlfriend, who was a cop." She beamed.

"Grand," Colin called back. "Christ, that's a bit dark isn't it?" he muttered to Niall. "Thought Americans were meant to be cheery."

But Niall only smiled as he poured a pint. "She likes dark stories."

"Niall!" his father bellowed from the kitchen.

"Coming, Da," he called and set the pint in front of Darragh before heading into the kitchen. He found his father with a small notepad and pen in hand.

"I'm putting the orders in for Pátrún," he said.

"Oh." *Shit.* "I'll have my list for you Sunday. By dinner."

Owen's bushy eyebrows knit together. "Can't be any later than that. And I'll need to taste this dish first."

"Right," Niall said. "No problem. I'll cook it for you Sunday too. Give Mam a break." He grabbed a plate of mussels on his way out and set them down in front of a waiting patron at the bar. "Shit, shit, shit," he muttered as he walked away.

"Everything all right?" Cordelia was looking up at him from over the top of her book.

"Da needs to make the order for Pátrún," Niall explained.

"And you still don't know what you're cooking."

He shook his head. She closed her book and rested her chin in her hand. Her hair glowed like molten gold in the light of the overhead lamps.

"You're reminding me of me," she said.

Niall raised an eyebrow. "Have you discovered some latent ability to cook since Monday?"

She grinned. "Not even a little. More like, you're reminding me of how tight I was holding on to my photography and how it actually made me a worse photographer. The more pressure I put on myself, the more I failed to live up to this crazy standard I'd set in my head." She tapped on the camera sitting beside her plate of spaghetti. Niall had never seen her go anywhere without it. "This was such a gift, you know. I'm glad I bumped into you on that dock. I mean, thank god my dad's camera can be fixed. But having a new one, it's like . . . pressure's off. I can see clearly again. You should try that."

"Not sure what you mean," Niall said. "The extent of my photography skills is *pull out iPhone and press button*."

"I was talking about the pressure you put on yourself," she said. "I mean, forget finding the perfect balance or whatever. Say you were cooking dinner for me and Róisín. What would you make for us?"

"I'd make colcannon the way Róisín likes it. So she wouldn't be able to complain."

Cordelia laughed. "Excellent, because I've been wanting to try this colcannon now that I've heard so much about it. What else?"

"That depends," Niall said. "What kind of meat do you like?"

"Lamb," Cordelia said at once.

"All right," Niall said. "So we've got colcannon and lamb. We need a veg."

Cordelia wiggled on her seat and thought for a moment. Niall liked this game. It was far more fun than stressing about what his father would and wouldn't approve of.

"What about carrots?" she said. "Róisín has tons of carrots in her garden."

Niall could feel the menu coming together. Make a rub for the lamb—something spicy, maybe Indian inspired. Glaze for the carrots. Balsamic? That was too basic. He could do better.

"Oh my god, I can literally see the wheels turning in your head," Cordelia said. "Do you need me to write this down or anything?"

He shook his head and tapped his temple. "It's in the vault," he said. Then he wondered if she'd get the callback to their morning at the Black Fort.

"Does this mean I'm part of the Fellowship now?" she asked.

Niall shot her a wry look. "For someone who claims not to be a nerd, you seem to know an awful lot about *The Lord of the Rings*."

She blushed. "My brother was really into the books."

"Niall!" Shauna called from the other end of the bar. Cordelia picked up her book again.

Lamb chops, colcannon, and carrots, Niall thought to himself.

He'd have to ask his mam to invite Cordelia over for Sunday dinner.

14

Cordelia sipped her tea and reveled in the weak sunshine streaming in through her front windows.

As she waited for Toby to FaceTime her from their vacation home, she sat at the table editing some of the pictures she'd taken at the Black Fort. The one she liked best was of Niall with a pebble in mid-throw, his arm in an arc-like motion, the clouds swirling behind him, a spray of seawater crashing up against the cliffs. There was so much movement to draw the eye. She really wanted to put it on her Instagram.

She still hadn't posted anything. She was worried that once she did, everything would change. The lightness she had begun to feel, the freedom and ease of her photography, would all get strangled by the pressure of expectation.

She picked up her phone and texted Liz.

So I want to put this shot I took of Niall on my Instagram, she wrote.

Instantly, a typing bubble appeared.

YES! I've been telling you to put your pics up, they're AMAZING. Send it to me!!! I've been dying to know what Niall looks like.

Cordelia had been specifically avoiding sending any shots of Niall to Liz. But in this shot, you could only see part of his face. So she texted it to her. Then she waited. And waited.

Finally, Liz responded.

W O W

Cordelia let out an embarrassingly high-pitched giggle.

Cordie, it's INCREDIBLE. You MUST post it. Put the ones from the session up too. And the Seal Colony. You've taken so many fantastic pictures.

Cordelia sighed. *Ok.*

Can I pls get one of Niall's actual face now? Liz added the pleading eyes emoji.

Fine, hold on.

She searched her photos and found one that took her breath away. Niall, standing over the potatoes in his kitchen. His eyes were bright and teasing, the dimple barely making an appearance. His hair flopped down over his forehead.

She didn't let herself think too hard. She sent it off to Liz then turned her phone upside down, her heart racing. After only a few seconds, her phone began to ping wildly.

"Jesus, Liz," Cordelia muttered. There was a long series of texts.

O

M

G

WHAAAAAT

Cordie

STOP IT

He's gorgeous!!!!!

I mean, I'm gayer than gay but that man is DIVINE. Can he have a twin sister who is also a lesbian so you can introduce me???

Cordelia let out a breathy chuckle. *Sadly, he is an only child.*

Just my luck.

You've got Meena anyway, Cordelia reminded her. She expected some snappy reply and was surprised when Liz didn't text back right away.

Liz? No response. *Ok, now I'm freaking out.*

Don't freak out. I didn't want to interrupt your trip.

What's going on??

Meena and I broke up. But it's FINE.

Cordelia gripped the phone hard. *WHAT? When? Why?*

She could practically hear Liz's sigh through the tiny letters on her screen.

We broke up the first week you were there. I didn't want to say anything because I didn't want you to worry. Because IT IS FINE. We both weren't feeling it anymore. We were more friends than lovers for a while. We're still friends. We're actually having dinner on Thursday. She's sleeping with some finance dude that her father approves of I guess.

Meena was bisexual but Cordelia had sort of forgotten that since she'd been dating Liz for so long.

Are you sure you're okay????

I. AM. FINE. It's actually been nice to be single. I like having some me time.

Cordelia bit her lip. She felt terrible that Liz hadn't told her all this right away.

Omg, I can feel you stressing through the phone. Stop that. I'm really okay.

I love you to pieces, you know that right?

I do.

Cordelia saw the time.

Shit gotta go, FaceTiming with the fam in a few.

Tell Gary I say hi, Liz wrote with a winky face.

Cordelia sent back an eye roll.

Be nice, Liz said. *It's not the worst thing that your mom is happy with her boyfriend.*

You sound like Niall.

OH MY GOD DO I???

Cordelia grimaced. She shouldn't have said that. Just then her phone pinged with a text from Niall. A jolt ran through her as she read it.

Glad you're coming tonight. Think you'll like the menu xx

Cordelia stared at those two little exes, her heart thumping hard against her ribs. Exes stood for kisses. But maybe it was just an Irish thing. Should she send exes back?

Her phone began to ring and she answered it, smiling as her niece's face filled the screen.

"Auntie Cordie!" Grace shrieked.

"Hi, Grace!" Cordelia said. "Oh my god, look at you. I love that headband!"

Grace was wearing a band with pink satin kitty ears on it.

"Gary got it for me," she said, beaming.

First test, Cordelia thought. "Wow. That was super nice of him."

"He got a Batman mask for Miles. Ow, Miles, stop it!"

Miles pulled the phone away from his sister, and Cordelia laughed to see him with the black mask over his eyes, one of his front teeth missing from his big smile.

"Hi, Auntie Cordie," he said. "Look, I lost another tooth!" He smiled wider.

"Way cool," Cordelia said. "Are you guys having fun at the cabin?"

"Yeah!" they both cried in unison.

"There's a pool," Miles said.

"We saw a baby deer," Grace added.

"All right, you two, don't hog the phone." The camera swirled around, giving Cordelia a glimpse of a cozy living room with lots of teak paneling and plaid pillows before Nikki's face appeared.

"Hey, Cord," she said. She looked tired.

"Hi, Nikki," Cordelia said. "How's it going?"

"It's nice to be out of the city for a bit. How're things in Ireland?"

Cordelia glanced out the window. "Well, it's not raining today."

Nikki laughed. "We've been loving the photos you've sent. The kids think you're hanging out with leprechauns."

"I haven't met one yet," Cordelia said. "Though Róisín probably has some stories she could tell them."

"I want to see a leprechaun!" Miles shouted from off screen.

"Shush, Miles, where's your father? Toby, your sister is on the phone!" Nikki called. She spoke to Cordelia quietly. "Your mom and Gary are out by the pool. Do you want me to go get them or would you rather not?"

Cordelia appreciated how Nikki never pushed her. "No, it's fine, I'd really like to say hi. To both of them," she added.

Nikki winked. "Got it. Kids, go get Nana and Gary," she said as she passed the phone over to Toby. Cordelia heard the sounds of running and screaming and then a door slammed. Toby's face appeared on the screen.

"Hey," he said stiffly.

"Hi," she replied. She felt a twinge of guilt for the fight they'd had before. Seeing their faces reminded her how much she missed her family. "How's it going there? Looks like Gary got the kids some good loot."

Toby relaxed a bit. "Yeah, he's really spoiling them. And Miles keeps losing his teeth. I swear, that kid is going to bankrupt us. Oh, here's Mom and Gary." Toby shot Cordelia a warning glance that was entirely unnecessary since she'd already decided to be nice.

Her mother's face appeared. She was tanner than usual and wore a floral bathing suit with a white lace shawl around her shoulders.

"Cordie!" she said with a huge smile.

"Hi, Mom," Cordelia replied. "You look great. Is that a new suit?"

"Yes, I picked it up in Tuscany. How are you, darling? Every thing okay over there? The light looks gloomy, what time is it?"

"It's just after three," she said. "And it's actually sunny today."

Louise pursed her lips. "It doesn't look very sunny."

Cordelia willed herself not to get defensive. "It's Ireland, Mom. You get used to it. Hey, can I say hi to Gary?"

May as well do it now while she was still in a somewhat positive mood.

"Of course! Gary, come say hi."

Gary's weathered face appeared on the screen. He was a big burly man with a wild thatch of graying hair and a large nose that reminded Cordelia of Darragh.

"Hey there, Cordelia," Gary said.

"Hi. How was Italy? The pictures looked great."

"It was fantastic. I think your mother wants to move there."

"Oh shush, I never said that," Louise said, pushing her face into the screen. "Jon is a lovely young man, Cordelia. You'd really like him. And the villa is just stunning. You know, it's so sad to think of him alone in all that space."

Was her mother seriously trying to push Gary's son on her?

"Yeah, well, it's a villa in Tuscany so I'm sure he's coping okay," she said. "How are you guys enjoying the place in the Berkshires?"

"It's great," Gary said as Louise said, "It's a bit small but the pool is nice."

"We wish you were here," Gary added.

"Maybe we could come visit you!" Louise said suddenly. "Gary, wouldn't that be nice, to go and visit Cordelia on—what's the name of the island again, sweetheart?"

"Inishmore," Cordelia said through clenched teeth. "Mom, I don't know if—"

"That's a great idea, Louise," Gary said.

Nikki's face appeared behind them, her eyes wide, and Cordelia could tell she was trying to find a way out of the situation.

"You know," she said, "it's an awfully long trip."

"Not as far as Italy," Louise insisted.

"It's not just the flight," Cordelia said. "There's a train and a bus and a ferry and . . . I don't know where you'd stay, Mom."

"We'd stay with you, of course. Aren't you renting a house?"

"It's a cottage. It's basically three rooms."

Gary seemed to take the hint. "Louise, we don't want to be inviting ourselves into Cordelia's vacation."

"It's not really a vacation if she's living there for three months, is it?" Louise said. "Jon was perfectly happy hosting us." Cordelia wondered very much if that was how Jon would have put it—her mother was a pretty exhausting houseguest. "Doesn't that Alison girl run a bed and breakfast? Cordelia, didn't you say Alison ran—"

But before her mother could finish the sentence, the front door burst open and Róisín stormed in, bringing a gust of cool air and the scent of thyme.

"There you are!" she cried. "Come on now, I've got some New Zealanders down the harbor waiting on you."

Cordelia blinked. "Huh? Róisín, I'm on a phone call with my family."

Róisín brightened. "Are you now," she said, coming over to the table. "Hello, Cordelia's family."

Louise and Gary looked astonished at this wild woman in her overalls.

"Hello," Louise said. "I'm Louise James. You must be—"

"Ah, so you're the overbearing mother, are ya? Then you must be the boyfriend Cordelia's got a stick up her bottom about. Nice to put faces to names."

Cordelia felt mortification crest over her scalp in hot prickles as she heard Nikki give a snort of laughter.

"I beg your pardon?" Louise said, aghast. "Overbearing?"

"Sorry, no time to chat," Róisín said. "Got to take this one down to the harbor. Where's your camera? The New Zealanders won't wait all day."

"I have no idea what you're talking about, Róisín," Cordelia said.

"Christ on a cracker, girlie, I'm saying I got some well-paying clients for ya! Showed them a few of your photos o' me and Brigid, they went over the moon for them. Your wan Cordelia is a fine photographer, Louise, if you don't mind me saying. Very fine indeed."

"My what?" Louise said, bewildered.

"It's an Irish expression, Mom," Cordelia explained. "'Your wan' means 'your woman.'"

Louise looked absolutely baffled. Nikki, it seemed, couldn't help herself—she grabbed the phone from them.

"Hi Róisín, I'm Nikki, Cordelia's sister-in-law," she said.

"Ah, yes," Róisín said. "I've heard about you too. She likes you best. Where's the brother, though, eh? What's his name again?"

"Toby's right here," Nikki said gleefully. Cordelia was glad someone was enjoying this. Nikki shoved the phone in Toby's face and he gave a small wave.

"Uh, hi," he said.

Róisín peered at the screen. "So you're Toby. Cordelia, he's not near as ugly as you said he was. Oh, I'm just teasing you, boyo, she thinks you're grand. Now if you don't mind, we've got some New Zealanders to photograph and then Niall's dinner to get to. You know all about Niall, of course. Cordelia, did you tell them about Niall?"

Oh no, Cordelia thought as her mother called out, "Who's Niall?"

"Sorry, got to go, clients are waiting," Cordelia said. "Love you guys, bye!"

"Cordelia Marie, who is Nia—"

Cordelia pressed end and the phone went dark. Róisín cackled.

"They're a fine bunch, aren't they? Come on, shake your stumps. It's a gorgeous day for a photo shoot."

Cordelia bet the idea of her mother visiting was right off the table, thanks to Róisín. She grinned as she grabbed her raincoat and camera and left the cottage.

"How's it going in there?"

It was the fifth time his father had posed that question from the other side of the kitchen door.

"It's fine, Da," Niall called back, the same response he'd given each time.

"Owen, leave the boy alone," Róisín shouted from the living room. Niall bent to take the carrots out of the oven—he tossed them and put them back in for ten more minutes.

"It smells amazing, doesn't it?" he heard Alison say. There was a light tap on the door. Niall stormed over to tell his father off once and for all, but instead came face to face with Cordelia.

"Can I hide out in here?" she whispered. "Your dad keeps pacing up and down the hall, then glaring at me."

"Oh god, sorry about that," Niall said, ushering her inside.

"It's fine, I mean, I get it," Cordelia said. "Last time I came for dinner I basically told him he was a shitty father. Oooh, it really does smell amazing."

Niall looked around at the mess—he usually kept a cleaner kitchen but he was too nervous to worry about that today. He lifted the top off the pot of colcannon and made sure it was still nice and warm on the back burner.

But he could feel Cordelia's presence even when his back was turned, like she was a sun pulling him into orbit. It was massively distracting.

"D'you mind juicing that lemon for me?" Niall asked her.

She raised an eyebrow. "You trust me?"

He chuckled. "You just cut it in half and squeeze it through that strainer there."

Niall set the lamb chops to sear in the cast iron pan and turned to see Cordelia squeezing the lemon with intense concentration, her lips pouting slightly, the crease between her eyebrows more of a dent. How could squeezing a goddamn lemon cause such a visceral reaction in him? He wanted to smooth the dent away with his fingertip. He wanted to see if her lips were as soft as they looked.

He needed to stop looking at her so much.

Cordelia finished with the lemon and held up the juice like she'd won first place in the currach races. "Ta-da!" she exclaimed, the freckles dancing on her left cheek as she smiled. Niall felt something molten and shivery slip into his stomach.

Whatever his expression was, it made her face change. Her eyes went wide and her breath hitched. Niall quickly grabbed the lemon juice and turned to make the sauce. He focused very hard on adding Dijon mustard, honey, and olive oil to the lemon juice.

"Whisk that for me, will ya?" he asked, handing the bowl to her without looking.

She took it, their fingers brushing together, and Niall felt shivers run across his skin. He kept his eyes focused on the lamb. When the chops were well seared, he turned them over to cook on the other side.

"Right," he said, wiping his hands on a towel. "That's done, then."

The problem was, now there was no place else for him to look but at her. She was watching him with a clear, open expression, her lips slightly parted, the whisk moving around in slow circles. He should probably tell her that wasn't how you whisked a sauce. But words had deserted him completely.

Niall felt a line of energy connecting them, as delicate as a spider's web but crackling with heat. Or maybe that was just the stove. He didn't know. He didn't care. He couldn't stop looking into her eyes. He wanted to see her thoughts. He wanted to feel her hand in his again, like he had on the cliffs at the Black Fort.

She took half a step toward him.

The door burst open and Róisín strode in. Cordelia jumped so hard she spilled some sauce on her shirt.

"What the hell is taking so long?" Róisín said. "If you're to be making something that smells as good as this, Niall, you need to be making it faster. Oh, Cordie, look you've gone and spilled sauce on your jumper. Fiona! Cordelia's spilled sauce, go fetch her another jumper. We can wash this one."

Niall's head was spinning. He hardly had a second to think before Cordelia was whisked out of the kitchen. But Róisín stopped at the door and winked.

"What?" he said dumbly.

"Oh, don't you *what* me," she said. "There's more things cooking in this kitchen than lamb. Christ, I could cut the tension in here with a knife." She grinned at him. "I'll have Alison come and help you with the plates."

Dinner turned out to be a smashing success.

But Niall barely tasted the food.

He was hyperaware of Cordelia sitting next to him, now wearing one of his mother's old button-down shirts. Róisín kept giving him significant glances that Colin quickly picked up on. Niall had almost forgotten that the point of the evening had been to impress his father until Owen put his knife and fork down.

"So," Owen said. "What's in the rub for the lamb, then?"

"Smoked paprika, cumin, chili powder, bit o' thyme and oregano, salt and pepper," Niall recited. Thank god he hadn't forgotten his own recipe.

"And the glaze on the carrots?"

"Butter, brown sugar, honey, chili flakes, and sea salt."

"Mm."

"The colcannon is *excellent*," Róisín added. "No fecking kale, thank Christ."

"Mm," Owen said again.

Colin shot a low thumbs up over the edge of the table.

"It'll do," Owen said finally. "We'll put it on the menu."

Alison clapped and Róisín raised her glass as Fiona cried, "Oh, lovely!"

Cordelia was a sun once again pulling him toward her. He couldn't resist turning to meet her gaze. Her cheeks were seashell pink, her smile shy as she raised her glass of wine.

"Congratulations," she said.

He clinked her glass with his.

"So," Colin said as they walked home that night, Pocket at their heels. "That was interesting."

"I know," Niall said. "I can't believe Da is letting me put something on the menu. Never thought I'd live to see the day."

"Your da would be a fool not to serve your food," Colin said. "That wasn't what I was talking about."

"What were you talking about then?"

"Cordelia." Colin was grinning at him.

"What d'you mean?" Niall asked, trying and failing to sound casual.

"Well," Colin said, opening the front door. "She couldn't stop staring at you all through dinner, now could she?"

Niall felt himself pinned to the ground, his knees locking together, his heart pounding in his ears. Colin chuckled softly at his expression, letting himself inside and leaving Niall like a statue on the doorstep.

15

Cordelia woke the following morning and gazed up at the ceiling.

All she could see were Niall's eyes.

Had she imagined that moment in the kitchen? She was probably being pretty obvious. But she couldn't stop thinking about him. Those tousled jet-black locks, the shadow of stubble across the hard line of his jaw, the tempting curve of his mouth . . .

She picked up her phone to text Liz, but it was the middle of the night in New York and Cordelia wasn't altogether sure she was ready to hear what Liz might have to say. Her mother had sent an endless stream of texts in various forms of *Who is Niall?* and Cordelia was ignoring them all.

Liz would be encouraging for certain—she'd probably dance a jig and set off some fireworks. Cordelia James crushing on a guy at last. But then Liz would probably tell her she needed to "make a move" or "go for it," and Cordelia didn't think she was ready for that. Besides, what if Niall didn't want her to make a move? He probably didn't. He definitely didn't.

Cordelia threw off her blankets and padded into the kitchen to make coffee. She banged open drawers and slammed a mug on the counter with unnecessary force. She didn't *want* to be crushing on someone! Especially not a guy who was still grieving another relationship.

Just friends, just friends, just friends . . .

But she didn't want to be just friends.

"Ugh!" she cried, running her fingers through her hair. Wanting someone like this was awful. Why did people do it? She felt on edge and buzzy, like there was a swarm of bees in her chest. She waited for the kettle to boil and her thoughts drifted back to that one long moment in the kitchen when she thought she was going to explode into flames if she stood there a minute more without touching him.

She poured the water over the grounds and opened her computer. It was time to post some photos—Colin and Alison and Róisín had all given their permission for her to use their images last night. But Cordelia hadn't asked Niall if she could use his yet.

Should she text him? No, it was probably too early. But they'd been texting for a week now. Surely it wouldn't be weird to reach out. She picked up her phone, then put it down.

There was a knock on the door and Cordelia jumped up off her stool. Was that Niall? Would he be standing on the other side, with his beautiful blue eyes and thick black hair and broad shoulders, waiting to say *Hello let's make out*?

Shit, she was still wearing her sweatpants and Mets tee. The knocking came again and she hurried to the door, taking a deep breath before opening it.

Alison stood on the doorstep. "Morning," she said cheerfully.

Cordelia's chest deflated. "Oh. Hi."

Alison laughed. "Expecting someone else?"

"No! No. Sorry. Come on in. Want some coffee?"

"That'd be grand." Alison stepped inside and took her jacket off. "Gran's on her way down now. Told her I'd drive up and get her but you know her and the damn car."

Cordelia poured Alison a cup. "Yeah, she's really stubborn about that."

"I pick my battles now," Alison said. "It's no trouble for her to walk down to the cottage. Anyway, you should get ready."

Cordelia stared at her in confusion.

"To meet Cian Byrne," Alison said. "To go over taking the photographs for Pátrún. It's this weekend, remember? Hence the delicious dinner at the O'Connors' house last night?"

Cordelia slapped her hand to her forehead. "That's right. Give me two minutes."

"Take your time," Alison called as Cordelia hurried into her bedroom. "Gran loves pissing off Cian Byrne."

"Why is Róisín coming again?" Cordelia asked.

"To piss off Cian Byrne!"

Cordelia laughed. When she was dressed, she got back to the kitchen and found Alison looking at a picture of Niall on her laptop.

"Christ," she said. "You really captured him."

"Oh." Cordelia folded her arms over her chest to stop them shaking. "Um. Yeah. Thanks. He's . . . yeah."

Alison raised an eyebrow. "Look at your face, my god. Cordie, I won't pry if you don't wish to speak about it."

"No, I . . . there's nothing to speak about. I mean, nothing's happened."

"But you want something to happen," Alison said knowingly.

"Well . . ." Cordelia gave up. She needed help. She was floundering on her own. "Yeah. I guess. But obviously he's super torn up about his ex."

"Still torn up about Deirdre? No, I don't think so," Alison said. "When he first walked off that ferry I thought I would be knocked clean over by the rage rolling off him. Angry and bitter and sad, he was. Not anymore, though. Not by a mile. And then last night at dinner, I mean . . . lord, the sparks were flying." Cordelia's head snapped up. Alison was grinning. "Think everybody noticed except Owen—he was too bothered by how delicious that meal was. Oh, I hear Gran coming."

"Wait, *everybody* noticed?" Cordelia said, panicking, as the front door burst open and Róisín strode into the kitchen.

"Well, look who's dressed and out of bed. It's a miracle. Americans, Alison," she said, shaking her head.

"Yes, Gran," Alison said. "But as you can see, we're both ready to go."

"Just a minute, now." Róisín walked up to Cordelia and leaned in as close to her face as her height would allow. "Niall's a fine thing, as I've said before. And he's a good man. So if you do anything to hurt him or break his heart, I'll murder you in your fecking sleep. Clear?"

Cordelia blanched. "I don't want to hurt him, Róisín. I haven't even—I mean—nothing's actually happened yet!"

"Hasn't it? Christ, girlie, what are you waiting for! Didn't you hear me say he's a fine thing and a good man? Can't let him go slipping between your fingers. Now, let's get a move on. It'll be a grand day if I can be getting Cian Byrne to start tearing his hair out before noon." She cackled as she left the kitchen. Alison came up and put an arm around Cordelia's shoulders.

“This is going to be quite a week,” she said.

The days passed in a blur and before Niall knew it, Friday had come and the first day of Pátrún began.

The pub had been growing busier, and he'd seen Cordelia twice when she came in to have dinner with Alison, but he'd hardly been able to speak to her, it had been so packed. Róisín had come by O'Connor's on Wednesday for a whiskey and asked him rather pointed questions about whether Niall was fully over and done with “that fecking trollop,” as she called Deirdre.

And he was. He didn't need to stew over Deirdre anymore. His brain was no longer interested. Where once he'd clung to his misery as a way of keeping Deirdre close, now he felt himself release it like the string of a balloon, watching it float away and not really caring where it might blow off to.

And he realized he desperately wanted Cordelia James. Well, he'd probably realized that sometime between helping her over the stone walls by the Black Fort and shoving sauce at her in his parents' kitchen, but still. The thought was there and it wasn't going away. He just hadn't worked out what to do about it yet.

“Niall!” his father shouted from the kitchen. The pub was closed, but there was a lot to do before they opened for lunch. Niall was working tonight but had the next two days off—his father wasn't about to let him miss the currach races. He, Colin, and Alison were on a team.

Niall hurried through the swinging doors. A large bowl of mixed spices was sitting on the counter. Owen pointed.

“There,” he said. “I've made your rub for the lamb.”

"Oh," Niall said. "Great."

"Go on then," Owen said. "Try it. Got to make sure it's as good as it was on Sunday."

Niall could not recall a single time his father had ever asked him to approve anything in this kitchen. He quickly rearranged his face and stirred the bowl, tasting the spoon.

"Just a dash more paprika and it'll be perfect," he said.

Owen grunted and grabbed the smoked paprika from the shelf.

Colin popped his head into the kitchen. "Niall, come help me with the lights."

Niall washed his hands and headed outside. Strings of fairy lights lined the windows and the roof of O'Connor's. Colin was hanging large lanterns on tall posts up and down either side of the road. Already Cottage Road was filling with people, tourists stopping to check the menu in the glass stand by the door. Niall felt a burst of pride, knowing that *his* dish was on that menu—Owen had new ones printed yesterday. They were calling it St. Enda's Lamb.

"Best food you'll find in all of Inishmore," Colin said to the passersby. "Come by tonight for live music!"

"You're a regular one-man billboard," Niall said, laughing.

"I want every tourist in this town to eat that lamb of yours," Colin said. "Every islander too. Give your da something to think on."

There was a clopping of hooves behind him.

"Hiya, Róisín, Cordelia," Colin called. Niall almost dropped the lantern he was holding. Cordelia wore an orange blouse with small white flowers on it, her raincoat resting over her lap, her camera slung across her chest. Niall couldn't imagine a lovelier sight.

"Hi," she said as they rolled up. "I'm heading to shoot the sandcastles down by the harbor." Was it Niall's wishful thinking or did she seem to be only speaking to him?

"Grand," he said.

She smiled playfully. "Róisín says you two used to make really shitty ones when you were kids."

Colin roared with laughter and Niall shot Róisín a rueful look. "You aren't supposed to be telling her things like that."

"I tell her what I please," Róisín said, patting Cordelia's knee. The cart rolled off down the road but Niall saw Cordelia turn back to look at him. He hoped he'd see her at the bar tonight. Maybe, amid all the music and good cheer, he could finally work up the courage to do something about these feelings buzzing inside him.

"Our sandcastles weren't shite," Colin said as Niall handed him another lantern.

"I hate to break it to you, mate," Niall said. "But they were bloody awful."

Cordelia crouched in the sand as two young boys carefully tipped a bucket packed to the brim on top of the low platform of sand they'd spent the past half hour perfecting. There were adults skilled in the art of sandcastle construction as well—one creation in the shape of a whale was particularly impressive—but these boys had so much giggly enthusiasm. Cordelia's shutter click-click-clicked. She squinted down at the screen.

Perfect, she thought. Then she glanced back toward the town behind her, foolishly hoping Niall might be coming down to the beach. *He's working*, she reminded herself. A couple of fishermen drinking bottles of beer were hanging around on the docks.

Tourists crowded the Sweater Market and Róisín was gesturing wildly as she told the story of Finn McCool and the salmon of knowledge to a group of gathered children.

Flags were strung up all along the harbor, and there was a platform where musicians were playing. Cordelia wandered over and took some shots of a woman and her son holding hands as they danced what looked like some sort of jig—she wasn't all that familiar with Irish step dancing. The mother and son finished and people clapped, but the music kept going. A man in a suit got up and performed a series of kicks and turns. Cordelia cheered along with the crowd and the man finished and took a bow.

Róisín took her to a big field where there was a massive tug-of-war happening. After that she was whisked away to where some teenage girls were in a competition to be named the Queen of Pátrún, and then Cian wanted her to take photographs of him and some rowers from Galway. He dragged her all through Kilronan, and by the time she was released, the weather had changed and she was exhausted and cold and there was mud all over her jeans.

She walked by O'Connor's on her way home, hoping she might be able to grab a minute with Niall. She was beginning to worry she'd imagined that moment between them. But the pub was filled to bursting, people spilling out onto the street, Colin's music wafting into the cool night air. She tried to peek inside but it was too packed. All hope of seeing Niall died and she plodded back to the cottage, trying to ignore the sinking in her stomach.

The next day was gray and overcast.

The chill from the night had grown colder. Cordelia wore fleece-lined leggings, a green striped sweater beneath her raincoat, and an Aran wool scarf as she walked with Róisín down to the harbor. The streets were even fuller today.

"Everybody's come to watch the currach races," Róisín said. "The team from Inisheer is the one to beat. They've won the past three years running."

"What about Niall's team?"

"Ah, they're fucked. Have you seen Colin Doyle's spindly arms? I could use 'em for my needlework. It's good of Niall to have asked Alison to row with them, though—she loves the water, that girl, just like her grandfather did. Some o' these island boys, they don't much like girls to be rowing with them."

"Niall's not like that," Cordelia said.

Róisín patted her arm. "No," she agreed. "He most certainly is not."

The flags that lined the harbor were flapping about wildly in the wind when Róisín and Cordelia arrived at the docks.

"Look, they're getting the currachs out now," Róisín said. She marched up to the wall surrounding the harbor and shouted down to the beach. "Good luck, you bastards!"

There were many men and a handful of women carrying the long slender boats out to the water, each one with a number painted at its prow. But Cordelia only had eyes for Niall. He, Colin, and Alison were carrying a currach with the number 4 painted on it. Niall wore track pants and a maroon hoodie, his black hair tangled by the wind. Cordelia felt a tightening in her stomach.

"I'm going to go down there and get some better shots," she said. She climbed down the steps to the beach, crouching to take a few pictures before heading over to Niall and the others.

"Hiya," Niall said, smiling as she approached them.

"Hi," she said breathlessly. She turned to give Alison a hug. "Good luck, you guys."

"We're going to need it," Colin said, coming over to them with three life jackets hanging from his arm. "Have you seen the boys from Inisheer? Christ, we're fucked."

"Just think about after, Colin," Alison said, "when we can have a whiskey by the fire at O'Connor's and say at least we tried."

"I could do with a bit less cold and a bit less wind, but that's Inishmore, isn't it," Colin said. "Right, let's get the damned currach into the water and get this over with."

Cordelia had to agree the weather wasn't great for water-based activities. She looked up at Niall, who was putting on his life jacket. "Please don't fall in. The ocean looks scary."

"Don't worry, see that tugboat out there?" He pointed to a small white boat floating out in the harbor. "That'll be following us the whole time."

"Are you sure?" she asked.

Niall's eyes grew soft. His hand twitched like he wanted to touch her, and Cordelia wanted that too—she wanted him to wrap his arms around her and press his lips against her hair, and tell her everything would be okay. But then Colin called out for him, and Niall hurried to push the boat off. Cordelia stayed on the beach for a few minutes, walking up and down to get a variety of angles and compositions, but her lens always drifted to currach number 4. Then she went back up to watch the race with Róisín. Brogan, one of Róisín's neighbors, stood at the end of the long pier with a rifle in one hand.

"What's that for?" Cordelia asked.

"He'll shoot to start them racing," Róisín explained. "And then one shot when the winner crosses the line."

Fiona hurried up to them, her curls even wilder than usual in the wind. "I haven't missed it, have I?"

"No, they're just setting up," Róisín said.

"Good. Owen's popping into the pub and then he'll be down."

It was a bit weird standing next to Niall's mom feeling all the feelings Cordelia felt about Niall. She excused herself as Niall's father came up, pretending she needed to get some pictures from the other end of the harbor, all the while mulling about these new, strange, wonderful and confusing feelings she'd developed.

She was attracted to Niall. She wanted more than just friendship with him. There it was. She had to admit it head-on. But it was delicate as a soap bubble—giving words to this thing growing inside her chest might pop it. What if Niall didn't feel the same way? No matter what Alison or Róisín might say, they weren't him. They didn't know.

She hopped up onto the harbor wall. The currachs were lining up along a rope strung out from the pier—she zoomed in on number 4. Niall was seated at the stern of the boat, Alison in the middle, Colin by the prow. The water was choppy and growing rougher by the minute. Cordelia glanced at the tugboat, grateful for its presence. She took a shot of the onlookers, crowded around the harbor in windbreakers and thick woolen hats. You'd never guess it was June, Cordelia thought wryly.

Róisín was gesturing to her to come join them, so she jumped down off the wall.

She got there just as Brogan fired the rifle and the race began.

"Go number four!" Fiona cried out as the currachs began to slice through the water, the long wooden oars cutting into the waves, the boats rocking from side to side.

"Come on, Alison!" Róisín cried.

"Pick up the pace, Colin, you reedy bastard," Owen shouted.

"I don't like the look of those waves," Róisín said darkly.

"They'll be fine," Owen said. "Niall knows what he's doing."

"Does he now?" Róisín said sardonically. "You might try telling him that to his face every once in a while."

"Where are they going?" Cordelia asked, searching for the finish line. She didn't like the look of the waves either—she didn't know anything about currach racing, but the way the boats were tilting side to side was making her uneasy.

"They circle the harbor there," Owen said, pointing. "And then go round that buoy and back to where Brogan stands."

It looked to be a long way. Niall's boat was definitely lagging behind. Currach number 2 was well ahead of the rest as they reached the buoy.

"It'll be the Inisheer lads winning again this year," Owen said, shaking his head. He kissed Fiona on the temple. "I'm off back to the pub."

Cordelia's fingers were getting cold, her knuckles stiff. She blew on them to keep warm, then lifted her camera to her eye so she could see Niall more clearly. The wind had picked up and the waves were growing foamy and white-tipped. Through her lens she saw him shout something to Alison. Alison turned to say something to Colin just as a wave swept up against the side of the boat. Cordelia watched in frozen panic as the currach vanished from sight behind a wall of water.

Then the wave sank back into the sea and there were only two people in the currach instead of three.

16

"*Niall!*"

Cordelia barely registered it was she who was screaming before she sprang into action, adrenaline flooding her veins. She thought she heard Fiona shout, but Cordelia was already gone, pushing through the crowd to get to the pier. She reached the steps and stumbled down them as she heard someone shout, "Look! They've got him!"

She spared half a second to watch Colin and Alison haul Niall up out of the water by his life preserver, the tugboat coming alongside them—then she was running again. Her boots slapped against the cement as she rocketed down the pier. It seemed to take forever; the pier was like an endless stretch of road jutting out into the ocean and Cordelia couldn't run fast enough. The tugboat pulled up and Brogan grabbed the ropes as other men jumped off the boat to secure it—but Cordelia only had eyes for Niall.

He was wrapped in a heavy blanket and Alison was helping him off the tugboat and onto the pier.

"Niall!" Cordelia cried again and without stopping to pause or think or consider, she flung herself into his arms and pressed her mouth against his. He was frigidly cold, his body shaking, and she kissed him like she could breathe her own warmth into him, her fingers tangled in his cold, wet hair. His lips were icy but they melted against hers, soft and eager. His hands came up to press against her back. He tasted like the sea.

From somewhere at the edge of her consciousness, Cordelia heard the sounds of cheering. Niall gave a deep, shuddering breath and Cordelia went absolutely rigid. There were people *watching*. Tons of people. People she knew. People Niall knew. Niall's *mom*.

Cordelia felt the blush run from her scalp all the way to her toes.

"I should get myself dumped in the ocean more often," Niall murmured in her ear, sending shivers down her spine.

Cordelia realized she was still holding onto him. She stepped away quickly, her cheeks burning. Fiona and Róisín were hurrying up and Cordelia moved aside, trying to hide herself in her scarf.

"Niall, my god, are you all right?" Fiona said.

"I'm fine, Mam," Niall said.

"It was my fault," Colin said. "Didn't see the wave, didn't turn the right way in time."

"It's all right," Niall said as Fiona rubbed his arms. "Mam, I'm *fine*. Could do with a change of clothes."

"Your da's getting hot whiskies and stew set up for you all down the pub," Fiona said. "I'll run back to the house and grab you some fresh clothes."

"That'd be sound, thanks, Mam." His eyes slid to Cordelia and she turned away flustered. What had she been thinking? What was *he* thinking? Why had she gone and done that in front of so many people?

Róisín was embracing Alison. "They shouldn't have had the races today," she said. "Not in this water."

"If I ever volunteer to do this again, Róisín, I give you full permission to smack me upside the head," Colin said. "That was absolutely fecking awful." He turned to Niall. "I'm so sorry, mate."

Niall waved him off as they made their way down the pier. Cordelia made sure to walk behind in step with Alison, who kept glancing Cordelia's way, a big smile on her face. The cheers erupted again when they reached the roads of the harbor, people calling out Niall's name and wishing him well. Cordelia was pretty sure they were cheering for her too, but she tried to block it out.

Stepping into O'Connor's was like stepping into a hot bath on a winter's day. Owen had saved them the couches and chairs surrounding the crackling fire. Cordelia had a brief moment of panic—where should she sit? Would Niall want to sit by her or not?—before he disappeared into the kitchen to change out of his wet clothes.

"Well," Róisín said, settling herself into the armchair closest to the fire. "This has been a currach race to remember."

No one had mentioned the kiss, but Róisín was looking very smug and Alison couldn't stop grinning.

"Are you all okay?" Shauna came hurrying over. "Niall's just told us what happened. I've given him towels to dry off and I'm making some whiskies now. Owen'll bring the stew out in a moment."

"That'd be grand," Colin said as Fiona burst through the doors with a pile of folded clothes in her hands.

"You are all the talk of the town," she said. "Aoife got the whole thing on video, she's bringing it over now." Cordelia blanched. *On video?* "Cordelia, be a dear and take these to Niall, would you? I brought some extra jumpers for you two as well," she said to Alison and Colin.

Cordelia had only just taken off her jacket and turned to find the clothes shoved into her hands. "Okay," she said numbly.

She shot an uncertain glance at Alison, who jerked her head toward the kitchen and mouthed, "Go on." Cordelia stumbled back behind the bar. She'd never been in the kitchen before. She pushed through the swinging doors and saw Owen ladling stew into shallow bowls. Cordelia's knees locked but Owen glanced up, saw the clothes in her hands, and said, "He's in the back room."

"Okay," Cordelia said again, feeling very much like she was walking through water herself. There was a door off to her left—she knocked on it and glanced behind her. Owen was leaving the kitchen with the stew.

"Yeah?" Niall called. Cordelia opened the door and slipped inside.

"Your mom brought some clothes for—" Her brain screeched to a halt as she saw Niall standing there, shirtless, a towel in his hands, his wet track pants clinging to his legs.

His chest was covered in fine black hairs. His shoulders were broader than she'd imagined, the curve of his bicep glistening wet, the flat planes of his stomach giving way to a V of muscle that disappeared beneath the waistband of his pants. Cordelia had to physically haul her eyes up to his face, her cheeks on fire.

"You're blushing, Miss James," Niall said.

"I'm always blushing," she croaked.

Niall chuckled. "Are those for me?"

Cordelia looked down at the clothes in her hands. "Oh. Yes. Here."

She held them out, her arms shaking. Niall filled her vision. He was so beautiful it hurt.

He came over and took the clothes from her. His chest was so close. She wanted to reach out and run her hands over him to see if the hairs were fine or coarse. She wanted to trace the lines of his waist and feel the sharp points of his hip bones. And at the same time she wanted to run away and hide. The feelings were so potent they were baffling. Her mind could not sort them out. Everything was Niall.

"That was awfully nice, what you did out there," he said softly.

She tried for a casual laugh, but it came out like a cough. "You mean embarrass you in front of the whole town?"

"I'm not embarrassed."

Her breath caught in her throat. His eyes were sapphires today, dark and glittering and endless in their depth. She could feel her pulse all over her body, from the fluttering in her toes to the faint throb between her thighs.

"Oh," she said. "That's . . . good."

Niall put the clothes down on a stool and took another step closer to her. Cordelia felt panicky and eager all at once. Her skin thrummed, calling to him, every strand of her hair alight.

He leaned forward so that their mouths were only inches apart.

"I'm all cold and wet," he said. "Or I'd kiss you again."

Her head was spinning. He smelled like salt water and driftwood.

"I already kissed you when you were cold and wet," she pointed out weakly.

"So you did," he whispered, and then his mouth was on hers. She melted against him, her arms wrapping around his waist, her hands sliding across the smooth, damp skin of his back. Her lips parted as his tongue slipped inside her mouth, and she felt a flame ignite in her chest. She wanted more of him, of this, of everything—she teased his tongue with hers, lapping up his briny flavor. His mouth was warm and sure, his hand moving to cup the curve of her neck. She shivered at its chill.

"Right, sorry," he said, pulling away.

"No," she said, clutching him closer, bringing him back to her, and he chuckled against her lips, kissing her again eagerly. She pressed herself against him until—

"Gah!" she cried. Her sweater had absorbed the water on his skin. There was a dark spot on the green stripes where his torso had been. "Oh shit. Ugh, Niall!"

Niall was laughing.

"Stop, this isn't funny." Cordelia pushed against his chest, torn between embarrassment and desire. "Your *mom* is out there!" she hissed. "She's going to know."

He caught her hands and held them to him so that she could feel his heart beating beneath hard muscle. "Know what?" he asked, faking innocence.

"Know we've been . . . you know . . . kissing!"

"I'm pretty sure that cat left the bag when you jumped me on the pier," Niall said, bringing her mouth back to his. She succumbed, her palms sliding down his stomach, his lips moving in perfect time with hers.

"I thought you were dead," she murmured as he traced a line of kisses across her cheek to the curve of her ear.

"It was extremely heartwarming to see how much I'd be missed." He took her earlobe in his mouth and tugged it between his teeth, and she thought she might faint right here in this broom closet.

"Wait, no, seriously," she said, pushing him away. She could not go out there and face, well, literally everyone with her cheeks on fire and her sweater all wet. "I need to be presentable. You need to get out of those pants."

She clapped her hands over her mouth and Niall let out a bark of a laugh. "I think I rather like Flustered Cordelia," he said, handing her the towel. "But you're right, we mustn't be making out in the back room like a couple of teenagers. Go on, then. I'll be out in a minute."

The towel was still dry on one end and she did the best she could to get the dark spot out.

"Very presentable," Niall said.

"I'm going to need a *lot* of whiskey," Cordelia said.

"You and me both."

He looked positively giddy, and Cordelia knew if she stayed in here a moment more she was going to start kissing him again, so she slipped out of the room and fled the kitchen. There was a bowl of stew and a steaming glass mug filled with hot whiskey and a thick slice of lemon waiting for her at the table.

"Cordie, you've got something on your jumper," Róisín said and Colin snorted into his drink. Cordelia looked down in a panic, her face burning.

"Jesus, I've never seen someone turn so red so quickly," Colin said. "Róisín, have you ever seen anyone turn so red so quickly?"

"I cannot say that I have, Colin."

"Stop it, both of you," Alison chided them, as Cordelia began to scoop spoonfuls of stew into her face, partly because she needed somewhere else to look and partly because she was famished.

"Niall's back," Róisín said after a few minutes and Cordelia almost choked on a potato. There was a smattering of applause from the patrons at the bar.

"All right, boyo?" Darragh called.

"Grand, Darragh," Niall said. "It's a gorgeous day for a swim, don't you think?"

That set the bar laughing. Rain had begun to fall outside, spattering against the windows and whipping about in the wind. Cordelia noticed a lot of people glancing at her, so she hid her face in her drink.

"There's food here for you, Niall," Alison said as Niall sat down beside Cordelia.

"Thank god, I'm starving," he said. He seemed so at ease as he helped himself to the stew, and Cordelia wondered if maybe he really wasn't embarrassed by her display.

"Nearly drowning will give a man an appetite," Róisín said.

"He was only in the water for about ten seconds before we pulled him out," Colin protested.

"Let's throw you in there next time, see what you have to say about it."

"Niall, you've got to see this," Fiona said, hurrying over. She held out an iPhone and Cordelia saw the whole scene play out again on the small screen. She watched, mortified, as she flew down the pier, hearing the voice of Aoife behind the camera saying, "Oh look, there goes Cordelia," before Cordelia ran right into Niall and started kissing him. Aoife said, "Aw, isn't that lovely," and there were cheers along with some wolf whistles. Aoife called to someone behind her, "He's all right! They've got him on the pier now."

Fiona was smiling at her. She patted Cordelia on the arm and said, "You're a good lass." Then she started to fuss over Niall, insisting he eat more stew and going to get him another hot drink.

There wasn't much to photograph because of the rain, so an hour later, Cordelia found herself in Fiona's car alone with Niall as he drove to his house. She'd offered to come with him, thinking they needed a moment by themselves, plus she was very much over the looks everyone in the bar kept shooting at the two of them.

Though now that she and Niall *were* alone, she didn't know what to do. She should probably be playing this cool. But she was terrible at playing things cool.

"You're awfully quiet," Niall said as he parked at the end of the drive. Rain spattered against the windshield.

"I'm fine," Cordelia said in a voice too high to be normal. "You should get inside. You've had a day."

"That I have," he said. He turned to her. "Coming?"

She ducked her head in a nod and they hurried into the house. Niall hung up their coats as Pocket trotted up, tail wagging. The silence seemed to expand around them. Niall scratched Pocket behind the ears. Then he leaned his forehead against Cordelia's.

"So," he said.

"So," she replied. There were things she knew she should be saying, but she couldn't stop staring at his mouth. Her fingers trembled. She wanted to kiss him so badly it scared her. "Um, why don't you go sit down? I'll make some tea."

Niall hesitated, like he was gauging her reaction. Then he said, "That'd be grand. Come on, Pocket."

The dog happily followed him to the couch as Cordelia made her way down the hall. Once in the kitchen, she pressed her back to the door, clutching her hands to her chest. Her heart careened wildly against her ribs. It was disorienting, like she'd shed the skin of the person she'd been yesterday and emerged as someone entirely new. She set about filling the kettle and taking out mugs when another thought crashed into her.

Sex. She and Niall were all alone in this house. Was he expecting them to sleep together? Should they? Was she ready? It had been almost three years since she'd slept with anyone. What if she was bad at it now?

The high-pitched shriek of the kettle startled her out of her thoughts. She filled the mugs carefully, her hands shaking, and headed down the hall to the living room.

Be cool, she told herself.

But she needn't have worried.

Niall was snoring softly as she entered the living room, Pocket curled up against his side. Cordelia smiled and put the mugs down on the coffee table, then grabbed a blanket from where it hung on the back of an armchair. She gently laid it over Niall's legs and gave Pocket a parting pet before quietly slipping out the door and walking back to the cottage.

17

Niall woke the next morning with the sense that he was floating in some half-remembered dream.

Yesterday's events filtered back to him—Cordelia kissing him on the pier, her hands on his bare skin in the back room, the feel of her mouth, her warm body against his. She'd been gone by the time Colin woke him up from where he'd fallen asleep on the couch, but there'd been a text from her on his phone—*Can't wait to see you tomorrow.* Niall grinned and checked it again, just to remind himself this was all real. What a change a month made. He blinked around at his room, seeing everything with fresh eyes. He found he couldn't stop smiling as he padded down the hall to take a shower.

The sun was shining today, reflecting his mood. He felt like a kid on Christmas. He couldn't wait to see Cordelia.

He tried on almost every shirt in his wardrobe before dressing in a blue-checkered button-down and a pair of dark jeans, then headed downstairs to make coffee. By the time Colin wandered in, bleary-eyed and yawning, Niall had made a full fry up: eggs, rashers, sausage, beans, roast tomatoes, and fried bread.

"Jesus," Colin said as Niall poured him some coffee. "Are we expecting the whole town this morning?"

Niall shrugged. "Felt like cooking."

"Look at you and that big dopey grin," Colin said. "What happened yesterday after you left the pub? I thought Cordelia might still be here when I got home, to be honest."

"I fell asleep."

"I know. It was me who dragged you up those bloody stairs to bed. So." Colin slid onto one of the stools, rested his chin in his hands, and batted his eyelashes. "That was quite a performance on the pier."

"It wasn't a *performance*," Niall said, moving to serve up some eggs.

"Fair enough, but it was like something out of a movie. And then you two go making out in your da's back room—what are you, seventeen?" Colin hooted with laughter.

Niall flushed. "Who said we were making out in the back room?"

"Please, brother. She came out with her jumper all wet and I thought she was going to melt into the floorboards, she was blushing that hard." He got up and threw his arms around Niall. "This is grand, mate, just grand. I'm happy for you."

"Thanks, Colin," Niall said. "I'm happy too."

"Course you are, can't get that damned smile off your face. Right." He sat down again and started cutting into a sausage. "This looks fecking fantastic. Oh, what a joy and wonder it is to be so right. I knew it. The moment she walked into O'Connor's and called you an arsehole I thought, that's the woman for Niall."

Niall rolled his eyes. "You did not."

"I did!" Colin popped some sausage into his mouth. "I told you she was easy on the eyes."

"Not the same thing."

"Well, if I had said 'Here now, Niall, that's the girl that's going to be mending up your broken heart in a month's time,' I think you might have chucked me through the window."

Niall grinned. "I might have," he admitted.

They finished their breakfast and left the house together. All traces of yesterday's cold and wind had vanished and Inishmore shone like an emerald. Niall inhaled deeply, grass and ocean scenting the air in an intoxicating combination. God, he really was going to think everything was sunshine and roses today.

"I'll just pop up to the cottage then," he said to Colin, but Colin pointed behind him.

"No need," he said. Róisín and Cordelia were coming down the road in the cart.

Cordelia smiled at him so big and bright that Niall was struck dumb—she was sunlight incarnate, she was everything good and green in the world. She wore a white sundress with a gold print under a pale yellow cardigan.

"Aren't you looking mighty fine this morning, Niall O'Connor," Róisín said as Cordelia hopped down off the cart. Niall had wondered if she'd perhaps want to keep some polite distance, but she skipped over and threw her arms around his waist like she had been waiting for this same as he had.

"And a good morning to you," Niall said, pulling her even closer.

"Sleep well?" she asked.

"I did. For, like, twelve hours. Sorry for passing out on you."

"You needed it. Hey, Colin."

"Morning. Ready for the Guinness races today?"

"The what?"

"We've got to be watching the hookers first," Róisín said.

"The *what*?" Cordelia yelped as Niall helped her into the back of the cart, Colin climbing into the front.

"They're boats," Niall explained with a chuckle.

Róisín turned to fix Niall and Cordelia with a serious look. "I'm telling you both now—brace yourselves. You two are the talk of Kilronan. Aoife put that video up on one o' them SnapFaces or what have you."

"Didn't think you'd be one for looking at social media," Niall said.

"I'm not! But the prodigal son and the American girl, well, that's a fine story for Kilronan to be chewing on."

"Hey, Niall, speaking of social media . . ." Cordelia took her phone out of her pocket. "I'm going to start posting on my Instagram again. And there's one picture I really want to put up first. It's a little nerve-racking, sharing my work after so long. But this one is, um, pretty special to me."

"All right," Niall said, a bit confused.

"Would you be okay with this?" she asked, holding up her phone.

It was a photograph of him at the Black Fort, in profile, his arm arcing in a half circle as he cast a stone over the cliffs, the smoke-gray clouds swirling behind him. For a moment, Niall was speechless. The picture truly encapsulated the timelessness of the cliffs, and he suddenly felt like he was right back there, on that day. It made his chest ache in a way he could only describe as homesickness—as if Cordelia had been able to capture exactly what he loved about not just Dún Duchathair, but Inishmore itself.

"Wow," he said. "Cordelia, that's . . . that's stunning."

"I won't put it up if you feel uncomfortable," she said quickly. "I know you don't like having your picture taken."

"I may be changing my mind about that," Niall admitted.

Cordelia's whole face brightened. "Really?"

"Well, I have been told I make a good—"

"Don't say it," she said, pinching his lips together and grinning. "Okay. I'll do it." She took a deep breath like she was about to plunge from the cliffs themselves.

"This is really hard for you, isn't it," Niall said.

Her mouth twisted, the little dent forming between her brows. "I stopped posting when Dad died. And then the first thing I did post, maybe like a year after his death, went nowhere. It was just a bland shot from inside my local café—nothing interesting or moving about it. But I attached so much importance to other people liking it, you know? All those clicks, all those little hearts, the constant pings telling me someone thought I had value. And you know people on the internet, it's brutal. No one liked my new stuff and people had to tell me *why* they didn't like it, and it just made me doubt myself and my work even more than I already did. But I've turned off my notifications. I want to post this because it's a beautiful and meaningful picture of someone who is beautiful and meaningful to me." She glanced at him shyly. "It's not about getting likes from strangers. It's about sharing my art."

Niall had never been called beautiful or meaningful before. Cordelia saw things in him he'd never seen in himself. The sensation ballooned in his chest—he felt the exact same about her. She was beautiful and meaningful and so much more.

He leaned in and kissed her softly.

"Oi! No kissing in my cart," Róisín called.

"Christ, d'you have eyes in the back of your head?" Niall said.

Cordelia busied herself preparing to post the picture. She titled it *Niall at the Black Fort* and added some hashtags about Inishmore and street photography. Then she took a breath, her face screwed up in fear and anticipation, and hit the post button.

"There," she said, exhaling in a rush. "I did it!"

"Congratulations," Niall said, wrapping his arms around her and kissing her temple. His heart swelled up with pride. He hoped those stupid people on Instagram appreciated how incredible she was, how much love and care went into her photography.

"All right," Cordelia said, putting her phone away and rubbing her hands together. "Bring on the hookers."

Niall laughed.

They spent the morning and most of the afternoon at the harbor.

They couldn't have asked for better weather for the last day of Pátrún. There was music on the docks and a warm breeze in the air. The red sails of the hookers dotted the water, which was serenely periwinkle today. Cordelia flitted about, standing on the stone wall surrounding the harbor or crouching by the musicians to get a shot of some kids dancing a céilí, a traditional Irish folk dance. But she would always return to him, to hold his hand, or kiss his cheek, or just be near him.

They did seem to be something of a celebrity couple, as Róisín had warned. Even those who weren't from Kilronan smiled knowingly or patted Niall on the back or wished them well. When it came time for the Guinness race, Niall declined to participate—he'd had enough racing for this season. But he helped his father pour out the beers.

"What's this all about?" Cordelia asked, as she snapped some pictures of the two of them. "Drinking as much Guinness as fast as you can?"

"No," Owen said emphatically. "See these trays here?" Cordelia nodded. "Each runner gets a tray and a full pint and they've got to balance it using only one hand. They race up the road to where we've set the finish line. Fiona's up there now."

"Oh fun!" Cordelia exclaimed. "I'm going to go check it out."

She left them alone. Niall poured another pint as his father wiped down the trays.

"So," Owen said at last. "You and the American, eh?"

Niall supposed he should have been ready for this. "Her name's Cordelia, Da."

"I know her name."

Niall bit back a retort. He didn't want to fight with his father about Cordelia. It didn't much matter what Owen thought about her one way or the other.

"Never thought I'd see the day a stranger would come into my house and tell me how to love my son," Owen said after a pause. Niall stopped pouring.

"Are you still mad about that?"

"I wasn't mad then and I'm not mad now," Owen said. "Don't be giving me that look, it's true. Not *mad*—that's not the right word. I was taken aback, sure." He put down the tray he was cleaning and sighed. "I know I've been hard on you, Niall. But you've got to know that when you left, well, to me it felt like you was slapping me in the face. That you looked down on all I did and all I'd worked for—this place, this town, this island, all of it. O'Connor's . . . it's in my blood and bones. It's a part of the family. And it felt to me like you were spitting on it."

"Da, I wasn't—"

"Let me finish, now." Owen held up a hand. "You're a right talented young lad. And I think I didn't want to admit that because it made me feel like I was a poor bumbling sod who only knew how to make a stew. But it isn't about me, is it? You're my son. You're my only child. And what that Amer—what Cordelia said that night, well, it's been ringing in my ears ever since."

Owen clapped Niall on the shoulder and pinned him with his gaze. "I'm proud of you, Niall. I'm proud of the man you've become. I'm proud of you going and trying t'do your own thing in Dublin and I'm proud that you came back when you needed help. And you're a damned fine chef. Damned fine. So I thought, you know, perhaps you could come up with a few more things we might be putting on the menu."

Niall thought he might have to physically pick his jaw up off the floor.

"Da," he said, bewildered.

"I'm not offering you the crown jewels." Owen flushed and picked the tray back up. "Will you be adding more dishes to the menu or no?"

"I will," Niall said quickly, eager to seize the moment before it passed. "I'd love to."

"All right then."

Niall finished pouring the last pint and set it down beside the others. "It was you, you know," he said quietly.

"It was me what?"

"Who first inspired me to start cooking. I remember coming in here, following you around the kitchen like a shadow, watching you make the chowder or steam the mussels. You had this confidence, like you were in command. The way you'd mince and simmer and boil and stir and then suddenly there was a meal all ready to be eaten. It was like magic." He finally glanced up at Owen. "You're the reason I started cooking in the first place, Da."

Owen swallowed hard. "Well," he said. "I didn't rightly know that."

"How's it coming along in here?" Colin said, bursting through the doors.

"Hold your damn horses, Colin Doyle, or today I'll be dumping *you* in Kilronan Harbor," Owen said.

Colin raised his eyes to the ceiling. "I am never going to live that down, am I."

"Nope," Niall said cheerfully. "Call the lads in, the pints are ready."

Cordelia was waiting for him outside. "Your dad didn't seem to want me around. I think he seriously hates me."

"He doesn't, in fact," Niall said and then he told her what had transpired after she left.

"Niall, that's amazing!" she said. "I mean, duh, your food is insanely delicious, but I'm so glad your father is finally acknowledging that."

Niall wrapped her up in his arms. "Thank you," he murmured.

"Roger, look, it's that cute couple from the race yesterday!" an American tourist exclaimed to her husband as they walked past. "You guys are adorable!"

"Róisín wasn't exaggerating," Cordelia said as Darragh appeared behind them.

"Hello, lovebirds!" he said. "Now I don't normally hold with foreigners coming and snatching up our fine young Irishmen, but for you, Cordelia, I will make an exception."

"That's grand of you, Darragh," Niall said dryly.

Colin and some other men were lining up with their Guinness and trays. Alison rushed up to them, her cheeks ruddy, her auburn hair coming out of her ponytail.

"Howya," she said. "I didn't miss it, did I? Cordie, I saw that photo you posted of Niall at the Black Fort, gosh it's a beauty. Oh look, there they go!"

Niall turned to see Colin power-walking as fast as he could, his eyes fixated on the pint balanced on his tray.

"Go Colin!" Niall shouted as Alison whooped and Cordelia clapped. One of the boys from Inisheer was close behind him but Colin was walking in quick measured steps, keeping a foot ahead. Another runner's tray tilted but he caught it before it fell, beer slopping over the rim of the glass, and everyone cheered. The man bowed and left the race, chugging his beer as he went.

"I like this much better than the currachs," Cordelia said.

"I don't know," he murmured in her ear. "Not much chance of getting pulled out of the water and kissed by a pretty girl." His eyes traced down to where her hair fell over her shoulder, glowing against the print of her sundress. "Sorry, but . . . are those pineapples on your dress?"

"They are."

"Let me guess—Liz got it for you."

Cordelia laughed. "No, this one I bought myself."

"You like to have food on your clothes, don't you?"

"Am I making you hungry?" she teased. Her top teeth pressed into her bottom lip as she looked up at him from beneath thick lashes.

He groaned. "You're making me something, that's for sure."

She giggled and ran her hand down his chest. Niall caught it and kissed her palm.

"Think you could make a meal out of pineapples?" she whispered.

"I'm certain of it," he said, his voice rough. She tilted her head toward him, her mouth curving into a wicked grin that set Niall's pulse racing.

"He won!" Alison cried suddenly.

They broke apart and Cordelia threw her arms up in a V of victory.

"Yeah, Colin!" she cried.

Colin was standing down the road next to Fiona, holding his beer aloft. The crowd whooped and Niall watched as Colin proceeded to drain his entire glass dry.

"Let's get locked!" Colin shouted and the crowd cheered again.

"Oh, lord," Niall said, then turned to Cordelia. "You ready for a night of good craic?"

"Born ready," Cordelia said, slipping her hand in his.

The afternoon melted away into evening and Niall couldn't remember when he'd had a better day.

And it wasn't in the usual way he had begun to think about his life, the Before Deirdre and After Deirdre times. It was that he simply could not recall ever feeling happier, or more at peace, or filled with such contentment. Who would have known this feeling would exist in Inishmore of all places? He sat at a table with Cordelia by his side, smiling the same smile that he had woken up with that morning.

"Another round for you all?" Shauna said bustling up to the table. "And will you be wanting any food?"

"Lamb!" Cordelia, Alison, and Róisín all cried together, then burst out laughing.

"Then I've got terrible news," Shauna said with mock solemnity. "We've sold out o' the lamb I'm afraid."

"You didn't," Alison gasped as Róisín drained her whiskey and slammed her tumbler down on the table.

"That's what I like to hear," she said.

Cordelia touched his knee under the table and beamed. "I knew it."

Shauna winked. They ordered some other items, but Niall wasn't interested in food. He wanted to whisk Cordelia out of the pub and down to some dark corner of Kilronan where they could be well and truly alone. The pineapple dress was driving him mad, her legs long and lean under its skirt, the tops of her breasts peeking out from the low neckline.

She kept glancing up at him like her thoughts were in line with his. Colin was playing a cover of Taylor Swift's "I Forgot That You Existed" and Róisín launched into one of her many stories, this one about the time the púca saved Brigid's life by telling Róisín not to go to the Wormhole, and then it turned out a freak storm swept in and several sheep were lost.

"So you see," Róisín said as Shauna brought their drinks, "he's not a bad púca. Not like the one in Inishmaan. That one's a right menace. Always sits on the left-hand side." She took a sip of her fresh whiskey. "I wish he'd thought to warn me about Aidan, though," she said, her eyes turning misty.

"My granddad," Alison explained.

"He loved the sea. Couldn't pull him away from it if I tried." Róisín gave Niall and Cordelia a wobbly smile. "You two make a very fine pair indeed," she said. "Love is a precious thing. We think it'll be around forever, but it won't. You need to grab it and hold it close for as long as you've got."

"All right now, Gran," Alison said.

"What? Everyone in town has been saying what a fine pair they make. I'm not trying to gossip."

Niall chuckled. "What are you on about, you're always trying to gossip."

"You know me too well. Oh look! They're setting up for the dancing. I was wondering when Colin was going to play some real music and not whatever the feck that was."

"Taylor Swift," Alison said.

"Eh? Who's he? Never mind, Alison, help me up." Róisín sprang to her feet before Alison even had a chance to move. The doors to the pub were being propped open. People spilled out onto the street with their drinks, laughing and chatting as Colin moved to set up outside. Fergus had come with his bodhran and Eoghan had his melodeon too. Cormac was getting his violin out of its case.

"I'm just going to check on Da," Niall said.

He skirted around behind the bar and Shauna was there, pouring two shots of whiskey. She pressed one into his hand.

"To your success," she said. "Sláinte."

"Sláinte," Niall replied with a grin.

The whiskey burned in his chest, giving heat to the desire building in him, this twisting unflappable want. The band started up playing traditional folk tunes—Niall recognized "The Auld Triangle." He saw Alison leading Cordelia outside and hurried back to the kitchen. He didn't want to abandon the pub if it needed him. He grabbed the rack of dirty dishes on his way in.

"All right, Da?" he said.

His father was wiping down the countertops.

"That's it for food," he said. "It'll be just drinks from now on. The dancing has started, has it?"

"Yup," Niall said, putting the rack in the dishwasher and heading back outside. He spotted Cordelia holding Alison's hand as Alison tried to teach her one of the céilí dances. Her skin glowed in the light of the lanterns, her golden hair spilling down her back, and Niall's groin ached just looking at her.

"Niall!" Alison called, waving him over. "Colin's going to start 'The Walls of Limerick.' You and Cordie be partners. I've been spoken for by this handsome gent, haven't I, Liam?"

She gestured to a young boy of about ten grinning at her side.

"You were racing currachs yesterday!" Liam exclaimed.

"I was," Niall said.

"You fell in the harbor."

"I did."

Liam pointed at Cordelia. "And she kissed you!"

"You're a regular commentator," Niall said, ruffling his hair.

Liam puffed out his chest. "I'll be racing meself when me mam says I'm old enough. I'll be winning too!"

"I don't doubt it."

"All right, folks, pair on up now!" Colin said into the microphone. Niall held out his hand to Cordelia.

"I'm going to majorly screw this up," she warned him as she took it.

"It's been years since I've danced a céilí myself so we're basically even." Her hand was so small and soft. Niall wanted to kiss it.

The music started up and Niall and Cordelia turned to face Alison and Liam.

"Okay, now we go forward," Niall said.

"I don't get the skippy hoppy thing," Cordelia said as they danced toward the opposite couple.

"That's okay, just make it up," Niall said. "Now back. Now we go forward again."

"Now we switch sides!" Alison said and she and Cordelia were spinning around each other so that Alison was next to Niall.

"I'm so confused," Cordelia said, laughing. Niall switched sides with Liam so that he was next to Cordelia again.

"Now take Liam's hand," Niall said as he took Alison's. They danced out away from Cordelia and Liam and then back toward them. "And now we spin," he said, grinning. He held both her hands in his and maneuvered her around in a circle.

"Ahhh!" Cordelia cried as she stepped on his foot.

"You're fine," he said. "Now we stand."

He slid a hand around to position her beside him as Alison and Liam started the dance again with another couple. He let his palm linger on the curve of her waist. She looked up at him, her lips slightly parted, her eyes twinkling in the little white lights, and he felt something catch in his chest. Then the song ended and everybody clapped as Colin cried out, "Okay, next up, 'Haymaker's Jig'!"

"D'you want to dance another?" Niall asked.

Her answering smile was luminous. "Yes, please!"

They got into two lines. Cordelia was able to watch his mam and Darragh going through the steps before the line shifted and she and Niall had to do them. They spun and twirled, and even when she was stepping on his foot, Niall could not remember ever having more fun at a dance. They danced another and another, and by the time they'd finished the "Fairy Reel," Niall was out of breath from all the laughing and spinning.

"Okay, we're going to slow it down now," Colin said, leaning close to the microphone. "Give a break to all you dancers and a chance for all the lovers out here to get a little closer. Let's take it back to America, 1964."

He started up a rendition of Otis Redding's "These Arms of Mine" and Niall turned to Cordelia. Her eyebrow was curved like a question and he smiled softly in answer. She lifted her arms and he pulled her to him, his hand finding the small of her back and pressing her close. Their fingers entwined and she looked down, her forehead grazing his shoulder.

Niall ducked his head and murmured, "What are you doing?"

"Trying not to step on you," she said.

"Cordelia." Could she hear the tremble in his voice?

"Yes?"

"I don't care if you step on me."

All he wanted was to see her face. They turned in a slow circle. Niall was only vaguely aware of the other dancers, their blurred shapes and colors—there was nothing for him but Cordelia, the curve of her cheek, the slope of her nose, the warmth of her palm. Her hips swayed against his body as she moved and the ache grew within him. He turned her around so that they were moving in a bigger circle, away from the crowds and the lanterns. They reached the opposite side of the road and danced into the darkness until Niall suddenly found his back pressed up against a tree. The lights of O'Connor's glowed and twinkled behind Cordelia, turning her into a fairy right out of one of Róisín's stories. They'd stopped moving but he still had one hand in hers and his fingers were splayed wide across her lower back. He could feel her breath soft on his neck, and the thrum of her heart against his own.

"Niall," Cordelia whispered. And he gave in at last.

Her mouth was soft and warm, her lips gentle as they molded around his. Then she opened for him with a tiny moan. She tasted sweet and tart, like honey and red wine. Niall spun her around to press her against the tree, their kiss deepening, their tongues slick and hungry. She released his hand so she could curl her fingers in his hair, clutching him closer, and he wanted it too, he wanted to unzip his skin and let Cordelia touch every part of him, his mind and body and soul.

He brought his hand to her neck, tilting her head so that their kiss could become even more profound. He tugged her lower lip between his teeth, sucking it gently before sliding his tongue back to taste her again. Her hair was like silk across his knuckles. Her bergamot-pine scent was everywhere.

She pulled away, gasping for air, and he moved his mouth to her throat, unable to stop, unable to not touch her. His heart pounded out a heavy rhythm and every part of him burned for her. He kissed the dip in her collarbone and then left a trace of kisses up to her chin and she blissfully pulled his mouth back to hers. Niall let his fingers trace the strap of her dress, teasing the soft line where it hugged her breasts. Cordelia gave another tiny moan and Niall thought he might go mad with the wanting.

"Will you walk me home?" Cordelia whispered in his ear.

"Yes," he whispered back.

18

The walk back up to the cottage took much longer than usual, but Cordelia wasn't complaining.

This whole day had been like a dream, from the moment she woke up to the moment Niall pressed her against that tree. She wanted to pinch herself. It couldn't be real, couldn't be physically possible to contain this much happiness. She thought she might burst into a thousand pieces.

They kept stopping to kiss every five steps or so. They could barely keep up a conversation; the only dialogue they needed was touch—Niall's mouth on hers, her fingers in his hair, his hands on her waist. She felt alive in a way she hadn't ever before—alive and luminous, like there was a lantern glowing inside her, shining its light through her every pore.

But by the time they reached the cottage, the warm glow had turned to frazzled sparks. She knew herself well enough to know she couldn't go any further without a sense of where things stood. So as Niall kissed her by the front door, in that way that made her toes curl and her breath go ragged, she called on all her willpower and pushed him away.

"Wait," she gasped.

"Right, sorry," he said, breathing heavily. For a second she was tempted to pull him back to her, to lean into the kiss like she wanted to. Her eyes hovered on his mouth.

"Cordelia?" Niall said warily. "Are you all right?"

Be cool, she reminded herself.

"What are we doing?" she blurted out.

Niall raised his eyebrows. "Uh . . ." He looked around. "We're at the cottage."

"No I know where we are, but what are we"—she gestured back and forth between herself and him—"doing?"

"Kissing?"

"Niall. Seriously."

"I'm serious." He cocked his head. "Are you asking, like, what are my intentions?"

Her palms tingled and she pulled at the hem of her cardigan. "Yeah. I guess. I mean that sounds kind of old fashioned but . . . I can't just casually sleep with somebody, okay? That doesn't work for me."

"Good," Niall said, dipping to kiss the base of her throat. "It doesn't work for me either."

"Okay." Cordelia felt a thrill run through her. "This isn't like anything I've ever done before."

His nose traced the line of her neck to nuzzle against her ear. "How so?"

"I mean . . . you're my neighbor." She gasped as his hand slipped beneath her cardigan to stroke the smooth skin of her back. "Your parents are my neighbors. We're in this tiny little town and everybody knows everything about everyone—"

"This is true," Niall said. He frowned and pulled away. "Are you . . . embarrassed? To be spending time with me?"

"What? No!" Cordelia said quickly. "Not at all. I want to spend *more* time with you."

The words slipped out before she could stop them. In her experience, blurting out her feelings like that usually sent a guy running for the hills. But Niall only smiled. The moon was bright above his head, the stars twinkling in a canopy of black.

"I want to spend more time with you too," he said softly.

All the air left her in a giant whoosh. "You do?"

He quirked an eyebrow. "Was I not making myself clear just now?"

"That was kissing," she said. "That doesn't mean . . . that could be . . . I don't know. This is not how dating in New York works."

His mouth pulled up at one corner. "I hate to break it to you but we're very much *not* in New York."

"I know." She looked down, resting her hands on his chest, fiddling with one of the buttons on his shirt. She wanted him so badly it hurt. "I told you at the Black Fort, it's been a really long time since I've been with anyone. And I'm out of practice with, well, everything to do with relationships. And I'm probably messing this up right now. I don't do casual things. I don't fall for people lightly."

She took a deep breath. May as well say it straight and get it over with.

"And I'm pretty sure I've fallen hard for you. You've made me feel alive for the first time in years—for the first time since my dad died, if I'm really being honest. But if you're not ready or if me being too serious like this scares you, then you should tell me now. I'll understand."

She finally dared to peek up at him and saw a bemused yet slightly playful expression on his face. He reached up to tuck a lock of hair behind her ear and his hand lingered at her neck.

"When I first met you," he said, "I was in such a dark place, I was sure I would never be able to open myself up to someone else. You pulled me out. You've made me feel alive again too." He wrapped one arm around her waist and leaned his forehead against hers. "You being serious like this doesn't scare me," he whispered. "It thrills me."

Cordelia felt an opening in her chest, like a flower turning its petals to the sun. "Really?"

"Really. Christ, I've been dying to kiss you since the Black Fort."

She let out a tiny gasp. "You have?"

He nodded. "Didn't know how you felt, though."

She winced. "I think I made myself abundantly clear."

"You did. And it was gorgeous. I'll never forget the sight of you running up to me on that pier."

Her heart was racing, unable to believe this was really happening, unable to compute that he was telling her he felt the same way she did. "But I'm only here until the end of August," she said. "What then?"

"I don't think we need to go worrying about that just yet," Niall said. "You might not like me anymore in a couple of months."

"I already didn't like you," she pointed out. "And look where that got us."

Niall laughed. "Fair play." He tilted her chin so that her eyes met his. "Have I proved my intentions now? Or do I need to get you a claddagh ring? Maybe let you wear my school jacket?"

"Do you have a school jacket?"

"No. But if I did, I'd let you wear it." He batted his eyelashes. "Cordelia James, will you go steady with me?"

It was her turn to laugh, and it was clear and bubbly and for a moment the stars seemed to shine even brighter. "Yes," she said, leaning in to kiss him, his lips already so familiar. She ran her hand down his chest and Niall gave a little purr of pleasure, a visceral sound that tugged at the string connected to the pit of need low in her belly. She felt all her fear and anxiety melt away, leaving only a warm thrumming behind.

"Do you want to come inside?" she asked coyly.

The inside of the cottage was dark.

Niall hadn't been here in years. He could smell Cordelia's bergamot scent beneath the wood polish and wool. Cordelia put her bag down and closed the door, and Niall was there in an instant, his hands in her hair, his mouth covering hers. God, he would never tire of kissing her. Her lips were so soft—he took the lower one between his teeth and tugged on it gently, eliciting that tiny moan from her again. In one swift movement, he slipped her cardigan off her shoulders and it fell softly to the floor. He pushed her back against the door, his hardness pressing into her thigh, but she seemed to welcome it, twisting in his arms and kissing him with more force, her hand dropping so she could run her fingernails over the bulge at his inseam. He groaned against her mouth.

His hand moved from her hip to the curve of her waist, playing over her ribcage until he reached her breast. He swept his thumb across the soft fabric, feeling her nipple beneath. She wasn't wearing a bra. He brushed her nipple again and again until it hardened into a tight peak. Cordelia dug her fingers into his back, giving a little shudder.

"I need you in my mouth," Niall said roughly, and she gasped as he slid the strap of her dress down and tugged at the neckline, exposing one perfect breast, soft as satin and begging to be kissed. He took the whole thing, sucking on her and flicking the nipple with his tongue until she cried out. Then he gently slid the dress back into place.

"What are you doing?" she panted.

His mouth moved to her ear. "Taking my time," he murmured.

She was so impossibly lovely. He didn't want to rush anything. He wanted to sip her slowly and savor every last drop. He wanted to feast on her until the sun rose and still be hungry for more. He slipped his other hand beneath the hem of her skirt and stroked the delicate skin of her thigh. Her breath caught as he hitched her leg up to his hip, sliding himself further between her legs. His mouth explored the length of her collarbone, dipping down to kiss the valley between her breasts. The hand at her thigh moved to grip her ass, lifting her up so that he could press deeper against her.

"You're so fucking hard," she whispered in his ear and it was like a shot of pure ecstasy through his veins. She began to fumble with the buttons on his shirt, but when he went to help her, she stopped him. "Keep those hands where they were," she growled and he chuckled, breathless, loving the sound of her ordering him around.

He traced a finger down her chest and ran his palm over her breast again, that teasing nipple still hard and calling to him. He needed to work on the other one. It took all of his self-control not to rip the thin cotton dress off right there.

Cordelia reached the last button and slid his shirt off his shoulders, letting it puddle on the floor. Then her hands were on him and he couldn't think, he couldn't see, he could hardly breathe . . . everything was Cordelia. She kissed along his shoulder, then gently bit his neck, making him gasp. Her fingernails raked through the hair on his chest, her palms resting at his hips, one index finger swooping teasingly beneath the waistband of his jeans while the other went to cup his cock, rubbing her palm up and down in a steady repetitive motion that had his knees going weak.

"You're killing me, woman," Niall moaned.

"Take my dress off," she whispered.

Niall needed no further instruction. His hands found the zipper at her back and he peeled the dress off so that Cordelia stood before him in the moonlight, naked except for a pair of cotton underwear designed to look like a slice of watermelon.

"Oh," she said, realizing she was wearing yet more food. She grinned sheepishly. "I didn't do that on purpose. It's laundry day."

Niall chuckled, tracing the line of fabric across her stomach and feeling the goose bumps blossom on her skin. "Let's see if they taste as good as they look," he said, and got down on his knees. He kissed her just below her belly button and then looked up at her. Her breasts swelled, both nipples hard in the cool air, and Niall couldn't resist reaching up and pinching one pert bud between his fingers. She gasped and bit her lip and Niall's cock grew so hard it hurt. She brushed a lock of his hair away from his face and let her hand fall gently against his jaw. He turned his head to kiss her palm, then gazed up at her again.

"Cordelia James," he said. "You are so beautiful."

Her eyes widened a fraction and her lips parted but Niall couldn't wait. He kissed her mound softly, reveling in the moan that escaped her, louder and more primal than the little ones before, and he couldn't wait to set her truly free, to learn how to make those moans grow in pitch, to understand her inner workings until he had her shuddering.

He hooked a finger around the watermelon underwear and pulled it aside, tasting her at last. She was wet and ready and he slid his tongue along her clit, feeling her thighs quiver, pressing his hand flat against her stomach to hold her upright. He licked and sucked at her, sensing when she tightened and when the wetness flowed, falling into a pattern of gentle circles around her clit, sinking lower and lower toward her opening.

"Niall," she gasped as he slid a finger inside her. "Wait."

"I can't," he murmured against her.

"Oh god," she said and he tilted his head to see she was gripping her hair with one hand. "I think I'm going to fall over." She met his gaze. "Bedroom."

That was the only word that could have gotten him to move from what he considered to be the most perfect spot in the entire world. His knees creaked as he stood, kissing her deeply and then bending to sweep her legs out from under her, cradling her against him as she shrieked.

"You bastard!" She giggled, swatting his chest.

"And a very strong bastard at that," he said with a grin. She wrapped her arms around his neck and arched up to kiss him.

"More please," she whispered.

"Oh yes," he murmured in agreement. He wasn't done with her yet. Not by a long shot. He strode through the small living room with Cordelia in his arms.

"Wait, the lights," she said.

"Fuck the lights," Niall growled.

Cordelia was a tangled, twisted up, writhing knot of pleasure.

Her skin was on fire. Her heart pummeled against her sternum. The tender spot between her thighs seemed to have its own heartbeat and Cordelia ached for Niall's mouth on her again. He carried her easily as he kicked open the door to the bedroom and laid her down gently on the bed. He towered over her, his skin shining like pearl in the dim light spilling through her bedroom window, his eyes dark as lapis.

"You still have pants on," she said, sitting up. "No fair." She unbuttoned his jeans and left a trail of kisses across his stomach, feeling the muscles clench and tremble beneath her lips. She lay back and waited as he took his shoes and socks and jeans off before crawling across the bed to stretch out alongside her, his head propped up on one hand.

His fingertips ran from her throat down her chest, between her breasts and over her stomach until he was slipping his fingers over her clit. She gasped, tension coiling inside her at his touch. He grinned and stroked her gently, like he had all the time in the world. He started doing that circular thing he'd been doing earlier with his mouth and Cordelia groaned, spots of light flashing in the edge of her vision. He dipped to suck at her breast again, biting ever so gently on her nipple and Cordelia had to suck in a scream.

"You're so tense," Niall murmured, moving to take her other breast in his mouth. Cordelia's head spun, the waves of sensation forming a delicate buzz across her skin. There was a taut silken line connecting all the way from her nipples down to her clit, and just when she thought she was going to faint or shatter, he slid his fingers inside her again.

She cried out and Niall shifted his position so he was hovering over her, balanced on his forearm while he teased and stroked her, dipping in to touch her G-spot and then sliding back out to run his fingers in that goddamn miraculous circle. She brought his mouth to hers fiercely as her thighs clenched together around his hand, her hips arching to coax him deeper. She was right on the edge of that ultimate release, but she didn't want to give in yet. She didn't want a single scrap of fabric between her and Niall when she did.

"Take them off," she pleaded and he didn't need any more encouragement. With one swift pull, the watermelon underwear was yanked off and tossed aside.

"Yours too," she whispered against his cheek. She felt him move on the bed and then heard the soft sound of his boxers falling to the floor.

Cordelia had thought that whenever she felt comfortable enough to have sex again, she would be shy and awkward, embarrassed by her nudity or second-guessing herself. But not with Niall. He looked at her like a man dying of thirst looked at a jug of water, like she was the most precious jewel he'd ever seen. She *felt* precious. Precious and sexy and alive and *happy*. She'd never felt such pure elation, like she was floating. The rules of gravity no longer applied.

She let her gaze travel across his shoulders, down his chest, to the V of muscle she'd seen in the back room yesterday. Was it only yesterday? Niall was full and hard and she reached down and took his cock in her hands, marveling at the softness of skin over hard muscle. She heard his breath catch and she grinned wickedly, stroking him as gently as he'd stroked her, looking up to see his jaw clenched.

"Now who's tense?" she teased.

He gave a throaty chuckle. "You're going to be the death of me."

Cordelia gripped his shaft tighter and he moaned. "Not tonight, let's hope."

In a sudden burst of sassiness she didn't know herself capable of, she pushed him down on the bed and straddled him, pressing her breasts against his chest, slipping her tongue back inside his mouth, and all the while her hand pumped and stroked at his cock, sometimes firmly, sometimes softly.

"I want you inside me," Cordelia growled. "I need you inside me."

"Oh shit," Niall muttered. Cordelia sat up, wondering if this was the moment when her dream was punctured. Niall saw the shock on her face and sat up too. "I don't have any condoms," he explained. "I used to keep some in my wallet but I stopped after . . ."

Relief melted through her. "Oh," she said. "I'm on birth control and I've been tested."

"Me too," he said, and she was grateful he didn't have to pull away, grateful she didn't need to pause this insatiable hunger for even an instant.

Cordelia lay on her back against the comforter and then Niall was hovering over her, stroking her hair away from her face.

Her nipples grazed his chest as he slowly entered her, taking his time, making sure she was comfortable. She could feel it now, how every motion, every movement was made with her in mind. He knew how long it had been for her. He knew her fears and hesitations, her anxiety. But as he slid inside her, Cordelia let out a sound she hadn't known she was capable of making, a sort of gasping wail of utter desolation and joy.

Niall's head dropped to her breasts. "Oh my fucking god," he said. "Cordelia."

"More," she gasped and he slid even deeper. He filled her up and she scratched at his back, panting, reveling in the pressure of his cock, the heavy, slow movements across her G-spot. It was a dizzying, mindless pleasure, and Cordelia felt her universe expand and contract, every particle of her being focused on the point between her legs. When Niall reached down and stroked her clit as he pumped, she thought she might explode, burst into a million glittering particles and get swept away in the wind.

He increased the pressure and speed. Cordelia wailed again, her back arching, and he took the moment to flick his tongue across her nipples, first one then the other. Cordelia let out a moan that resonated through her whole body and Niall murmured something in her ear, but she couldn't hear, she couldn't think, she couldn't see, she was one radiating pulse of sensation. The tightness was gathering, she could feel it, could feel how slick she was over him, her wetness growing. She could feel it build in him too, feel him grow even harder, push even deeper, and just when she thought she couldn't take it anymore, just when she was about to scream and beg for sweet release, his cock plunged deep and his fingers lit up the seam within her and she felt herself tearing in two, pleasure ripping through her body in hot, endless waves—she cried out his name as she shuddered against him, over and over, the orgasm taking her to a place she'd never known, sparks exploding in her vision. She was a vessel of pure ecstasy and she felt him coming too, felt him surge within her, setting off another wave of toe-clenching, mind-numbing shudders.

Her body shivered once more and then they both went still. Niall's hair was damp with sweat, his chest heaving. They lay in silence for a moment. Cordelia felt oddly loose, like all her joints had come undone. She stroked a hand through his hair and he shivered and tried to move, but she clutched him close, a sudden pang of fear seizing her, though she couldn't say why or what she was afraid of. Just that she didn't want him to leave, didn't want the glorious pressure of his body to go away.

"I'm just cleaning up, love," he murmured, and her heart flipped at that word, so small and simple yet so potent. He slid out of her and she felt the ache he left behind. Her sex was throbbing and tender, yet she wanted him again already. She heard the faint sound of his movements and then he was back, cradling her against his chest.

She felt his lips press against her hair as she traced patterns lazily across his skin. His heart beat heavy against her cheek and it was the most beautiful sound she'd ever heard. Her body was weightless, her legs like jelly. She felt as if she'd been melted down and reforged.

"Are you all right?" Niall whispered after a moment. She tilted her head to gaze up at those startling blue eyes she had come to love so dearly.

"I'm perfect," she said.

19

The first thing Niall noticed when he woke up the next morning was the ache between his thighs. His body felt rubbery and raw, but in a good way, like he'd been stretched by a rolling pin.

The second thing he noticed was the gorgeous, golden head tucked in the crook of his arm. Cordelia looked so peaceful as she slept, her breathing slow and even. She was tangled up in the sheets, one breast peeking out to reveal a pale pink nipple. The sight had him growing hard again. He hadn't been able to see all of her colors last night, the delicate cream-peach of her skin, the sunshine gold of her hair, the blush of her lips.

He didn't want to wake her, but he really needed to piss. He extracted himself as carefully as he could and hurried to the jacks. When he came out, she was awake and watching him, a quiet smile playing across her mouth, that one breast still exposed and taunting him. He licked his lips, remembering how good she'd tasted.

"Good morning," Cordelia said.

"Morning," Niall said, crawling back into bed and kissing her. Her arms came up to wrap around him, her fingers tracing down the length of his back. Niall slipped his tongue inside her mouth, not caring about morning breath, not caring about anything except being close to her. She responded in kind, opening herself for him, and he slid his hand down her waist, hitching up her thigh so he could settle between her legs. Her heel dug into his back and she lifted her other leg so that both were wrapped tight around him.

"I've got you now," she said, grinning. "You can't go anywhere."

Niall knew without a doubt there was nowhere else in the world he would ever want to be. "I'm your prisoner then," he said, bringing his wrists together over her head. "Do what you want with me."

She giggled and he felt it in his own body, the movement of her chest and stomach. His cock nudged her thigh and she gave a little moan, not the orgasm-inducing wail from last night that made him harder just remembering it, but the tiny coo of pleasure that he knew meant she was warming up.

"I'm hungry," he said.

"I can see what food I've—"

"Not hungry for food," Niall growled in her ear, then he tugged the sheet out of the way and scooted down the bed so he could take her in his mouth.

They fell into a heap together on the bed, breathing heavily.

"Holy fuck," Niall gasped.

"Holy fuck," Cordelia murmured in agreement. For one blissful moment, everything was in its exact right place in the world. The planets had aligned, the order of the universe restored, and Cordelia James was in his arms.

Then her stomach growled.

"Oh," she said, embarrassed and Niall chuckled against her neck.

"Shall I make us some breakfast?" he asked.

"Yes please!" she said eagerly. He got up and got her a towel from the bathroom, then threw on his underwear and jeans and headed into the kitchen. The day was cloudy but the sun peeked through in some spots. Niall had no idea what time it was. He had no idea what day it was. He thought he could live in this cottage forever, surviving on nothing but Cordelia.

He opened the fridge and gasped. "What the fuck . . ."

Cordelia came into the kitchen wearing a pair of striped sleep shorts and a hooded sweatshirt, her hair tied up in a messy bun. Only the sight of her loveliness could distract him, however briefly, from such horrors.

"Cordie," he said, "what is *this*?"

She beamed. "You've never called me Cordie before." She looked from him to the open fridge and her face fell. "Oh."

"I thought Róisín was exaggerating," Niall said. Inside the fridge there was a solitary apple, three different kinds of cheese, and two Mars bars.

"I told you I don't know how to cook," she said, coming up to wrap her arms around his waist.

"You do know how to eat, though, right?" Niall said.

"I go to O'Connor's for that," she insisted.

"Okay," he said, closing the fridge door. "We're going to the market today. Cooking isn't rocket science. I can show you some really easy things to make."

"All right," she said happily, leaning up to peck him on the lips and then prancing off into the living room. "I hope nobody was upset we sort of disappeared from the party last night."

"It's called an Irish goodbye," Niall said, pouring coffee grounds into the French press and putting water on to boil. "I promise you, no one was surprised. Bet you'll be getting some sass from Róisín today, though. So will I, come to think of it." There was silence from the living room. "Cordelia?" Niall called. "You okay?"

More silence. Niall hurried out of the kitchen and found Cordelia in the middle of the room, her purse hanging limp from one hand, her phone clutched in the other, a blank look on her face.

"What?" he asked, coming to her side. "What's happened?"

"Liz texted me last night," she said, bewildered. Niall leaned over to see a string of texts growing more frantic.

Cordelia!!!!

CHECK YOUR INSTA

NOW

Hello??? Girl that pic is blowing UP

People are loving it!! You need to post more. Right now. ASAP.

Hi are you alive answer me please.

"Did you check it?" Niall said. Cordelia shook her head. She blinked up at him. He smiled softly and kissed her temple. "Go on then."

She sent a quick text to Liz saying *Sorry, I'm alive, checking now!* Then she switched over to the app. Niall took note of her handle—@cordjamesshoots—and then found himself staring at the picture of him at the Black Fort. By the little heart in the left-hand corner was a number—20.3K.

"Holy shit," he said. "That's quite good, isn't it?"

Cordelia was staring at the number with a look of shock or horror, he couldn't tell.

"Cord?" he said. "It's good, right?"

She looked up at him with tears in her eyes. "It's so many," she said. "I've never . . . all these people like my photo? Niall!" She flung her arms around him. "Oh my god. Oh my god!"

She pulled back and stared at the screen. The photo had already received more likes, even in the time she'd been standing here. Professional photographers were commenting on the color and the composition and the lighting while other people commented on the location. Niall read some along with her.

I've always wanted to go to the Aran Islands!

That's Dún Duchathair.

Look at those clouds! 😍

"They love it," Niall said proudly.

"Look, there are some about you," Cordelia said.

Hellooooo, Irish hottie!

That is a good-looking man on a good-looking cliff.

Another was just a series of fire emojis.

"Ah," Niall said, rubbing the back of his neck. "Well. Huh."

Cordelia pressed her face into his chest and began to laugh. She laughed and laughed and Niall held her, grinning.

"Think this is funny, do ya?" he teased. "Your man is quite popular with the Instagram folk it seems." It was a bit weird, but Niall didn't care. He only cared that Cordelia was happy and getting the accolades she deserved.

"My Irish hottie," she said, leaning up on her toes to kiss him.

There was a pounding on the door. "Oi!" Róisín called.

"Shit," Niall said, hurrying to pick his shirt up off the floor. He was buttoning it up as Cordelia opened the door.

"I'm surprised you knocked," she said wryly.

"I didn't want to disturb," Róisín said.

"You always want to disturb."

Róisín cackled. "Well, I didn't want to burst in on Niall in naught but his birthday suit."

Cordelia turned bright red and Niall groaned. "Enough of that, Róisín, you've got to see this."

"My picture," Cordelia said, still sounding stunned as she handed Róisín the phone.

"Now that's a grand photo of our Niall, isn't it." She patted Niall on the shoulder. "Is that at the Black Fort? Oh yes, wait, I see the title now: *Niall at the Black Fort.*" She frowned. "That's a bit obvious, isn't it, Cordie?"

"People like it," Cordelia said.

"Of course they do, they'd be blind not to." Róisín gave back the phone. "Go on then, put one up of me. That's what the people are really wanting to see."

Niall laughed and Cordelia blinked at them. "Should I?"

"Yes!" Róisín cried as Niall nodded.

"Okay," she said, and Niall's stomach flipped to see the pure, unadulterated joy on her face, the excitement as she scrolled through her photographs. She chose the black-and-white one of Róisín and Brigid, the first picture of hers Niall had ever seen.

"Maybe tell one of Róisín's stories along with it," he suggested.

"Yes!" Cordelia exclaimed. "Like *Humans of New York.* Except it's *Humans of Inishmore.* I could do a whole series! Róisín, tell me the story of how the púca saved Brigid again."

"Ah, well, it was a cold and windy day, it was," Róisín began as Cordelia's fingers flashed across her keyboard. "And he was in the shape of a rabbit, a big brown hare with these golden eyes and sharp, pointy ears . . ."

Cordelia's head was still spinning as she followed Róisín up to the house on the hill.

Niall had gone back to his house to shower and change. The paints had finally come and Róisín was eager to get Cordelia back to work. She was mixing colors to find the perfect yellow for the St. John's wort when her phone began to ring.

"Who's that?" Róisín asked from the other side of the table where she was shelling peas.

"It's Liz," Cordelia said, answering the FaceTime call.

"Hi hi hi!!" Liz's face appeared on the screen. "Look at you, going all balls to the wall with Instagram now. I love it. The Róisín pic is gorgeous. And that story is hil—"

"Niall and I are together," Cordelia blurted out. Róisín grinned to herself and pretended to be very busy with the peas.

Liz's eyebrows shot up her forehead. Her red-painted mouth formed an O. She blinked, inhaled deeply, then shouted, "WHAT?! When? How? Cordie!! I need details. Have you kissed him? Have you slept with him? Was it good? When did this happen??"

"Judging by the fact that he was shirtless in her house not an hour ago, I'd say it's going fairly well," Róisín said.

"Is that Róisín?" Liz said eagerly. "Hi, Róisín!"

"Hello yourself," Róisín said, coming around the table so Liz could see her.

"He wasn't shirtless," Cordelia insisted.

"His buttons were done up all wrong," Róisín said dismissively. "Now let me tell you, Liz, those two have been dancing round each other since her first day on the island—"

"I know, right?" Liz added.

Róisín launched into the tale of the currach races and the kiss on the pier.

"Cordelia Marie James," Liz said, enunciating each syllable. "This is even better than the Instagram thing!"

"It's pretty crazy," Cordelia admitted.

"Not crazy. Blissfully, amazingly, wondrously perfect. Oh, Cordie. No one deserves this more than you. I'm so happy for you guys."

"Thanks," Cordelia said, grinning. "I'm happy too."

"Of course you are, look at you, you're glowing! Have you told your mom yet?"

Cordelia's face fell and her stomach dropped. "No," she said. She looked down.

"Shit. I shouldn't have said that. Don't let her rain on this day! You don't have to tell her anything you don't want to."

"She'll just be insufferable if I do," Cordelia said. "Like this somehow proves her point."

"You let that mother o' yours get in your head far too much," Róisín said, going back to the peas.

"I agree," Liz said. "So what if she thinks that? It doesn't make her right and it doesn't make all her pushing okay. And she has nothing to do with you and Niall. Niall and Cordelia! Even your names sound perfect together."

"You're right," Cordelia said, straightening.

She wasn't going to let her mom ruin this for her, either by crowing about how right she'd been all along or by instantly pushing Cordelia to get married and have babies. No, Cordelia was finally full and truly happy and she wasn't about to let Louise James interfere with that.

20

The month of July was the happiest month in the history of Cordelia's life.

She spent every minute she could with Niall. He took her around the island and let her take more photographs of him for her Instagram. Her following was growing by the day, each new photograph and story garnering more and more attention and acclaim. Ever since Róisín began boasting about Cordelia's posts, it seemed like the entire island had signed up for Instagram. And those who hadn't were always badgering Niall to show them the pictures on his phone, usually during one of his shifts. He didn't seem to mind, though. Whenever someone asked, Cordelia noted the shine of pride in his eyes. She'd never been with a man who lifted her up so completely, who believed in her through and through.

The islanders had clamored to be featured on her feed and Cordelia found her work cut out for her—every local had a lot of stories in them. But she discovered her patience again, and her good humor, chatting to everyone with ease and drawing out their tales with care and skill, whether it was talking to Aoife O'Shea about the death of her husband or watching Liam Sullivan practice his currach rowing. Colin was a popular subject, much to his delight, as was Pocket—any picture that featured the border collie immediately shot up with likes and comments.

But Niall was the secret star, Cordelia knew. Her love for him shone through every shot.

"You make the island come alive," he told her once. "In a way I hadn't ever really seen before. I think this is the first time I've felt proud of my home."

Cordelia had kissed him then. If she had her way, she would have spent ninety percent of her time kissing Niall. Or in bed with Niall. Or naked with Niall. If the world were to end this very moment, she would want to spend her last seconds in Niall O'Connor's arms.

In the back of her mind, of course, there was the constant nagging fear, the ticking of the clock that meant her time on Inishmore would come to an end. But, she always reminded herself, it was still July and she wasn't about to ruin a good thing by fretting over it, as Róisín would say.

She'd told Nikki and Toby about Niall, but she still hadn't managed to bring it up with her mother yet. Louise had texted a few times with links to more articles and another dating app (Luck of the Irish), so Cordelia guessed Toby hadn't spilled the beans yet. But she hadn't responded to her mother at all. She didn't want to lie but she didn't want to tell the truth either. As the month dragged on, though, Cordelia knew it was only a matter of time before she'd have to say something. Her mother had started calling, once last week and then three times this week. Cordelia couldn't avoid her forever.

But today, Cordelia was focusing on the task at hand—which was Niall teaching her how to cook. He spent every night at the cottage now, and her fridge was always stocked with fresh greens, eggs, milk, poultry, and cheese.

Well, she was trying to focus on the task at hand. It was very difficult with Niall standing there looking so confident and hot as he cracked another egg and added it to the bowl.

"An omelet is a simple thing," he said as he began to whisk, beating the eggs into a yellow fervor.

"Mmhm," Cordelia said, coming up behind him and pretending to be observant.

"It doesn't take long to make and it's a good way to get veg and protein."

"Veg and protein, yup."

She caught the faint scent of his driftwood smell and it sent small shivers straight down to her thighs. His shirt was open at the collar and she leaned her head against his arm as he showed her how to properly clean a mushroom. Her hands wandered to his waist, skimming the top of his jeans.

"Are you even listening to me?" Niall asked, looking down at her with a mischievous gleam in his eyes.

"Hm?" she said as she slid her hand down between his thighs. She felt him stiffen beneath her fingers.

"You are a wicked, wicked woman," he murmured as she stroked him into hardness.

"Who, me?" she said, batting her eyelashes and raking her fingernails over his jeans. He gasped.

"Goddamn you," he said, turning in her arms to kiss her, his mouth taking hers just the way she liked it. She melted against his chest, keeping one hand on his cock, and pushed him back against the countertop. Her tongue played with his as she unbuttoned his jeans and reached down beneath his boxers to take him in her bare hands. She loved the way she could feel the muscle grow and expand beneath her fingers. And she wanted to be in command. So she sank down onto her knees on the kitchen floor and took him in her mouth.

Niall groaned with pleasure, clutching the back of her head. She let his cock sink deep in her throat, then pulled out and licked a long line from the base of his shaft to the tip. "Christ," he gasped as she traced her finger around the tip before sucking it, gentle at first and then harder, sinking him back into her mouth, her tongue exploring every inch of him. Niall yanked his shirt up over his head and then bent to lift hers off too. She loved going braless around the house with him for this very reason. Her breasts spilled out and she raised herself up to rub them along his cock before pulling it to her mouth once more. She licked and sucked until all of a sudden she found herself flat on her back on the kitchen floor.

"Goddamn you," Niall murmured again, yanking down her shorts, and she wriggled out of them gladly, tossing her underwear aside. Niall slid his cock inside her and she whimpered. He was so hard, hard and ready, but she still wanted to be in command.

"Get on your back," she whispered in his ear.

He followed her orders to the letter. She crawled on top of him, straddling him and grabbing his wrists to place his palms over her breasts.

"Fuck," Niall moaned as she slipped his cock inside her again, plumping her breasts with his strong hands, dragging his fingers over her nipples. She took him fully deep, deeper than he'd ever been, and they both cried out in unison. Cordelia began to rock in time to the motion of his hands as they pulled and teased and stroked her, her nipples tight buds when he rolled them between his fingers, shooting lightning bolts of pleasure right to her clit. She rubbed against him and his hands came to clutch her hips, helping her, holding her firm. She placed one hand on his chest as she rode him hard, unleashing herself, letting the want and the need take over as she drove him deeper, nudging her G-spot, coaxing it as Niall surged inside her, his hips bucking. She felt it coming like a tickle in the back of her throat or a prickling along her scalp—he hit just . . . right . . . *there*, and she was done, her body shuddering in ecstasy and Niall reached up to squeeze her breast as he came inside her, the two of them rocketed into the heightened planes of pleasure.

She fell forward and kissed him on the nose.

"Wicked . . . woman," he panted, tucking her hair behind her ear.

"Would you have me any other way?"

"I would not."

He kissed her and then she eased herself off of him, grabbing a tissue from the table to clean herself.

"Right," Niall said, pulling his jeans back on and standing. "I'm showing you how to make this bloody omelet, then I'm taking a shower. Can't be going to the pub all sexed up."

Cordelia laughed. "Yeah, that's more of an *at home* look."

A couple of hours later, Cordelia had made an omelet that she knew she would never succeed in making again without Niall's help, and they were both showered and dressed and on their way to O'Connor's.

"Huh," Cordelia said as they walked. "I've got two missed calls from Toby."

"Should you call him back?"

"Not yet," she said, slipping her hand into his. Her phone rang again. "Ugh, god, Toby," Cordelia muttered, silencing it.

"Call him," Niall said.

"I will. I just need a glass of wine first. I feel another Big Brother Lecture coming on."

"That can be arranged, I think," Niall said, opening the door to the pub.

There was a tall woman at the bar with Róisín, her back to them, wearing a big furry hat and a peacoat.

"Ah, there she is," Róisín said, pointing. The woman turned around.

"Cordelia!" she exclaimed.

Cordelia's mouth fell open. "Mom?"

"Cordie, look, your mam's come all the way from Russia to see you," Róisín said, giving a sardonic glance at Louise's hat. "How's the weather in Moscow, Louise?"

Niall choked on a laugh but Cordelia was in a complete state of shock.

"Well, come give your mother a hug," Louise said. Shauna was staring unabashed from behind the bar, wiping the same glass over and over again. "Gary's just in the bathroom. This place is so cute! And you," Louise said, looking Niall up and down. "You must be Niall."

Cordelia still hadn't moved. Niall prodded her gently in the back, then took her elbow when that didn't work. Cordelia felt like she was walking on wooden legs.

"I am," Niall said. "It's very nice to meet you."

"It's wonderful to meet you too," Louise said.

"What are you *doing here*?" Cordelia demanded, finding her voice at last.

"I told you we were going to come visit," Louise said.

"You did not," Cordelia said. "Mom, you did *not* tell me that."

"We talked about it when I was at the cabin with Nikki and Toby."

"That—that was like a month ago!" Cordelia cried.

"You know, if you'd actually pick up your phone when I call this might not have come as such a surprise," Louise said tartly. She turned to Niall with a Cheshire cat smile. "Now, Niall—" she began.

"How do you know about Niall?" Cordelia said.

"Cordelia, I follow you on Instagram," Louise said. "Besides, your brother told me. Toby can't keep secrets."

"Traitor," Cordelia muttered.

"I should probably get—" Niall began, but Louise cut him off.

"Oh, but Niall, you've got to meet Gary. Gary!" Louise motioned to a burly man with thick graying hair. "Gary, this is Niall, Cordelia's boyfriend."

"Mom!" Cordelia said loudly. "I don't . . . I thought I told you not to come."

"Yes, but that was then and this is now. You have a boyfriend I needed to meet! And anyway I found a fabulous deal for the hotel on Groupon. Oh, don't make that face, we're only here for one night and then we're off to tour Dingle."

"Dingle's grand," Niall said. "You'll love it. Very beautiful."

"That's what we've heard!" Louise exclaimed. "Such a nice young man," she said to Cordelia. "I don't know why you were hiding him from me."

"I wasn't hiding him," Cordelia insisted.

"And so handsome!" Louise cried.

"*Mom!*" Cordelia snapped.

"Are you staying for dinner?" Róisín asked. "They've got to have dinner here, haven't they, Cordie? Must try one of Niall's dishes. He's got three on the menu now," she said proudly.

"Oh, you're a chef, are you?" Louise said, brightening. "Well, of course we'd love to stay."

"Let's get you set up with a table then," Róisín said, grinning at the glare Cordelia shot her and bustling Louise and Gary over to one of the tables.

"I've just got to check in with Da," Niall said.

"Don't leave me," she hissed.

He kissed her quickly. "Be right back. Come on, Róisín. Da needs to talk to you too."

It wasn't a very good lie, but Róisín happily followed him back into the kitchen.

"Aw, isn't that sweet," Louise said, sinking into one of the chairs and taking off her ridiculous hat. "He's very good-looking, Cordelia. And he seems so nice. A chef! That's a good job."

Cordelia was busy texting Toby under the table.

MOM IS HERE.

I know, that's why I keep calling you. Answer your damn phone next time, sis.

Ugh. Not helpful. Cordelia was glad when Shauna bustled over.

"Evening, Cordie," she said, glancing eagerly at Louise and Gary. Cordelia sighed.

"Shauna, this is my mom, Louise," she said. "And this is Gary."

"Howya," Shauna said. "We love having your daughter here on our little island, Mrs. James."

"Aren't you sweet to say so," Louise said, beaming.

"What can I get for you?" Shauna asked.

"Wine," Cordelia said. "A lot of wine. Like, all of it."

"Cordie, you are so silly," Louise said, laughing and slapping her arm playfully. "I'd love a glass of white wine, Shauna."

Gary ordered a Guinness and Shauna bustled away.

"So," Cordelia said, fixing a fake smile onto her face. "When exactly did you make this plan?"

"We've been following along with your pictures—they're really lovely, Cordie—and I thought what a marvelous island this seems to be, and I wished we could see it too. And then Toby told us about Niall, though of course I had my suspicions already—I mean, he seemed to be prominently featured and I admit I was hoping that maybe—"

"Yes, yes, but when did you buy tickets? Where are you even staying?" Cordelia wondered what was taking Shauna so long with the drinks. She kept glancing at the kitchen doors waiting for Róisín or Niall to come out and save her.

"The Killarney house or something, Gary, what was it called again?"

"The Kilmurvey House?" Cordelia said.

"That's the one," Louise exclaimed.

The Kilmurvey House was one of the nicest hotels on the island.

"We didn't mean to intrude," Gary said. "Your mother was very eager to see where you've been living."

He looked just as relieved as Cordelia when the drinks arrived. She wondered if he'd had any hesitations about this trip but had been steamrolled by her mother.

"We're not intruding, how could we be intruding, we're only here for one night," Louise said dismissively. "I want to hear more about . . ." She glanced around and lowered her voice. "Niall."

"You don't have to whisper, Mom," Cordelia said. "Everyone knows we're together."

"So . . . he *is* your boyfriend, then?" She bit her lip, her eyes bright.

Cordelia groaned. "Yes, he's my boyfriend."

Louise clapped her hands and beamed at Gary. "I knew it! I knew she'd find someone here. Gary, didn't I tell you? I said she's been so sad and so lonely, maybe this trip will do the trick."

"No you didn't," Cordelia said, exasperated. "That is the opposite of what you said."

"Louise, come on, don't embarrass the poor girl," Gary said as Cordelia downed half her wine in two large gulps and signaled Shauna for another glass.

Louise looked flustered. "I only want you to be happy, Cord."

"Do you?" Cordelia demanded. "Because if you really wanted me to be happy, you would have listened to me when I said don't come."

"I don't know why you're being so difficult," Louise said.

"*I'm* not being difficult!" Cordelia cried. All the anger and resentment and pain she had been holding onto came boiling up to the surface. "*You're* the one who's jetting around the world and acting like a teenager. *You're* the one who plows through every conversation like you know all the fucking answers. *You're* the one who's been trying to push a man on me like that will somehow solve all my problems. *You're* the one who acts like Dad never existed or mattered at all. I mean, Jesus, Mom, did you even love him?"

People were definitely staring now. Cordelia was vaguely aware of Niall and Róisín hovering by the kitchen doors. She didn't care. Her pulse was pounding in her ears.

All the blood drained from Louise's face. "How dare you," she said. "How dare you even ask me that."

Gary was very pointedly looking at the posters on the walls. Cordelia had had enough.

"Excuse me," she said and pushed away from the table, storming out the front door. The air was chilly and damp. Cordelia's face was hot, her eyes filling with tears that spilled over, dripping down her cheeks.

"Cordelia."

She turned around, and her mother was standing there with her arms crossed over her chest. "Do you honestly believe I never loved your father?"

Cordelia threw her hands up. "I don't know, you seemed to get over him pretty quickly."

"Excuse me?" Louise's nostrils flared. "Cordelia Marie, I've missed your father every single day since he died and I will miss him every single day until the day *I* die. He was the love of my life. Don't you ever question that again, do you hear me?"

"Then how come you started dating Gary so fast? And why do you keep pushing me to get a boyfriend like I'm a carton of milk about to expire?"

Louise's whole face changed and she suddenly seemed to wilt. "I know I've been a bit much, with all the dating apps and whatnot."

"You think?"

"But Cordie . . ." Louise's breath hitched and a tear glistened in her eye. "I thought I'd have so much more time with Chris. I thought we had forever, or as close to it as we could get. And then he was just *gone*. My entire life as I knew it vanished in an instant. Your father left for work on a normal Wednesday and never came home. And it hit me how little time we have. I only ever wanted you to know that kind of love too, and to have it for as long as you could. To me it seemed like the longer you waited, the less you would get. And maybe that sounds silly—but Toby doesn't need my help or advice and Nikki has her own mother to turn to. I thought I could help you. I wanted you to feel loved in the way that you deserve. But I don't seem to be able to do anything right, do I?"

Cordelia didn't know what to say. They hadn't ever really talked about the day her father died.

"And as far as Gary goes, well . . . it didn't feel fast. Not to me, anyway. I was so lonely, Cord. So achingly, terribly lonely. And do you really think you would have liked anyone I dated, whether now or ten years from now?" Cordelia pursed her lips but didn't answer. "No, you wouldn't have. And to be honest, I don't like being on my own. I like being in a partnership, part of a team. But maybe I should have considered that what works for me doesn't work for everyone. So . . ." She shrugged. "There. That's it. You can judge me all you want now. We'll cancel the hotel reservation and leave tonight. I really truly didn't mean to upset you. But don't you ever—*ever*—doubt the love I had for your father."

"Oh, Mom," Cordelia said. She wrapped her arms around Louise and breathed in the scent of Chanel No. 5 and cashmere. Cordelia remembered how her mother used to make instant hot cocoa and let Cordelia put as many marshmallows in as she could. She recalled the time when Louise had stood up to the parent of a girl who was bullying Cordelia in middle school. It was like ever since her father died, Cordelia had turned off all the good memories of her mother, choosing only to focus on the ways in which Cordelia felt Louise was letting her down. But she was the one who was always dodging her calls or cutting off a conversation. She'd been pushing her mother away instead of having an honest talk with her.

"I love you, Mom," Cordelia murmured into her mother's shoulder.

"I love you too, baby girl." Louise pulled away and smoothed Cordelia's hair back.

"I think I just wanted everything to go back to how it was before," Cordelia said. "Before Dad died. But that's not possible, is it. And I guess it felt like you didn't see me as a fully whole person because I wasn't in a relationship."

"Well, I did," Louise said firmly. "I've always seen you as one of the most marvelous gifts in my life. Look at all you've accomplished! How could any mother not be proud?"

"I wish you'd say that more," Cordelia said quietly.

Her mom paused. "I should. You're right."

Cordelia bit her lip. "I didn't think about you being lonely. I guess it's a little weird to think of your parents as, like, people with wants and needs."

Louise laughed. "I hate to shatter the illusion, but we are."

"I *am* happy for you," Cordelia said. "That Gary makes you happy. He's a nice guy. I know I've been a little . . . resentful."

"A little?" Louise said, raising an eyebrow.

"Okay, a lot. But I'll try to be better from now on."

Louise smiled. "Me too."

"Right, is all the fighting over and done with?" Róisín said, throwing open the door and standing with her hands on her hips. "Mothers and daughters need a good row every now and then, but there's drinks to be had and food to be eaten—I think poor Gary is about to pass out under the table if we don't get some good Irish stew in him. Cordie, Niall's joining us for dinner, I had Owen call in Rory McDermott to help out at the pub. Well, what are you waiting for, come in, there's a chill in the air and I don't like the look of those clouds."

Without waiting for a reply she turned around and stalked back inside.

"She's a bit pushy, isn't she?" Louise said. Cordelia burst out laughing.

"She is," she agreed, looping her arm through her mother's. "You two will get along just fine."

21

Niall and Cordelia walked back to the cottage in silence after dinner.

He held her hand, letting her work through everything that had transpired that evening. Louise was a whirl of frenetic energy, bouncing from one topic to the next with dizzying speed. Gary was like a rock, sure and steady and always there to gently nudge her back on course. They seemed like a good match. Niall wasn't about to say that out loud, though.

"Gary's pretty nice, I guess," Cordelia said as the cottage came into view.

"I was just thinking that," Niall said with a smile.

"Yeah, I know, I could tell you guys were hitting it off." She huffed and leaned her head against his shoulder. "Ugh, damn my mom. But also . . . I'm glad she came. We needed to clear the air. I get where she's coming from now. And I think she gets me too."

"I'm glad I got to meet her," Niall said. It was nice to feel like he was part of her life from America. He'd spoken with Liz on

FaceTime but that wasn't the same. He wished he could meet Toby too, and Nikki and the kids. His stomach gave an unpleasant lurch, another reminder of the approaching end to her time on Inishmore. What were they going to do about that? Neither of them had mentioned it, and Niall definitely didn't want to be the first one to bring it up. He'd been idly wondering if there were some way he could go to America with her, but visas were hard to get and expensive. Him following her seemed the best option—she had a life back in New York she needed to return to. Niall had nothing keeping him in Ireland.

"I'm glad you got to meet her too," Cordelia said, unlocking the door and stepping into the cottage. "I swear, she looked like the cat who ate the canary, grinning at us through the whole meal."

"She's happy you're happy," Niall said, ducking to kiss her neck and pulling her back against his chest.

"I'm more than happy," Cordelia said, leaning into his embrace as his hand slipped under her sweater to stroke her stomach. "I'm elated. I'm jubilant. I'm—"

"You're a bloody thesaurus, that's what you are," Niall said, his hand moving up her torso to skim the line of her bra.

She twisted in his arms. "Let's go to bed," she whispered.

The next day they went with Róisín in the cart to pick up Louise and Gary and do some sightseeing before their ferry left in the afternoon. Róisín took them to the Seven Churches, and then Dún Aengus, finally stopping by the Wormhole.

"Now," Róisín said as they clambered across the grassy cliff to stare down at the perfectly rectangular hole below, the ocean churning beneath it as the tide rose. "You'll hear this referred to sometimes as the Serpent's Lair, but its rightful name is Poll na bPéist. Looks man-made, doesn't it? But it's not. One hundred percent natural, it is."

They climbed down to get a closer look, and Niall stopped to offer Louise his hand. "Why thank you," Louise said. "You are quite a gentleman, Niall. I'm so very glad my daughter met you."

"I'm glad I met her too," Niall said.

"I haven't seen her this happy in a long time." Louise glanced over to where Róisín was pointing out something to Cordelia and Gary. "She and her father were very close."

"She's told me some about him," Niall said. "He seemed a good man."

"He was," Louise said, and she swallowed. "My Cordie has been alone for so long." She looked up at him with hazel eyes, the exact same shade as her daughter's. "Have you two talked about what happens when this summer ends?"

"Oh, ah, not yet, no," Niall said scratching the back of his neck. "But I promise you, Mrs. James, I'd gladly follow her wherever she goes."

Louise tightened her silk scarf and shot him a rueful smile. "Good," she said. "That's all I wanted to hear."

Róisín drove them back to the hotel and they said their goodbyes. Niall saw Cordelia talking quietly with her mother, looking a little exasperated, but then she hugged her tight.

That night, as Niall held a sleeping Cordelia in his arms, he thought about what he'd said to Louise, and the truth of his words seemed to shimmer in the darkness around him.

He would follow her anywhere. He just needed to sort out how.

The days slipped by, and before Niall knew it, the second week of August was staring him in the face.

The more he willed time to slow down, the faster it seemed to go. And still he and Cordelia did not talk about her leaving. It became an ugly pulsing thing between them that they both seemed determined to ignore, even as it grew larger and more urgent.

Finally, Niall realized that if they didn't talk now, the thirty-first of August would arrive before he had a chance to do anything. He told her to meet him at the Black Fort that afternoon, then hurried to prepare a picnic, bringing a tarp to put under the blanket in case the ground was wet. It was a fine day, the air warm, the sun shining, and he picked a spot well away from the fort—a little cove of ancient stones that offered protection from any prying eyes but was still on the cliffs of his very favorite spot in all of Inishmore.

She tramped up to him wearing that shirt dress from the first Sunday dinner they'd spent together, kicking off her rain boots and kneeling down to kiss him.

"What's all this?" she asked.

"I made us a little picnic," Niall said, opening the bottle of wine and pouring it into two plastic cups. He'd brought cheese and pickle sandwiches, a bag of salt and vinegar crisps, and some fresh cut fruit. For a while they ate and drank and chatted. Niall felt the need to say what he had come here for squirming in his chest and ready to burst free like that scene in *Alien*. But Cordelia seemed remarkably at ease, holding up her camera to take a quick shot of him with his mouth full.

"That one is not going on your Instagram," he said as he wiped his mouth with a napkin.

"Nope," she said, grinning. "This one is just for me." She sighed and gazed out over the ocean. "I'm going to miss this place."

And there it was—his opening. "Cordie," he said and she turned at the seriousness of his voice. "We need to talk about the end of the summer."

Her face blanched and he saw how much the subject had been gnawing at her too.

"Shh," she said, crawling over to him and pressing her lips against his. "Not now."

"Yes, now," Niall said, willing himself not to get distracted as she kissed the line of his jaw.

"I'm not wearing anything under this dress," she whispered.

"Oh god," he murmured, his cock stiffening. He flipped her over onto her back and she shrieked with delight. Her hair spilled across the blanket like a river of sunlight and she was looking at him from beneath heavy-lidded eyes, toying with the button on her dress before opening it to reveal a tantalizing glimpse of skin and the curve of her breast. Niall bent to kiss that curve, then he popped open the next button.

"We are going to have this discussion," he said, his lips brushing against her sternum.

"Mmhm," she murmured. He unbuttoned another button, sweeping the fabric aside to expose one breast to the sun.

"You'll be leaving soon," he said, kissing in a circle all around her nipple. "And we can't keep pretending like you aren't."

"Mmhm," she murmured again and he kissed the underside of her breast, where the skin was soft and tender. "You're killing me."

"We're having a talk," Niall said, unbuttoning the dress down to her belly button. He kissed down her stomach, pausing to suck at her ribs or bite softly against her side. She was squirming beneath him, her hands in his hair, her stomach muscles clenching. "Don't be trying to distract me."

"I would never. Do you have any ideas?"

Niall returned to her breasts to tweak one nipple between his thumb and forefinger, pinching it nice and hard and tight. "Ideas about what?" he said roughly in her ear, his fingers moving to the last two buttons on the dress. It fell open, revealing Cordelia, naked and perfect and bathed in afternoon sunshine. Niall's cock ached at the sight of her.

"Ideas about what we should do post summer," Cordelia said, arching her back. He slid down so that his face was at her stomach, kissing her hip and then the crease of her thigh, sinking low so that his nose grazed her sex. She was already wet, and it took all of Niall's focus not to take her right then and there.

He couldn't help flicking out his tongue to taste her briefly, though, and she gave that little coo of pleasure he'd grown to love so much.

"I don't want to stop seeing you," he murmured into her thigh.

"I don't want to stop seeing you eith—ohhh," she said because those words were all the encouragement he needed. Niall's tongue ran up the length of her pussy, sucking at her and making little circles as he drew nearer to her opening. Cordelia's legs spread wide and she gasped as he slipped a finger in, tracing the lines inside her, probing a little deeper each time. Fuck, she made him so hard, all her little moans, the sweet taste of her, the way her ass clenched when he hit a certain spot. He gripped it now, plunging his mouth into her, groaning against her clit, and she cried out and clutched his hair. He could feel her tighten, feel her wetness growing, and he stopped and moved back to kissing her inner thigh, his hands still cupping her ass, tilting her this way and that.

"Please," she moaned. "I want you inside me."

"Not yet," he growled, feeling her go like putty in his hands, moving back to take her other breast in his mouth, so pert and perfect, sucking at her nipple until he felt her fingernails rake over his back, and she bit him hard on the shoulder. "Hey!" he said, coming up to kiss her. "That hurt."

"You . . . are . . . killing me," Cordelia panted. Niall slid his hand down to finger her clit again. It was so swollen, so tender, and she gasped and clutched at him, her hips coming to buck against his hardness.

"You still want to be with me," he said, needing to make sure that in this one sense at least they were on the same page. "Even after the summer's over?"

"Yes," she moaned, rubbing against him, her fingers scrabbling at the base of his tee and tugging it up. Niall paused to yank it over his head and then he was back, her nipples grazing his chest, his lips on hers, his hands slipping beneath her to grab her ass again and press her against his hardness. "I want to be with you no matter what," she said. "No matter where, or how. I don't care. I love you, Niall."

As soon as she said it, he felt her freeze up. He pulled back and looked at her, her sweet delicate features pulled together in fear, her wide careful eyes.

"I love you too," he said, and she melted against him. Niall could wait no longer. This wasn't how he had planned for this to go, but it was so much better than he could have ever hoped. He loved Cordelia and she loved him. He needed to show her that.

He couldn't wait to take his jeans off, just unbuttoned them and slid his cock out. He hooked an arm around her, turning her on her side and hiking the fabric of her dress up and out of the way. Thank god he'd picked this hidden spot. But maybe he'd known he wouldn't be able to stop himself from taking her on this, their cliff.

Her ass pressed against him and he grunted, sliding his hand between her thighs again. She moaned and lifted her leg and when

Niall entered her, they both gasped. He slipped into her like they'd been made for each other, getting so utterly, blissfully fucking deep. He made lazy circles over her clit with one hand while he fucked her, his cock growing with each pump, his other hand moving to grip her breast.

"Harder," she moaned and he gladly obliged, sinking further into her warm wetness, feeling her muscles contracting around him, stroking his cock with their own tiny shudders. He yanked the collar of her dress down and sucked on her shoulder as he worked her, and her hand moved to grab his ass, pulling him closer, deeper, lifting her thigh so he could angle to that spot inside her and as he stroked her clit with sure quick movements, he felt it coming, felt the gathering within, tight and wet and ready. And he was ready too, his cock about to burst, and he pumped faster, unable to stop, unable to focus on anything but the slippery bead between his fingers and the velvet-softness around his cock. She was incredible, she was everything, and he loved her, he loved her more purely and deeply than he'd ever loved anyone before, and he whispered it in her ear over and over as they climaxed together, both of them crying out in unison. Cordelia made a wild shriek and he felt it against his cock, against his fingers, against his chest, felt her break free and shudder as she came over and over, and he spent himself inside her.

They lay together, panting, their bodies slick with sweat. Niall didn't know if he'd ever be able to move again. His heart was pounding against her back and she trembled in his arms. She lifted his hand that was still pressed against her sex, took it to her mouth, and kissed his fingers.

"I love you," she said quietly.

"I love you," he whispered back.

They lay together, the warm August air caressing their skin.

"What do we do?" she said. "I mean, how do we . . ."

"Don't rightly know. We could get married, I s'pose." As soon as he said it she stiffened. "Sorry, I didn't—"

"Are you serious?" she asked, twisting in his arms so that their noses were almost touching. Niall hadn't really been thinking when he'd said it, but now he was, and while the idea seemed crazy, it was also . . . appealing. Like the answer he'd been looking for but just couldn't see.

"I mean . . . yes?" he said. "I know it's nuts but . . . we could. Then I could come back to New York with you."

She blinked. "You want to come to New York with me?"

He chuckled. "Did you not hear me say I don't want to stop seeing you?"

"Yes, but I thought . . ." She frowned. "I thought you would want us to stay in Ireland. If you wanted us at all."

Niall leaned in to kiss her. "You are daft sometimes, you know that? What would I be staying in Ireland for? You've got a whole life in New York. I thought maybe you'd not mind if I was part of it."

"Mind?" Cordelia said, sitting up so fast it was alarming. "Niall, are you serious?"

"You've got to stop asking me that," Niall said, laughing and slipping his jeans back up over his hips before propping himself up on his elbow.

"But . . . but what would you do in New York?"

"I don't know. Find a job. I've heard there are a fair few restaurants and pubs out there, you know." He leaned down to kiss the top of her knee. "Cordelia, I want to be a part of your life. I don't want to be anywhere you're not."

She clapped her hands over her mouth and tears filled her eyes.

"Here," Niall said, reaching down to pluck a long, tough blade of grass. He wound it into a circle and tied it together, then slipped it onto her ring finger where it hung loosely. His heart thrummed with excitement, his throat tight, his own eyes prickling with tears. "Cordelia Marie James, will you marry me?"

Cordelia stared at the circle of grass. "Can I have a second?" she asked quietly. "Just the night, to think this over. I want to be with you," she said, leaning down to kiss him. "But this is, I mean . . . marriage is a big deal, Niall."

"I am aware," he said teasingly. "Already having been engaged once before."

"And we've only been together like, a month."

"Feels longer to me, I guess," Niall said, embarrassed. He stood and grabbed his shirt, yanking it on. He was probably being stupid. She was right, this was way too fast.

"Wait, stop," she said, buttoning her dress and standing up so she could press her cheek against his chest. "I'm not saying no. And it does feel like we've been together for—well, a lot longer than a month. And I want you to come to New York with me. I do. One hundred and ten percent. I just need a second to process. Is that okay?"

Niall knew he was being foolish. Just because he was ready to jump in with both feet didn't mean she was. And she was glad of him coming to New York with her—that was huge. He could spend the night coming up with other ways to get there if he had to. He would do anything as long as it meant he could be with Cordelia. This wasn't like any relationship he'd had before—never had he felt so comfortable, so much himself. Never had he shone love on someone and felt it reflected back to him in equal fashion. When he was with Cordelia, he was home. He loved everything about her, from her passion for her art to her wisecracks to her sweet blushes of embarrassment.

If there was one thing of which he was certain, it was that he didn't want to live a life without Cordelia James in it. So if she needed a night to think, well, he would gladly give it to her. One night was nothing in the grand scheme of forever.

He kissed the top of her head and held her close. "Of course," he said. "I understand completely."

He was distracted during his shift that evening.

"Where's Cordelia tonight?" Colin asked him during a break. Niall pulled him aside and told him what had happened on the cliffs.

"You *proposed*?" Colin yelped gleefully.

"Keep your voice down," Niall said. He didn't need that news getting around Kilronan. "She hasn't said yes yet."

"But she will," Colin said, a merry gleam in his eye. "How could she not? Feck, should've thought of that meself instead of entering that lottery they have."

Niall's eyebrows rose. "I didn't know you entered the US green card lottery," he said.

Colin shrugged. "It was before your mam asked me to come here," he said. "Anyway, haven't heard anything and don't expect to. Your way is better."

"You think?" Niall said. "You don't think it's too fast?"

Colin clapped a hand on his shoulder. "I hate to break it to you, mate, but commitment has never been your problem."

"What's my problem?"

"Choosing the right bloody girl. And Cordelia is the right bloody girl."

A bubble of happiness swelled in Niall's chest. "She is."

"Come here, you," Colin said, wrapping him up in a bear hug. "I'm so happy for you, Nie. Truly."

"Don't say that until tomorrow," Niall warned him.

Colin pretended to lock his lips and throw away the key.

The next morning, Niall was trying to read *The Irish Times* over his coffee but couldn't stop glancing at his phone. Would Cordelia text him? Would she just come by? It was the first night he'd spent alone since Pátrún. He hadn't liked it—it made him even more certain of his decision. Of course he would marry Cordelia. He never wanted to spend another night without her.

There was a knock on the door and Niall jumped. *Here we go,* he thought. He couldn't wait to see Cordelia's face again, no matter what choice she made.

"You're up early," he said as he opened the door. His heart stuttered to a halt.

The woman standing before him wore a Burberry trench and Prada boots, her sleek chestnut bob exactly the same as he remembered.

"Hello, Niall," Deirdre said. "Can I come in?"

22

For a second, Niall couldn't move, or think, or breathe.

"What the *fuck* are you doing here?" he demanded when he finally found his voice.

"I need to talk to you about something," Deirdre said.

"No, you don't," Niall said. "There's absolutely nothing in the world that you could have to say to me that I'd want to hear."

Deirdre's eyes went wide under the thick line of her fringe. "I deserve that," she said. "But please, Niall—"

"If you came here to apologize, Deirdre, you're about three months too late."

"I didn't," Deirdre insisted. "I mean, I did, but that's not . . . there's something I need to talk to you about. I was hoping you'd hear me out."

"Well, you hoped wrong," Niall said, moving to close the door. Deirdre stepped forward and put her hand out to stop him.

"Five minutes," she said. "That's all I ask. Five minutes of your time to let me explain. If you don't like what I have to say, you'll never hear from me again. I promise."

Niall gritted his teeth. He knew how stubborn Deirdre could be, and he saw the distinct set in her jaw that told him she would wait on his stoop all day, and he couldn't have that. Better to get this over with and send her on her way before Cordelia came round.

"Five minutes," he said.

Cordelia was propped up against her pillows, the ring of grass perched on her knee.

She'd hardly slept that night. And it wasn't just the hamster wheel of thoughts circling around in her head. She hated sleeping without Niall next to her. Her bed had felt huge and lonely. She'd lain awake, staring at the ceiling, her mind turning over his proposal again and again and again.

She loved Niall, she was certain of that. But marriage? That was something other people did. People who had been together for years. It wasn't something you decided at the end of a summer so you could stay with the man you loved.

Was it?

She had resisted calling Liz for help. She wondered a little what her mother might say. But in the end, it would be her decision to make and she didn't know if she needed any other cooks in this particular kitchen. It seemed insane to spend the summer on an island and come home engaged. She could only imagine what she herself would say if she heard about someone else doing it. *That's crazy. It will never work. Too soon. Just wait till they really get to know each other. Divorced in six months.* But if the snide remarks of other people were the only thing preventing her from saying yes . . . well, that didn't seem like a very good reason, either.

But was Cordelia ready to jump into a marriage with Niall? She didn't know anything about being married. She barely knew anything about relationships. But being with Niall was so effortless. Like falling into a soft bed at the end of a long day. He was what she thought about each morning when she woke up. He was what she looked forward to every day. He was her safe harbor. How could she give that up?

But what if it doesn't work out? What if you get all the way to New York and he leaves you? Or you realize you don't like him all that much. Or he cheats on you. Or you cheat on him. Or you become totally incompatible. Or he starts to drive you crazy leaving all his dishes in the sink.

But the more she considered those options logically, the less likely they seemed. Sure, they could grow apart and go their separate ways. But that happened with couples who had been together far longer than she and Niall—that could happen to any relationship. It didn't seem like a good reason *not* to try. As for the cheating, she would never, ever do that to Niall. And she couldn't imagine, what with his past, him ever doing that to her. As far as leaving dishes in the sink, that actually sounded more like something she would do.

Of course, he would have quirks that would bother her, and she him. Wasn't that the nature of being close with someone? And what was the alternative? Maybe try to do long distance, but honestly, she didn't think she could handle that. It might be fine at first, him coming to visit or her going back to Ireland, but she knew that she was the kind of person who needed someone there. Long distance was not going to work for her. And she didn't think it would work for Niall either.

So she had two options, as she saw it. She could let fear, or the rules of society, or other people's opinions dictate what she did with her life. Or she could jump into the deep end with him. She could say yes to his proposal. They could probably get married here on Inishmore—it might be nice, she thought. Alison could stand for her and Colin for Niall. Niall's parents would be here. And they could do another celebration in New York. Not a big white wedding, god no, but a small party for friends and family. Her mom would be thrilled. She could see it now, Miles and Grace all dressed up, Toby and Niall bonding over a couple of beers.

And then Niall making himself at home in her little Morningside Heights apartment. Cozy Sunday mornings in bed with coffee and the *New York Times* crossword. Watching the leaves change in Morningside Park. Pasta at Il Cantante, her favorite Italian place down the street. Maybe Niall could join one of the soccer leagues in Central Park. He could find a job at an Irish pub easily enough. She could take that job Liz had offered. They would have a life together, one Cordelia could suddenly see so clearly and wanted so badly she could taste it, like warm chocolate on the back of her tongue.

She realized with a startling certainty that she wasn't afraid of being with Niall for the rest of her life—no, that sounded like absolute heaven, more dream than reality. And that's what marriage was. A promise for life.

She picked up the grass ring and slipped it onto her finger. A shiver ran deep through her belly.

Did I just get engaged?

Wait, she had to tell Niall yes first. *Yes.* Another shiver. She leaped out of bed, tossing on the closest clothes she could find. The morning was misty and cool and she walked the long drive to the white house with her heart pounding a painful beat. Her spine was buzzing as she reached the door and she raised her hand to knock when she heard the voices, very clearly, like they were standing just on the opposite side.

She froze. Quite literally—it felt like her muscles turned to ice, her blood frosting over in her veins. Because there was a woman speaking to Niall and somehow, through pure instinct, Cordelia knew exactly who it was, though she'd never heard the woman's voice before in her life.

"Thank you," the woman said.

"Don't thank me, Deirdre," Niall said brusquely. "You've got your five minutes. What do you want?"

Cordelia stood on his stoop, listening hard.

Niall's arms were crossed so tight over his chest he thought he might be cutting off his circulation.

Deirdre's pink-painted mouth turned down and her face puckered. Niall knew that look.

"I fucked up, okay?" Deirdre said. Well, she was acknowledging that, at least. "I was a complete and utter arse. I'm so, so sorry. Truly, Niall. I don't think I'll ever forgive myself for what I did to you."

"Thought you said you didn't come here to apologize," Niall said. "Does Patrick know you're here?"

"Patrick and I aren't together anymore," Deirdre said tightly. She sighed and threw out her hands. "He was a fecking nightmare, honestly. Controlling and wasteful and . . . well, you probably don't need to hear about that."

"Nope."

"I bought him out and started with a new partner. The pub's doing really well. You'd be so proud. We're booked clean through the holiday season. And my new partner, well . . . he's the reason I came here to talk to you."

"Are you fucking him too?" Niall asked.

Deirdre pursed her lips. "No," she said. "He's Ritchie Malcolm."

"What?" Niall yelped, the name temporarily yanking him from his anger. "Ritchie—like, *the* Ritchie Malcolm?" Ritchie Malcolm was one of the most famous restaurateurs in the UK. He'd opened restaurants all over the world. And he was now an investor in Niall's pub?

It's not your pub, he reminded himself.

"The very same," Deirdre said, looking both pleased and relieved. Niall pulled himself together. Deirdre did not get to come to Inishmore and wave Ritchie Malcolm in his face like Niall should be cheering for her. "And here's the thing, Nie—"

"Don't call me that," Niall snapped.

Deirdre had the decency to look ashamed. "Right, sorry." She took a breath. "He wants to open a second location. For the pub. He's already got the perfect property scouted in London. The floor plan is basically identical and he's got all these teams on call to start the renovations."

"A second location?" Niall asked, dazed. "In London? Are—are you serious?"

"Yes," Deirdre said. "It's a grand space. And Ritchie is keen to get it opened. He's willing to do a rush job to get it running by December, in time for the holidays. But there's one catch." She worried at her lower lip. "He wants you to be involved, Niall. It was the food that got his attention. He wants to add a couple of new things to the menu, you know, appeal to the London crowd.

And he won't do it without you. He wants you to be the chef. Making all the calls in the kitchen. It's what you've always dreamed of—"

"Don't talk to me about my dreams, Deirdre," Niall snapped.

Deirdre's expression turned mournful. "I know," she said. "I know how much I hurt you."

"Do you?"

She didn't seem to know what to say to that. "I can't change the past," she said quietly. "But this is too good an opportunity to pass up, Niall, and you know it. Head chef in your own kitchen, serving your own food, in London! You'll get the experience and the credibility that you deserve. Because you *do* deserve it. And I'm so sorry I fucked all that up for you. I know the Fallen Star was your baby. I want to make things right."

"And are you part of this?" Niall asked acidly. "Will you be in London organizing the opening?"

"I will," Deirdre said. "But I'm only trying to make up for the wrongs I've done. I'll not be bothering you if you don't want me to—I'll stay out of your way completely. Think about it! Working with *Ritchie fecking Malcolm*. And he's a huge fan of your food, Niall. That's what got him interested in the first place—he read about the pub in the *Times* and came in for dinner one night at the bar. Patrick and I were already having, erm, issues."

She coughed and rubbed the back of her neck, but Niall didn't give two shits about what had happened with her and Patrick. All he could think was that Ritchie Malcolm had eaten his food. And Niall hadn't even gotten to be there.

"Anyway, we hit it off and he immediately thought of a property he had in Camden, how perfect it would be for a second location, how great the menu would translate. We've been hammering out the deal all summer and there's just one final detail left to sort out."

"Me," Niall said.

"You," Deirdre agreed.

They stood in his front hall in silence for a moment.

"You can't show up here and spring this on me, Deirdre," Niall said. "How did you even find me, anyway? How did you know I was in Inishmore at all?"

She blushed. "Someone showed me this Instagram photographer's work. She's got tons of photos of you."

Niall scraped a hand over his face. To think Cordelia had unknowingly brought Deirdre back into his orbit.

Deirdre cleared her throat delicately. "Is she your girlfriend?"

"I'm not talking to you about her," Niall said.

She swallowed hard. "That's perfectly fair. Of course. Right. Look, here's all the information, your salary and the shares you'd own, the contract, some sketches of the place, a potential wine list . . ." She reached into her bag and took out a huge folder. "Think it over. But Ritchie needs to know soon, if we're to greenlight this."

"How soon?" Niall asked.

"Within the next two days. If you agree, we'll need you in London immediately."

"Fucking Christ," Niall said, snatching the folder. "No pressure, eh? No rush. You couldn't have fucking called?"

"Would you have answered?"

"No," he admitted.

"You deserve this, Niall," Deirdre said. "I'll never forgive myself for what I did to you. I'm only trying to make amends—trying to make things right. Or at least do what I can." Her eyes filled with tears. "I really am sorry."

"I don't want your apologies, Deirdre."

She ducked her head. "Fair enough. I'll leave now. You can reach me at Kilmurvey House. I tried to keep well clear of Kilronan—if Róisín finds out I'm here she'll probably throw me off a cliff." She chuckled weakly, but Niall's mouth was set in a hard line.

"You aren't being fair," he said. "You do realize that, don't you? Coming back with no warning, offering me . . ." He waved the folder. "All this. I've got a life, you know. One that you are now once again blowing up. You offered me my dream before, remember? And look how that turned out."

She gave him a brittle smile. "Well, there's no danger of me sleeping with Ritchie—he's extremely gay."

"I don't fucking care who you sleep with. That's not what I mean."

She blinked. "Right."

Niall rubbed his temple with the heel of his hand. "I need time to think about this."

"Of course." She turned and opened the door, and Niall's heart rammed itself into his throat as he saw Cordelia standing on his doorstep.

Deirdre was the kind of woman who looked like she'd stepped right out of an advertisement in *Vogue.*

Maybe if the situation had been different, Cordelia might have felt embarrassed by her faded jeans and tank top with the words *It's Guac O'Clock* printed across the chest. But this was the woman who had broken Niall's heart. Cordelia pulled herself together and called on her inner New Yorker.

"Hi," she said tartly, staring Deirdre directly in her dark brown eyes. "I'm Cordelia. Niall's girlfriend."

Deirdre's perfectly threaded eyebrows flew up her forehead. "Oh, hi!" she gushed in a voice too bright. "I'm Deirdre. It's nice to meet you."

Is it, though? Cordelia thought as Niall said, "Deirdre was just leaving."

"Right," Deirdre said, looking back and forth between Cordelia and Niall like she could somehow size up the depth of their connection. Then she walked past Cordelia, leaving the scent of jasmine in her wake.

"Sorry," Niall said, stepping back so Cordelia could stumble her way inside. "I didn't know she was . . . she came to talk to me about . . ."

"I know," Cordelia said. "I heard."

Niall blinked. "You did?"

He had a thick folder in his hands, full of all the things Deirdre had mentioned. Cordelia thought about the words *contract* and *salary* and *shares.* She didn't know much about the restaurant industry, but she could tell by Niall's reaction that this was a huge deal.

"So she wants you to open another restaurant?" Cordelia asked.

"Yeah," Niall said. "It would be the Fallen Star but in London."

"And this Ritchie guy won't do it without you?"

"So it would seem." He shook his head. "I can't. It's crazy. Plus it involves being around Deirdre, which, no fecking thanks. Come here," he said, wrapping his arm around her waist and pulling her in for a kiss. "I'm sorry about this. I was shocked to see her here."

Cordelia kissed him back mechanically, her mind racing. "What do you mean, you can't?" she said, extracting herself from his arms. "It sounds like an incredible opportunity."

"Well, of course, I mean Ritchie Malcolm is one of my heroes. He's a virtual god in the restaurant world. But Cordie, I can't go skipping off to London. How would that even work?"

"I don't know, but I bet you could figure it out," Cordelia said. "Isn't this what you've always wanted? You'd have your pub back but even better. Because you'd be working with your literal *hero*." What was he not getting about this? "Your own restaurant in London, Niall! I mean, my god. How can you say no to that?"

"Come with me then," Niall said, stepping toward her. Cordelia probably should have seen that coming. And for one fleeting moment, she tried to imagine it. But the pictures were hazy and incomplete, nothing like the crystal-clear future she had seen for them in New York.

Because there was no future for Cordelia in London.

"I can't," she said. "I have to go back to the States when my visa ends. You know that."

"You could get another tourist visa. Come for another three months."

"I need to get a job when I get back to the city, Niall," Cordelia said. "And what would I do in London anyway? I can't work there."

"You could keep doing your Instagram thing."

"That isn't a job."

"I'll support you."

"I can't let you do that." She saw he was going to argue so she added, "I don't *want* you to do that. I need to be able to take care of myself."

"What about us, though?" Niall asked. "What about . . . what we talked about yesterday at the Black Fort?" His face turned apprehensive.

And Cordelia saw, with a sudden, vicious clarity, that she had to lie to him. She had to tell him no. Because she couldn't let him come to New York and work in some random pub when he had this incredible chance to make a name for himself, to run his own place, his own kitchen. She wasn't about to let him give up on his dreams because of her. And she couldn't give up her independence to follow him to London, unable to earn money of her own or stay long term. The thought of rejecting him was a hot stabbing pain straight through her breastbone. But the thought of him missing out on this opportunity was unacceptable.

She clenched her jaw and forced her face to stay neutral.

"I can't marry you, Niall."

She saw pain flicker across his face and hated herself for it. "Why not?"

"It's too soon. It's too much. Marriage? Really? We barely know each other."

"But . . ." Niall blinked. "I thought you felt the same as me."

Her stomach quivered and she strained to keep her voice steady. "You can't miss out on this kind of opportunity over a summer fling. That would be insane."

Niall looked like she'd slapped him. "Fling?"

"Look, we've had fun, right? Let's just leave it at that." She felt the tears start to form and blinked them back. She had to get through this. She couldn't break down or he'd know. He'd see through her. And he wouldn't leave. If there was one thing that became achingly clear in this moment, it was that she loved Niall too much to let him give this up for her. "You should go to London."

Niall's eyes filled with tears and Cordelia almost broke. "What are you saying, Cord?" he said quietly.

Cordelia took a deep breath.

"I don't *want* you to come to New York with me, okay? We've had a fun summer and all, but our lives are just too different. You've got your career to pursue and I'm finally getting back in a groove with my photography."

"I don't care that our lives have been different," Niall insisted. "I wouldn't care if we came from different planets. You brought me back from the abyss, Cord. You've given me a life worth living. You think I wouldn't give up anything, *anything* at all to be with you?"

The pain at hurting him was a violent, slavering monster inside her. She knew what she had to do even as the monster tore at her ribs and shredded her heart.

"You say that now but you don't really know, Niall. You could end up resenting me. Things could get messy. It's not worth the risk. I've already got a life in New York and you aren't a part of it. You wouldn't . . . fit." Her voice almost cracked, the lie too vicious to be borne.

"You don't want me," he said.

She steeled herself for the final blow.

"No. I don't want to marry you. So there's nothing stopping you from London. Go. *Go,* Niall." She chanced a look in his eyes and they were the softest, saddest blue she'd ever seen. She needed to get out of this house, away from him, before she crumbled into a pile at his feet and begged him to ignore everything she'd said. She caught one last glimpse of his stricken face before she turned and fled back up the road to the cottage.

Róisín found her there an hour later, sobbing into her pillow.

"My god!" she exclaimed. "Cordie, love, what's happened?"

Cordelia crawled across her bed and laid her head in Róisín's lap, the grass ring clutched in one hand as she told the whole story from Niall's proposal to Deirdre's arrival.

"You can't ever tell him I was going to say yes," Cordelia said, sitting up suddenly. "He can't know. Because then he'll say no to Deirdre's offer and he needs to go to London, Róisín. He deserves this. He—"

"Quiet yourself, girl, I won't be saying anything." Róisín studied her with dark, discerning eyes. "You really do love him."

"I do," Cordelia said. The sobs took her again, and she cried into Róisín's lap, her heart cracked wide open, its edges so sharp and jagged it hurt to breathe. Everything before her was blank, an endless march of time, the world drained of color because there would be no more Niall in it. She hadn't understood how vibrantly he'd painted her life until now.

Her phone pinged and she ignored it. But then Róisín shifted on the bed and said, "Who's Kate Sarkesian?"

Cordelia sat up. "What?"

Róisín held up the phone. "You've got an email from her."

Cordelia grabbed the phone, her head spinning. "She was the editor for my coffee table book," she said, moving to open the email. "I haven't heard from her in years. I wonder what she . . ."

Her voice trailed off as she read.

Hi Cordelia,

I hope this email finds you well. I wanted to reach out because I've been following your Instagram and I am just loving all the pictures and stories you've been posting! In fact, my team and I love them so much, we'd like to do another book with you—one that will feature your work from Inishmore. I'm not sure when you're back Stateside but I'd love to set up a time to meet and go over . . .

The rest of the email blurred as more tears filled her eyes. Another book. They wanted another book. If she'd received this email yesterday, Cordelia would have been running down the road to tell Niall. As it was she could only sit and stare at the tiny letters on the screen, her limbs drained and lifeless.

"She wants me to do another book," Cordelia said thickly. "With the pictures I took here."

"Well," Róisín said, one wizened hand coming to grip Cordelia's shoulder. "That's grand, isn't it?"

Cordelia nodded and more tears spilled down her cheeks. Róisín wiped them away gently. "What a day this has been for you, girlie," she said. "I'll make some tea."

Cordelia sank back onto her pillow as Róisín headed into the kitchen. Her world had turned completely upside down, and Cordelia didn't think it would ever feel righted again.

23

"She didn't," Colin said for the fifth time.

"She did," Niall said wearily. He stared at the empty fireplace, a tumbler of whiskey in his hand, his ass in the same spot on the couch it had been for hours, ever since Cordelia had broken up with him and left. Colin had found him there, sitting in agonized silence. Not crying, no, that would come later. Niall was just . . . blank.

"It doesn't make sense," Colin said. "You two are meant for each other! I don't believe her, Niall. There's got to be some other—she can't—I mean, you guys are—fucking Christ, does Deirdre have to ruin everything?"

"Cordelia's right, though," Niall said thickly. "I've got to go to London."

"Sure, yes, I agree with you on that despite Deirdre the fucking trollop being part of the deal. But Cordie could go with you!"

"She doesn't want to, Colin, you dumb bastard, haven't you been listening? *She doesn't want me.*" Niall sprang to his feet so suddenly Colin leaned back in his chair. Niall slammed his whiskey down on the side table and started pacing around the room. "I never should have proposed. Scared her right off, I did. Great fucking job, Niall. Am I some sort of cosmic joke? Is this the universe's way of letting me know I should throw in the towel on love? I *love* Cordelia, Colin. I love her so much it hurts. And I went and fucking lost her, all because I had to open my damn mouth and propose. Who proposes after a month? Nobody. Of course she said no."

"But it felt like the two o' you had been together for ages," Colin insisted. "I never seen you like that with anyone—not even Deirdre. Christ, if I'd thought it was a crazy idea I would've told you so."

Niall slumped back down onto the couch. "Leave me be," he mumbled. "I can't talk about this anymore."

"You sure?"

"Go, Colin!"

"All right," Colin said and headed down the hall to the stairs. Niall heard the light tread of his footsteps and then his door closed.

And at last, Niall allowed himself to cry.

There was one thing he had to do before he agreed to Deirdre's deal.

Niall left the house early the next day, unable to help glancing up toward the cottage. There was no sign of Cordelia. He trudged to the yellow farmhouse, and the look on his mother's face when she opened the door said it all.

"Who told you," he asked bluntly.

"Róisín might have stopped by last night." Fiona gathered her son up into a hug. "Oh, my sweet boy. I don't understand. What happened? You two were so perfect together."

"Where's Da?" Niall said. He didn't want to talk about Cordelia. He couldn't. He wanted to close that door in his heart and lock it up tight, never to be opened again.

"He's in the kitchen," Fiona said. Niall stalked past her and into the kitchen where his father was frying up some eggs and rashers.

"Róisín told you, then," Niall said without preamble. His father whirled around.

"Christ, you gave me a fright," he said. Then he took in his son's face. "Aye. She told us. Not much in the way of details, though."

Niall's throat tightened, the ghost of the iron spring clenching in his chest. "Did she tell you about Deirdre?"

"She said she made you an offer. Something about London?"

Niall sank down at his kitchen table and the whole story spilled out. He'd never been one for heart-to-hearts with his da before, but he needed his father's perspective. Part of him wanted to tell Deirdre to go fuck herself and march straight back up to the cottage and beg Cordelia to take him back.

"What do I do, Da?" he asked bleakly. "I don't want to work with Deirdre, but it's Ritchie Malcolm. I mean—"

"You've got to go, son," Owen replied. He placed a plate in front of Niall and sat at the table with him. Two fried eggs stared up at Niall like yellow eyes. "Cordelia is right about that. You've got to go to London."

Niall stared at his plate. How different this should have been, telling his father he was off to work with Ritchie Malcom. He should be jumping for joy.

"I hate to see you like this," Owen said. "'Specially when you're finally getting the chance you deserve. I don't rightly know why Cordelia said no to ya—I expect that's her business and not mine. Though I will say I wish she hadn't. I wish she'd said yes and gone there with you, like you wanted. But it is what it is. This is your moment, Niall."

"What about O'Connor's?" Niall said.

"O'Connor's will be fine," Owen said. "Your mam only said we needed help to get you home. As I'm sure you guessed. But there will always be a place for you here, Niall. No matter what. And, well . . ." His face turned pink and he shifted in his chair. "I'm no good at giving relationship advice, but it seems to me that if two people are meant to be together, they'll find their way back to one another. You aren't dead, either of you."

"That was pretty optimistic until the end there, Da."

Owen chuckled. "I told you, I'm no good at relationship advice. But for now, you've got to do what's best for yourself. Even if it means working with that floozie, as your mam would say."

Niall's head sank into his hands. "Yeah," he said. "You're right."

"Well, shite, better note the time and date," Owen said. "Never thought I'd be hearing those words coming out o' your mouth."

Niall gave him a grim smile. "May as well go get this over with," he said, rising up from the table. Now that the decision was made, he wanted to get out of Inishmore as fast as he could. He wanted to move, move, move so that he wouldn't have a spare moment to think. Thinking was like quicksand—it would pull him down and drown him.

He borrowed his mother's car and drove to Kilmurvey House. Deirdre was in the front lounge. She broke into a wide smile when she saw him, then tempered it the slightest bit.

"Good morning," she said. "Fancy a coffee?"

"I'm in," Niall said curtly. "When do we leave?"

Cordelia heard from Alison that Niall had left the following day.

Alison had tried talking to her about what happened, but Cordelia couldn't. She could no longer say the words out loud. She'd sent a cursory text to her mom and barely managed to get the whole story out to Liz over FaceTime.

Over the next two weeks, she felt like she'd been packed up in cotton. Her eyes itched all the time. Her chest was too tight. She couldn't sleep.

She had not been prepared for this constant, aching loss. It was like half of her insides had been scooped out. Not even the promise of a new coffee table book, a second chance at her career, could soothe the jagged pain she felt with every stilted beat of her heart. She couldn't find comfort in anything anymore, not photography, or her true crime books, or riding around in the cart with Róisín.

Niall was gone.

She stopped going into O'Connor's. She couldn't face the place without Niall in it—and Owen probably hated her for what she'd done. She went back to eating sad pasta alone in her front room. Once she'd tried to make an omelet and the memories it triggered were so brutal, she ended up sobbing on her kitchen floor. A hundred times a day, she would pick up her phone to text Niall. Or check to see if he had contacted her. But he never had and she never did.

She knew she would never hear from him again. She'd hurt him too badly. Why would he even *want* to talk to her? She'd eviscerated him and shoved him away. She hoped he was having fun in London. Not with Deirdre—no, she was far too selfish to hope for that. But she hoped things were going well. Róisín offered small morsels of information that Cordelia hoarded greedily.

Niall had arrived in London.

Niall had found a flat in Camden.

Niall had met with Ritchie Malcolm.

Niall was working on new menu items.

That was it. Four little details. Cordelia spun wild fantasies of him coming back to Inishmore, showing up at the cottage, declaring their love more important than anything else in this world. But he'd already declared that, and *she* had pushed *him* away! There was no one to blame for this but herself. She deserved every ounce of misery.

The night before she was set to leave Inishmore and head back to New York, Alison and Róisín came over. Alison made a chicken curry, the small kitchen filling with the smell of cumin and coriander—it only made Cordelia feel miserable. The scents and sounds of cooking were like their own special pain. Róisín pressed a glass of whiskey into Cordelia's hand.

"Now," she said. "I'd like to give a toast. When you first showed up here, girlie, I don't think it comes as a surprise to anyone that I wasn't too keen on the idea."

"Weren't you, Gran?" Alison said. "Gosh, what a shocker."

Róisín grinned at her. "But I've got to say, Cordie, it's been a mighty pleasure getting to know you this summer. And I do hope you'll not be a stranger. The whole island would love to have you back."

Cordelia wasn't so sure about that—she imagined Niall's parents weren't her biggest fans. She hadn't seen either of them since Niall had left.

"That we would," Alison said, raising her own tumbler. "And please do keep in touch, Cord."

"I will," Cordelia said, feeling the emptiness of the promise. "You've both been so wonderful." Her throat squeezed up. "I'll miss you guys."

Cordelia felt this horrible tug-of-war going on inside her. On the one hand, she couldn't wait to get off of Inishmore, to leave behind all the memories of Niall. On the other hand, those memories were all she had. She loved this island, more than she had ever thought she would way back when she arrived in June. So much had changed so quickly. Cordelia wanted to run to her bed and hide under the covers until her life righted itself again.

But life doesn't right itself on its own. She was the master of her own fate, just like Niall was of his. She had to move forward, as much as she didn't want to.

A few people came to see her off on the ferry the next day—Darragh and Brogan, Aoife and Fergus. And, to Cordelia's great surprise, Fiona and Colin and Pocket. Fiona didn't look the least bit angry with her—instead, she pulled Cordelia in for a hug.

"I packed you some food for the train," she said, pressing a warm paper bag into Cordelia's hand.

"Fiona, I—" Cordelia began, but Fiona shushed her.

"You take care of yourself now," she said, tears in her eyes.

"Don't be a stranger," Colin said, giving her one of his big bear hugs.

"I won't," Cordelia said.

Pocket nuzzled at her hand and she scratched the dog behind her ears.

"You've all been such wonderful friends," she said. "Thank you so much for—well, for treating me like family."

She got on the ferry and nearly broke down again, the memory of her first meeting with Niall all those months ago suddenly as clear and sharp as if it were yesterday. She stowed her bag and sank into her seat, the rain picking up just as the ferry pulled away from the harbor. Pocket ran down the pier, barking like mad. Cordelia pressed her hand to the window.

"Goodbye," she whispered.

The day was long and arduous. Ferry to bus, bus to train, train to plane. She barely noticed where she was or what was going on around her. She kept taking the grass ring out of her pocket and slipping it onto her finger. It represented a whole life she was meant to have—she couldn't bring herself to throw it away.

When her flight landed at JFK, Cordelia felt like she had traveled from another world, a different century, a new dimension. She waited among the crowds at the baggage claim, flinching every time she heard an Irish accent. She was so utterly wrapped up in her own misery that she didn't notice the balloons at first—or the sign with her name on it.

Standing by the exit was her family: her mom and Gary, Toby and Nikki, Miles and Grace holding up a homemade sign that read *Welcome Home Auntie Cordie!!* Liz was there too, running up to her before even the kids had a chance to move, throwing her arms around Cordelia.

"Oh my fucking god I missed you so much," she said in Cordelia's ear as Miles flung himself around Cordelia's legs.

"Auntie Cordie!" he cried. "Did you bring us any presents?"

"Miles," Nikki admonished, coming up to hug Cordelia after Liz finally released her. "Don't be rude."

"Of course I did," Cordelia said, smiling for the first time in so long she thought her cheeks might crack. "I got Aran sweaters for everybody. But you guys . . . I didn't know you'd all be here!"

"We had to give you a proper welcome back, didn't we?" Louise said, descending on her daughter and kissing her cheek. "How are you?"

Cordelia shrugged. "I don't know, Mom. Can we talk about it another time?"

"Of course, darling, of course."

"The kids worked all day on the sign," Toby said, grinning and squeezing her around the shoulders. "It's good to have you back, sis."

Cordelia's shattered heart thumped out a painful beat. She felt so much love fill her up, but there was sadness there too, because one kind of love was missing. And Cordelia didn't think she'd ever find it again.

"We thought we'd give you and Liz a lift back to Harlem," Gary said.

"Back to . . ." Cordelia looked at Liz. "Are you coming home with me?"

Liz beamed and held up a big tote bag. "I've got wine. I've got Jiffy Pop. I've got ramen—yes, I know, you're welcome. Thought we could do one of our extremely weird movie night mashups—*Notting Hill* for me, *Lost Girls* for you." She rolled her eyes. "I will put up with your murder shows just this once."

Cordelia felt the tears rush to her eyes and didn't realize until this moment how utterly terrified she'd been of being in her apartment alone.

"Auntie Cordie, tell us about your trip," Grace said, tugging her sleeve. "Did you meet any leprechauns? Miles said you would but I said they're not real."

"They are too!" Miles insisted.

"I did not meet any leprechauns," Cordelia said, taking Grace by the hand and heading to the doors. "But I can tell you about the púca that lives on Inishmore. And he *is* real. Róisín talks to him all the time."

"Whoa!" Miles said, then added, "What's a púca?"

Cordelia laughed and stepped out into the humid New York air. She managed to keep her spirits up as she said goodbye to Toby and the kids, promising to come visit them that week, then she and Liz piled into Gary's Jeep. Her breath caught in her chest at the first glimpse of the New York City skyline—it never got old, seeing it from a distance, the sun glinting off the skyscrapers, the Empire State Building shooting like an arrow toward the sky.

Liz helped her with her bags and they tumbled into her apartment together. Everything was just the same as she'd left it. Her little window garden of succulents. Framed prints hanging on the walls. Her portable kitchen island made her think of Niall and she turned away from it. Her bed was covered in the same paisley comforter. Photographs of her family on her dresser. She put her father's camera on her nightstand.

And next to it, she placed the grass ring.

She showered and changed into pajamas. Liz had one pot on the stove making ramen, the Jiffy Pop bag filling up with loud pops.

"Here," she said, pressing a glass of wine into Cordelia's hand. She served up the food and Cordelia scarfed the ramen down so fast she almost burned her tongue. Then she drained her glass and poured herself another.

"So," Liz said. "How are you doing?"

Cordelia felt the ramen threaten to rise back up her throat. "I'm . . ." She burst into tears, the sobs taking her wholly unprepared. "When is it going to stop hurting?" she whimpered. "I hate this, Liz. I wish I'd never met him. I wish I'd never fallen in love at all."

"No, babes, don't say that," Liz said. "You did what you thought was best—for you *and* for him. You wouldn't be happy if you were there in London, would you? I mean, think about it. He's probably working all the time, and with his psycho ex to boot. That would be a whole can of worms you don't need to get involved in. What would you do during the day? It wouldn't be like Inishmore—there's no Róisín to take you around in her cart. And what about this new book, huh?"

"Technically I could work on that from anywhere," Cordelia pointed out with a slight hiccup.

"Yeah, but isn't it better to be here where you can sit down with Kate? I remember for the last one there was lots of back and forth."

"You're just trying to make me feel better."

"Ding ding ding! What has she won, Johnny? Well, folks, let me tell you, Cordelia James has won an evening with her best friend, who is about to shower her with alcohol and compliments! But wait, there's more . . ." She hurried to the fridge and rummaged inside. "Guac and queso dip!" Liz declared, holding up two takeout containers.

"Is that from Cantina?" Cordelia exclaimed.

"It is indeed," Liz said, opening the two tubs and grabbing a bag of chips from the cupboard. "I can't make things better for you. I can't make Niall pull his head out of his butt and come here to beg you to take him back."

"No, Liz, he needs to be—"

"I know, I know, it's his special opportunity blah blah blah. I don't have to be that magnanimous. My only priority is to make you feel loved. By smothering you with Mexican food. You didn't get much of that in Inishmore, I imagine."

Cordelia cracked half a smile. "No, definitely not."

"He'll come to his senses," Liz said, taking an enormous scoop of guacamole on her chip. "He has to. You two were—"

"Please," Cordelia said, holding up her hand. "Please stop. We were a moment, that was all." She plunked a chip into the queso. "I could see it, you know," she said quietly, not looking Liz in the eye. "I could see it so clearly. Him moving here. Our life together. I know marriage is a huge deal and it's pretty crazy that he proposed—"

"Yes, it is," Liz agreed. "I don't know what I would have said if you'd called me to ask my opinion first."

Cordelia got up and left the room. She came back with the grass ring and slipped it onto her finger.

"Is that . . . ," Liz asked.

Cordelia nodded. "He made it for me. I think . . . I want to wear it. Just for tonight. Is that okay?"

"Of course," Liz said. "Why wouldn't that be okay? You can wear it as long as you like."

She shook her head. "No, I can't. It's not . . . good for me. I need to move on, I know I do. But tonight I want to pretend. Pretend that he's packing up whatever he's got left in Dublin. That he'll be getting on a plane soon. I'll meet him at JFK. He'll get to see the skyline. He can tell me how little counter space I have and the importance of keeping my knives sharp. He could—" Her voice broke off, the tears falling thick against her cheeks. "Just for tonight," she whispered, clenching her hand into a fist.

"Just for tonight, then," Liz whispered, wrapping an arm around her.

24

"Five entrees for table fourteen!" Niall shouted to his sous chef. "And I need two pavlova and a lemon sorbet for twenty-two."

"Yes, Chef," Michel replied. The kitchen was a madhouse in that most wonderful way—flames leaping up from burners, meat sizzling, dishes clanking, knives chopping. There were colorful rows of sauces in squeeze bottles and clear plastic tubs full of vegetables. There was light banter from the line cooks. This was the only place where Niall felt alive anymore—here he was captain and commander, looking over every dish, ensuring each plate was perfect.

Deirdre poked her head into the kitchen. "I just sat a party of nine," she said. "Brace yourselves."

"Ah putain, Deirdre, give us a minute," Michel complained. "We're slammed."

"I'm sorry, I thought you wanted to be making money tonight," Deirdre shot back. "Shall I tell them to piss off?"

"Michel, quit whinging and see to those entrees. Deirdre, throw some complimentary champagne at them before they order," Niall said. "Give us a minute to catch up."

She smiled at him. "Sure thing." Then she vanished out the kitchen doors.

"Seriously, Chef," Michel said as he slapped two steaks into a fry pan. "You and her? I don't see it."

"Right, because it doesn't exist," Niall said. "Less talking, more searing."

There was no keeping secrets in a restaurant. Everyone from the hostesses to the busboys knew the whole sordid tale of Niall and Deirdre and the Fallen Star.

They didn't know about Inishmore, though. It had been over three months since Niall left the island, and he'd kept that part of his life locked up tight ever since he stepped off the plane at Heathrow back in August. The only way he could survive was by not thinking about it. Which had been pretty easy once he'd met Ritchie and they'd begun to work on the new menu, and renovate the space, and hire the staff. Niall had had to find a place to live and get to know the neighborhood. And Ritchie expected nothing less than one hundred percent total devotion to the pub. Not that Niall had seen much of Ritchie since that first crazy month. But the time commitment was fine with Niall. He didn't want to leave a fraction of space in his brain for anything else.

The rest of the night passed in a blur. The pub had officially opened a week ago and had been packed every evening, the kitchen straining at the seams. The work was so utterly, blissfully exhausting. All Niall needed to think about was making sure the right food got to the right table on time.

It was exactly how he wanted things to be.

Well, no it wasn't, but it was the only way to live any semblance of a life. Because Niall had a piece missing, a piece so huge it was shocking no one noticed it—sometimes he felt like he was walking around with only half a torso. Once there was a place where a soft, warm body used to fit snugly, where golden hair spilled into his hands. Now there was only a shadow. A shadow with a name too painful for him to even think, let alone speak it.

The dinner rush finally subsided around ten. Niall left the kitchen in Michel's capable hands and headed out to check on the bar.

"All right, Gemma," he said to the bartender, a no-nonsense woman with cat-eye glasses.

"Evening, Chef," she said as she removed the foil from a bottle of wine, expertly sinking in the corkscrew and popping it open.

"I've got that," Niall said. He liked being behind the bar after the kitchen calmed down. It reminded him of his roots. He liked talking to the customers, getting to know the regulars. "Who's it for?"

Gemma jerked her head. "Seat seven. You good, Chef? I was going to take a quick smoke break."

"Go," Niall said. There were only two tables left and a handful of patrons at the bar. Niall poured the wine. It was a cabernet—his stomach clenched. *Her favorite.* He put the bottle back and carried the glass over to the right person. It was a woman with blonde hair and Niall's heart somersaulted, but she turned and of course it wasn't *her.* This woman's hair was shorter and her eyes were blue.

"Cheers, thanks. Will, do you want a drink?" she asked the man taking off his coat and sitting beside her.

"God, yes," he said. He had an American accent. Niall wondered if this particular corner of the bar was haunting him on purpose. "And food too, if the kitchen's still open."

"It is," Niall said. "Open for another thirty minutes."

"Are you the chef?" the man asked.

"I am," Niall said.

"Not often I see a chef serving drinks," the man said. He held out his hand. "Will Kincaid."

"Niall O'Connor," Niall said, shaking his hand. He noticed Deirdre watching from the host stand. "I like to come out once the rush is over. I started my career behind a bar."

"I love that," Will said. "Most of the chefs I work with have egos the size of hot- air balloons. You'd never catch them behind a bar."

"You're in restaurants too, then?" Niall asked.

"I'm an investor," Will said. He looked around at the décor. "Ritchie did well for himself with this spot."

"You know Ritchie?"

"Oh, please don't get him started," the woman groaned. "The two of them are like little boys trying to one up each other all the time."

"Ritchie's a friend," Will said emphatically, and the woman rolled her eyes.

"Order a drink, for god's sake, Will. I'm Jules, by the way," she said. "And I have zero to do with restaurants except to go wherever Will recommends."

"I'm glad you two decided to stop by the Star," Niall said.

Jules cocked her head. "You look familiar, have we met before?"

"Don't think so. I only just moved here in August."

"I'll have a Sazerac," Will declared. Niall slid him a menu and went to make the cocktail. Two more people came in to sit at the bar, and Niall poured them some water and gave them menus as well.

"You don't have to work behind the bar, you know," Deirdre said, sipping a club soda at the service station. "This isn't O'Connor's."

Niall felt the blood drain from his face. He had told Deirdre in no uncertain terms when he'd joined this venture that the subject of Inishmore was strictly off limits.

"I know," he snapped. "I do it because I like it."

Her lips pursed. "Right. Sorry. Hey, who was that man you were talking to?"

"Will Kincaid," Niall said.

Her eyes popped. "Seriously?"

"You know him?"

"He's like the straight, American version of Ritchie. He just opened a place in Tokyo, I think." Niall could see the gears working. "This is fantastic. I've got to tell Ritchie he was in. Let me know what he orders, would ya? Let's comp them dessert."

Niall nodded as Will signaled to him.

"Ready to order?" Niall asked.

"Yes," Will said, rubbing his hands together. "We'll share the mussels to start."

"And I'll have the lobster risotto," Jules said.

"I'm trying to decide between the salmon and the lamb," Will said. "I think I'll do the lamb. I love a good hasselback potato."

"Right," Niall said. "Excellent choice."

It wasn't exactly the same as the lamb dish he'd made for O'Connor's, but it was close. He probably shouldn't have put it on the menu at all, but he hadn't been able to help himself. He wanted a tiny piece of her there.

"I bet you say that about every one of these dishes," Jules joked.

Niall's answering smile was tense. "Nah. The lamb is quite special to me."

"Oh really?" Will said, leaning forward. "Is there a story behind it?"

Niall realized the trap he'd fallen into. "Not really, no," he said quickly. "Reminds me of something I used to make at home, is all."

"Where are you from in Ireland?" Will asked.

"Oh, ah, Inishmore? It's one of the Aran—"

"Oh my god," Jules said. "You're *Niall*! Niall from that Instagram thing!"

Niall felt his insides turn cold. Jules was taking out her phone. "This photographer did a whole series on Inishmore—it's so cool, Will, let me show you."

"I don't—" Niall began but she was already scrolling through. "Look!" she said, holding up the phone. "It's you!"

Niall's vision blurred as he saw himself on the screen. It was a shot she had taken of him and his father filling the pints for the Guinness races at Pátrún. Niall's throat closed up remembering the dancing later in the evening, the walk to the cottage, the . . .

No. He slammed the door firmly on that night.

"Yup, that's me," he said.

"I love her work," Jules said, not realizing how close she was to shattering Niall into a thousand pieces by saying one simple name. "She's from New York," she explained to Will, "and she was staying on the island for the summer and interviewed all the locals. There's this one old woman, I forget her name—"

"Róisín," Niall said.

"Yes! She's so funny. How crazy to meet you! Small world. Oh!" she said, looking back at her phone. "I guess she's publishing a book about her time there."

She held up the screen again and Niall saw a post announcing the news.

"Oh," Niall said woodenly. "Cool."

Will seemed to pick up on his agitation. "Let's not keep you, if the kitchen's closing soon."

"Right. I'll get those orders in. Cheers."

Niall quickly placed the order then hurried out from behind the bar and down the hall past the kitchen. He leaned against the wall next to a mop and bucket, his heart hammering in his chest. He'd told himself he'd never look at those pictures again. The memories were too strong, bursting free from their cages. He jammed his knuckles into his eyes as if he could forcibly push them back to the dark recesses of his mind.

"Niall?" Deirdre appeared at his side. "Are you all right?"

"Can you get Gemma back behind the bar?" Niall asked, his voice strained.

"Of course. What happened?"

"Nothing," Niall said. "Nothing. I—I need to go. I have to go home right now."

"Okay." She looked worried and placed a hand gently on his shoulder. "Are you sure you're all right?"

"I'm fine. Michel can handle the last few orders, yeah?"

"Course."

"Thanks."

Niall grabbed his coat and left without saying goodbye. Usually he hung around after closing, grabbed a drink with the staff. But tonight he wanted to be alone.

He walked the chilly streets of London toward his flat. Three months, he should be over it by now. He thought he'd been doing so well. He thought he had managed to put the whole summer behind him. What a joke. He'd only hidden it behind a curtain, and now the veil had been lifted and he couldn't think about anything else except her. It felt like all he had been doing was thinking about her, even as he strained so hard not to.

December was here and Camden was gussied up for the season. Niall walked past storefronts lined with twinkling lights, Christmas trees sparkling in front windows, until he came to his apartment building. His flat was a modest one bedroom with a spacious kitchen. But right now there was only one place he wanted to be—in a small bed, in a small cottage, on a small island. But that may as well be on the moon. Besides, it wasn't the cottage that called to him. It was the woman who used to live in it. And she didn't want him.

She was making a book, though, he thought as he flicked on the lights and poured himself a whiskey. That was good. She must be so happy. It was what she'd wanted, to be sharing her work with the world again. Niall downed his whiskey and poured another. He took out his phone. Maybe he could text her. Say congratulations. That seemed a normal thing to do, didn't it?

He texted Colin instead.

She's making a book.

A few moments later, a bubble appeared.

I'm going to need a few more clues here, mate.

Niall swallowed hard. Colin knew how much Niall avoided saying her name. Or typing it. Or thinking it.

Out of her Instagram.

His phone rang.

"Shit," Colin said when Niall answered. "Are you okay?"

"Not really," Niall said and his voice cracked.

"Shit," Colin said again.

"You were supposed to be my lookout. Check her feed, let me know what's going on."

"Yeah, but it's been ages since she's posted—oh, I see it now," Colin said. "It was only yesterday she made the announcement."

Yesterday. Somehow it never ceased to demolish him, thinking of her living her life out in New York. Imagining her slender fingers typing out the words, the smile on her face as she glowed from the inside out, finally able to celebrate her big news. Did she ever think about him at all? Well, surely she must if she was doing a book on Inishmore. She'd have to look at his pictures at least. Did she feel anything when she did?

Stop it, he reminded himself. *She didn't want you.*

"Niall?"

"Yeah. Sorry."

"Look, I was thinking—"

"Gotta go," Niall said quickly, then he hung up without bothering to fumble around for an excuse. He sank onto his couch and stared at his phone with trembling hands.

"Fuck it," he growled. He opened Instagram and brought up her feed.

And there she was. Hair like sunshine. Little rabbit nose. She was holding out a champagne glass to cheers with the person holding the camera—Liz, Niall guessed with relief, based on the neon yellow nails. He didn't think he could handle it if she was dating someone else. He thought it might actually break him to imagine her sharing those photographs, their time together, with another man.

Her name burst through the dam he'd built up around it, spilling through his mind like water.

"Cordelia," he whispered. *Cordelia, Cordelia, Cordelia . . .*

He sat there scrolling through images of the happiest time in his life, until he reached the very first one she'd posted.

Niall at the Black Fort.

Niall felt something tear inside his chest. He hung his head in his hands and wished more than anything to be back on that cliff.

25

"Cordelia?"

"Hm?" Cordelia snapped her head up and blinked around the small conference room. Kate was looking at her expectantly.

Cordelia had been tuning out a lot. For the past few months it was like her mind couldn't stay put. It was always floating away, off across an ocean.

"We need more pictures of Niall," Kate said. "You've hardly given us any."

"There's the one at the Black Fort," Cordelia said.

"You can barely see his face. Women love him, Cord. He needs to be featured."

"Right," Cordelia said. This was not the first time they had had this conversation.

It had been nice to finally announce the book deal last week. Cordelia was glad she'd gotten everyone on Inishmore to sign waivers for her to use their photos up front, so she didn't have to go asking for their permission now. She had been selling lots of prints off her website too. And she'd taken the job Liz had offered as some part-time freelance work. Things were looking up in so many ways.

But she wasn't happy.

She tried. She pretended. And she knew she should be grateful for her change of fortune—it was what she'd wanted after all, wasn't it? She *was* grateful. But nothing was going how she'd imagined it. Everything seemed colorless, like a poor copy image of a life when Cordelia had once known the bright and vibrant original.

She should be over Niall by now. It was foolish, not to mention downright masochistic, to cling to the memories of him so tightly. But she couldn't help it, couldn't stop herself from revisiting their time together in every spare second she had. Or during important meetings where she should be paying attention.

"What did you bring for Pocket?" Kate asked, and Cordelia pulled up the photos on her computer.

"She's so cute," Kate's assistant Miriam gushed. "Did she really just wander around the island?"

"Yeah," Cordelia said, looking forlornly at a picture of Pocket smiling with her tongue hanging out, sitting on a stone wall with a bunch of sheep behind her. "One time she showed up at my door and herded me to Niall's house for dinner."

The memory made her eyes itch and her throat clench. She wished she hadn't brought it up. But that was what she was here to do—go over the memories of that summer again and again and again.

"Aw! That's adorable," Miriam said. Cordelia forced herself to stay present for the rest of the meeting. But she was grateful when Kate said, "All right, I think this is a good start. Get us more shots of Niall by next week, yeah?"

"No problem," Cordelia said. It felt like a giant fist had clamped around her lungs—the longer she looked at the photographs she'd taken that summer, the harder it was to breathe. She gathered up her things and checked the time. She was meeting her mother for lunch in Brooklyn.

It was one of those cold, clear December days in New York where you could walk on the sunny side of the street and feel almost warm. Cordelia put her earbuds in and headed to the F train, skirting a hotdog vendor and a group of tourists off to see the tree at Rockefeller Center.

Her phone pinged and her heart skittered in her chest. She needed to stop reacting like that. You'd think after three months she'd get that Niall was simply never going to reach out to her. And yet she still clung to the hope that he would.

Why wasn't she over this? She was never getting into a relationship ever again. No wonder she'd avoided them all those years. It wasn't worth this pain.

How'd it go? Liz had written.

Good, Cordelia wrote back.

Come out with me and Meena later! We're going to Trailer Park.

Cordelia paused outside the subway station. It was nice that Meena and Liz were still friends, but Cordelia always ended up feeling like a third wheel anyway. Like a mopey, miserable third wheel.

I can sense you trying to come up with an excuse, Liz wrote. *I will not believe a single thing you say. See you at 7:30* 😘

Cordelia sighed. It wasn't like she'd had any pressing plans.

See you then, she texted back.

She got off the train at Smith Street and headed toward the café where she was meeting Louise. It was a cute little French spot, the door wrapped like a gift, the bar adorned with sprigs of holly.

Christmas music played quietly over the speakers. Louise sat at a table in the corner, sipping a latte, and she waved Cordelia over.

"Hi, Mom," Cordelia said, unwrapping her scarf from around her neck and kissing her mother on the cheek.

"How'd the meeting go?" Louise asked eagerly.

"Fine. They want more pictures of Niall." Even saying his name out loud hurt.

"Of course they do, the photographs you took of him are stunning." Louise pursed her lips. "How are you doing, sweetheart? And don't say fine. How are you really doing?"

Cordelia shrugged. "Terrible?" she offered. "I mean, I got everything I wanted. I went to Inishmore to recharge my work and now I've got this book and my online store is doing well but . . ."

"But you lost something too," Louise said. "It's okay to mourn that."

Ever since she'd come back home, Cordelia and her mother had been having more and more lunches together or dinners at the house with Gary. Louise had ceased all relationship pushiness and had morphed into Cordelia's biggest fan, always asking her about her work or wanting to see what she'd shot that day. Cordelia had started working on a new project—going to find the places where her father felt most alive to her. Telling his story through photographs. Louise would help her by offering suggestions of spots to go or reminiscing about the places Christopher James had loved. Cordelia was glad of it—glad to feel close to the only parent she had left.

"Did I do the wrong thing?" she asked. "I was going to say yes. Should I have, I don't know, gone to London?"

"First of all, darling, I don't think rushing into marriage would have been the best thing for you. I know I was the one pushing for that, but we've all learned a bit, haven't we?" She smiled and squeezed Cordelia's shoulder. "I don't think you would have been happy going to London because you would be going for him. You're such an independent spirit, Cordie."

"Yeah," Cordelia said. "I guess."

"What I don't understand is why you don't call him," Louise said. "Or go visit! London is an easy trip from New York."

"Mom, I can't just show up in London," Cordelia said.

"Why not? It's romantic."

"It's embarrassing. If he wanted to talk to me, don't you think he would have reached out by now?"

"Well, have you reached out to him? No. So maybe he's in London thinking the same thing. I saw you two together, remember. I saw the connection you had. That doesn't come around every day."

"But you just said I made the right choice by saying no to him and coming home!" Cordelia cried.

"I'm flattered that you suddenly put so much stock in what I say," Louise said. "And I *didn't* say don't be together. I said there was no need to get married. You two acted like it was marriage or nothing. You're both smart people who could have sorted things out another way. Cordelia, it's your life. If you want him, go get him. I really don't see the big deal."

"If Gary moved away would you jump on a plane to 'go get him'?" Cordelia demanded.

"Without a second thought," Louise said.

"Oh." Cordelia sat back in her chair with a huff.

"Actually," Louise said, toying with her napkin. "There is something I wanted to talk to you about."

"What, are you and Gary getting married?" Cordelia was joking, but Louise didn't say anything. "Mom? Wait, are you getting married?"

"We're talking about getting engaged," Louise said delicately.

"Seriously?"

"I wanted to speak with my children first," she said. "And he wanted to talk to Jon too, obviously. But . . . well, he makes me so happy, Cord. It's been almost a year together and neither of us are spring chickens. We know what we want. But I wouldn't want you to think I didn't care about—"

But Cordelia was throwing her arms around her mother. "Mom, that's so great!"

"Is it?" Louise said, bemused.

"Come on, you know I got over all my Gary bullshit ages ago," Cordelia said. "He's a terrific guy who loves you and puts up with your crap."

"Oh shush," Louise said but she was beaming. "My god, I've been so nervous to tell you! Toby said I was being silly, but I was worried you'd be angry."

"You told Toby first?" Cordelia said. "Okay, well, *that* makes me angry." She grinned. "Aw, Mom. I'm really happy for you. Where's the ring?" She looked at her mother's hands.

"I don't need a ring," Louise said. "Rings aren't important. The promise is enough."

Cordelia's grin tightened and she thought of the grass ring she still kept on her nightstand back home. She knew she should put it in a drawer, or throw it out, but she couldn't bear to.

They spent the rest of lunch chatting about the meeting with Kate and Louise's new book club, leaving the topic of relationships behind. Cordelia wished she could believe her mother, that all it would take was a plane ride to London to tell Niall how she really felt. But she was sure he'd moved on. She bet there were girls falling all over themselves to date him. How could they not be? He was gorgeous, like Kate was always reminding her.

Later that evening, Cordelia headed out to meet the girls at Trailer Park. It was a small dive bar on 23rd Street, neon signs in the window, streamers hanging from the ceiling. The tables all had Formica tops and the seats were upholstered in colorful plastic. License plates and framed black-and-white photos hung on the walls. A bright red gas pump from the fifties stood at one end of the bar.

Liz and Meena were at a table in the back, a pitcher of margarita between them.

"Cordie!" Meena said, getting up to hug her. Meena had long glossy black hair and pale green eyes. "I'm so glad you could make it."

"You look amazing," Liz gushed. Cordelia immediately became suspicious.

"No I don't," she said, sliding into a chair as Meena poured her a margarita. "I look extremely regular."

"You always look amazing," Meena said, shooting Liz a sharp look.

"How was lunch with Louise?" Liz asked.

"Oh my god, you guys, guess what—Mom's *engaged*."

"What?" Liz shrieked as Meena cried, "No way!"

Cordelia told them the whole story, and at the end Liz raised her glass. "To Louise and Gary," she said. "Who would have fucking guessed."

"Me," said Meena as they clinked their plastic cups together. "I totally called it."

"You did not," Liz said.

"I did! No offense, Cord, but your mom is a handful. Once they hit the six-month mark, I knew Gary was going to be around for the long haul."

Liz rolled her eyes. "Sure, sure. Oh, Meena, tell Cordelia that story you were telling me about that client who tried to hit on you."

Meena worked for a high-powered defense firm—usually dealing with corporate assholes accused of embezzlement and things like that.

"What happened?" Cordelia asked. Meena launched into a tale of a seventy-five-year-old guy who kept calling her honey and said she looked "exotic."

"Ewwww," Cordelia said.

"Right?" Liz agreed. She glanced up and her eyes went wide. "Look, Meena, isn't that Jeremy from your office?"

Cordelia turned and saw a man walking up to their table, dressed in a suit, his brown hair slicked back on one side.

"Hey," he said.

"Jeremy," Meena said. "So glad you could join us."

Join us? Cordelia shot Liz a glare that she was studiously ignoring.

"You remember Liz," Meena was saying. "And this is Cordelia."

"Hi," Jeremy said, holding out his hand. "Nice to meet you."

Cordelia ignored it. "Liz, can I speak to you for a minute?" She didn't give Liz a chance to respond but walked over to stand by the gas pump.

"Okay, don't be mad . . . " Liz began but Cordelia was fuming.

"Are you serious? Are you trying to set me up with that guy?"

"No," Liz said. "I mean, not really."

Cordelia raised an eyebrow.

"I thought it could be fun!" Liz said. "No pressure or anything. Just . . . I thought it might be good for you to talk to other guys again. In a social setting."

"Why would you think that, Liz?" Cordelia demanded, tears springing to her eyes.

"Because you've been miserable, Cord. It's like you're drowning and I'm standing there watching you sink."

"And you thought Jeremy could be my life preserver?"

"No! A distraction, maybe. You don't have to marry the guy—" She gasped and clamped her hand over her mouth. Cordelia felt all the blood drain from her face. "Fuck. Cordie, I didn't mean that. Fuck, what a stupid thing to say."

"I'm not feeling well," Cordelia said. "I'm going home."

"Don't go," Liz pleaded. "I'll ask Jeremy to leave. I'm sorry, Cord. I fucked up."

"Yeah, you did," Cordelia said. She strode back to the table, grabbed her coat, and left the bar without a backward glance.

Later that night, Cordelia was lying in bed staring at the ceiling, wondering what Niall's day had been like and what he was doing now and what he would be doing tomorrow, when her phone buzzed. And yet again, even though she knew it was freaking pointless, she couldn't help hoping she would see Niall's name when she looked at the screen.

I am the absolute worst friend in the history of ever, Liz wrote. *Can you forgive me? I promise to never do anything like that again. I will get down on my knees and beg. I will crawl across broken glass. That was the epitome of stupid and I can't believe I hurt you like that.*

Cordelia gave a brittle smile. *As far as apologies go, that wasn't bad.*

Her phone immediately started ringing.

"Oh, Cord, I can't believe what an asshole I was," Liz said.

"It's okay," Cordelia said. "I shouldn't have just left." She rolled over onto her side. "Do you really think of me as drowning?"

Liz hesitated. "Don't you feel like you're drowning?"

A hot tear slid down Cordelia's nose. "Yes. But I thought I was hiding it better."

Liz chuckled. "You never were a very good actress."

"No. I guess not." She played with the edge of her pillowcase. "What do you think he's doing now?"

"Well, he's probably sleeping. Being five hours ahead of us and all."

"Do you think he ever thinks about me?"

"Yes, you silly dumdum! How could he not?"

Cordelia swallowed hard. "I wish it didn't have to hurt like this."

"Me too, babes," Liz said. "Me too."

There was a long pause. "You're probably right," Cordelia said. "I should start, like, getting out there."

"Nah," Liz said. "I was rushing you. Besides, Jeremy is super lame. He was just the only guy I could think of to invite. All the guys I work with are gay. I thought maybe a bit of flirting would do you good. But that's not you, is it? Sorry. I should have known better."

"It's okay," Cordelia murmured. The fact was, there was nothing anyone else could do or say to make things better for her.

She was going to have to get over Niall all on her own.

26

Niall couldn't wait for the holidays to be over.

Everywhere he looked, there were happy couples, holding hands or laughing over a glass of mulled wine or kissing in the middle of the street so that he had to navigate around them. This time of year brought with it an intense amount of pressure to be happy and in love. Niall was about as far from both of those things as he could get.

He was planning to spend his Christmas cooking boeuf bourguignon and drinking the bottle of fifteen-year-old Redbreast he'd been saving.

When he arrived to open the restaurant on Christmas Eve, he had to clear his throat so that the two people staring deeply into each other's eyes in front of the Star's glass-fronted doors would get out of the bloody way. What was it with couples and fecking Christmas? Why did Christmas have to equate with romance? Deirdre had hung mistletoe over the front door, insisting it was *cute* and that the patrons would *love it.* Niall glared at the small green plant as he entered.

Deirdre was sitting at the bar going over the books.

"Howya," she said. "Has it started snowing?"

"Not yet," Niall said, unwrapping his scarf and heading to the office to hang up his things before checking on the kitchen. Michel was doing prep.

"Salut, Chef," he said. Michel was exceedingly competent and Niall never had much to comment on, so he made himself a coffee and went out to sit beside Deirdre.

"How are we doing?" he asked.

"You know, in a few months, we might break even," she said, grinning. "Not bad, huh? I told Ritchie we should think of expanding."

"Expanding?" Niall said. "We only just opened."

"Yes, but we've got to capitalize on this success. America is the next frontier, I think. Wouldn't it be incredible to have a location in San Francisco? Or New York?"

Niall's stomach flipped, a stupid ray of hope lighting up his chest before he squashed it. *Even if you went to New York, it doesn't change the fact she doesn't want you*, he reminded himself. Also the idea of opening another location was quite frankly exhausting. Niall was barely used to the pattern of his life in London.

But that was Deirdre to a T. Always looking for the next thing. Always pushing for more. He couldn't help feeling like this place was more Ritchie and Deirdre's than it was his.

She put a hand on his arm and he jumped.

"Where did you go just now?" she asked, smiling.

"Sorry?"

"You've got that thousand-yard stare," she said. "I used to only see that when we went grocery shopping. Remember how you would stand in the produce section and stare at the same zucchini for ages?"

She was doing this a lot now, bringing up memories from their time together. It was getting on Niall's nerves. Working alongside Deirdre hadn't been the painful disaster he'd feared, but she was becoming a bit too cozy for his liking.

"I don't know, just thinking, I guess," he said. "I'm going to do some prep."

"Michel can do that."

"I want to do it, Deirdre."

"All right," she said primly, returning to the books.

Niall lost himself for a while, cleaning and chopping mushrooms, as Michel bantered with one of the line cooks in French.

Aside from the two new menu items, everything was the same as the Fallen Star in Dublin, right down to the kitchen floor that Patrick and Deirdre had fucked on. And since Niall hadn't actually opened that restaurant, he didn't feel much ownership over either locale. He couldn't believe he was admitting this, but he actually missed working at O'Connor's. He missed the way Darragh would joke with him, he missed Colin playing music every night, he missed Shauna's cheerful smile. He even missed his father's surliness.

Christ, would wonders never cease.

It's not only them you miss, he thought sourly.

The clientele in London was a far cry from Inishmore too. Niall was sick of having food sent back by people who didn't know how to order steak, or ridiculous substitution requests, or—worst of all—vegans. But what else could he do? Where else would he go? He was head chef. He should be fucking grateful. He'd gotten all he wanted.

It just didn't feel the way he thought it would.

"You okay, Chef?" Michel asked.

"Fine," Niall said. He was being absolutely ridiculous. Look at all he had. Look at what he'd achieved. And here he was, wishing he were somewhere else.

Service began and Niall lost himself in the flow and movement of the kitchen. It was a busy night—he could imagine the controlled chaos happening in the front of house.

"Roger, I need more mussels," he called to one of the line cooks. "Luis, don't you dare take that fucking risotto out looking like— Michel, where's the goddamn garnish for the risotto?"

"Here, Chef!"

"Oui, Chef."

"Mussels are up, Chef."

Deirdre burst through the kitchen doors. "Niall, you've got visitors!"

Niall thought he might throttle her—could she not see how busy he was?—when a familiar face peered around her shoulder.

"Out o' my way, you fecking trollop," Róisín said, pushing Deirdre to one side and eliciting a chortle from Michel. "Niall O'Connor, my god man, *my god*. Would ya look at this place?"

"Róisín!" Niall cried. "What are you doing here?"

"We came to see your restaurant, you daft bastard, what do you think?"

"We?" Niall asked and the unabashed hope in his voice rang so clear even Róisín heard it. Her mouth puckered.

"Your parents came too," she clarified. "But Owen said not to be bothering you in the kitchen during the dinner rush. Ha! As if

I could ever be a bother. Ooooh, that smells delicious," she said as a runner left with a tray of risotto and mussels.

Niall didn't know whether to laugh or cry. "Róisín, you gorgeous creature," he said, scooping her up in a hug. "Look, I'm totally slammed, let me—"

"Go on, you've got a job to do," Róisín said with a wave of her hand. "I'll not distract. But if you wouldn't mind sending some o' those mussels over to the table, I'd thank you for it."

"I'm sending you guys everything," Niall said. "Mam and Da are out there?"

Róisín leaned close. "Your da just about burst the buttons on his coat walking through the doors," she said. "He's that proud."

Niall felt a warmth spread from the center of his chest. Róisín turned on her heel, gave Deirdre a withering glare, and left the kitchen.

"Friend of yours?" Michel asked.

Niall smiled. "She's family."

Later that evening, once the rush was over, Niall was finally able to sneak out of the kitchen and see his parents.

"My sweet boy," Fiona said, enveloping him in a hug.

"Why didn't you tell me you were coming?" Niall asked.

"We didn't want to bother you," Fiona said.

"Didn't want to give you a chance to say no," Róisín said.

Niall looked to his father, suddenly nervous.

"How was the dinner, Da?" he asked.

Owen was shaking his head slowly. "My god, Niall," he said. "What a triumph."

Róisín and Fiona beamed at each other behind Owen's back. Niall's cheeks flushed.

"You liked it then?"

"Liked it? It's a proper place, isn't it, with proper food. That risotto is a bit rich for my taste, but you've done the salmon well."

"Shame about the trollop," Róisín said.

"Eh, you get used to her," Niall said.

Róisín shot him a piercing look. "Do you?"

"I just meant—"

"Give the boy a break, Róisín," Owen said.

"We hope this is a good surprise," Fiona said, worriedly. "We missed you so much and it's been ages since we've spent the holiday together and Alison gets all kinds of deals on hotels and whatnot, you know, and she saw one for London so we thought why not?"

"This is a grand surprise, Mam," Niall said. "I'm so glad."

"You don't look like you've been eating," Fiona said.

"I've been eating fine," Niall said, rolling his eyes. "You should come round my place tomorrow. I'm making boeuf bourguignon."

"Oh, are you having friends over?" Fiona said brightly.

Niall cleared his throat. "Ah, no," he admitted. "Just felt like making it is all."

"We'd love to come," Róisín said. "Seeing as you're the reason we're here in the fecking first place. London," she grumbled. "Don't see what all the fuss is about."

Niall gave them his address and directions from the hotel and hugged them all again, promising to see them tomorrow. He was heading back to the kitchen when he spotted a familiar face at the bar.

Will Kincaid gave him a wave.

"Will," Niall said, coming over to shake his hand. "Good to see you again! Happy Christmas."

"Merry Christmas to you too," Will said. "I'm off to the States tomorrow, but I had to come back for that lamb."

"I'm glad you did," Niall said. "Let me send you something. Have you tried the fried goat cheese?"

Will laughed. "I have not, but that sounds terrific. Oh hey, here's my card." He handed Niall a thick, cream-colored business card. "If you're ever in the US or Tokyo or Lisbon, look up my spots. I'd love to hear what you think."

"Grand," Niall said, pocketing the card. "I'll get the goat cheese and the lamb out for you straightaway. Gemma!" The bartender looked up. "Mr. Kincaid's drinks are on me tonight."

"You don't have to—" Will began but Niall insisted. He was feeling lighter. Maybe it was seeing his parents and Róisín. A little touch of Inishmore.

After the restaurant closed, the staff gathered for some drinks at the bar. Niall loved the time when the lights dimmed, the chairs were up on the tables, and the liquor bottles gleamed temptingly in their neat rows. He was sipping his second Jameson, feeling that lovely hum the whiskey brought with it, a softening at the edge of his mind, a gentle heat in the center of his chest. Michel was spinning Gemma around on the floor. Two of the waitresses were making out by the kitchen.

His da liked the place. Niall hadn't thought much about what Owen would say, assuming he'd never come to the Star. He'd made his father proud in his own way on his own terms.

He wished he could tell Cordelia.

Fuck it. He took out his phone, the Jameson making him brave enough. He brought up her number and began to type.

Hi Cord . . . No, that was too familiar. *So my da came by the restaurant tonight.* Well, that was crap—he couldn't just act like they hadn't spoken for months.

"All right," Deirdre said, putting down her glass of champagne. "I'm off. Niall, you're walking toward the tube, right?"

"Hm?" Niall said, glancing up. "Oh, ah, yeah."

"D'you mind walking me?"

"Sure," he said, getting up. He should be getting home too. Michel was giving him a look as he got his coat on, and Niall realized everyone else had left already.

"Joyeux Noël, Chef," Michel said, jamming his knit cap down over his brows and leaving. Deirdre was buttoning up her coat. Niall got his things and walked with her to the door when she suddenly grabbed his elbow and stopped him.

"What?" he asked.

She giggled and pointed to the ceiling. "Mistletoe," she said.

Then she leaned in and kissed him.

"Wait—fuck—Deirdre, stop it," Niall said, stumbling back.

"What?" she asked, her eyes wide.

"Are you fucking serious?" Niall said.

"I thought . . ."

"Thought what?"

"I mean." Deirdre gestured around. "This is our place, Niall. I thought you wanted—didn't you want—why did you agree to this?"

"I agreed because I wanted to work in my own bloody restaurant," Niall cried. "I told you when we started, this wasn't about me and you."

"Oh please," Deirdre said. "Men always say that. You didn't mean it."

"I did," Niall said, his head spinning. "And I do. Christ, did you only ask me to do this so we would get back together?"

"No," Deirdre said. "I mean, not *only*."

Niall waited. He knew her too well—she was keeping something back.

Deirdre looked flustered. "Ritchie did want you on board. After I told him how talented you were."

"After," Niall said, the back of his neck heating. "What you're saying is . . . he didn't insist on me."

"Well, no, I did. You're so talented, Niall, and I knew once Ritchie met you he'd feel the same way, but you're too stubborn. If I hadn't phrased it the way I did, you never would have come."

Niall thought he might throw up. "I can't believe this," he said. "I can't fucking believe this. Except I can. It's always about you, isn't it, Deirdre? About what you want. And you always get what you want, don't you? From your da, from Ritchie, from Patrick, from everyone. Well, you don't get me."

"Is this about her?" Deirdre demanded. "The girl from Inishmore? Carla or whatever?"

"Cordelia," Niall said through clenched teeth. "Her name is Cordelia. And no. Even if she'd never existed, even if I'd never met her, and you had come to Inishmore with the same lie you told . . . goddammit, Deirdre. You twist everything up. You manipulate the world to how you want it and expect other people to fall in line. Well, I'm done, all right? *I'm done.*"

"Niall—" Deirdre pleaded but Niall was so furious his ears were ringing.

"I quit," he hissed. "Find yourself a new chef."

And then he turned on his heel and stormed out into the snow.

"You what?" Fiona cried.

"I quit," Niall said for the third time.

"Oh, Nie," his mother said. "Was it . . . do you think that was necessary?"

"Yes, Mam, I do," Niall said. "This was meant to be *my* chance, not some way for Deirdre to sneak back into my life. I should have guessed."

"Fecking trollop," Róisín muttered.

"Owen, say something," Fiona said. His da was in the kitchen with him, peeling the pearl onions for the bourguignon. Niall glanced at him, but Owen shrugged.

"You can't make the man do what he's said he won't do, Fiona."

"But you said yourself that place was perfect."

"Aye, but only if it suited Niall, which it doesn't. Not anymore, at least." Owen waved a knife in Niall's direction. "And look at him now. He's got credentials. He's got experience. He can go anywhere."

Not anywhere, Niall thought dryly. He wasn't sure what he was going to do now. His phone pinged again and he ignored it. Deirdre had been calling and texting all day. But there was nothing she could say to change his mind.

Niall finished chopping carrots and wiped his knife clean.

"What about you, Róisín?" he asked. "You're being suspiciously quiet."

Róisín was sitting on his couch in her dungarees, a glass of Redbreast in one hand. "I was told very specifically by Fiona to keep my opinions to meself," she said.

Niall frowned. "And when has that ever stopped you from sharing them anyway?"

"Don't," Fiona warned.

"Don't what?" Niall asked, looking back and forth between them.

"Oh lord," Owen muttered, and then Róisín slammed her glass down on the coffee table and stood.

"She was going to say *yes*, you dumb bastard!" Róisín cried. "God, it's been eating me alive. But she only did it so he'd go to London, and Fiona, it's not worked out in London, has it?"

"But you promised her you wouldn't say anything," Fiona said.

Róisín huffed. "I told *you*, didn't I?"

"That's different and you know it."

"Can everyone slow down a minute?" Niall said. His pulse had kicked into a sprint, but he didn't want to get ahead of himself. Maybe he was misunderstanding. "What are you two on about?"

"Cordelia was going to say yes to you," Róisín said. "The day the fecking trollop showed up at your door. Do you hear me, boyo? She was going to say *yes*."

Niall blinked. He knew he understood the meaning of her words, but right now his brain could not compute. "But . . . she said she didn't want me."

Fiona's face creased and Róisín's nostrils flared.

"Well, that was a load of crap, now, wasn't it," Róisín said. "She knew you wouldn't go if she said yes to you. She couldn't go to London herself. Now, why on earth the two of you thought it was marriage or nothing in this day and age I'll never know, but there it is—she was going to say yes and she only said no because she loved you so damn much." She narrowed her eyes. "Have you been sitting here for months believing she didn't want you? Christ, Niall, I thought you were smart!"

Niall was still too bewildered to reply. He looked to his father for help.

Owen shrugged. "I told you," he said. "You're not dead, either of you. There's always hope."

"Did you all know?" Niall asked. "Did you all know about this?"

"Just Róisín," Fiona said quickly. "She only told us right before we came."

"I made a promise to Cordelia," Róisín said. "But I don't think keeping it is doing anyone any favors."

"What . . . I don't know what I'm supposed to do about this, Róisín," Niall said.

"Jesus fucking Christ, Niall, what are you, some kind of amateur? You get on a plane and fly to New York, for god's sake. Didn't think I'd have to sit here and explain it all."

"I can't just fly to New York," Niall protested, even as the idea tempted him.

"Oh, I'm sorry, did you have some other pressing matter to attend to here in London? Last I checked, you quit your job."

"But—she didn't want me," Niall said bleakly, and it hurt how much he had clung to that idea. He could feel it slipping away, feel hope springing up in its place, and he couldn't bear to be hurt again. Róisín seemed to see that in his face. She walked over and patted his cheek.

"Listen to me," she said. "I saw her, after it all happened. I sat there as she cried buckets into my lap. She loved you then and she loves you still. I can feel it in my bones. I'm always right about these things, aren't I, Fiona?"

"You are," Fiona said.

"And I can see plain as day you still love her too," Róisín said. "You're not happy here. Look at this flat. There's no character, no Niall. It's like a ghost lives here. You can work in a pub anywhere. There's only one Cordelia. You know where she is. Go get her."

Niall looked to his father again. Owen was searing the meat in a pan.

"I'm not one to argue with Róisín," he said.

Niall looked to his mother, who was trying and failing to suppress her smile.

"Go, Nie," she said. "It's what you want. I can see it in your eyes."

Niall felt dizzy. The thought of seeing Cordelia again was like a balloon expanding in his chest, his ribs straining against his skin like his heart might pop clean through.

"Can I?" he said, more to himself than anyone else. "Can I . . . go to New York?"

She was going to say yes.

"Course you can!" Róisín said, clapping her hands together. "Niall, get your computer. Fiona, pour us some more whiskey. Oh, this is a grand thing to be planning on Christmas Day, is it not?"

Niall found himself sitting on his couch between his mother and Róisín, looking at flights.

"This is insane," he said. "I don't even know where in New York she lives."

"I've got her address," Róisín said with a wink. "You two may have stopped talking but I've called her a time or two and Alison has checked in. She seems as mopey as you, to be honest. If I lived in New York, I'd have gone over to her place already to smack some sense into her."

She was going to say yes. Yes to him. Yes to them. Niall was still having difficulty processing it.

"Damn," Fiona said. "It looks like there isn't an open flight until December 31st."

"Well, book it!" Róisín said to Niall. "That's not more than a few days."

"Go on, lad," Owen said from the kitchen.

Niall grabbed his wallet. A few minutes later, he was the proud owner of a plane ticket from London to New York.

27

Cordelia was quite proud of herself, all things considered.

She'd spent Christmas Eve with Liz, drinking wine and watching Hallmark holiday movies. On Christmas Day, she'd gone to the brownstone in Carroll Gardens. It was fun to celebrate Christmas with the kids—Nikki had gotten everybody matching reindeer pajamas and Cordelia had spent the day in a onesie with Grace practically glued to her side.

She was determined to make merry and she had. She wouldn't let the lingering ache over Niall get in the way of celebrating with her friends and family. The week between Christmas and New Year's had that bizarre, timeless feel, as if she'd stepped into a wormhole where all the days blended together. But New Year's Eve had come and Cordelia was thinking that maybe this would be the thing that tipped her over the edge into actual happiness. A new year. A clean slate.

She'd even agreed to go to the New Year's Eve party Liz was throwing. Cordelia hated New Year's Eve parties as a rule, but she was willing to make an exception this year—staying home alone felt way too depressing. Plus, Liz's place was only three subway stops away. Cordelia could flee if she needed to.

She showed up at eight and almost immediately turned back around again. The place was packed, the music was loud, and Cordelia couldn't see anyone she knew. She was beginning to remember why she avoided New Year's parties in the first place. It was all too much—too much pressure to have fun, to get drunk, to kiss someone at midnight.

"Cordie!" Liz exclaimed, clearly well into the champagne already. "Come in, I want you to meet some people."

She allowed herself to be led around and introduced to other interior designers Liz worked with, and then Meena was there pressing a gin and tonic into her hand.

"She's gone all out, hasn't she?" Meena said, glancing around at the décor. Liz had those huge golden balloons that spelled out HAPPY NEW YEAR, and everybody got a pair of novelty glasses and a party horn when they arrived. Glittering beads hung in the doorways and a disco ball threw rainbow-colored light across the walls and carpet.

"Yes, she has," Cordelia said, gulping down half her drink and then going to the kitchen to make another one. She had to skirt a couple making out by the stove. Weren't people supposed to wait till midnight to do that? She threw some ice into her glass and grabbed the bottle of gin.

An hour later, Cordelia was not having any more fun than when she'd arrived. It was loud and hot in Liz's place, and she didn't really know anyone else besides Meena. People were dancing and laughing and kissing, and Cordelia felt like a visitor from another planet. It made her so sad all of a sudden. Like she didn't belong anywhere in this party, but even more than that, like she never would. She couldn't see this kind of joy for herself anymore.

Get up, get out there, and enjoy the day.

I tried, Dad, she thought weakly. Just then, some guy knocked into her, spilling her drink right down her shirt.

"Oh shit, sorry!" the guy said, but he was laughing and the girl he was with was laughing too. Cordelia was just. Fucking. Done.

"It's fine," she said through clenched teeth, then turned on her heel, grabbed her coat, and headed out into the cold December night. She decided to walk home—it would take her thirty minutes but was better than waiting for the subway with all the New Year's partygoers. She was turning into such a grouch. She texted Liz to say she'd left and apologized for not saying goodbye.

What had Niall called it? An Irish goodbye.

Her heeled boots were starting to hurt by the time she reached her apartment and she left a trail of clothes in her wake as she stripped and headed to the bathroom to run herself a shower.

What is Niall doing right now?

She had to stop thinking that, but it was like an evil little Whac-A-Mole lived inside her brain, popping up to wonder this same question every five minutes. It didn't matter what Niall was doing. She'd finally bit the bullet and sent nearly all of the shots she'd taken of him to Kate (let her decide which ones to use), so once this book was done, she could move on. Maybe that was what had been holding her back.

She turned the hot water off and changed into the reindeer onesie Nikki had gotten her. It was really comfortable, fleece lined with a zipper up the front, and Cordelia didn't care that she looked ridiculous, or that she'd left a New Year's Eve party to hang out at home, alone in silly Christmas pajamas. She put on an episode of

Murder in the Heartland, poured herself some wine, and boiled water for ramen.

She could have whatever kind of goddamn New Year's Eve she liked. This was as good as a party. Better even. Because here, alone in her apartment, she didn't have to pretend everything was fucking fine.

A thought occurred to her—she hesitated, then gave in. What did it matter? She was already the most pathetic sad sack the world had ever seen. May as well put the cherry on top.

Cordelia went into her room and picked up the grass ring from its perch on her nightstand. She still kept it there. Like a freaking masochist.

She slipped the ring onto her finger—the grass was brittle now but still held its shape. She stared at it for a moment, wondering what her life might be like if she'd been a bit selfish, if she'd said yes instead of no.

"Don't be stupid," she said out loud. Her mother was right, getting married was not the solution. She just wanted a world where she could be with Niall. That was all. But what's done is done, as her father used to say. She sighed. This was going to be the last time she wore his ring. She had to throw it away. It was time to move on.

I can wear it tonight, though, she thought viciously and stomped back to the kitchen to add the seasoning packet to her ramen. She was slurping her noodles and watching her crime show when the doorbell rang. She frowned and stayed where she was—maybe someone in the building was having a party and the stupid guests had gone to the wrong apartment. She certainly wasn't expecting anyone.

The doorbell rang again. Maybe Liz had come to try and drag her back to the party, though Liz had seemed pretty tipsy by the time Cordelia left. Then again, Drunk Liz could be very assertive.

The doorbell rang *again*.

"Okay, I'm coming," Cordelia snapped, storming over and throwing open her door.

Standing there . . . in her hallway . . . in *New York* . . . was Niall.

"Hello," he said quietly.

Cordelia just stared. He looked exactly the same—thick black hair falling over his forehead, a shadow of stubble across his jaw. His eyes were bluer than she remembered, as if her mind couldn't do them justice. He even smelled like Niall: driftwood and wool.

Oh fuck. She'd gone over the edge. She was actually hallucinating now.

Niall's brow furrowed. God, she'd missed that.

"Cordelia?" he said.

"Are you real?" she blurted out.

He blinked and then smiled so that his dimple popped. Cordelia felt something rip inside her chest. "Yes," he said. "I'm real."

"How—how are you here?" she asked. Her legs were beginning to tremble, her breath coming too quick.

Niall gave an embarrassed shrug. "Róisín," he said. "She, um, told me what you told her. After we . . . broke up. Please don't be mad, she wouldn't have, except that I quit the job in London and she said that she didn't need to keep her promise to you anymore, and anyway she said I was stupid to believe that you didn't want me. Well, she had a fair bit to say on the subject, as I'm sure you can imagine, but the point is she told me to get on a plane so I can tell you how I feel and so I did, though I couldn't get a ticket until today and I thought maybe you'd be out at a party or something, but I . . ." His voice trailed off. He shifted from foot to foot.

"Christ, have I fucked this up? Am I too late? I'll understand if you want me to go."

"Go?" Cordelia said. She was still trying to sort out everything Niall had said because it sounded very much like he'd missed her and wanted her back, but she had been so determined never to hope for that, it was messing with her head. "Why would I want you to go?"

Niall's cheeks turned pink. "I don't know if you've got another fella, or if you've moved on, or . . ."

The thing trying to claw its way out of her finally shook loose and Cordelia burst into laughter that was so loud it was borderline hysterical.

"Cord?" Niall said, looking really concerned now, and she couldn't blame him but she couldn't stop either. Cordelia laughed until her side ached, and then she finally gazed at him, standing in her doorway. Niall was real and true and *here*, and it felt like the sun rising inside her, it felt like the world had turned to Kodachrome colors, too dazzling to bear.

She held up her hand with the grass ring. A spasm of some strong emotion flashed across Niall's face at the sight of it.

"I haven't moved on," she said, and her voice broke. "And I don't have a fella. There's been nothing but you, Niall, all these months, I haven't been able to focus, I haven't been happy, I haven't been anything. I've—"

But she didn't get a chance to finish because in one stride he was inside her apartment, the door slamming shut behind him. He scooped her up in his arms and his mouth found hers, and Cordelia's heart was beating so hard she thought it might burst.

She kissed him like she was starving and he was her last meal. Her mouth was hungry for him, her lips greedy and insistent. She curled herself around him, her hands grappling at his peacoat, like she could tear through it and shred it with her bare hands. She wanted the curves of Niall's body, the planes of his chest, the dent of his hips, the rounds of his shoulders. She wanted to taste the base of his throat and the small of his back. She wanted to consume him whole. His hands sank into her hair as she fumbled with the buttons on his coat. She ripped it off and it fell to the floor.

She pulled back for a moment, drinking him in, still not quite sure this was real.

"Why are you looking at me like that?" he whispered. His voice was rough, sending shivers up her spine.

"I'm trying to decide if you're a hallucination."

He gave a low chuckle and she felt its echo between her thighs. "I promise you I'm real," he murmured. "Let me prove it."

He took her mouth gently then, his lips patient and sure. He kissed a little trail to her left ear and tugged her lobe between his teeth. Cordelia gasped, a flood of memories coming from that one little tug. He kissed another trail down her neck then along her collarbone.

"These are very nice jammies," he said, his hand teasing at the zipper.

Cordelia had completely forgotten what she was wearing and she blushed so hard her hair stood on end.

"Oh!" she gasped, her hands clapping over her mouth, but Niall just groaned.

"I forgot how gorgeous you are when you blush," he said, and his mouth came back to hers. He tugged at the zipper so that it opened down to the center of her breastbone, exposing a wide expanse of skin. He placed one hand across her chest, his thumb skimming the bottom curve of her breast, and Cordelia sucked in a breath.

"I feel your heart," Niall murmured in her ear. "My god, it's like a hummingbird."

"I want to feel yours," she whispered.

"As you command," he said, and in one fluid movement, his sweater was off. He stood in front of her shirtless, ivory skin covered in fine black hairs, and Cordelia thought this was too much, he couldn't possibly be for her. She was going to melt into a puddle on the floor or vanish in a puff of smoke. These feelings were simply too big for her small frame to contain. She pressed her hand against his chest and felt the steady thrum beneath her palm. He was breathing hard.

"You know," Niall said. "I had a whole speech planned."

"Did you?" Cordelia asked, marveling at the feel of muscle beneath skin, tracing her nails down his stomach and making him shiver. She hooked her fingers under the waist of his jeans.

"Yes, it was going to be—oh god," Niall moaned as she slid her hand between his thighs, feeling his hardness pressing against her palm. She couldn't help herself. Speeches could wait.

"I need to touch you," she said. "I need . . ."

"Me too." Niall scooped her up in his arms, like he had that very first night they'd made love. "Where's your bedroom?"

"Down the hall," she said.

Niall carried Cordelia without really looking where he was going.

He hadn't expected things to go this way, or if he had, not quite so quickly.

But he wasn't complaining. No, far from it. Niall could die right now and be perfectly content. He put her on her feet gently and then slid the zipper of her silly, adorable reindeer pajamas all the way down. She was completely naked underneath and Niall groaned again. His cock was straining to burst and she cupped him in her hands as the pajamas fell to the floor.

Niall eased her back onto the bed—she was beautiful, her skin like satin, her hair fanning out around her face. He knelt down so that her knees were even with his nose and kissed the tender skin of her inner thighs, feeling her shudder beneath his hands until his mouth reached her sex. Fuck, she was so wet already. Niall licked her in one long, slow line that had her gasping. And he knew this was no time for playing, no time for gentle teasing. This was pure, unadulterated need.

He released her only long enough to get the rest of his clothes off, then crawled across the bed to her side, his hand caressing her breast. Her hand slid between his legs, gripping his cock with sure, certain strokes, and he groaned as she slid one leg around him, angling herself.

"I need to feel you inside me," she said and he was hers to command.

He gripped her ass with one hand, the other sliding to cup her neck so they were face to face on their sides as he entered her. She gave for him and his breath snagged as he felt himself consumed by her. He nibbled at her lips, her cheekbones, her chin, a deep heat growing, a heat that called to him, beckoning, and his cock swelled to greet it.

"Niall," she whimpered and his willpower crumbled. He took her hard and fast and yet it wasn't enough, and Cordelia cried out for more as he flipped her on her back and she writhed beneath him, her hands scrabbling against his skin.

He came like a dam breaking, felt Cordelia's nails dig into him as she climaxed too, and everything felt far away as he was pulled into a vortex where nothing existed except Cordelia, the scent of her skin, the feel of her hair, the hot, dark, pulsing spot where the two of them became one.

He gave a last shuddering gasp and then fell still, his head resting on the pillow beside her, the warm shape of her body beneath him. Their hearts pounded against each other frantically. Her breath was a soft mist on his shoulder.

"Niall," she croaked after a moment. "I think you're crushing me."

"Shit," Niall said, springing up.

"No, come back," she gasped, reaching for him.

"I'm here," he said, cradling her against his chest. She twined her legs around his like she couldn't hold him tight enough. The bright lights of the city spilled in through her windows. Cordelia angled her head and gazed up at him, stroking the line of his jaw with her fingers.

"I probably should have shaved," Niall mused. "But I came straight from the airport."

"You came here," she whispered. "For me."

"I did." He kissed her softly.

"I was so sure you were having a great time in London." She sat up so quickly it startled him. "Wait, but . . . but the restaurant! What happened?"

"Let's not talk about that right this moment," Niall said, pulling her back to him. "Suffice it to say it wasn't what I thought and I quit. I'll tell you the whole story, I just . . . I need a minute. To be here. With you." He buried his nose in her hair, inhaling her bergamot-pine scent. "I never thought I'd get to do this again. Hold you like this. Christ, I never thought I'd see your face again."

She was quiet for a moment and then he felt something wet trickle down his collarbone. "Cordelia, are you crying?"

She sat up again, tears in her eyes. "I never should have said what I said," she burst out. "I'm so sorry, Niall, I didn't mean any of it, I only wanted what was best for you. I—"

"Hey," Niall said, sitting up and cupping her face in his hands. "It's all right. I understand. Thank god for Róisín. Don't know how she managed to keep that in all these months." He chuckled. "First time she's ever kept a secret in her life."

Cordelia laughed. "I miss her."

"She misses you too. But hey, she's very excited that she's going to be in a book."

He could feel the heat of her blush in the darkness. "You know about that?"

"I do."

She groaned and fell back onto the bed, her hands over her eyes. "You know, my editor hounded me for weeks for more shots of you. *Women love Niall*, she was always saying. Like yeah, I know, I'm one of them." She peeked up at him from between her fingers. "And now you're here. Naked in my bed. It's like . . . are you sure this isn't a dream? I can have very vivid dreams, you know."

Niall leaned down to kiss her. "This is not a dream. I promise, when you wake up tomorrow, I'll still be here. I'll be here as long as you want me."

"I want you forever," Cordelia whispered.

Niall took the hand where the grass ring he'd made all those months ago hung gently around her finger. He pressed his lips against it and smiled at her.

"Good," he replied. "Because I want you forever too."

EPILOGUE

Cordelia woke to gray light streaming through her windows.

At first she thought she was back on Inishmore. Partly because of the light, but mostly because of the man snoring gently beside her. Then the details of her bedroom filtered in. This wasn't Inishmore. This was New York.

And Niall was here.

She rolled over to look at him, his hair mussed, his eyes closed. He was so utterly perfect. She was still having trouble believing he was real, that he'd come all this way. For her.

One of his eyes cracked open, revealing a tiny slit of aquamarine. "Are you watching me sleep?"

"I am."

The other eye opened. "That's a bit creepy, you know."

She grinned. "I told you, I'm a creeper."

He chuckled and reached up to smooth her hair back. "What are you thinking about?"

"I love you," she said.

His thumb traced the curve of her lower lip. "I love you too."

She snuggled into the crook of his shoulder and he tucked her head under his chin. "What do we do now?" she asked.

"I think breakfast is a good place to start."

She rolled her eyes. "I mean . . . how long do I have with you?" Her heart kicked up a notch.

"Cordie, I'm not going anywhere," Niall murmured.

Cordelia's pulse seemed to freeze. "You're . . . not?"

"No. Where could I possibly go that would be better than here?"

She smiled against his chest. "Really?"

"I've always wanted to live in New York."

"You have not."

"Well, I haven't *not* wanted to live in New York."

Cordelia shifted back so she could see his face. "Are you serious? I mean, how, though? We're still in the same situation and I don't think marriage is—"

"Shh," Niall said. "One step at a time. You're right, we don't need to go jumping into marriage. But there's got to be another way. I've got three months to figure it out. And if not, I'll pop back to Ireland for a week and then come back. I'll sort something out, Cordelia. Not staying here with you, well, that's no option at all."

The reality was beginning to set in, and Cordelia felt so light she might soar right up off this bed and float around the ceiling. She jumped up so that she was on her knees, her palms on his chest.

"Oh, Niall!" she cried, leaning down to kiss him and then popping up again. He laughed. "Should we go to brunch? That's a very New York thing. New Year's Day brunch. We could go with Liz! If she's not too hungover. Oh my god, she is going to lose her shit when she sees you."

Niall was still laughing as he bent down to gather his clothes up off the floor. "You don't mind me staying with you, then? Since I don't have a place of my own."

"Are you kidding? I wouldn't let you stay anywhere else. This is . . . this . . . ahhh!" She threw her arms around him and kissed him again. "I'm sure we can figure out work for you. Maybe Meena has a connection—she knows, like, everyone. Or maybe . . ."

But Niall was looking down at his wallet and frowning.

"What?" Cordelia asked.

"I think," he said, slowly. "I think I just got an idea."

And he held up a business card with the name *Will Kincaid* printed on it.

"Who's that?" she asked.

"I'll tell you at brunch," Niall said, his eyes roving over her body before they both tumbled back onto the bed.

Cordelia felt all the scars and fractures of the past smoothed out beneath the touch of Niall's hand, the whisper of his breath against her cheek.

Her world had righted itself at last.

She looked at Niall and she was home.

ACKNOWLEDGMENTS

I wrote this book during the height of the pandemic when I was in a very dark place—like so many of us were—and it brought me such light, hope, and comfort but I never thought it would actually be published. Needless to say, I'm over the moon that it's made its way from my own personal security blanket to a real book, out in the big wide world. And I hope it's brought you some joy and comfort too, dear reader.

No book is ever written in a vacuum, though, and I have so many people to thank for their help in bringing Niall and Cordelia's story to light. First and foremost: Jess Verdi, the best editor any author could ask for. Thank you for your endless support, your keen insights, and your patience in answering all the million and one questions I peppered you with in my attempt to make this book as perfect and polished as humanly possible. You're the best and I love you forever. And because I must keep the tradition alive . . . Stefan's crying face.

Huge thanks to everyone at Alcove Press: Thai Fantauzzi-Pérez and Rebecca Nelson, my amazing production team; Dulce Botello and Mikaela Bender on the marketing team; Megan Matti and Stephanie Manova who got this book into the hands of foreign publishers; and Laura Apperson and Matt Martz. And to Ana Hard, thank you for the incredible cover! I couldn't have asked for better wrapping for this book.

Charlie Olsen, my incredible agent, thanks for sticking with me through the hard pandemic years. It's been a true gift always having you in my corner.

Marlies Hartmann, thank you so much for taking the time to share your vast wealth of photography knowledge with me and helping me bring Cordelia's perspective to light. It was a privilege to learn from you—and I have to give a shoutout to London too!

Caela Carter, I don't think I can write anything without getting your eyes on it first. Thanks for being so incredibly encouraging while I struggled with imposter syndrome.

Pep Funcia, mi Pepito abejito, you have brought so much joy into my life, I don't even know how to begin to thank you. From your unconditional support to the way you make me laugh to your reminders to relaja la raja when I get in my feels, I'm just so incredibly lucky to know you and to get to spend time with you every day. I love you corazón.

Ali Imperato, what would this book be without you? From the very first, you were there, demanding pages and keeping me going. You made me believe this was possible, and I truly could not have completed this story without you cheering me on. Thank you for being the most incredible friend.

To my amazing friends, Corey Ann Haydu, Alyson Gerber, Matt Kelly, Erica Henegen, Melissa Kavonic, Jared Wilder, Michelle Zink, Carissa Normil, Audrey Meihak, Lindsay Ribar,

Sadie Roberts, and Heather Demetrios, thank you all for your continuing support and for being a safe haven whenever I fell to pieces.

A million thanks to my family—to my mom and dad who have always supported me following my dreams, and to Ben, Leah, Otto, and Bea for being there and lifting me up and giving the best group hugs. I love you all and couldn't do this without you.

And to Faetra. I miss you every day.